YOUNG JUSTICE™

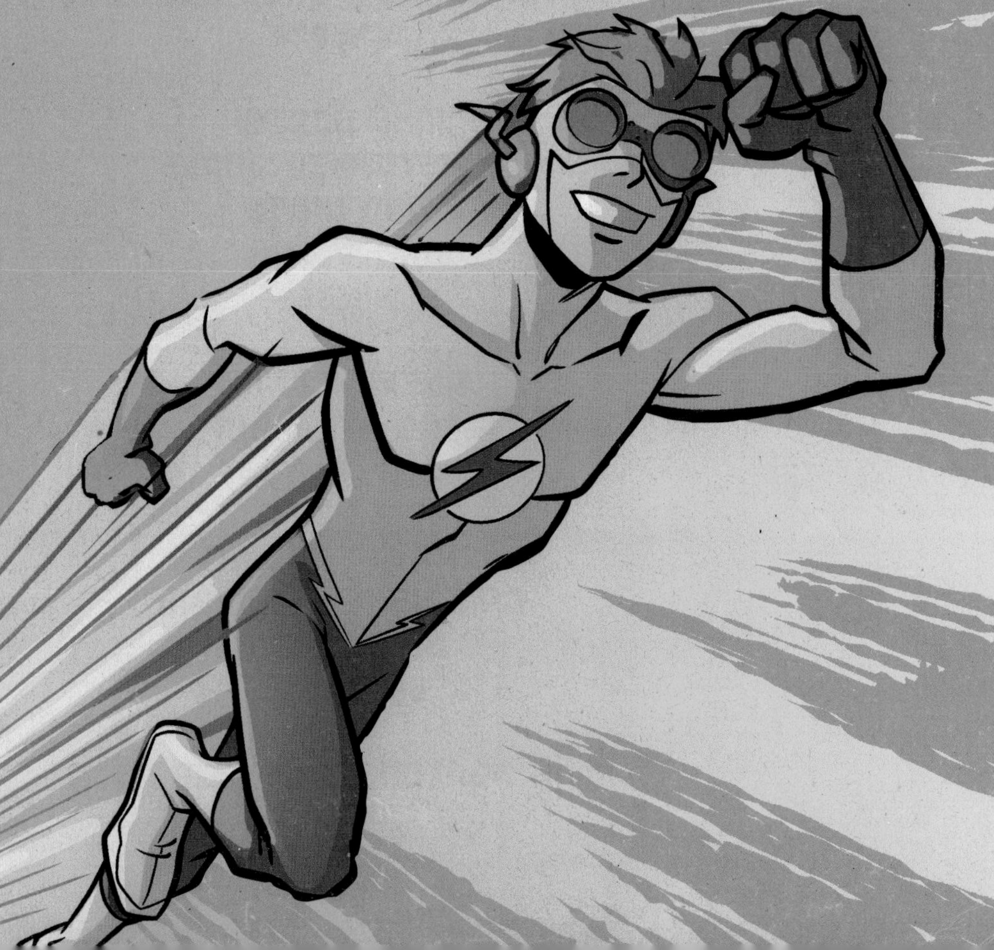

YOU JUS

ART BALTAZAR & FRANCO
KEVIN HOPPS & GREG WEISMAN
Writers

MIKE NORTON
CHRISTOPHER JONES
DAN DAVIS
JOHN STANISCI
Artists

ALEX SINCLAIR
ZAC ATKINSON
Colorists

TRAVIS LANHAM
CARLOS M. MANGUAL
DEZI SIENTY
Letterers

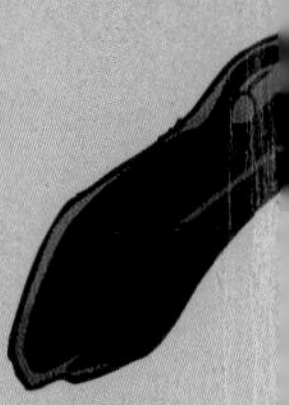

MIKE NORTON & ALEX SINCLAIR
Cover

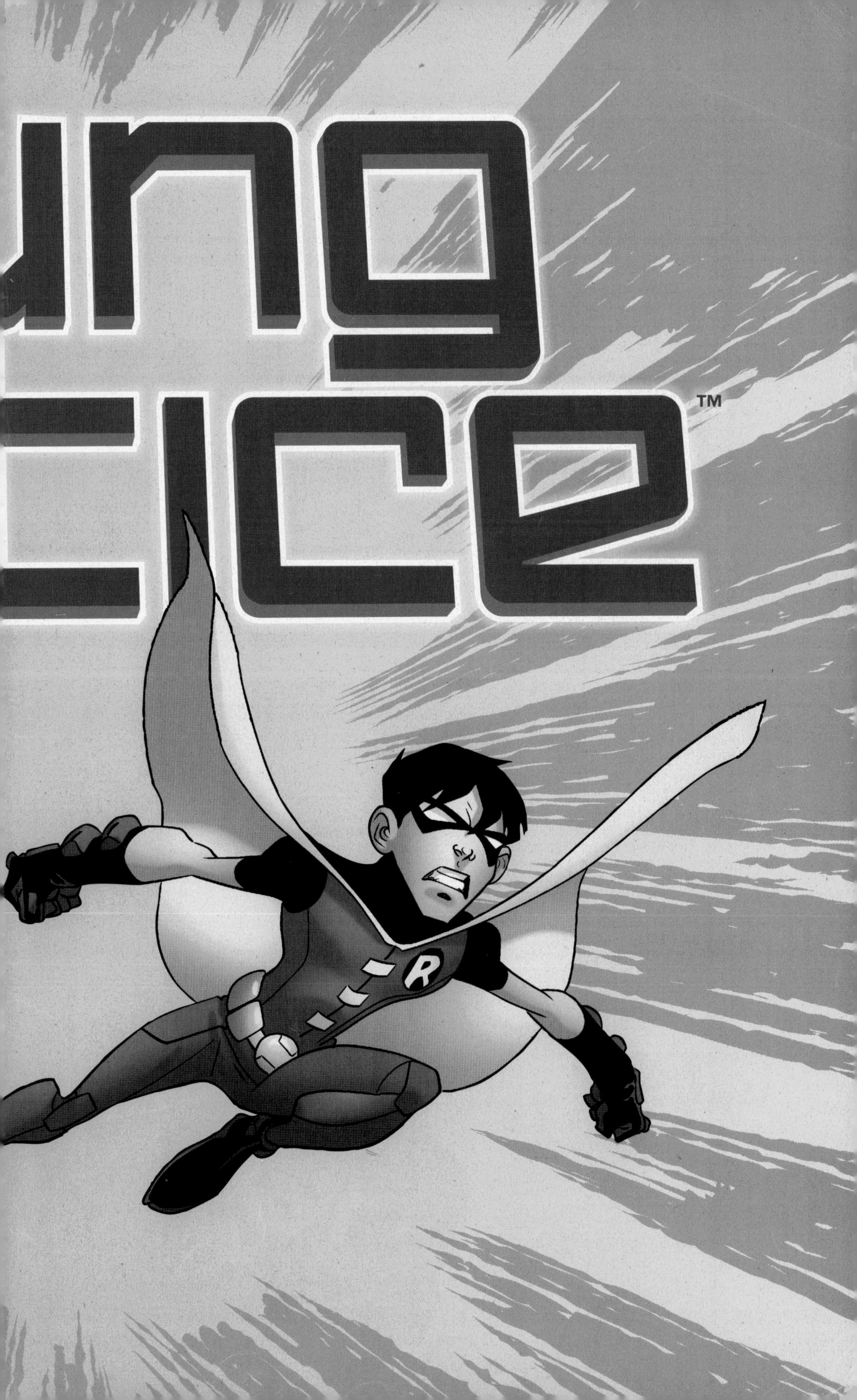

YOUNG JUSTICE

Published by DC Comics. Cover and compilation Copyright © 2012 DC Comics.
All Rights Reserved. Originally published in single magazine form in YOUNG
JUSTICE 0-6. Copyright © 2011 DC Comics. All Rights Reserved. All characters,
their distinctive likenesses and related elements featured in this publication are
trademarks of DC Comics. The stories, characters and incidents featured in
this publication are entirely fictional. DC Comics does not read or accept
unsolicited ideas, stories or artwork.

DC Comics, 1700 Broadway, New York, NY 10019
A Warner Bros. Entertainment Company.
Printed by Transcontinental Interglobe, Beauceville, QC, Canada. 11/22/13.
Fourth Printing. ISBN: 978-1-4012-3357-0

Library of Congress Cataloging-in-Publication Data

Baltazar, Art.
  Young justice / Art Baltazar & Franco Kevin Hopps & Greg Weisman
      p. cm.
  Summary: "Your favorite cartoon teen heroes are back in action! The Justice
League needed a covert team that could operate on the sly, so who better than
experienced crime fighters Robin, Kid Flash and Aqualad? Together with
Superboy, recently rescued from the top-secret Project Cadmus, and the
crush-worthy shape-shifting alien Miss Martian, these teens are ready to stop
being sidekicks and start taking down villains–like the League of Shadows and the
Joker–all on their own. But Superboy may have a secret mission of his own
to complete–destroying Superman!"–P. [4] of cover.
  ISBN 978-1-4012-3357-0 (pbk.)
  [1. Graphic novels.] I. Baltazar, Art. II. Hopps, Kevin. III. Jones, Christopher, 1969-
IV. Young justice (Television program) V. Title.
  741.5'973–dc23
                          2011287684

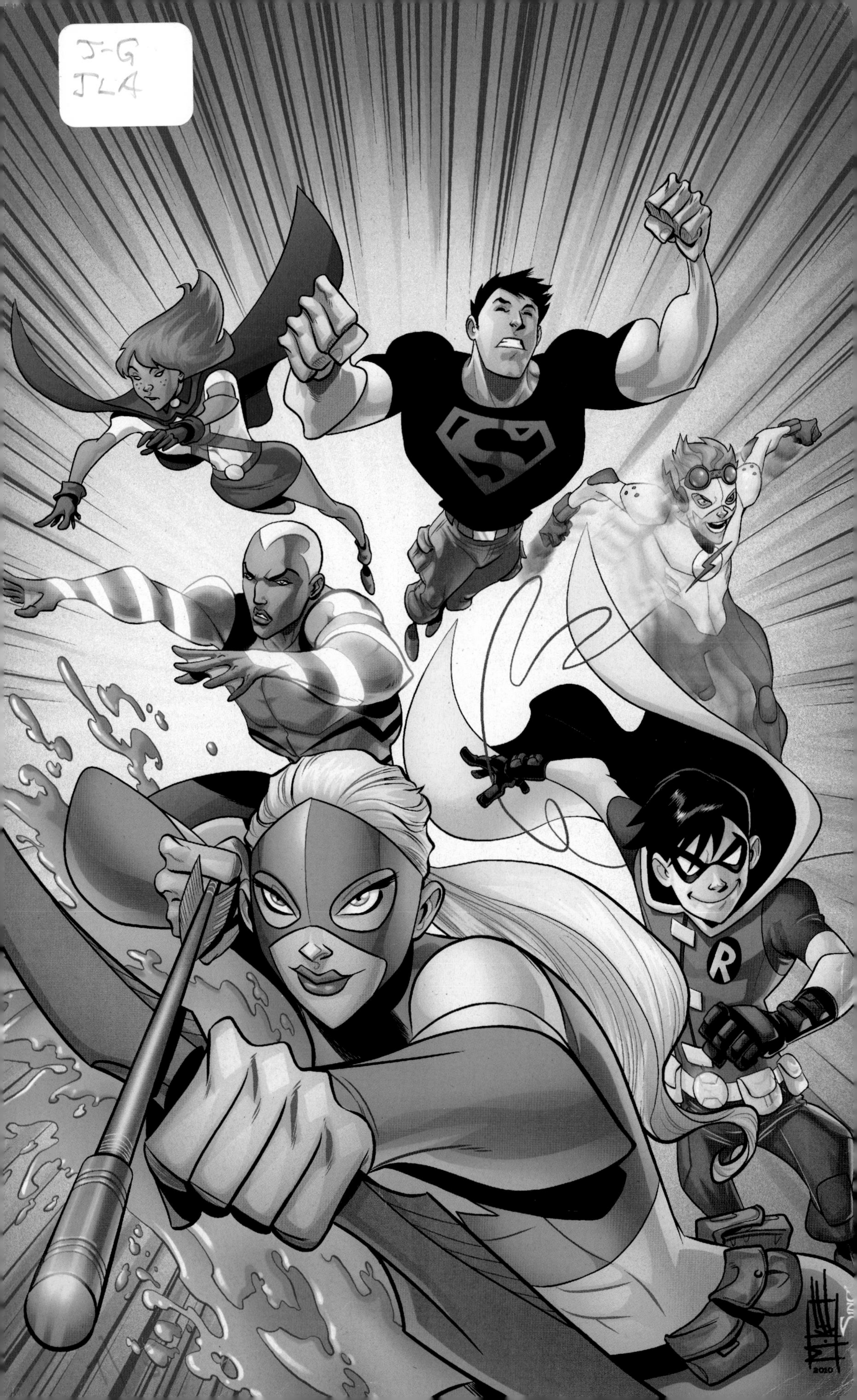

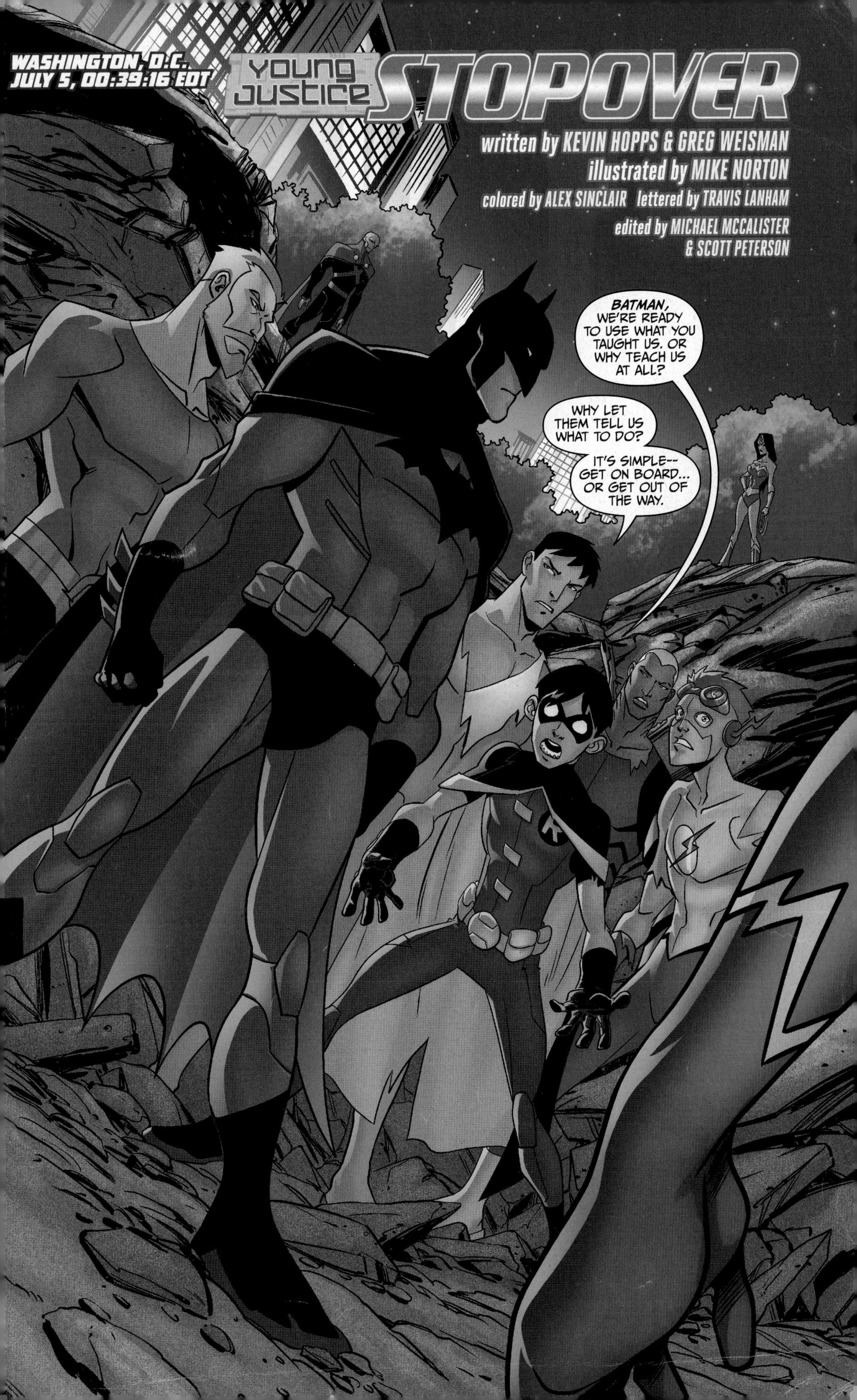
WASHINGTON, D.C.
JULY 5, 00:39:16 EDT
YOUNG JUSTICE
STOPOVER
written by KEVIN HOPPS & GREG WEISMAN
illustrated by MIKE NORTON
colored by ALEX SINCLAIR lettered by TRAVIS LANHAM
edited by MICHAEL MCCALISTER
& SCOTT PETERSON
BATMAN, WE'RE READY TO USE WHAT YOU TAUGHT US. OR WHY TEACH US AT ALL?
WHY LET THEM TELL US WHAT TO DO?
IT'S SIMPLE-- GET ON BOARD... OR GET OUT OF THE WAY.

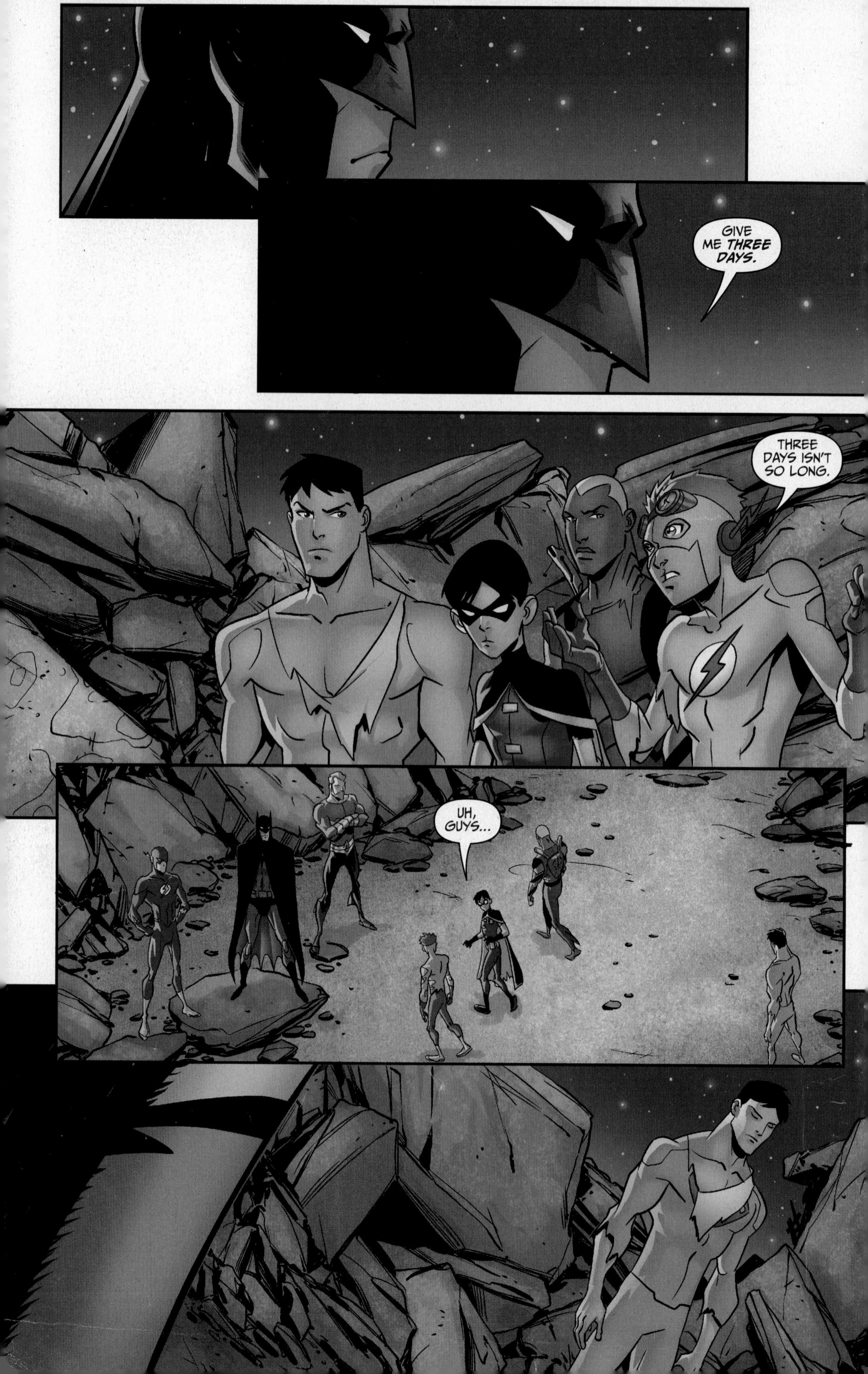
GIVE ME THREE DAYS.
THREE DAYS ISN'T SO LONG.
UH, GUYS...

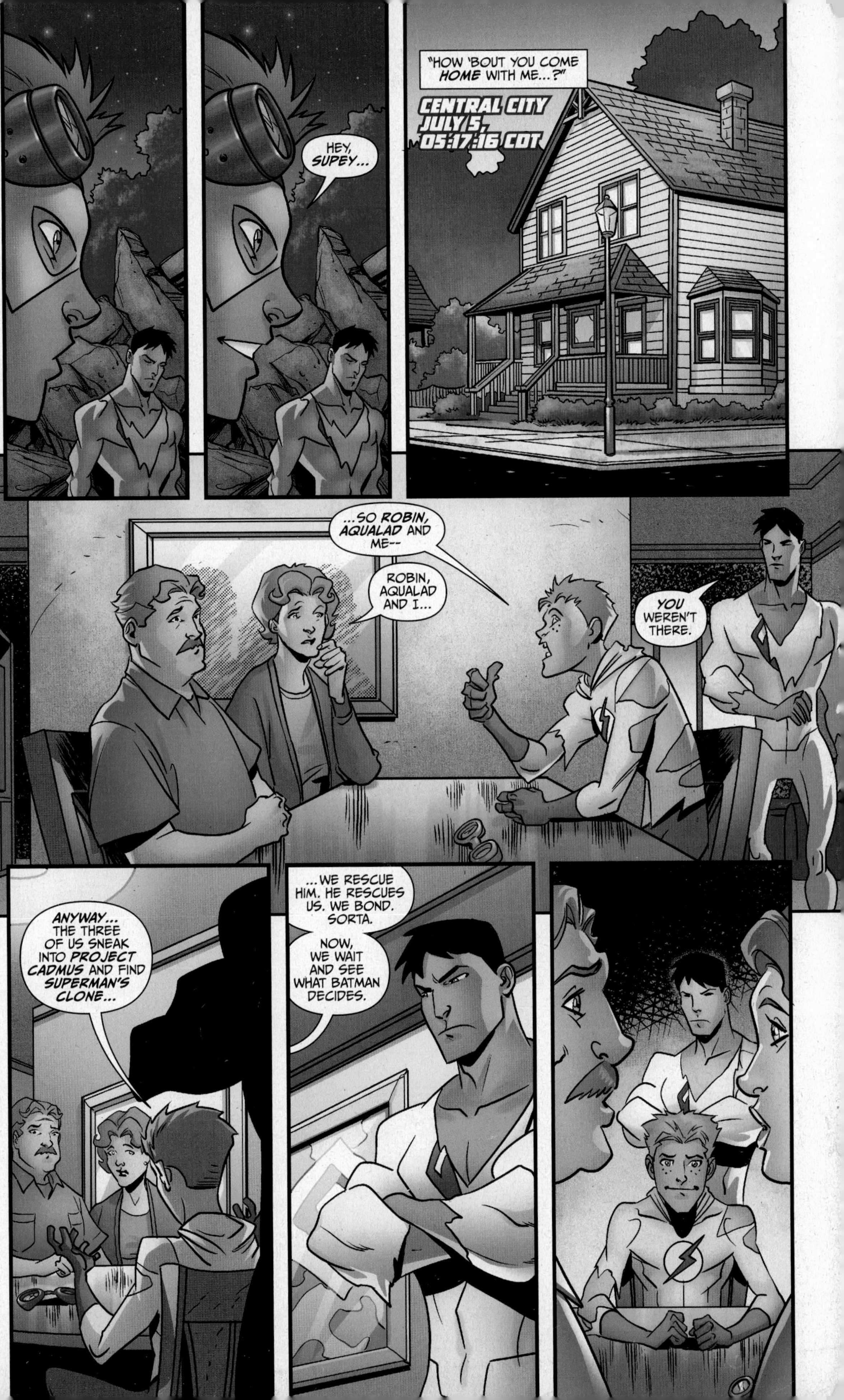
HEY, SUPEY...
"HOW 'BOUT YOU COME HOME WITH ME...?"
CENTRAL CITY JULY 5, 05:17:16 CDT
...SO ROBIN, AQUALAD AND ME--
ROBIN, AQUALAD AND I...
YOU WEREN'T THERE.
ANYWAY... THE THREE OF US SNEAK INTO PROJECT CADMUS AND FIND SUPERMAN'S CLONE...
...WE RESCUE HIM. HE RESCUES US. WE BOND. SORTA.
NOW, WE WAIT AND SEE WHAT BATMAN DECIDES.

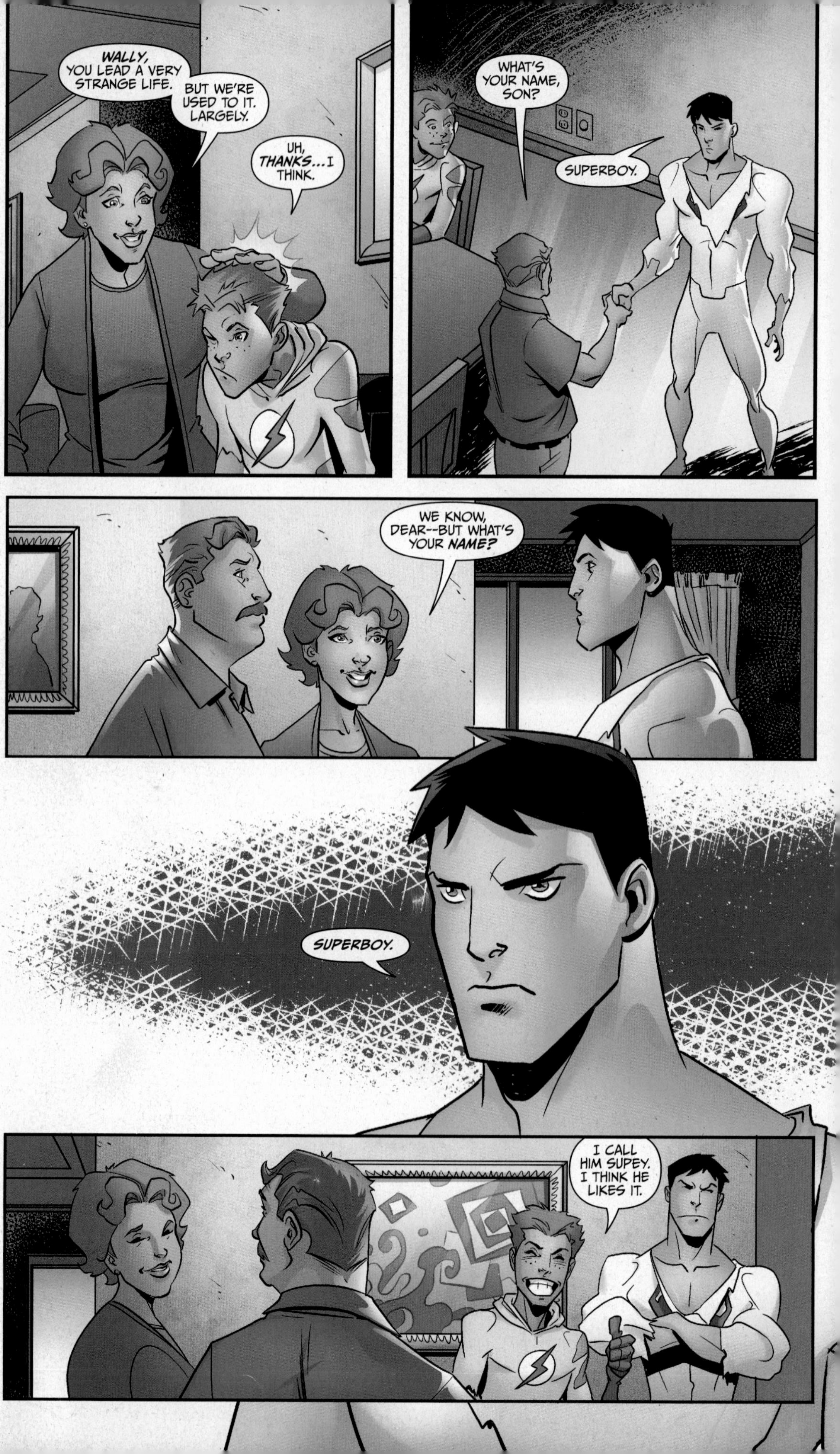
WALLY, YOU LEAD A VERY STRANGE LIFE.
BUT WE'RE USED TO IT. LARGELY.
UH, THANKS... I THINK.
WHAT'S YOUR NAME, SON?
SUPERBOY.
WE KNOW, DEAR--BUT WHAT'S YOUR NAME?
SUPERBOY.
I CALL HIM SUPEY. I THINK HE LIKES IT.

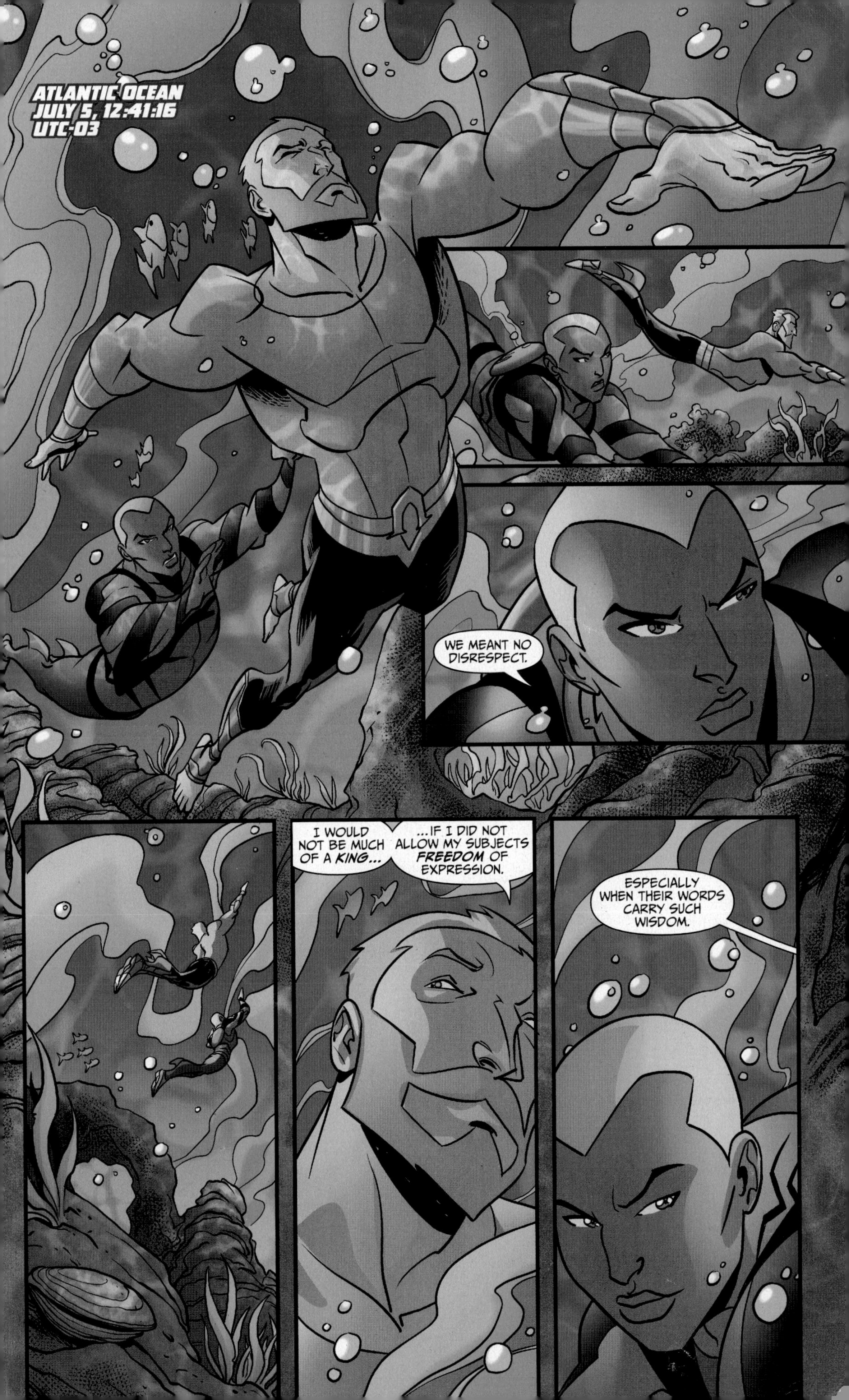

ATLANTIC OCEAN
JULY 5, 12:41:16
UTC-03
WE MEANT NO DISRESPECT.
I WOULD NOT BE MUCH OF A *KING*...
...IF I DID NOT ALLOW MY SUBJECTS *FREEDOM* OF EXPRESSION.
ESPECIALLY WHEN THEIR WORDS CARRY SUCH WISDOM.

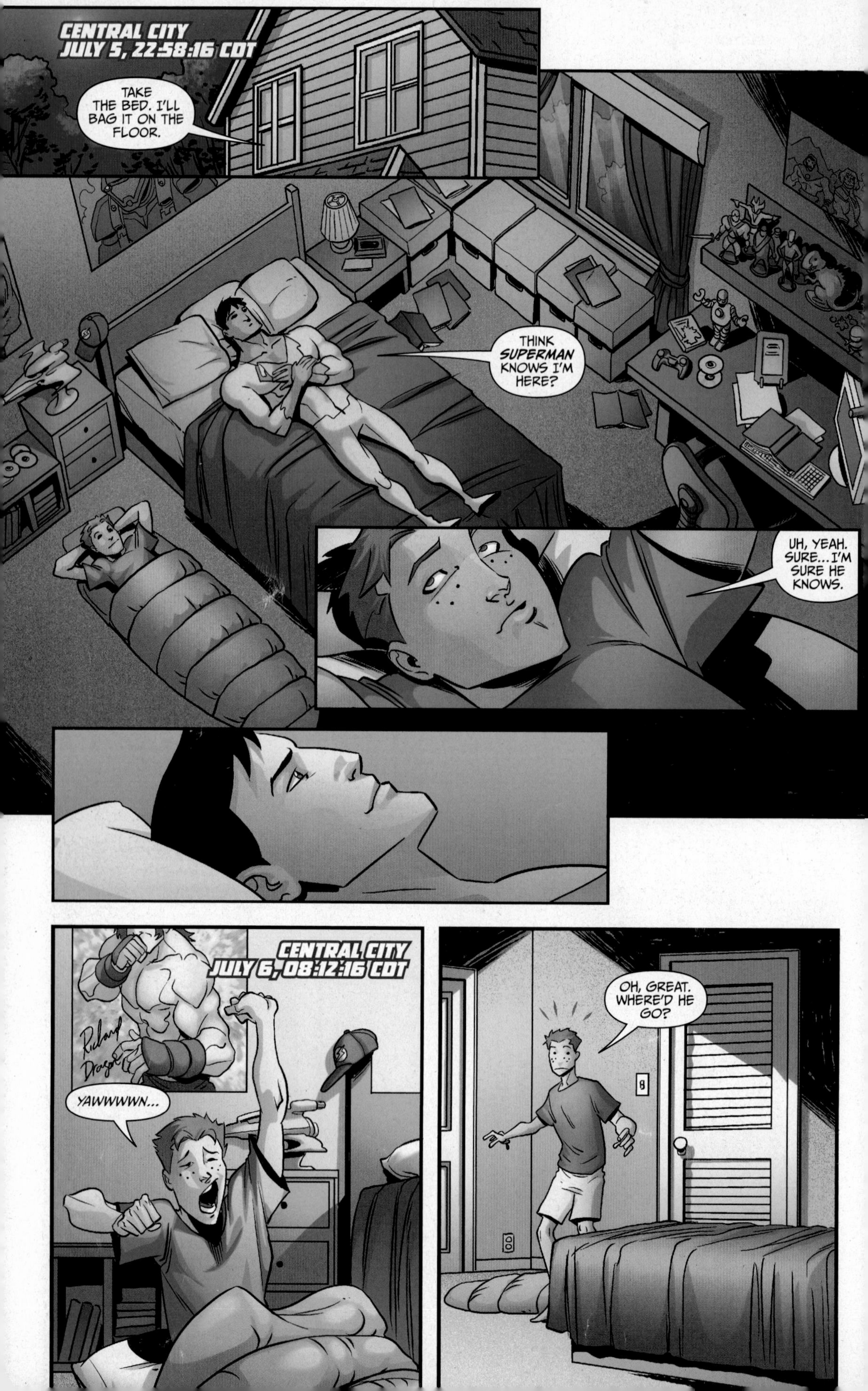
CENTRAL CITY
JULY 5, 22:58:16 CDT
TAKE THE BED. I'LL BAG IT ON THE FLOOR.
THINK SUPERMAN KNOWS I'M HERE?
UH, YEAH. SURE... I'M SURE HE KNOWS.
CENTRAL CITY
JULY 6, 08:12:16 CDT
YAWWWWN...
OH, GREAT. WHERE'D HE GO?

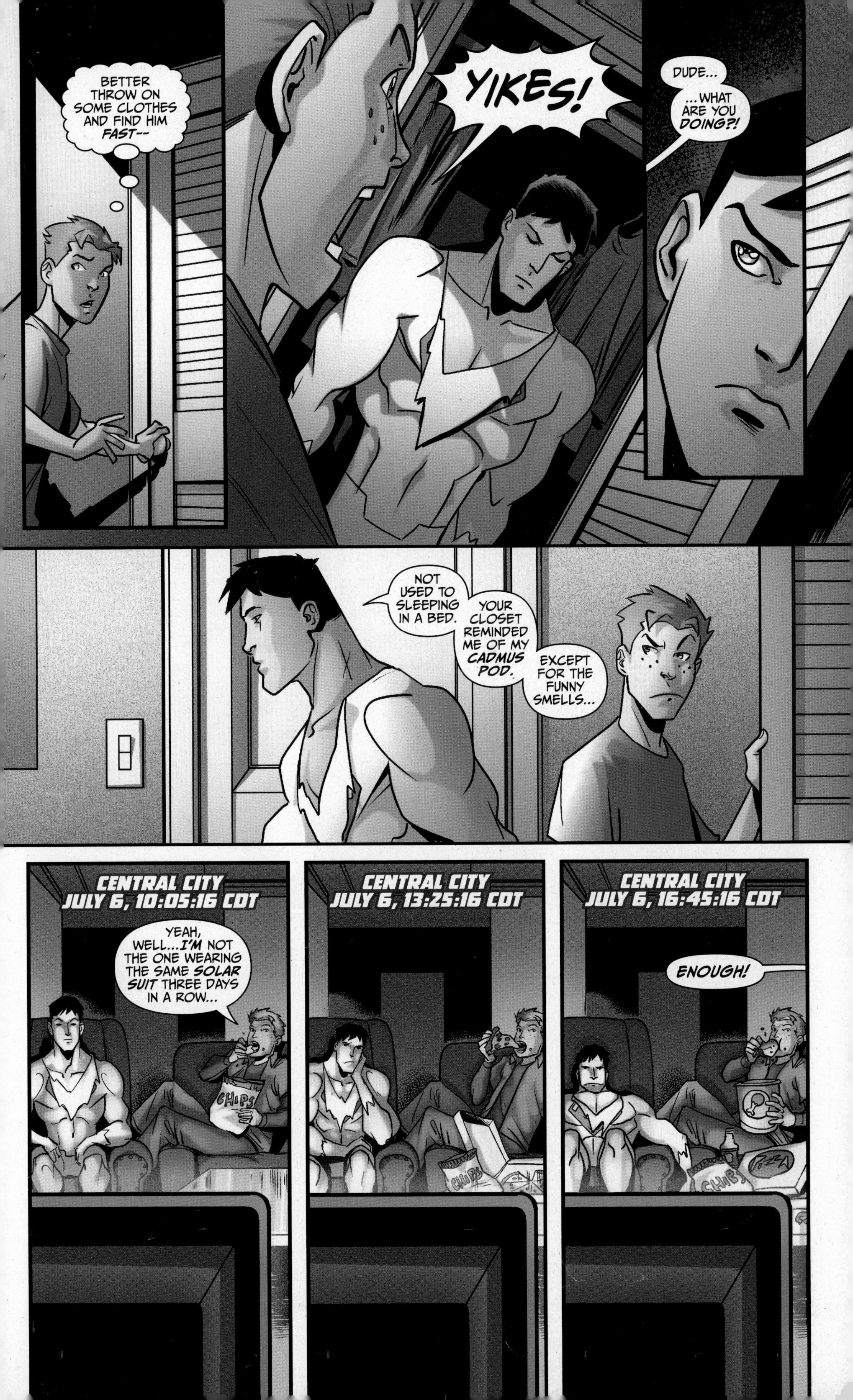
BETTER THROW ON SOME CLOTHES AND FIND HIM FAST--
YIKES!
DUDE...
...WHAT ARE YOU DOING?!
NOT USED TO SLEEPING IN A BED.
YOUR CLOSET REMINDED ME OF MY CADMUS POD.
EXCEPT FOR THE FUNNY SMELLS...
CENTRAL CITY JULY 6, 10:05:16 CDT
YEAH, WELL...I'M NOT THE ONE WEARING THE SAME SOLAR SUIT THREE DAYS IN A ROW...
CHIPS
CENTRAL CITY JULY 6, 13:25:16 CDT
CHIPS
CENTRAL CITY JULY 6, 16:45:16 CDT
ENOUGH!
CHIPS
PIZZA

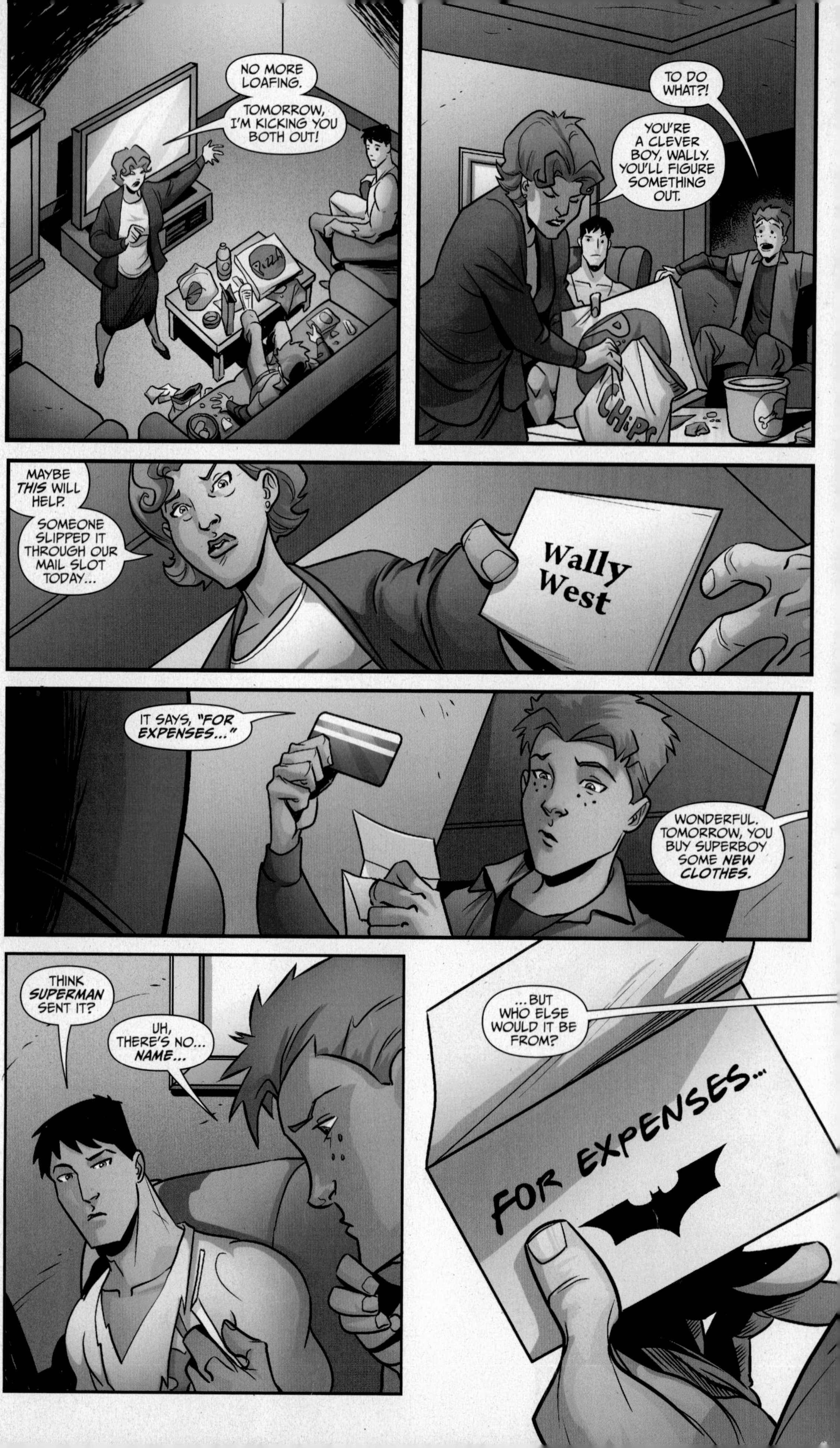
NO MORE LOAFING.
TOMORROW, I'M KICKING YOU BOTH OUT!
TO DO WHAT?!
YOU'RE A CLEVER BOY, WALLY. YOU'LL FIGURE SOMETHING OUT.
CHIPS
MAYBE THIS WILL HELP.
SOMEONE SLIPPED IT THROUGH OUR MAIL SLOT TODAY...
Wally West
IT SAYS, "FOR EXPENSES..."
WONDERFUL. TOMORROW, YOU BUY SUPERBOY SOME NEW CLOTHES.
THINK SUPERMAN SENT IT?
UH, THERE'S NO... NAME...
...BUT WHO ELSE WOULD IT BE FROM?
FOR EXPENSES...

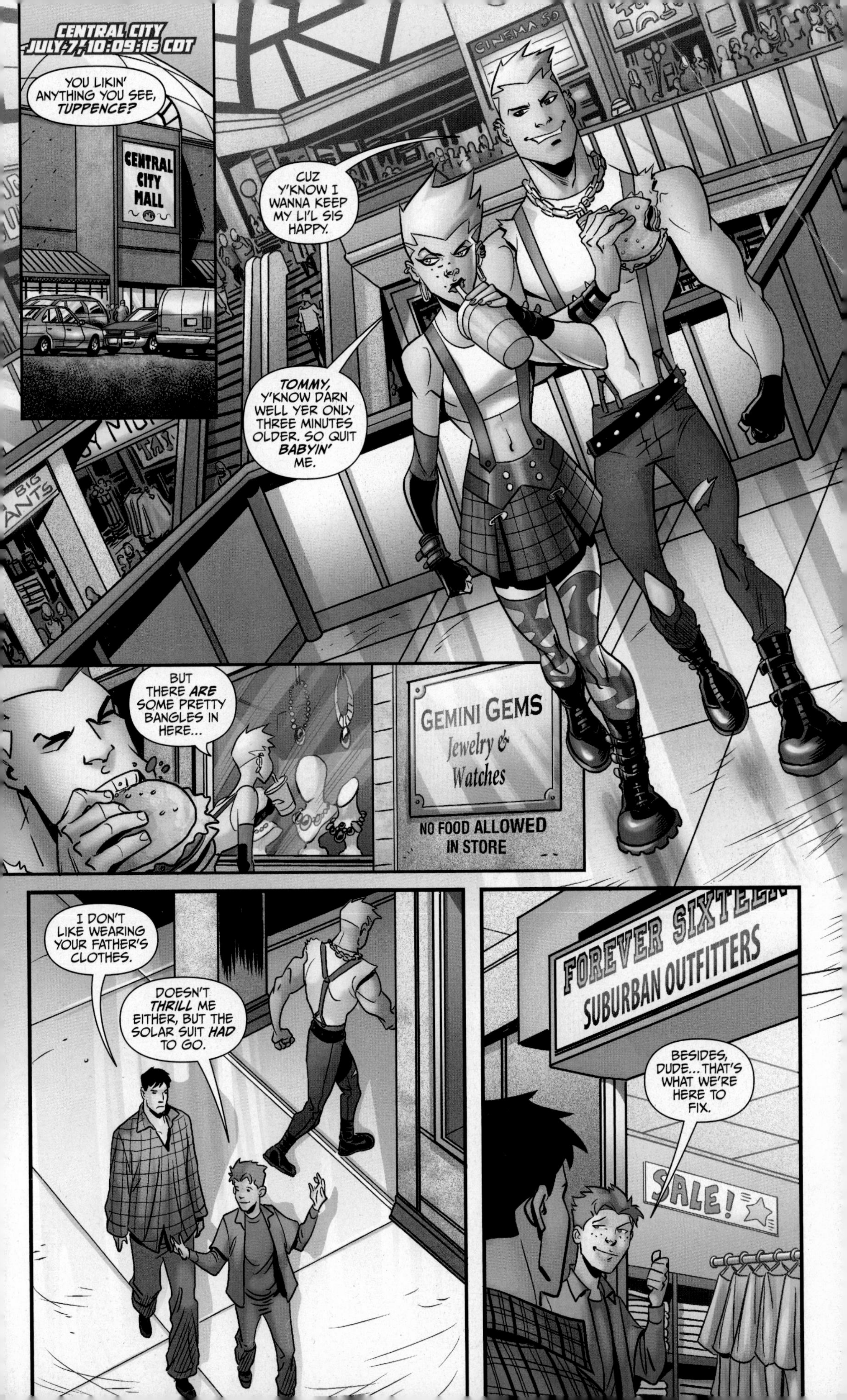
CENTRAL CITY
JULY 7, 10:09:16 CDT
YOU LIKIN' ANYTHING YOU SEE, TUPPENCE?
CENTRAL CITY MALL
CINEMA 50
CUZ Y'KNOW I WANNA KEEP MY LI'L SIS HAPPY.
TOMMY, Y'KNOW DARN WELL YER ONLY THREE MINUTES OLDER. SO QUIT BABYIN' ME.
BIG ANTS
BUT THERE ARE SOME PRETTY BANGLES IN HERE...
GEMINI GEMS
Jewelry & Watches
NO FOOD ALLOWED IN STORE
I DON'T LIKE WEARING YOUR FATHER'S CLOTHES.
DOESN'T THRILL ME EITHER, BUT THE SOLAR SUIT HAD TO GO.
FOREVER SIXTEEN
SUBURBAN OUTFITTERS
BESIDES, DUDE...THAT'S WHAT WE'RE HERE TO FIX.
SALE!

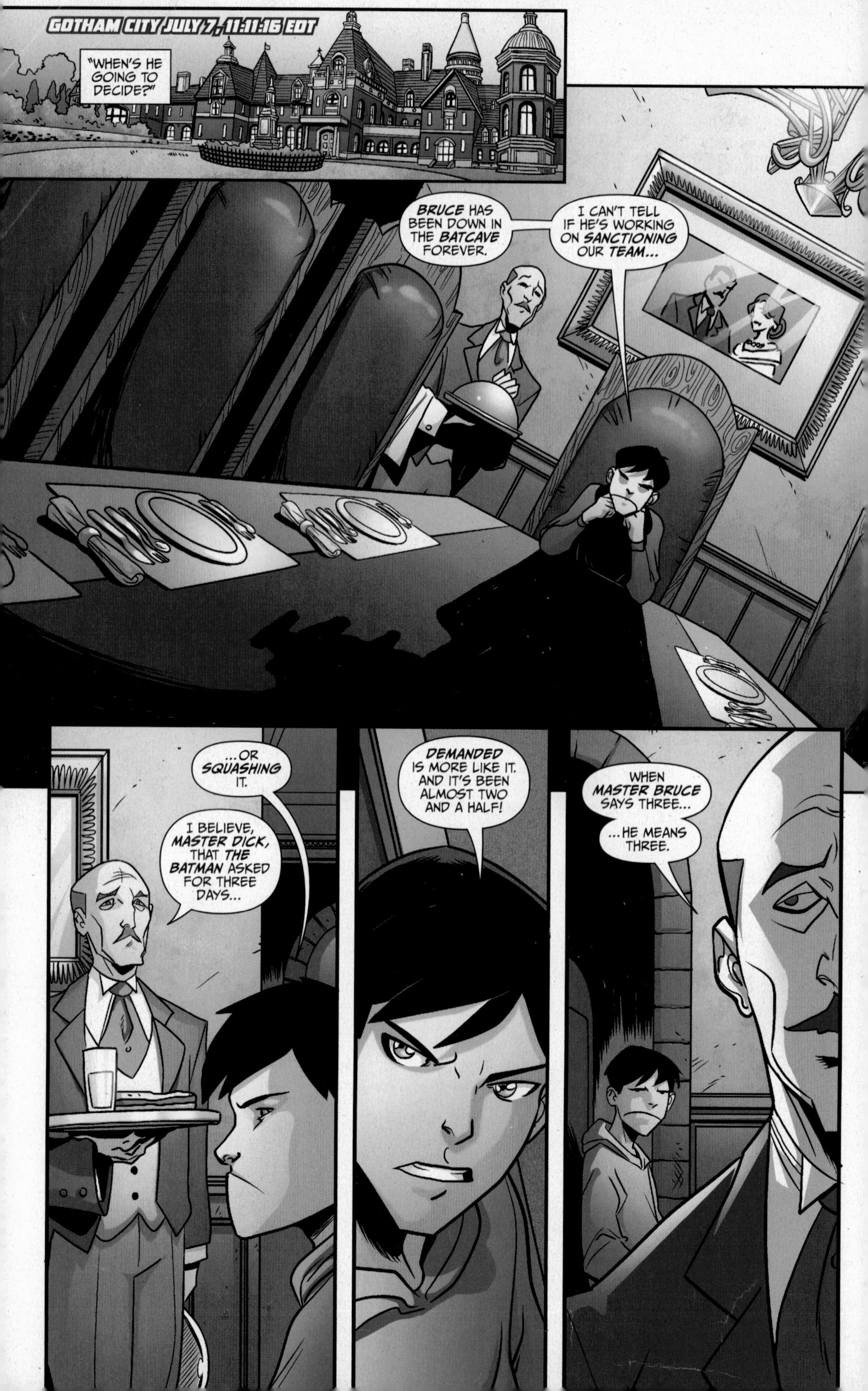
GOTHAM CITY JULY 7, 11:11:16 EDT
"WHEN'S HE GOING TO DECIDE?"
BRUCE HAS BEEN DOWN IN THE BATCAVE FOREVER.
I CAN'T TELL IF HE'S WORKING ON SANCTIONING OUR TEAM...
...OR SQUASHING IT.
I BELIEVE, MASTER DICK, THAT THE BATMAN ASKED FOR THREE DAYS...
DEMANDED IS MORE LIKE IT. AND IT'S BEEN ALMOST TWO AND A HALF!
WHEN MASTER BRUCE SAYS THREE...
...HE MEANS THREE.

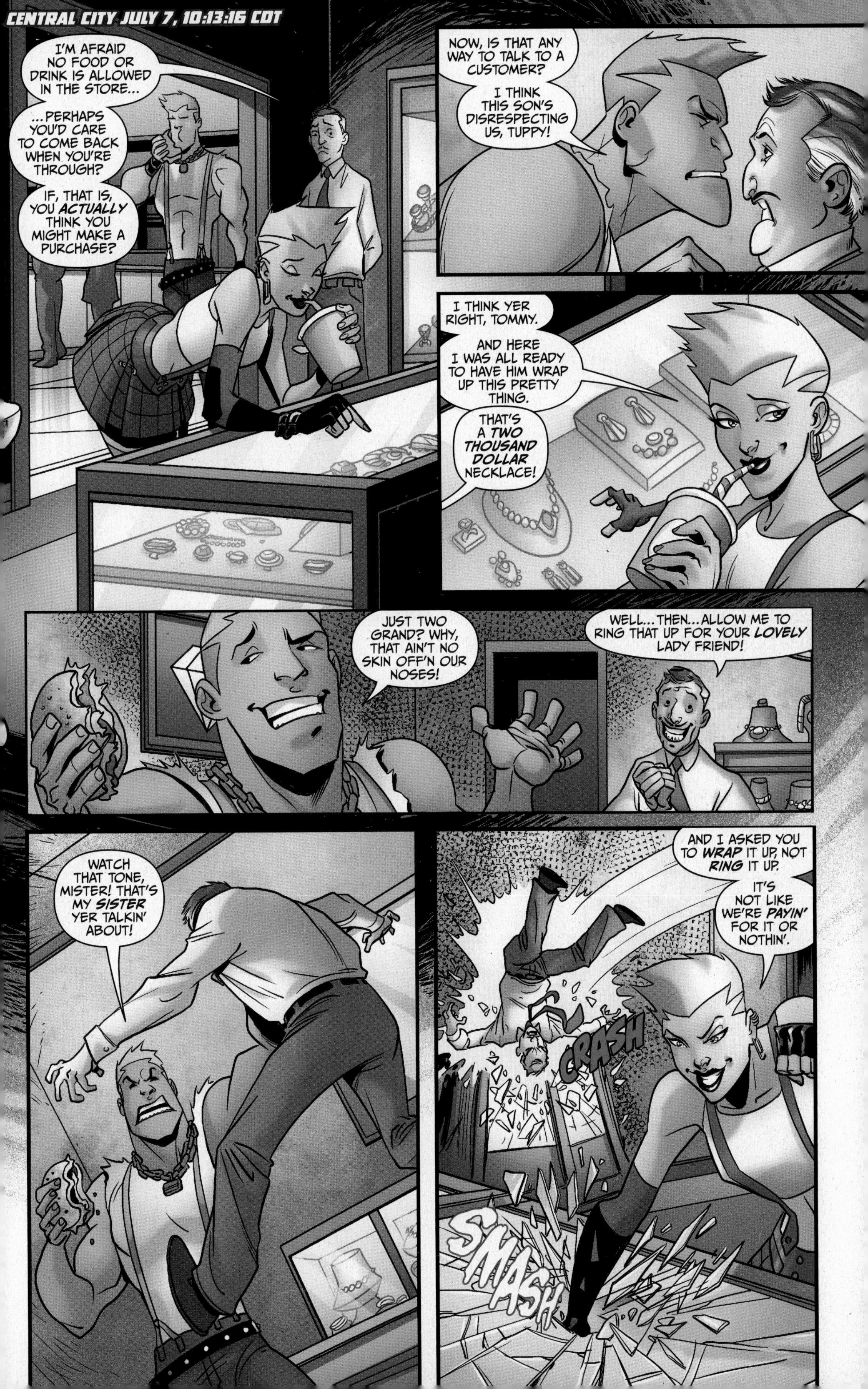
CENTRAL CITY JULY 7, 10:13:16 CDT
I'M AFRAID NO FOOD OR DRINK IS ALLOWED IN THE STORE...
...PERHAPS YOU'D CARE TO COME BACK WHEN YOU'RE THROUGH?
IF, THAT IS, YOU ACTUALLY THINK YOU MIGHT MAKE A PURCHASE?
NOW, IS THAT ANY WAY TO TALK TO A CUSTOMER?
I THINK THIS SON'S DISRESPECTING US, TUPPY!
I THINK YER RIGHT, TOMMY.
AND HERE I WAS ALL READY TO HAVE HIM WRAP UP THIS PRETTY THING.
THAT'S A TWO THOUSAND DOLLAR NECKLACE!
JUST TWO GRAND? WHY, THAT AIN'T NO SKIN OFF'N OUR NOSES!
WELL...THEN...ALLOW ME TO RING THAT UP FOR YOUR LOVELY LADY FRIEND!
WATCH THAT TONE, MISTER! THAT'S MY SISTER YER TALKIN' ABOUT!
AND I ASKED YOU TO WRAP IT UP, NOT RING IT UP.
IT'S NOT LIKE WE'RE PAYIN' FOR IT OR NOTHIN'.
CRASH
SMASH

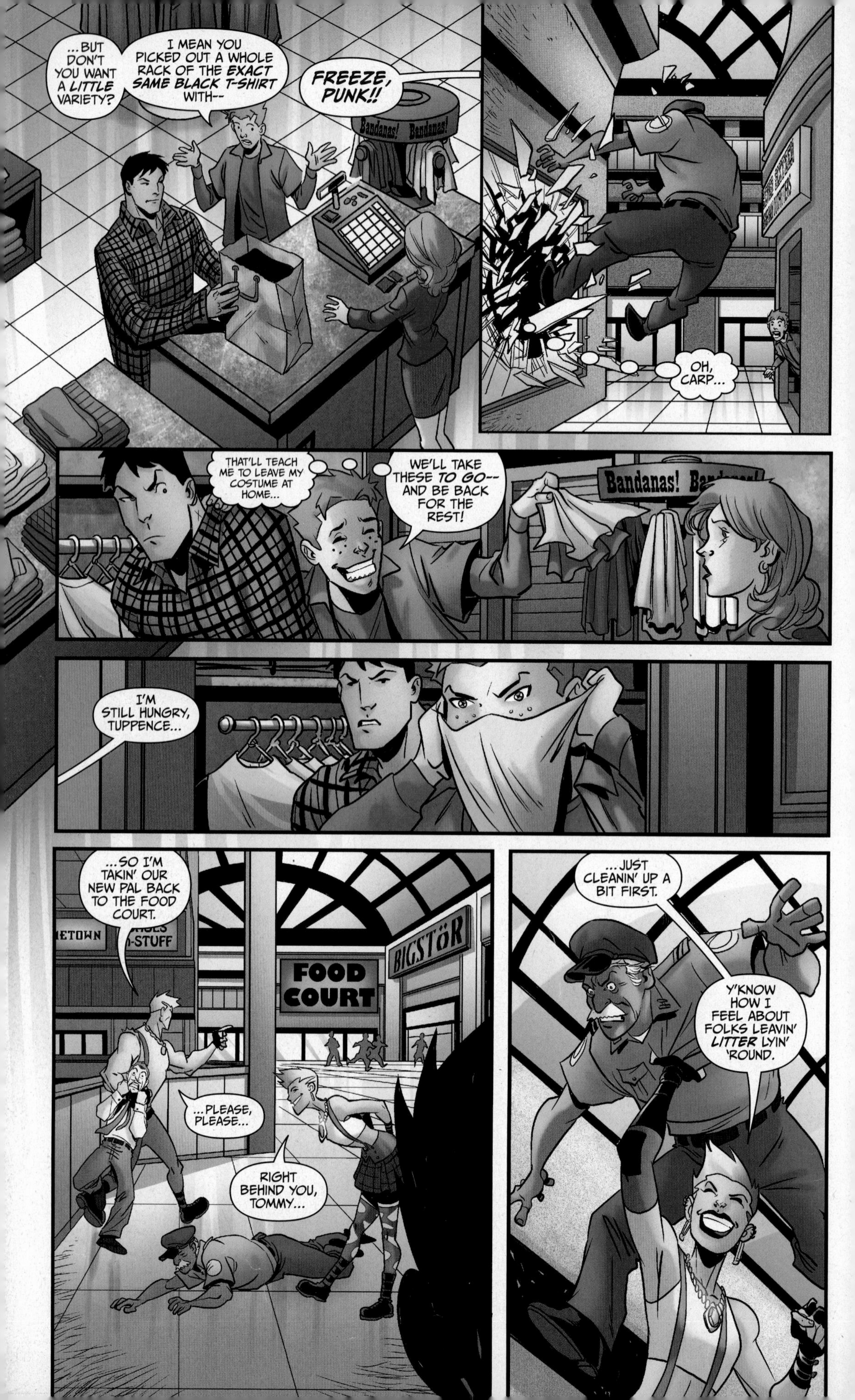
...BUT DON'T YOU WANT A *LITTLE* VARIETY?
I MEAN YOU PICKED OUT A WHOLE RACK OF THE *EXACT SAME BLACK T-SHIRT* WITH--
FREEZE, PUNK!!
Bandanas! Bandanas!
OH, CARP...
THAT'LL TEACH ME TO LEAVE MY COSTUME AT HOME...
WE'LL TAKE THESE *TO GO*-- AND BE BACK FOR THE REST!
Bandanas!
I'M STILL HUNGRY, TUPPENCE...
...SO I'M TAKIN' OUR NEW PAL BACK TO THE FOOD COURT.
FOOD COURT
BIGSTöR
...PLEASE, PLEASE...
RIGHT BEHIND YOU, TOMMY...
...JUST CLEANIN' UP A BIT FIRST.
Y'KNOW HOW I FEEL ABOUT FOLKS LEAVIN' *LITTER* LYIN' 'ROUND.

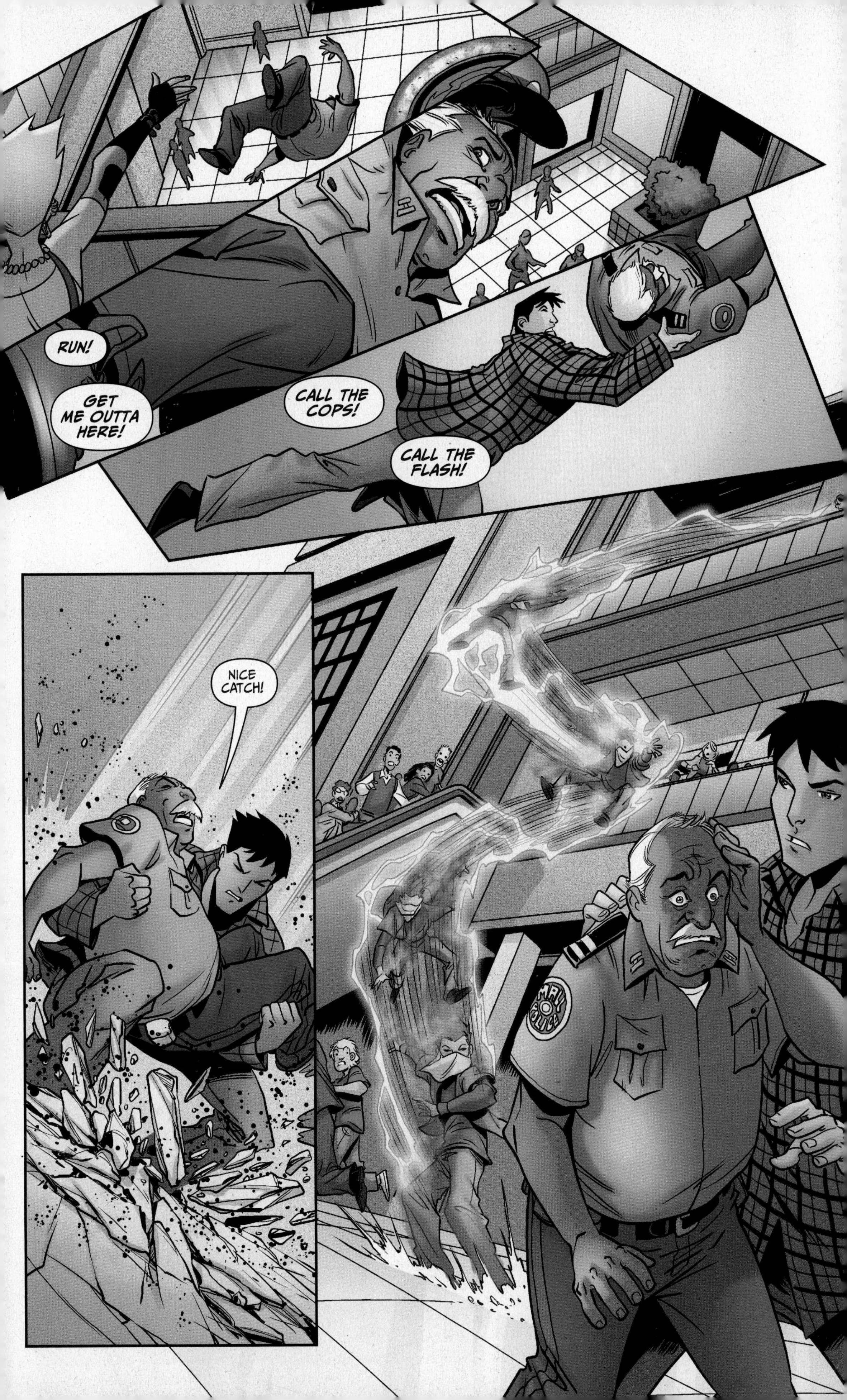
RUN!
GET ME OUTTA HERE!
CALL THE COPS!
CALL THE FLASH!
NICE CATCH!

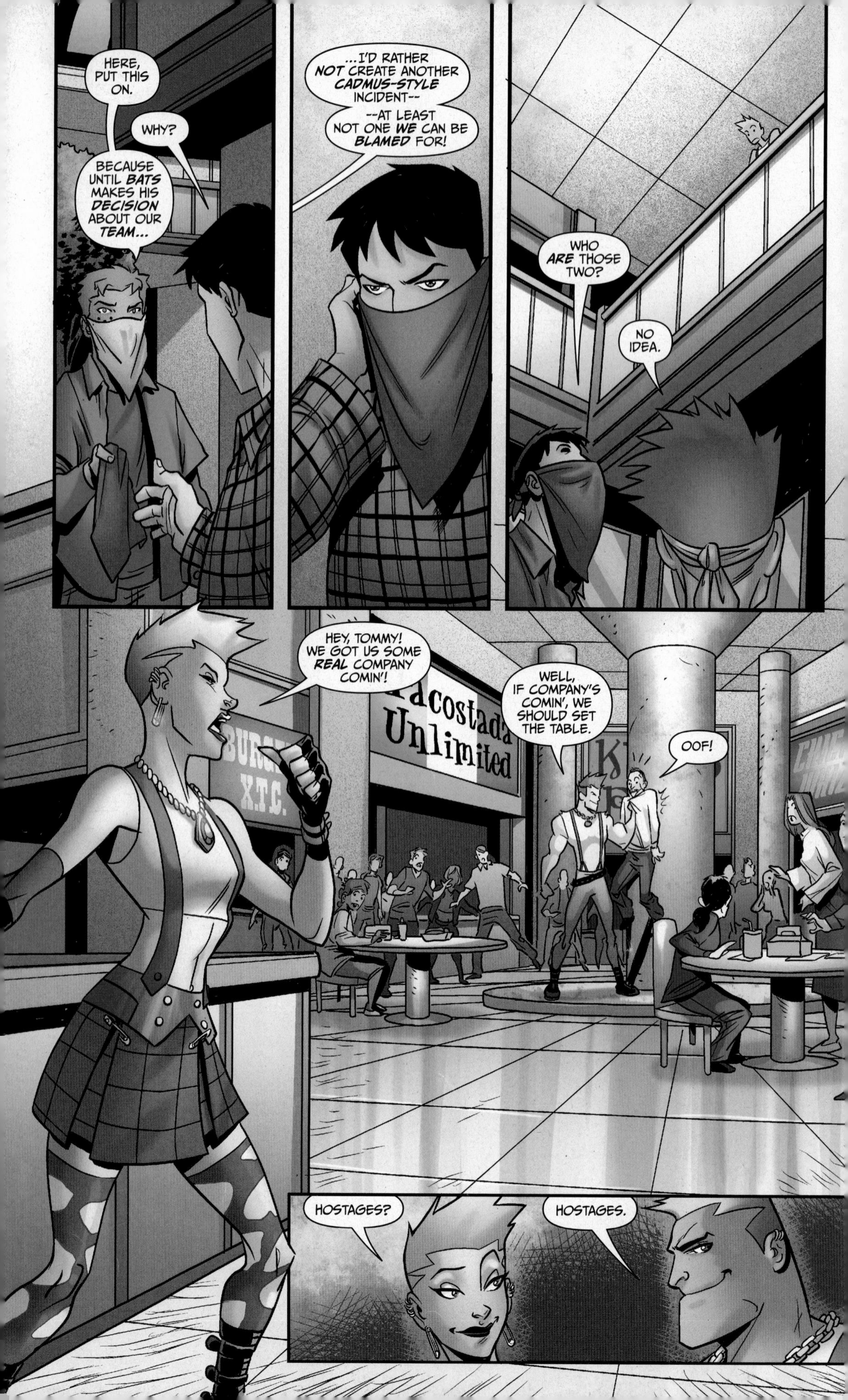
HERE, PUT THIS ON.
WHY?
BECAUSE UNTIL BATS MAKES HIS DECISION ABOUT OUR TEAM...
...I'D RATHER NOT CREATE ANOTHER CADMUS-STYLE INCIDENT--
--AT LEAST NOT ONE WE CAN BE BLAMED FOR!
WHO ARE THOSE TWO?
NO IDEA.
HEY, TOMMY! WE GOT US SOME REAL COMPANY COMIN'!
Unlimited
X.T.C.
WELL, IF COMPANY'S COMIN', WE SHOULD SET THE TABLE.
OOF!
HOSTAGES?
HOSTAGES.

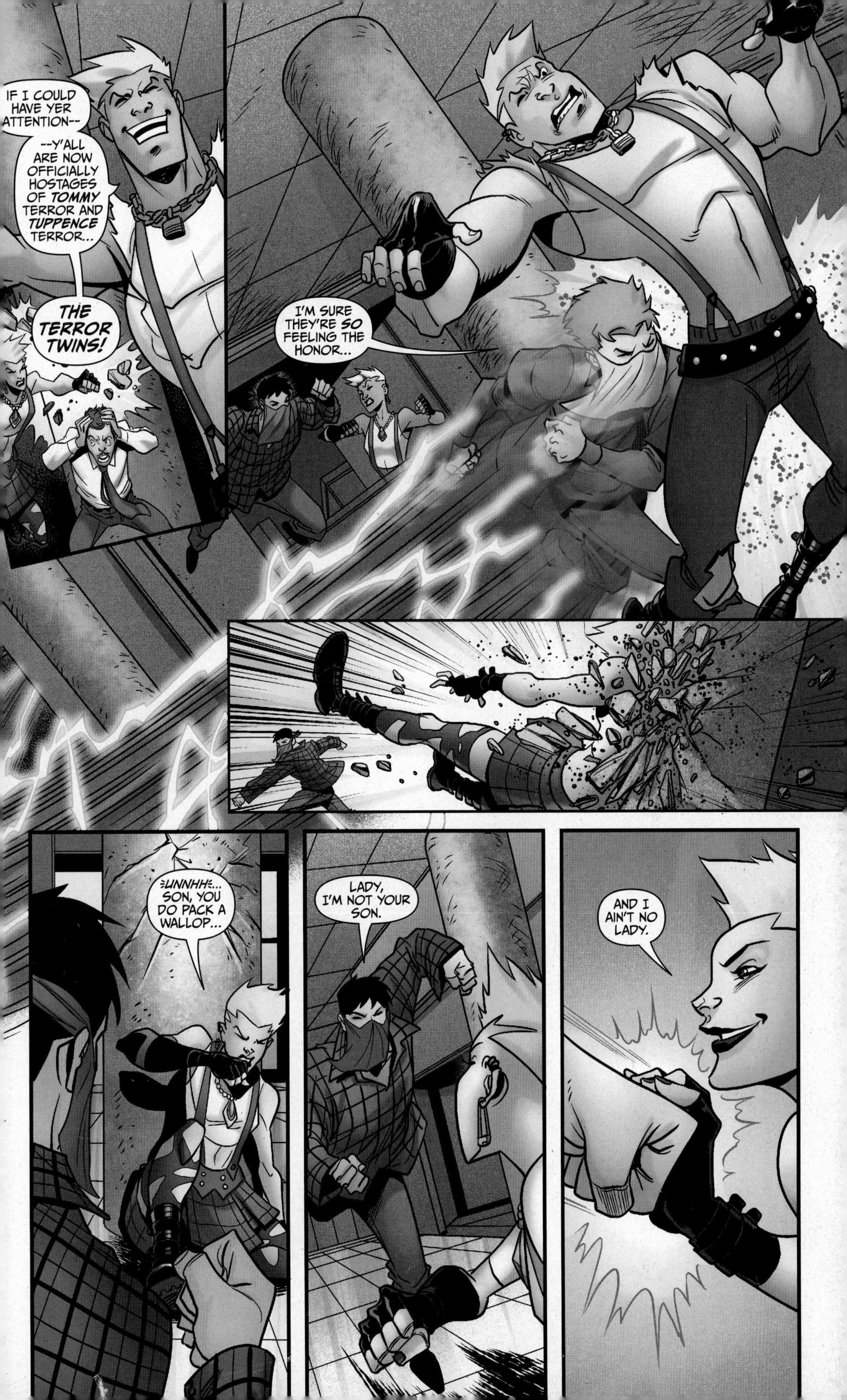
IF I COULD HAVE YER ATTENTION--
--Y'ALL ARE NOW OFFICIALLY HOSTAGES OF TOMMY TERROR AND TUPPENCE TERROR...
THE TERROR TWINS!
I'M SURE THEY'RE SO FEELING THE HONOR...
UNNHH... SON, YOU DO PACK A WALLOP...
LADY, I'M NOT YOUR SON.
AND I AIN'T NO LADY.

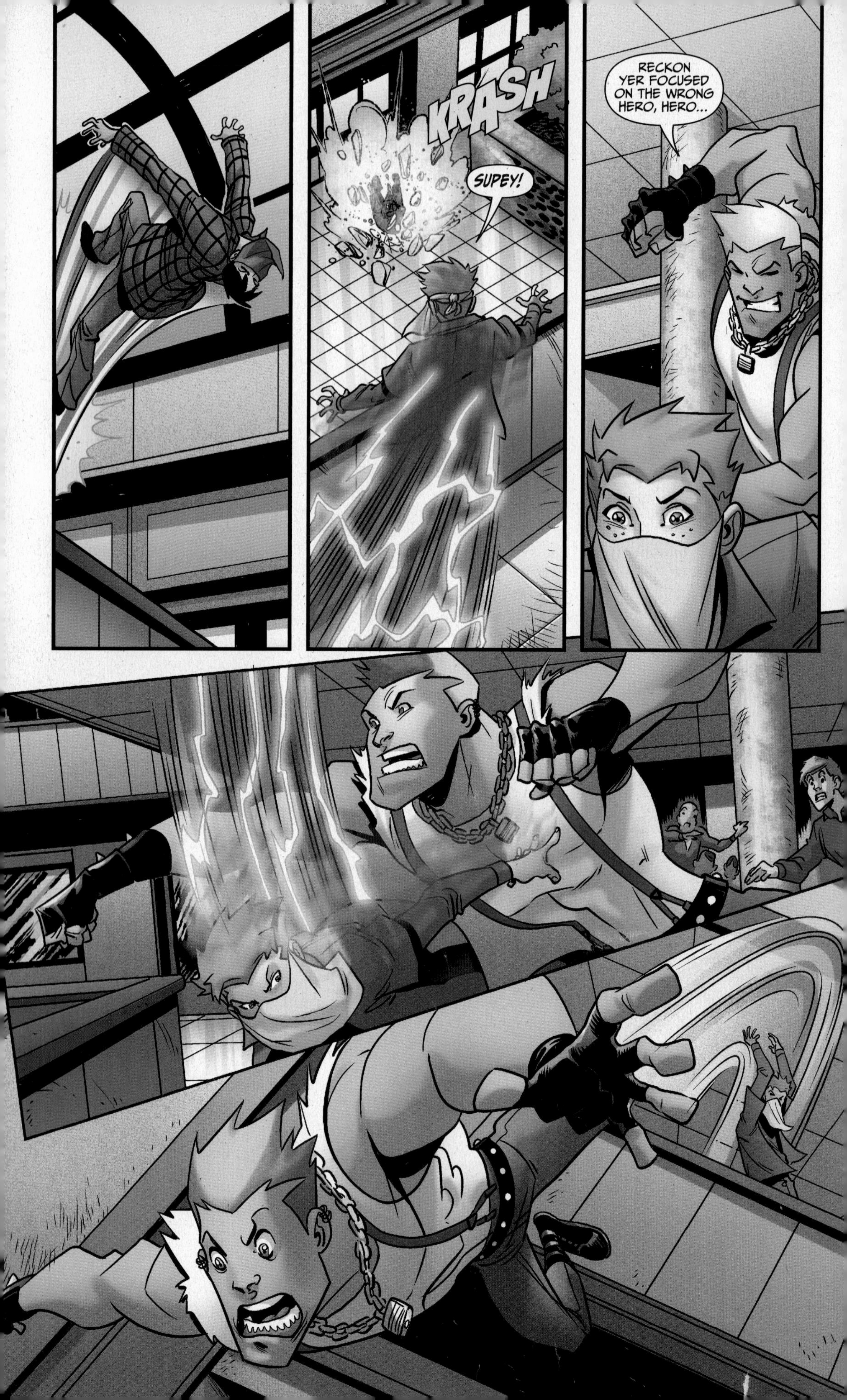
KRASH
SUPEY!
RECKON YER FOCUSED ON THE WRONG HERO, HERO...

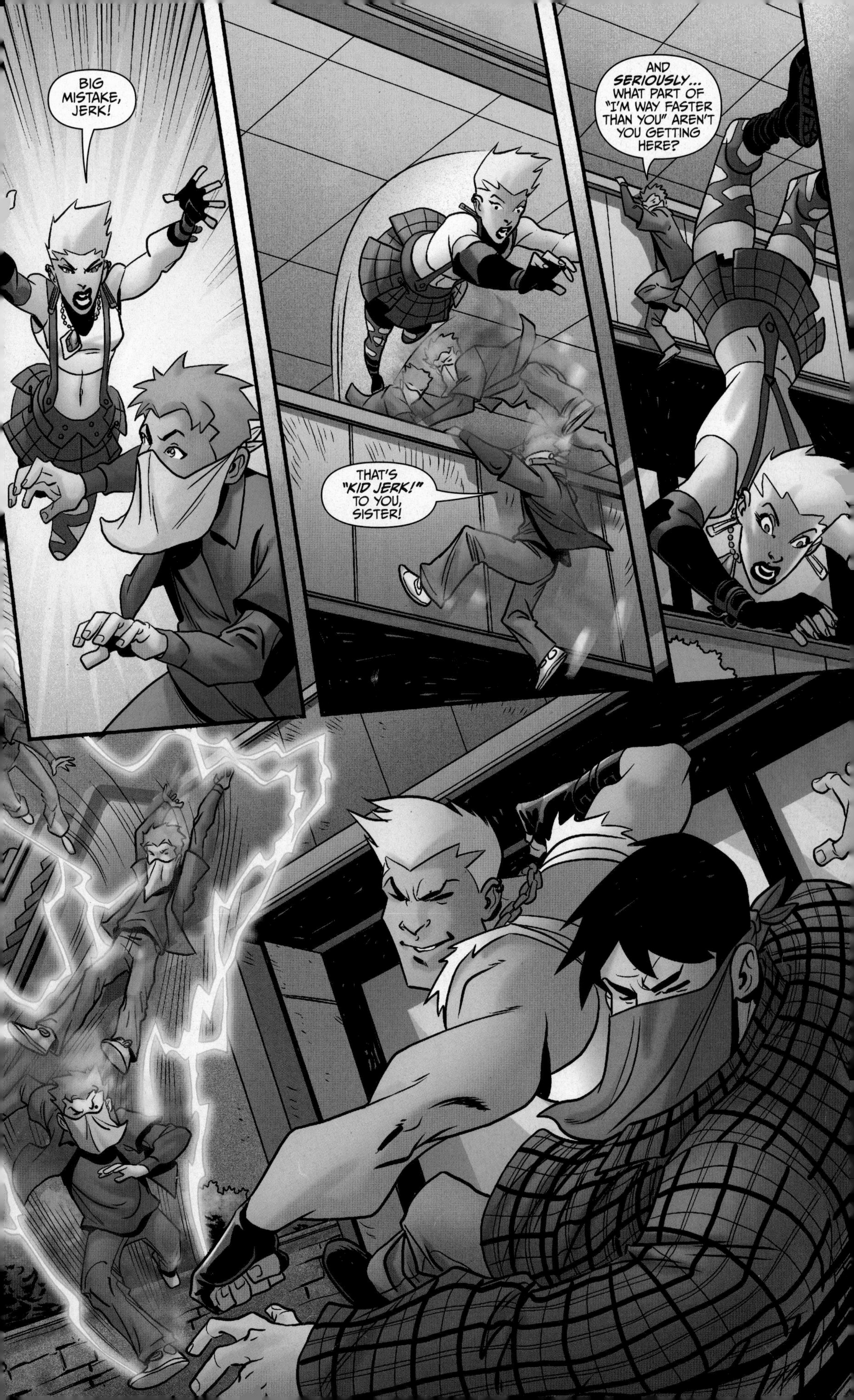
BIG MISTAKE, JERK!
THAT'S "KID JERK!" TO YOU, SISTER!
AND SERIOUSLY... WHAT PART OF "I'M WAY FASTER THAN YOU" AREN'T YOU GETTING HERE?

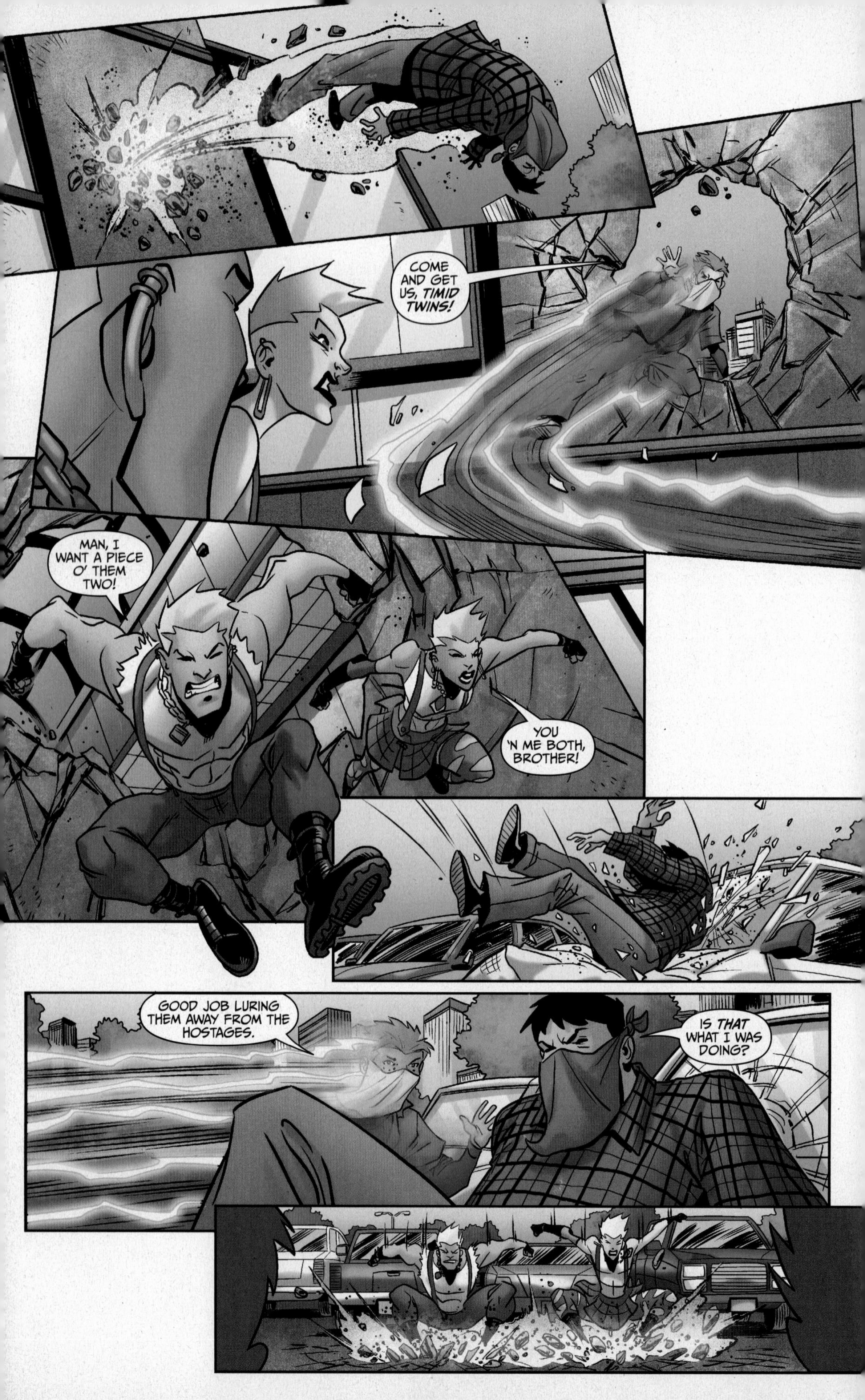
COME AND GET US, *TIMID TWINS!*
MAN, I WANT A PIECE O' THEM TWO!
YOU 'N ME BOTH, BROTHER!
GOOD JOB LURING THEM AWAY FROM THE HOSTAGES.
IS *THAT* WHAT I WAS DOING?

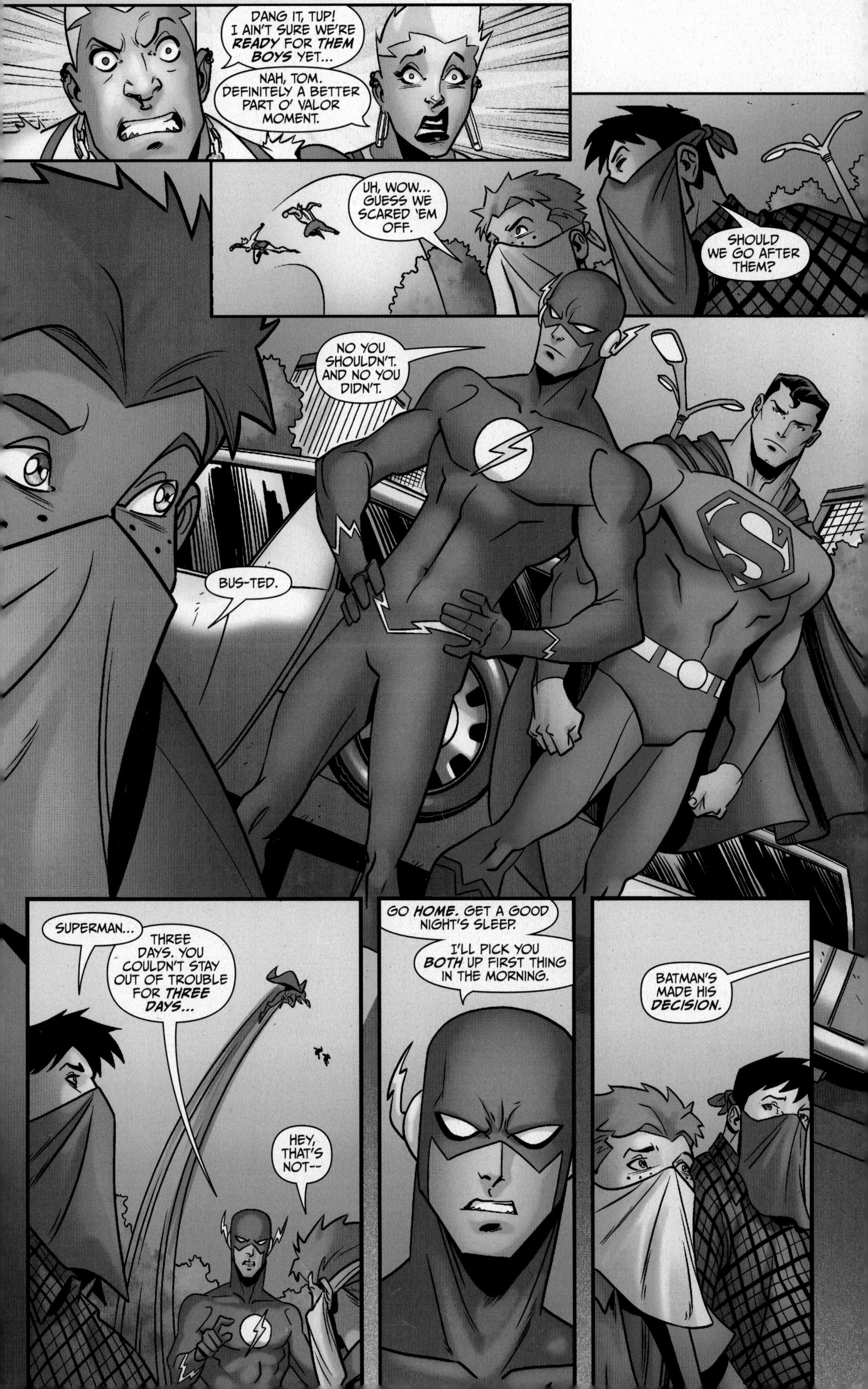

DANG IT, TUP! I AIN'T SURE WE'RE *READY* FOR *THEM BOYS* YET...
NAH, TOM. DEFINITELY A BETTER PART O' VALOR MOMENT.
UH, WOW... GUESS WE SCARED 'EM OFF.
SHOULD WE GO AFTER THEM?
NO YOU SHOULDN'T. AND NO YOU DIDN'T.
BUS-TED.
SUPERMAN...
THREE DAYS. YOU COULDN'T STAY OUT OF TROUBLE FOR *THREE DAYS...*
HEY, THAT'S NOT--
GO *HOME*. GET A GOOD NIGHT'S SLEEP.
I'LL PICK YOU *BOTH* UP FIRST THING IN THE MORNING.
BATMAN'S MADE HIS *DECISION.*

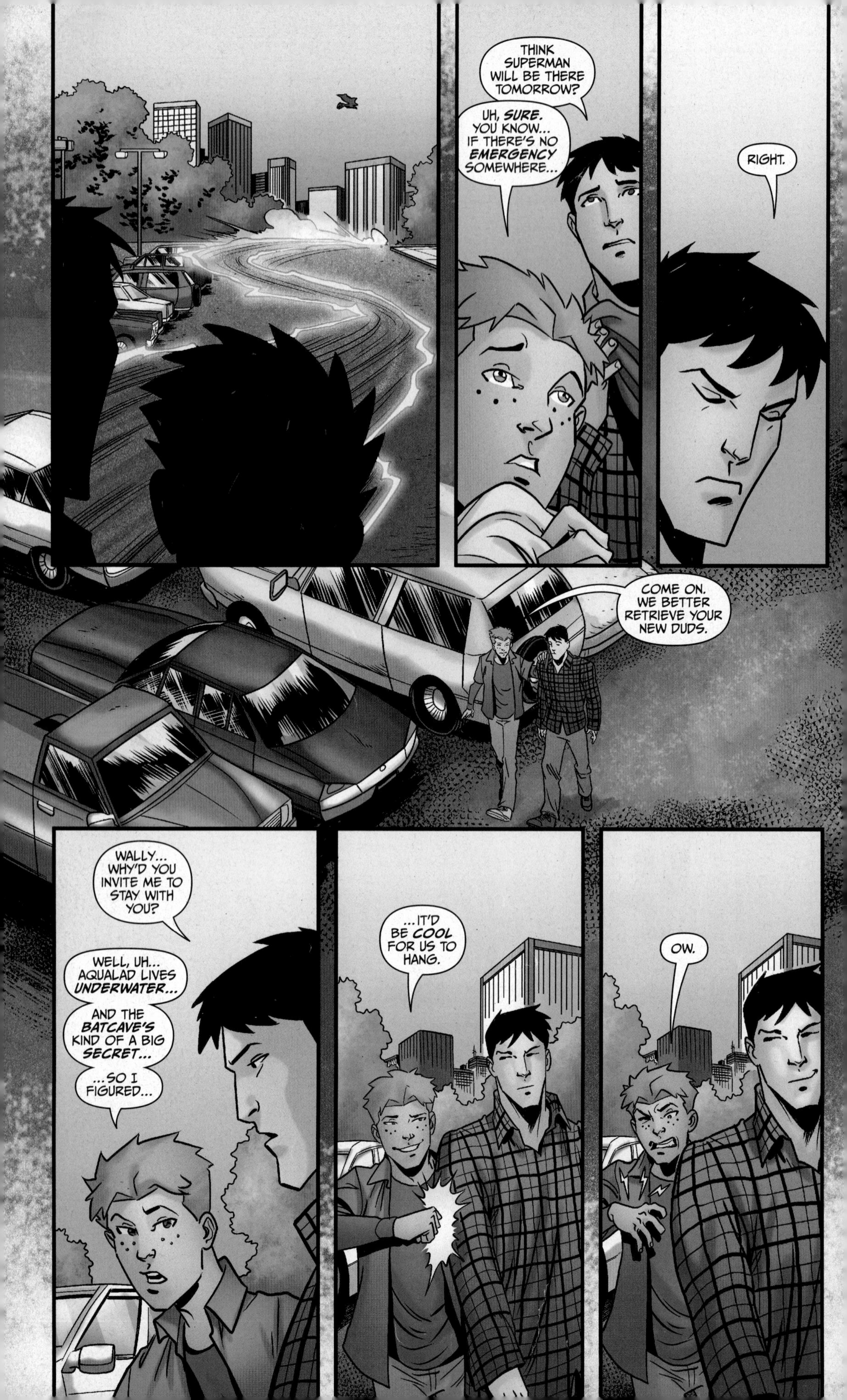
THINK SUPERMAN WILL BE THERE TOMORROW?
UH, SURE. YOU KNOW... IF THERE'S NO EMERGENCY SOMEWHERE...
RIGHT.
COME ON. WE BETTER RETRIEVE YOUR NEW DUDS.
WALLY... WHY'D YOU INVITE ME TO STAY WITH YOU?
WELL, UH... AQUALAD LIVES UNDERWATER...
AND THE BATCAVE'S KIND OF A BIG SECRET...
...SO I FIGURED...
...IT'D BE COOL FOR US TO HANG.
OW.

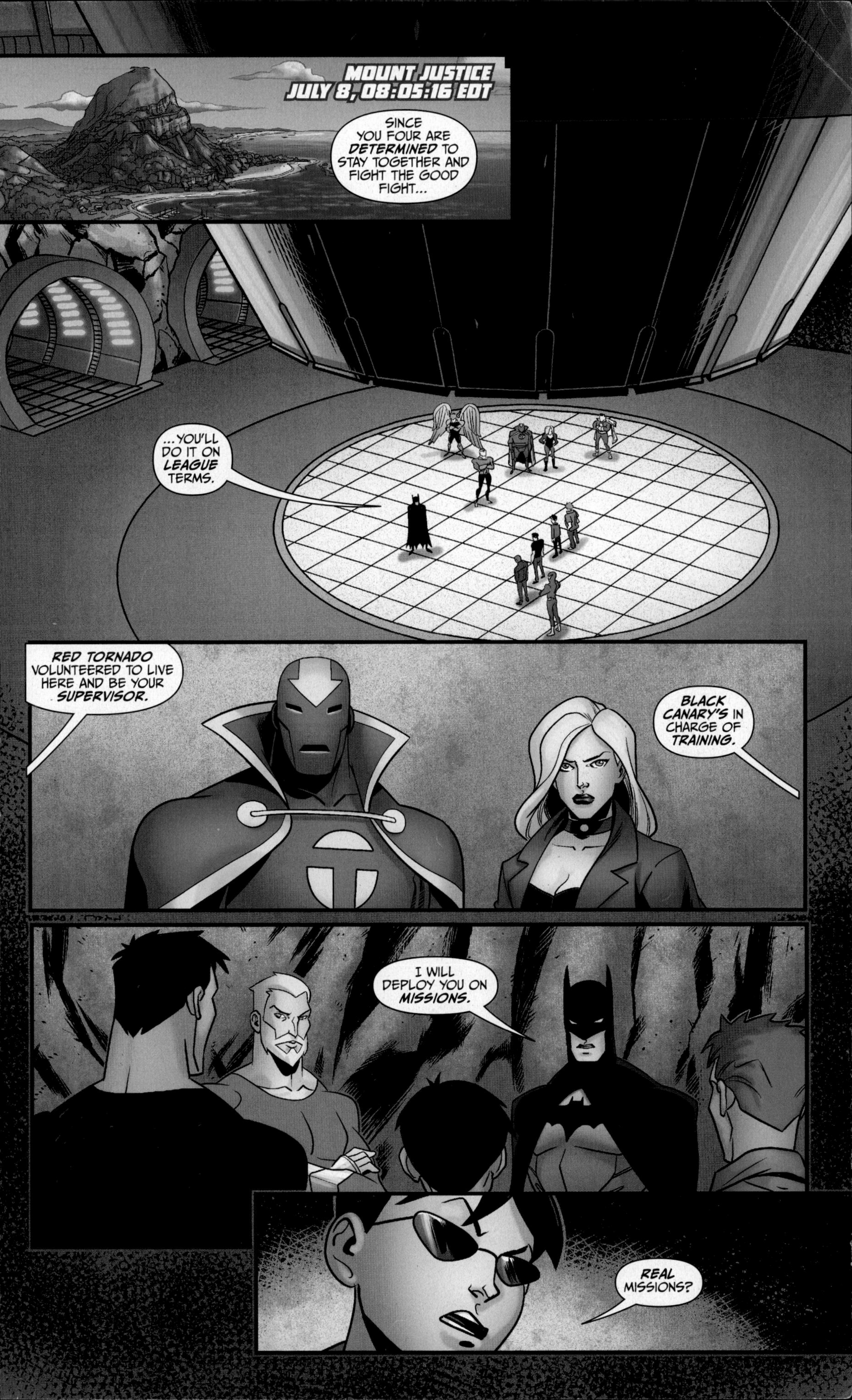
MOUNT JUSTICE
JULY 8, 08:05:16 EDT
SINCE YOU FOUR ARE DETERMINED TO STAY TOGETHER AND FIGHT THE GOOD FIGHT...
...YOU'LL DO IT ON LEAGUE TERMS.
RED TORNADO VOLUNTEERED TO LIVE HERE AND BE YOUR SUPERVISOR.
BLACK CANARY'S IN CHARGE OF TRAINING.
I WILL DEPLOY YOU ON MISSIONS.
REAL MISSIONS?

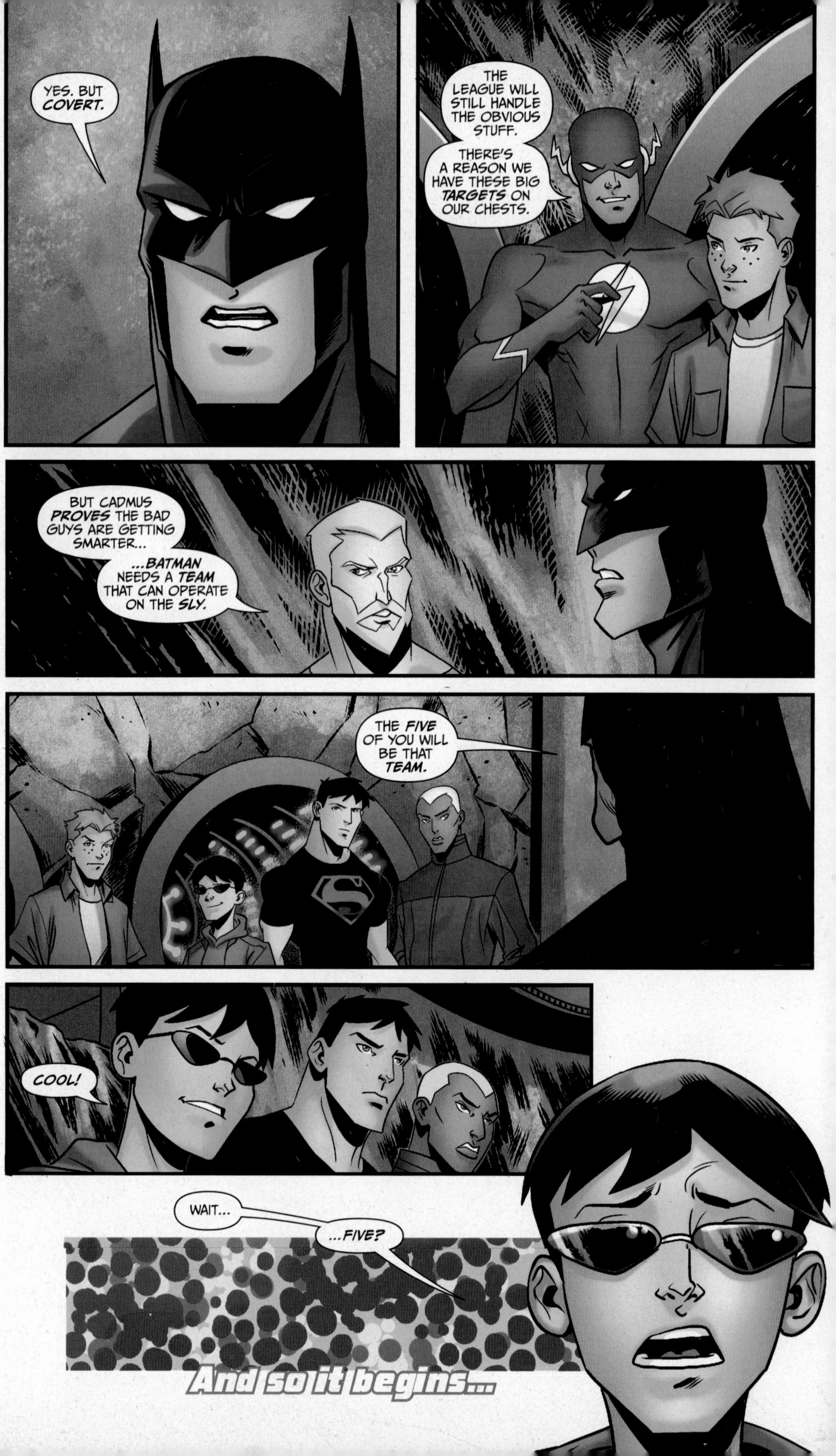
YES. BUT COVERT.
THE LEAGUE WILL STILL HANDLE THE OBVIOUS STUFF.
THERE'S A REASON WE HAVE THESE BIG TARGETS ON OUR CHESTS.
BUT CADMUS PROVES THE BAD GUYS ARE GETTING SMARTER...
...BATMAN NEEDS A TEAM THAT CAN OPERATE ON THE SLY.
THE FIVE OF YOU WILL BE THAT TEAM.
COOL!
WAIT...
...FIVE?
And so it begins...

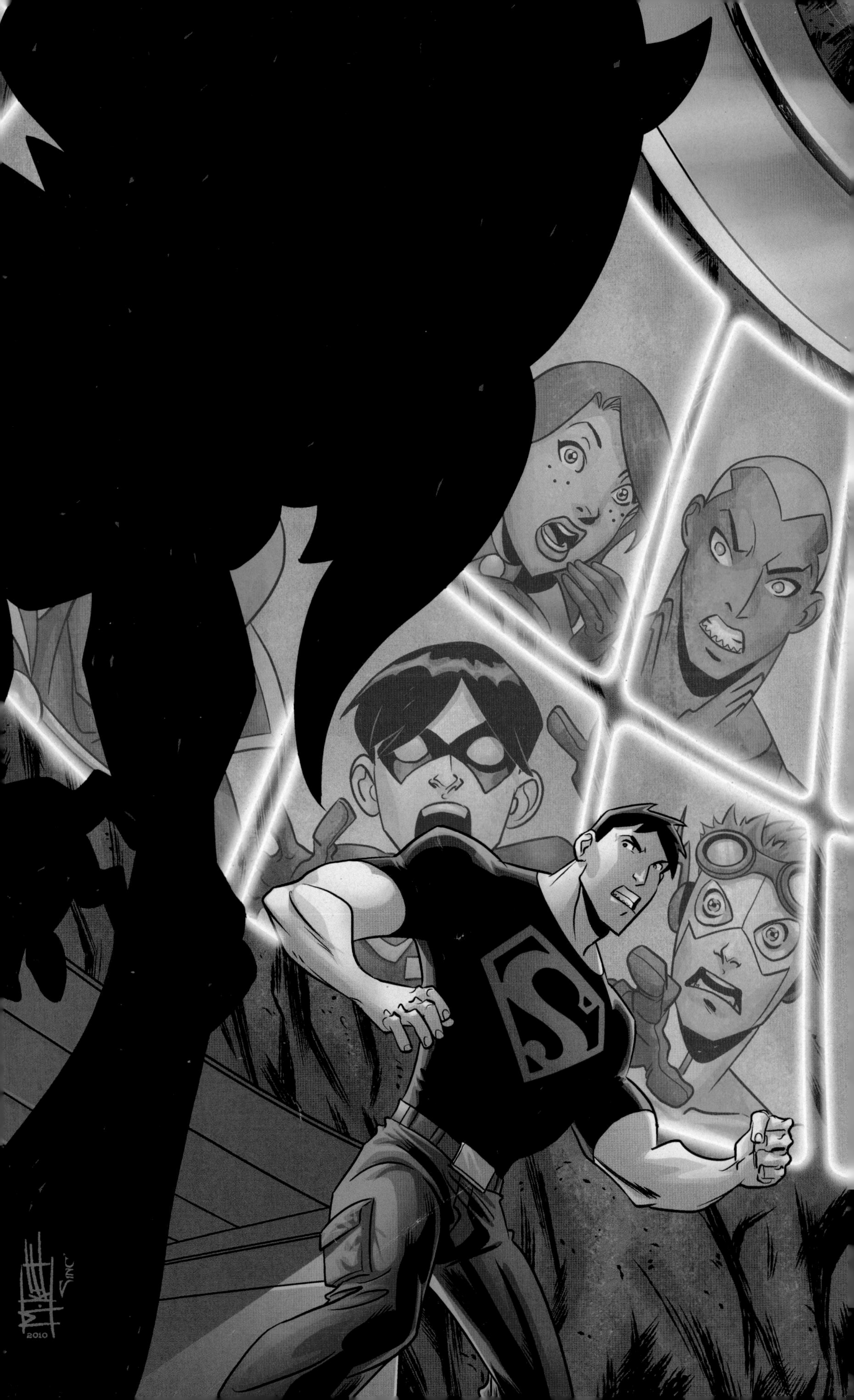

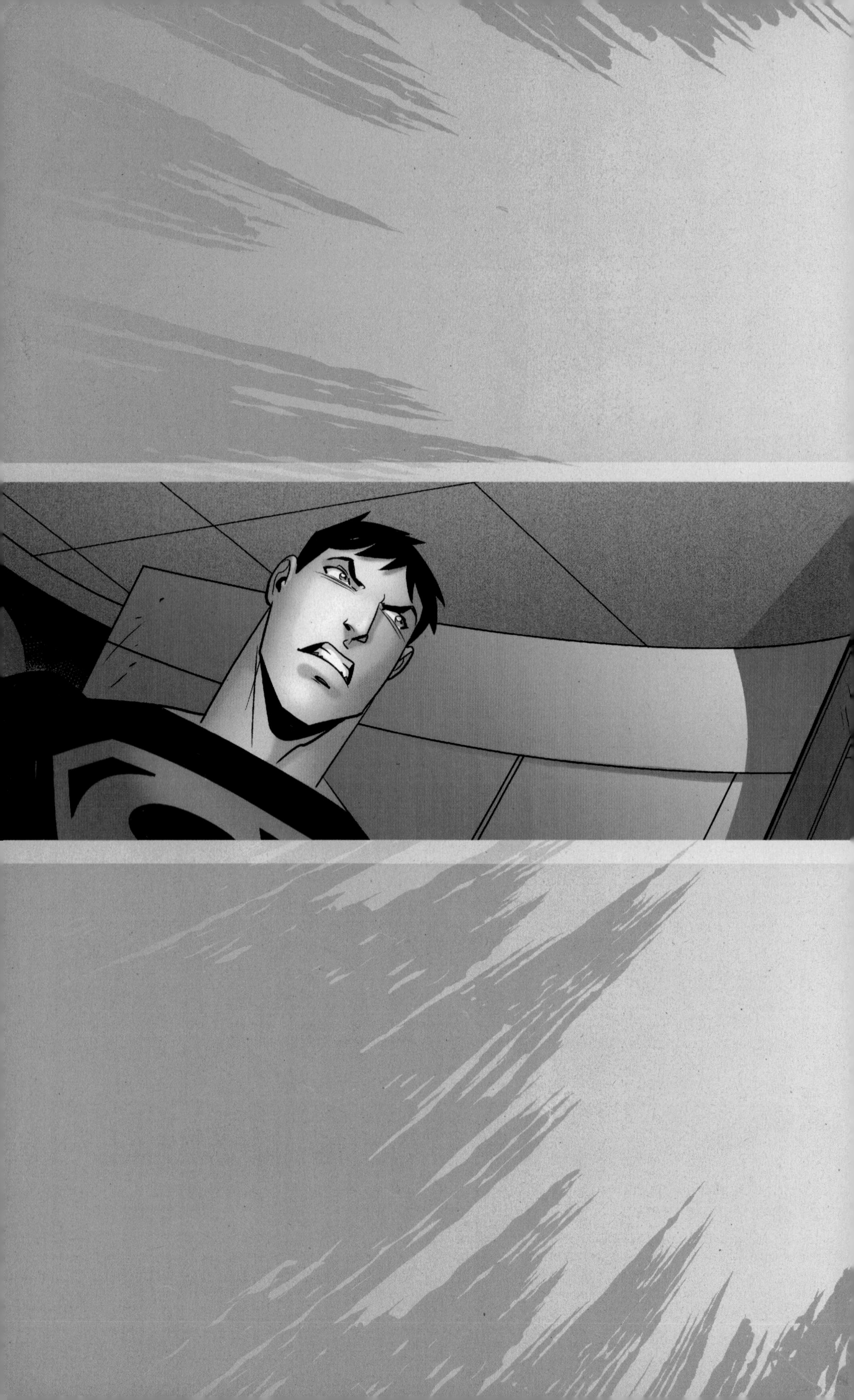

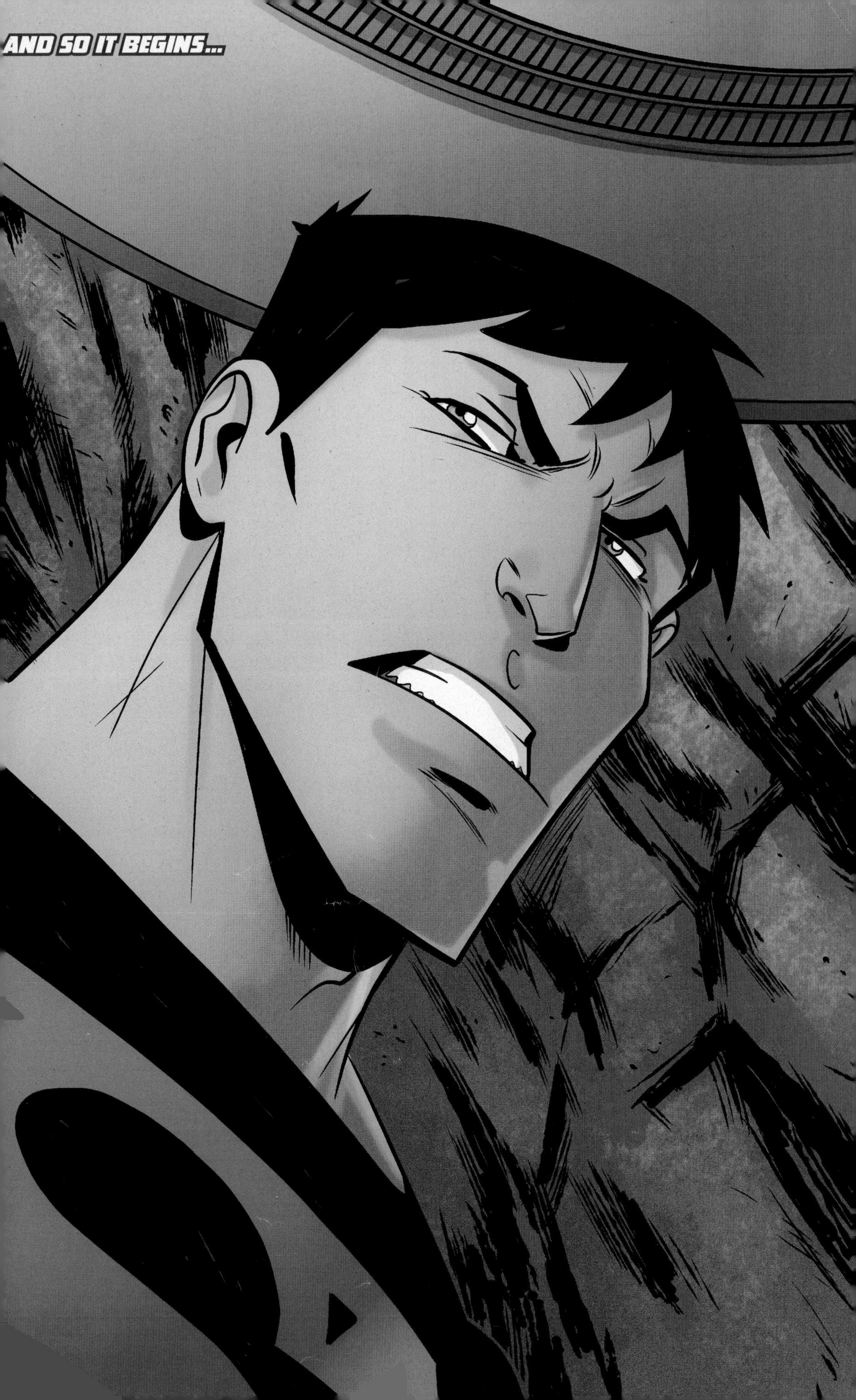
AND SO IT BEGINS...

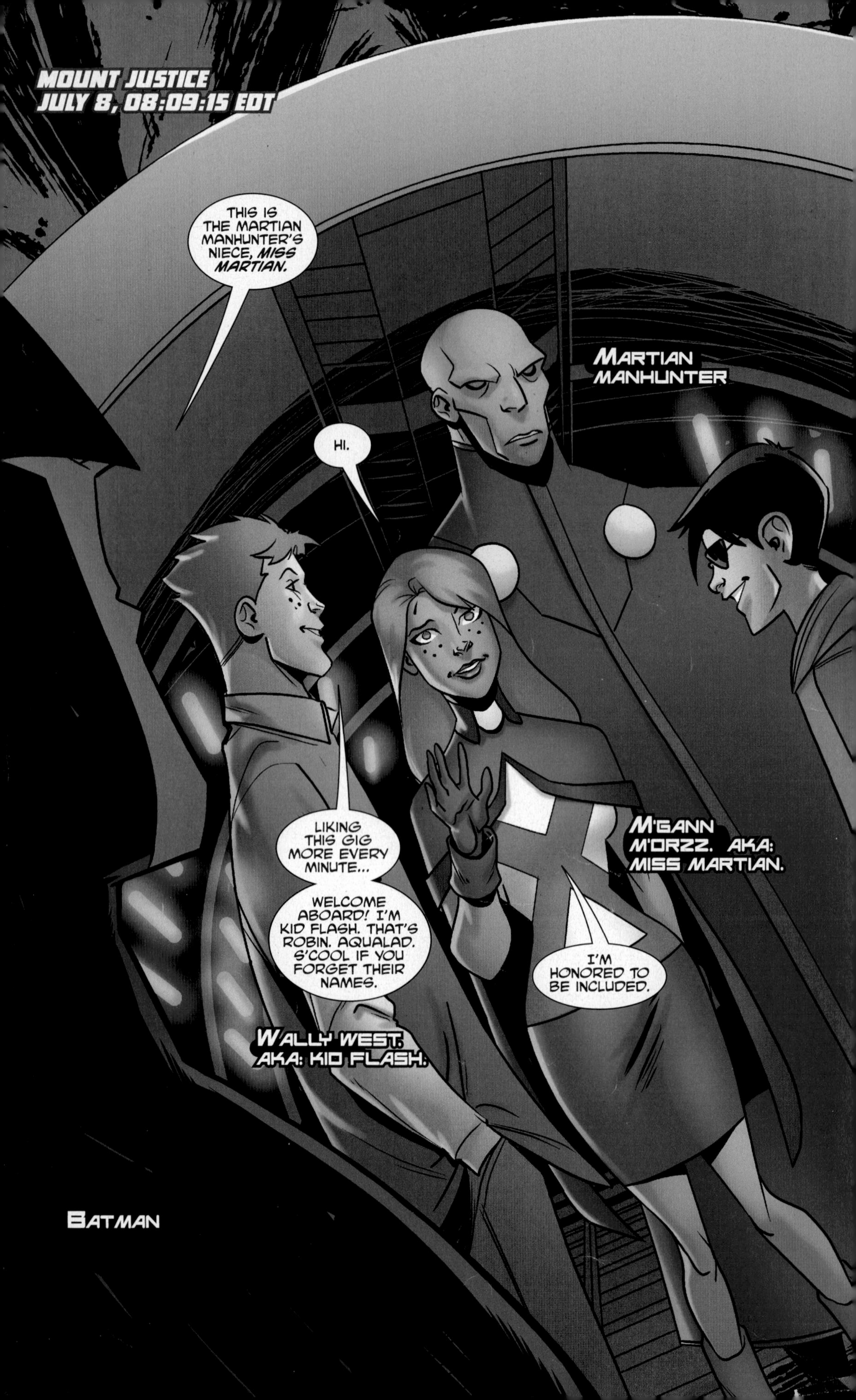
MOUNT JUSTICE
JULY 8, 08:09:15 EDT
THIS IS THE MARTIAN MANHUNTER'S NIECE, MISS MARTIAN.
MARTIAN MANHUNTER
HI.
LIKING THIS GIG MORE EVERY MINUTE...
WELCOME ABOARD! I'M KID FLASH. THAT'S ROBIN. AQUALAD. S'COOL IF YOU FORGET THEIR NAMES.
M'GANN M'ORZZ. AKA: MISS MARTIAN.
I'M HONORED TO BE INCLUDED.
WALLY WEST. AKA: KID FLASH.
BATMAN

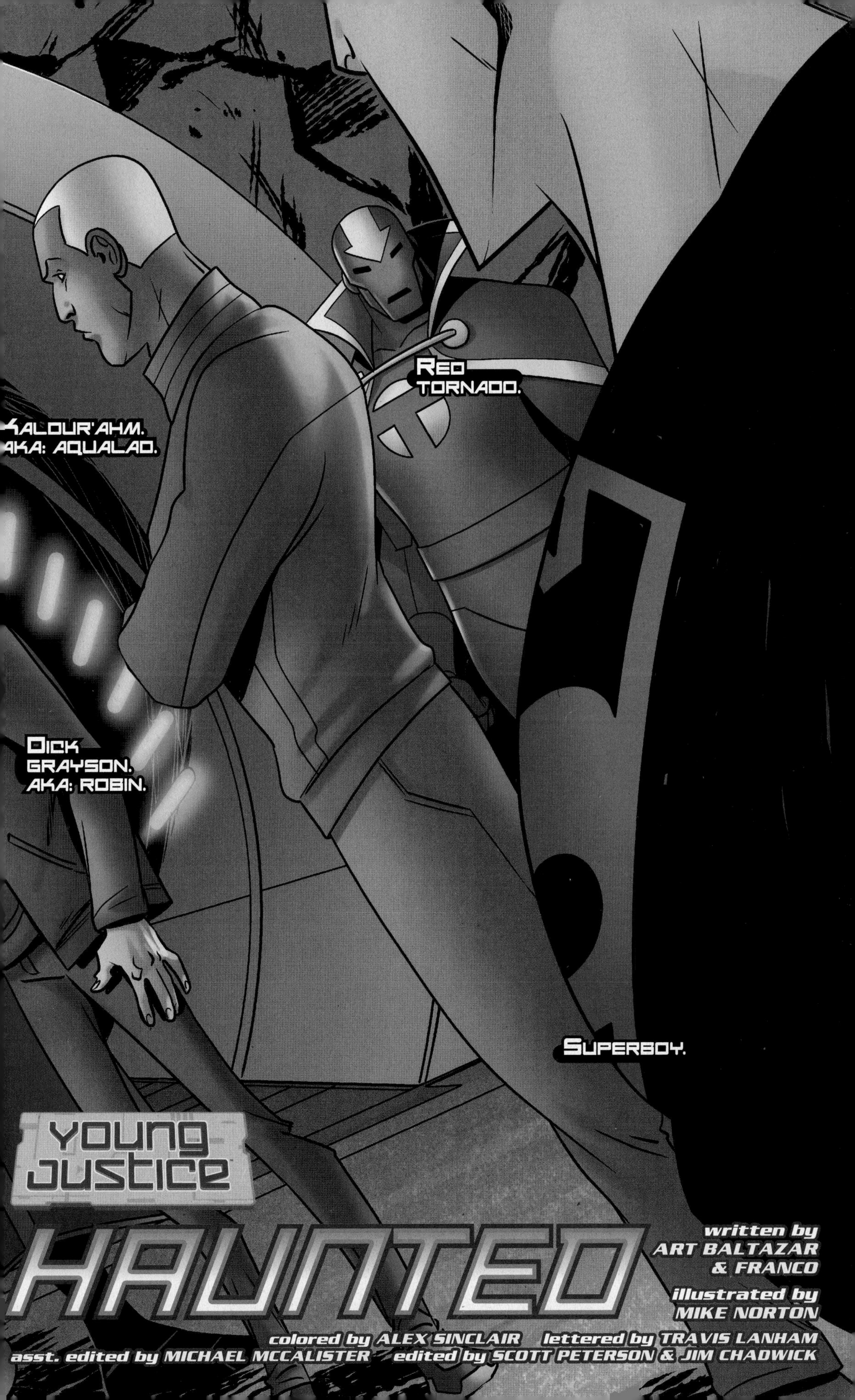
KALDOUR'AHM.
AKA: AQUALAD.
RED TORNADO.
DICK GRAYSON.
AKA: ROBIN.
SUPERBOY.
YOUNG JUSTICE
HAUNTED
written by ART BALTAZAR & FRANCO
illustrated by MIKE NORTON
colored by ALEX SINCLAIR
lettered by TRAVIS LANHAM
asst. edited by MICHAEL MCCALISTER
edited by SCOTT PETERSON & JIM CHADWICK

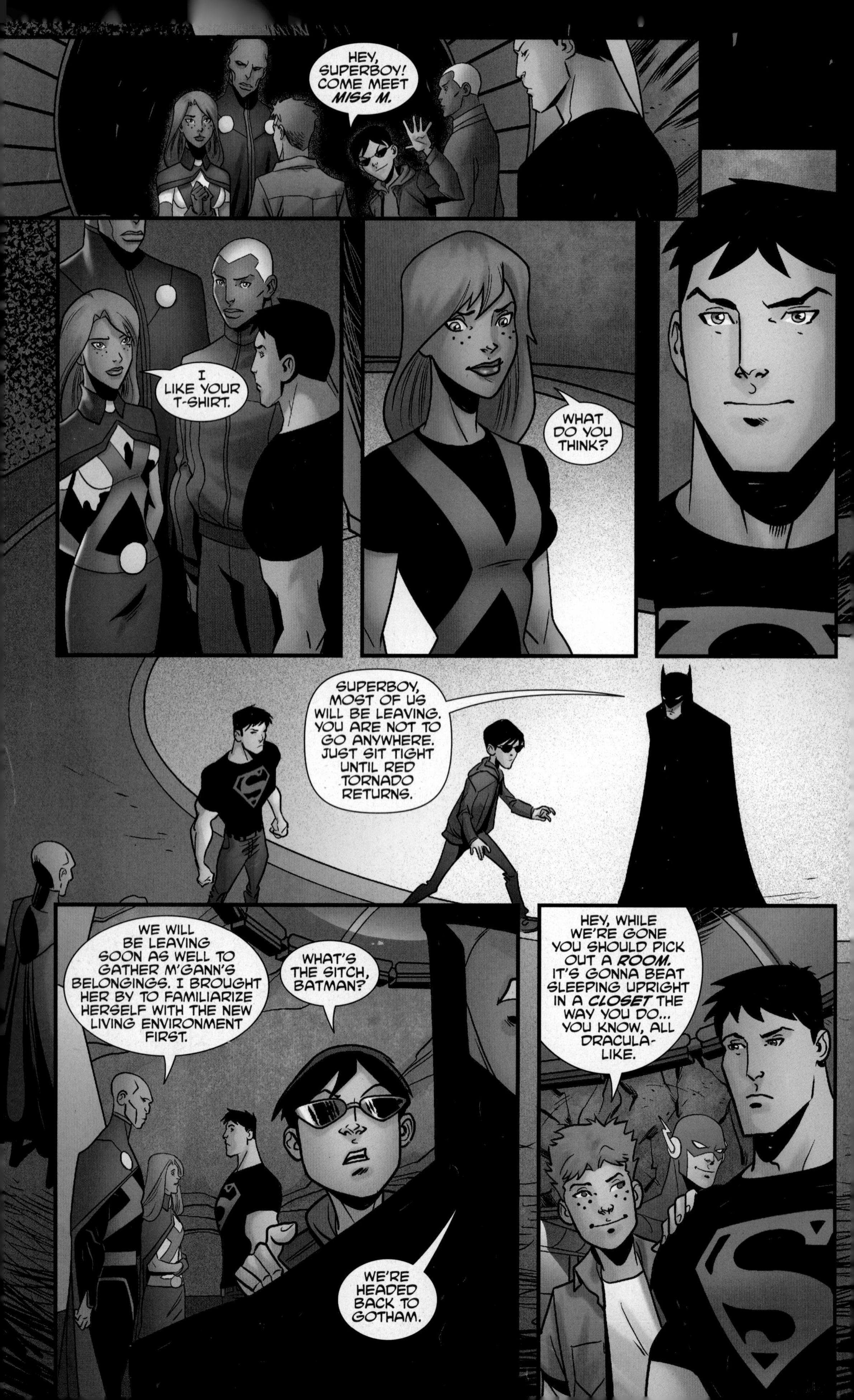
HEY, SUPERBOY! COME MEET MISS M.
I LIKE YOUR T-SHIRT.
WHAT DO YOU THINK?
SUPERBOY, MOST OF US WILL BE LEAVING. YOU ARE NOT TO GO ANYWHERE. JUST SIT TIGHT UNTIL RED TORNADO RETURNS.
WE WILL BE LEAVING SOON AS WELL TO GATHER M'GANN'S BELONGINGS. I BROUGHT HER BY TO FAMILIARIZE HERSELF WITH THE NEW LIVING ENVIRONMENT FIRST.
WHAT'S THE SITCH, BATMAN?
WE'RE HEADED BACK TO GOTHAM.
HEY, WHILE WE'RE GONE YOU SHOULD PICK OUT A ROOM. IT'S GONNA BEAT SLEEPING UPRIGHT IN A CLOSET THE WAY YOU DO... YOU KNOW, ALL DRACULA-LIKE.

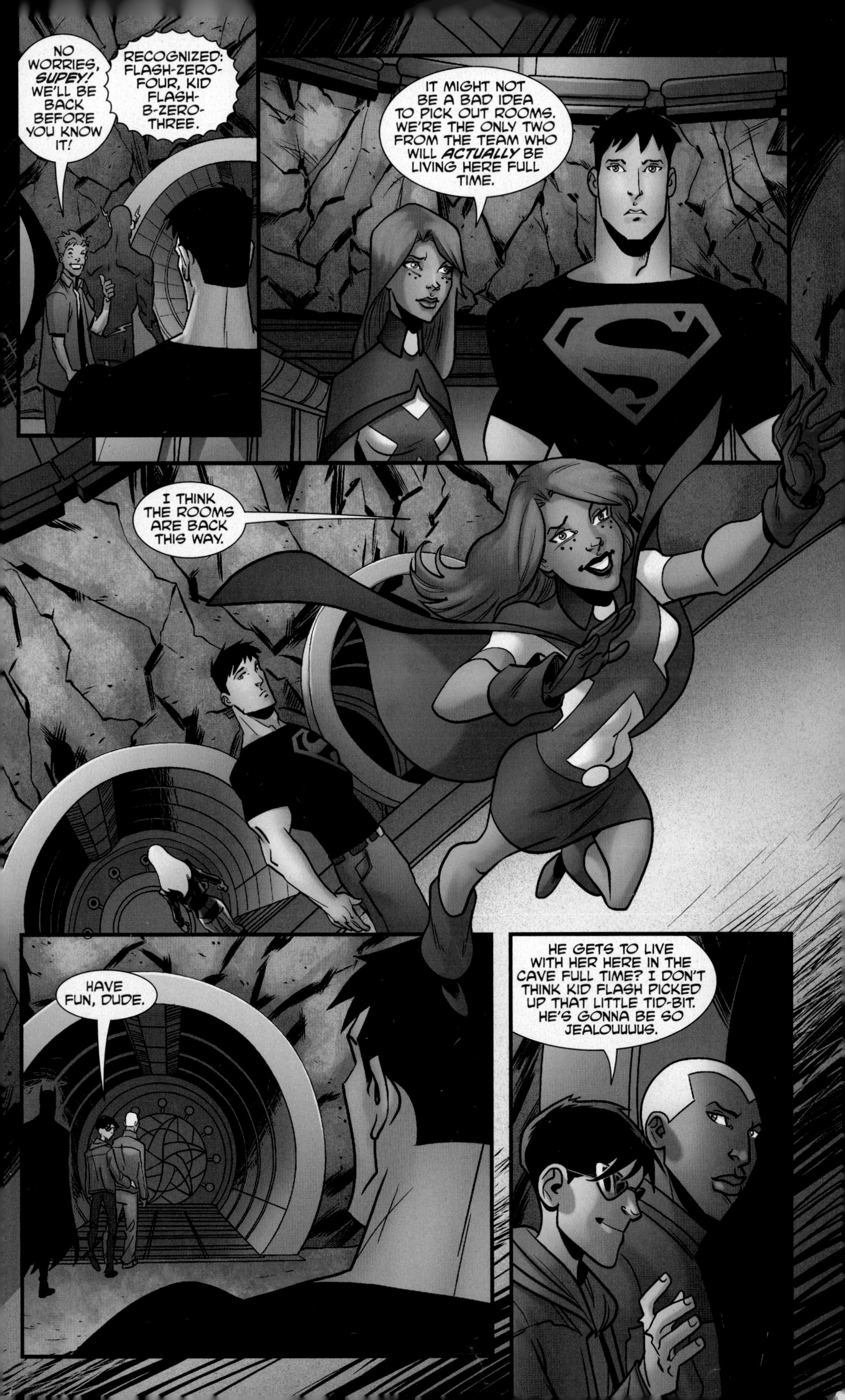

NO WORRIES, SUPEY! WE'LL BE BACK BEFORE YOU KNOW IT!
RECOGNIZED: FLASH-ZERO-FOUR, KID FLASH-B-ZERO-THREE.
IT MIGHT NOT BE A BAD IDEA TO PICK OUT ROOMS. WE'RE THE ONLY TWO FROM THE TEAM WHO WILL ACTUALLY BE LIVING HERE FULL TIME.
I THINK THE ROOMS ARE BACK THIS WAY.
HAVE FUN, DUDE.
HE GETS TO LIVE WITH HER HERE IN THE CAVE FULL TIME? I DON'T THINK KID FLASH PICKED UP THAT LITTLE TID-BIT. HE'S GONNA BE SO JEALOUUUUS.

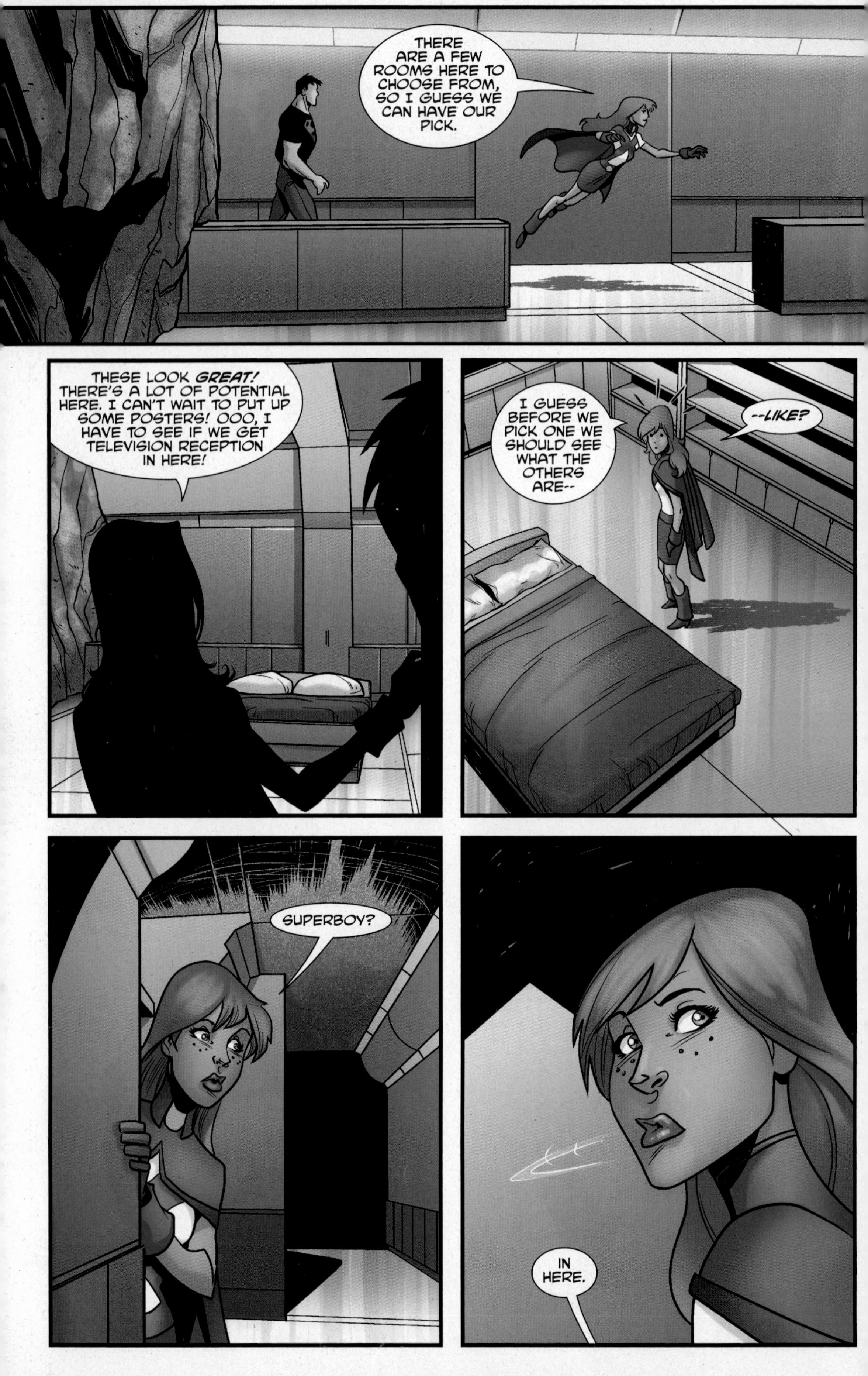
THERE ARE A FEW ROOMS HERE TO CHOOSE FROM, SO I GUESS WE CAN HAVE OUR PICK.
THESE LOOK *GREAT!* THERE'S A LOT OF POTENTIAL HERE. I CAN'T WAIT TO PUT UP SOME POSTERS! OOO, I HAVE TO SEE IF WE GET TELEVISION RECEPTION IN HERE!
I GUESS BEFORE WE PICK ONE WE SHOULD SEE WHAT THE OTHERS ARE--
--LIKE?
SUPERBOY?
IN HERE.

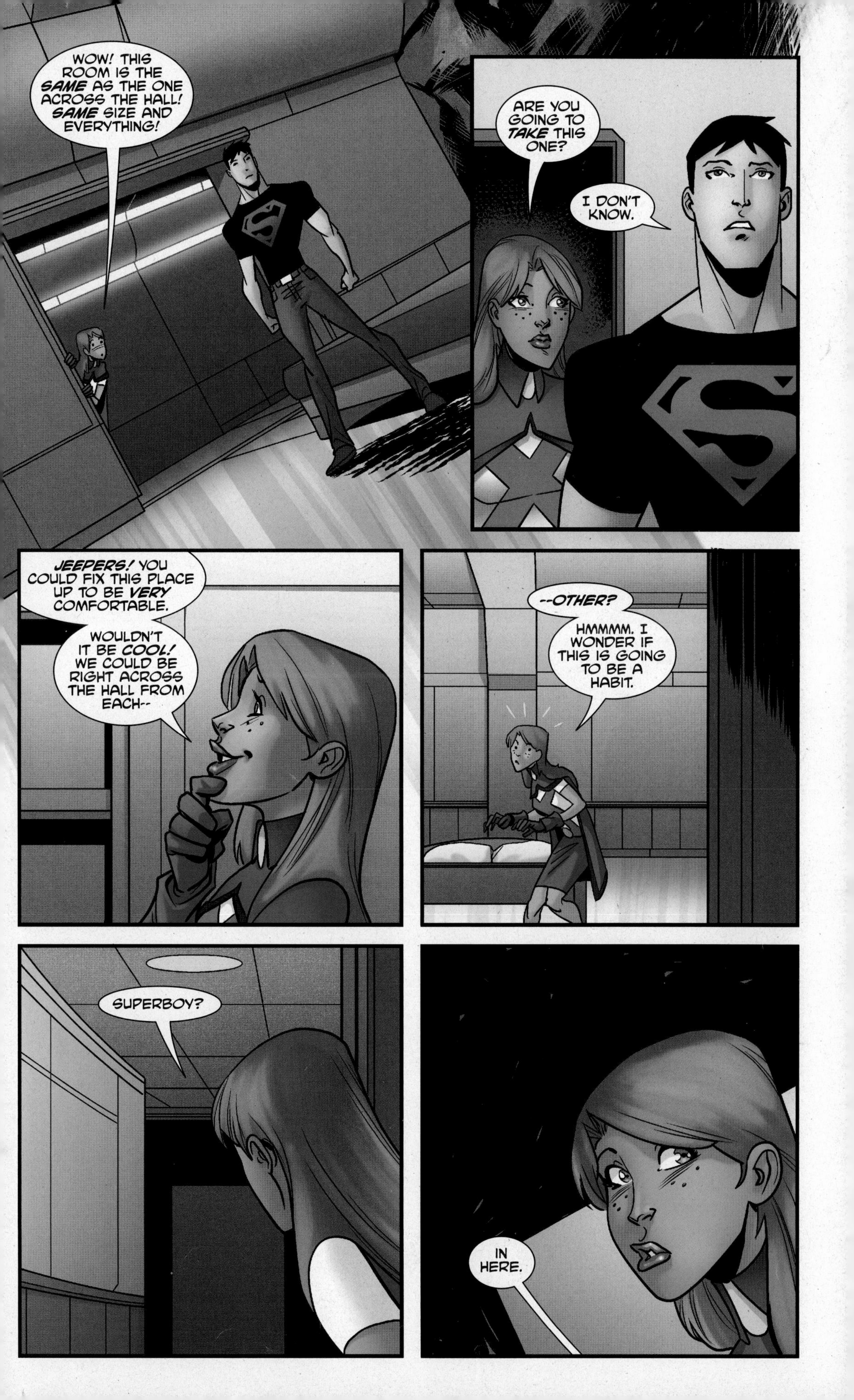

WOW! THIS ROOM IS THE SAME AS THE ONE ACROSS THE HALL! SAME SIZE AND EVERYTHING!
ARE YOU GOING TO TAKE THIS ONE?
I DON'T KNOW.
JEEPERS! YOU COULD FIX THIS PLACE UP TO BE VERY COMFORTABLE.
WOULDN'T IT BE COOL! WE COULD BE RIGHT ACROSS THE HALL FROM EACH--
--OTHER?
HMMMM. I WONDER IF THIS IS GOING TO BE A HABIT.
SUPERBOY?
IN HERE.

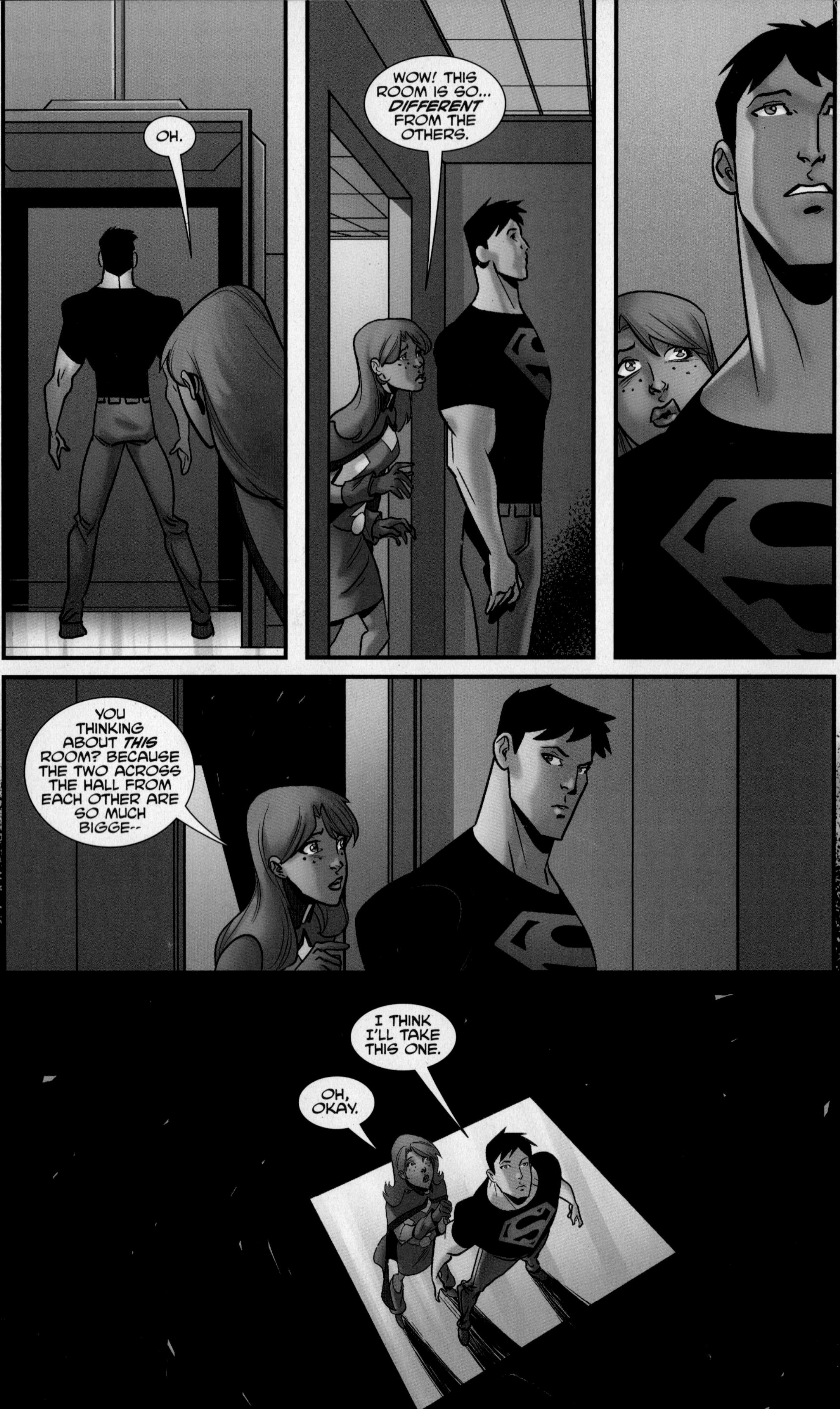
OH.
WOW! THIS ROOM IS SO... *DIFFERENT* FROM THE OTHERS.
YOU THINKING ABOUT *THIS* ROOM? BECAUSE THE TWO ACROSS THE HALL FROM EACH OTHER ARE SO MUCH BIGGE--
I THINK I'LL TAKE THIS ONE.
OH, OKAY.

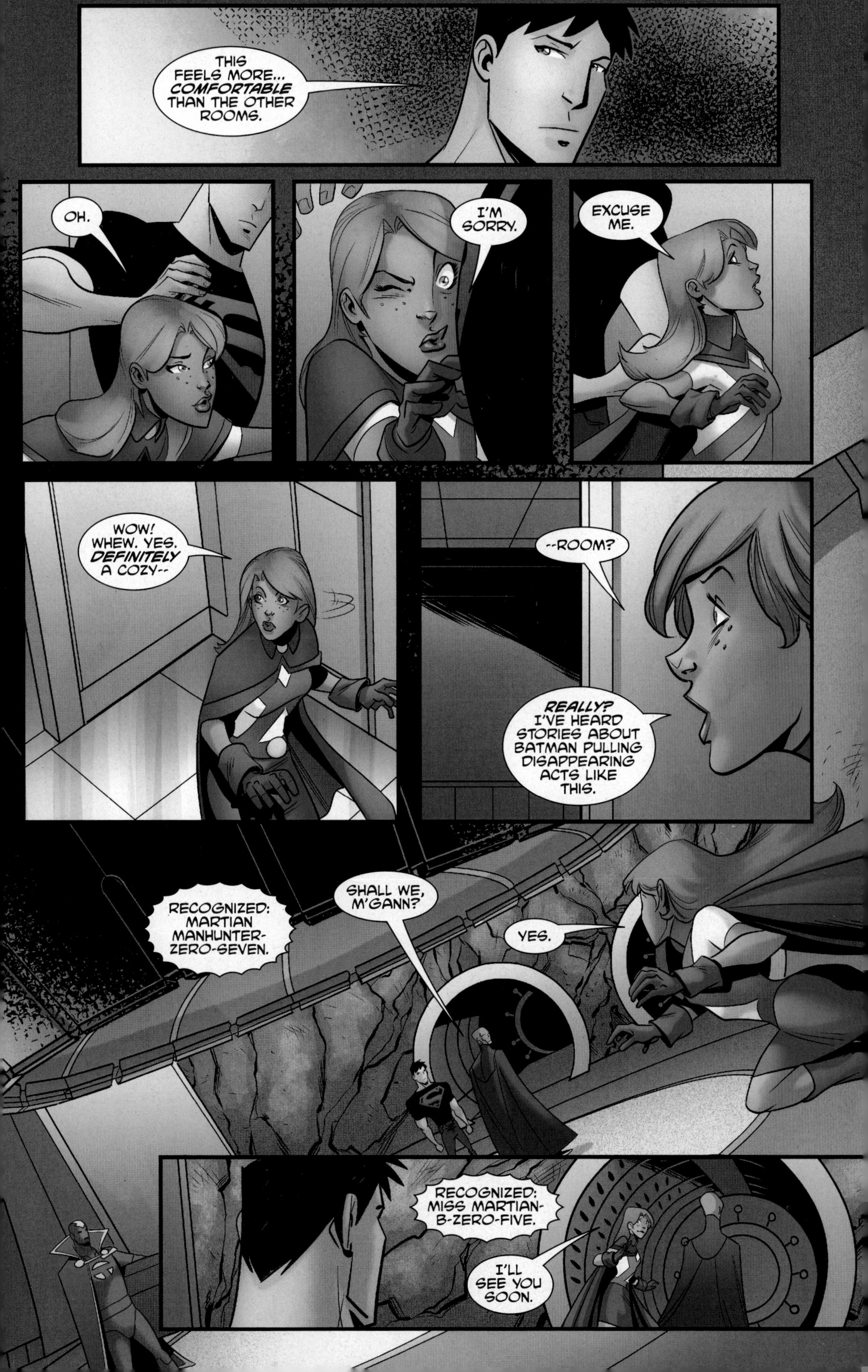
THIS FEELS MORE... COMFORTABLE THAN THE OTHER ROOMS.
OH.
I'M SORRY.
EXCUSE ME.
WOW! WHEW. YES. DEFINITELY A COZY--
--ROOM?
REALLY? I'VE HEARD STORIES ABOUT BATMAN PULLING DISAPPEARING ACTS LIKE THIS.
RECOGNIZED: MARTIAN MANHUNTER-ZERO-SEVEN.
SHALL WE, M'GANN?
YES.
RECOGNIZED: MISS MARTIAN-B-ZERO-FIVE.
I'LL SEE YOU SOON.

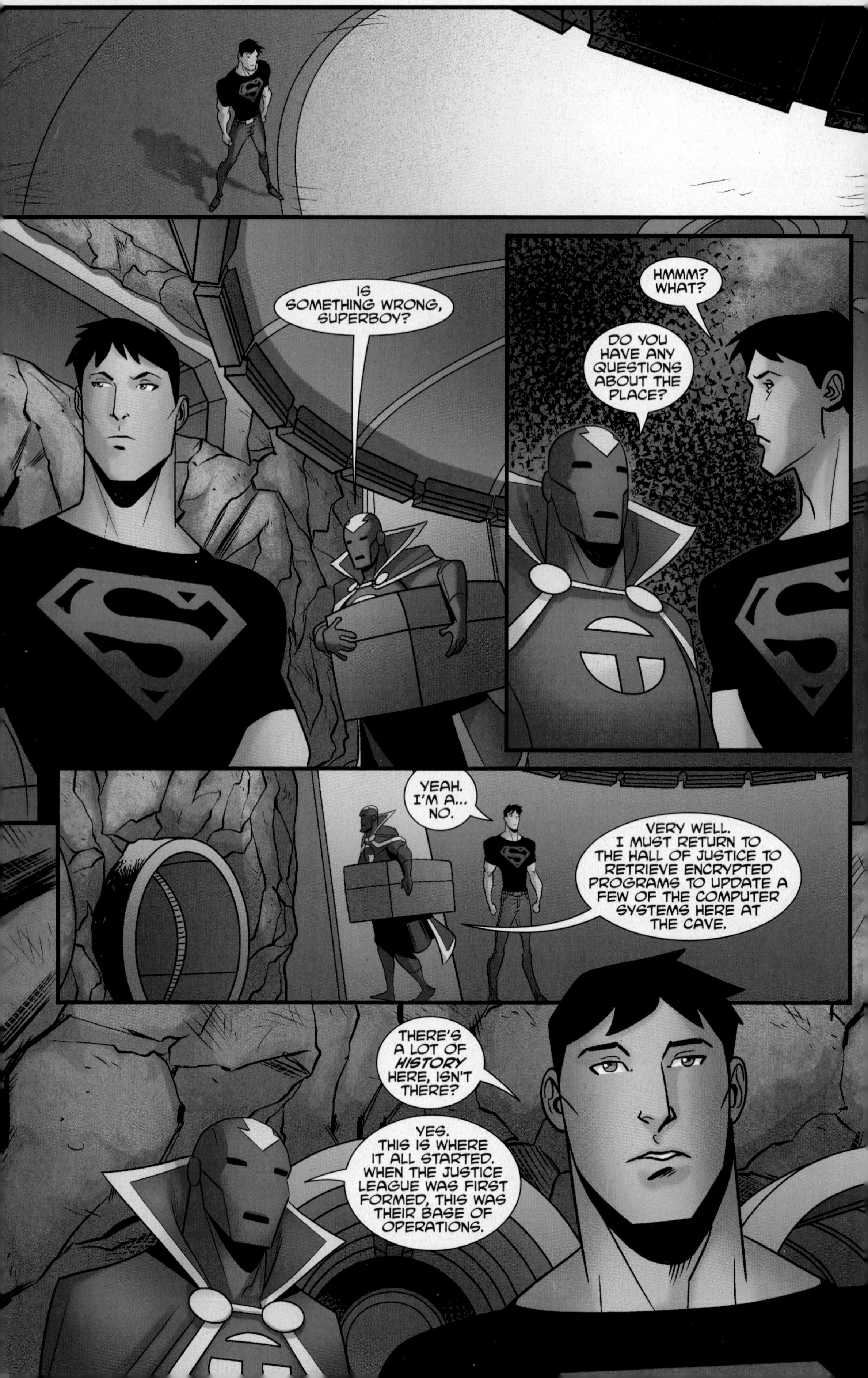
IS SOMETHING WRONG, SUPERBOY?
HMMM? WHAT?
DO YOU HAVE ANY QUESTIONS ABOUT THE PLACE?
YEAH. I'M A... NO.
VERY WELL. I MUST RETURN TO THE HALL OF JUSTICE TO RETRIEVE ENCRYPTED PROGRAMS TO UPDATE A FEW OF THE COMPUTER SYSTEMS HERE AT THE CAVE.
THERE'S A LOT OF *HISTORY* HERE, ISN'T THERE?
YES. THIS IS WHERE IT ALL STARTED. WHEN THE JUSTICE LEAGUE WAS FIRST FORMED, THIS WAS THEIR BASE OF OPERATIONS.

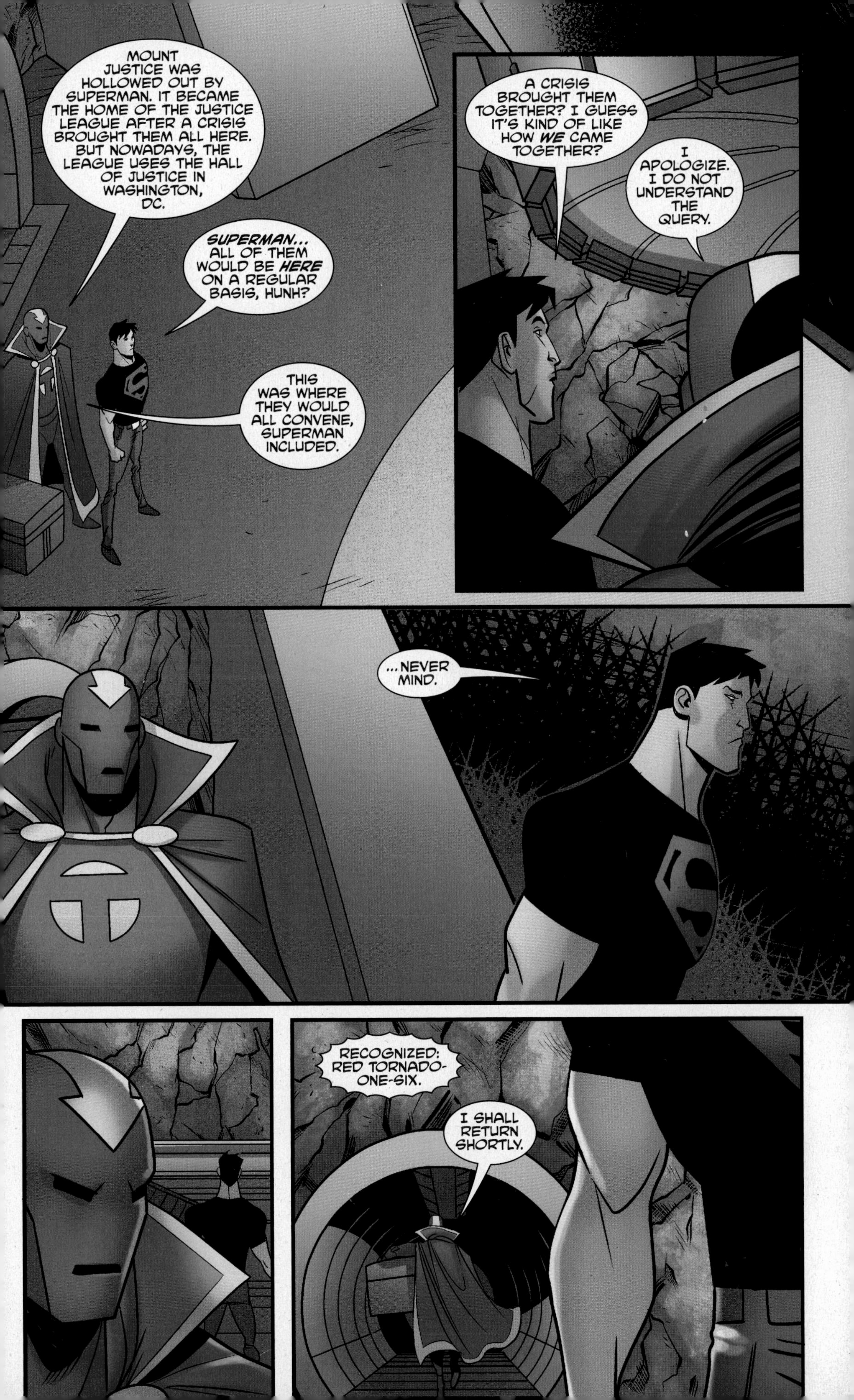

MOUNT JUSTICE WAS HOLLOWED OUT BY SUPERMAN. IT BECAME THE HOME OF THE JUSTICE LEAGUE AFTER A CRISIS BROUGHT THEM ALL HERE. BUT NOWADAYS, THE LEAGUE USES THE HALL OF JUSTICE IN WASHINGTON, DC.
SUPERMAN... ALL OF THEM WOULD BE HERE ON A REGULAR BASIS, HUNH?
THIS WAS WHERE THEY WOULD ALL CONVENE, SUPERMAN INCLUDED.
A CRISIS BROUGHT THEM TOGETHER? I GUESS IT'S KIND OF LIKE HOW WE CAME TOGETHER?
I APOLOGIZE. I DO NOT UNDERSTAND THE QUERY.
...NEVER MIND.
RECOGNIZED: RED TORNADO-ONE-SIX.
I SHALL RETURN SHORTLY.

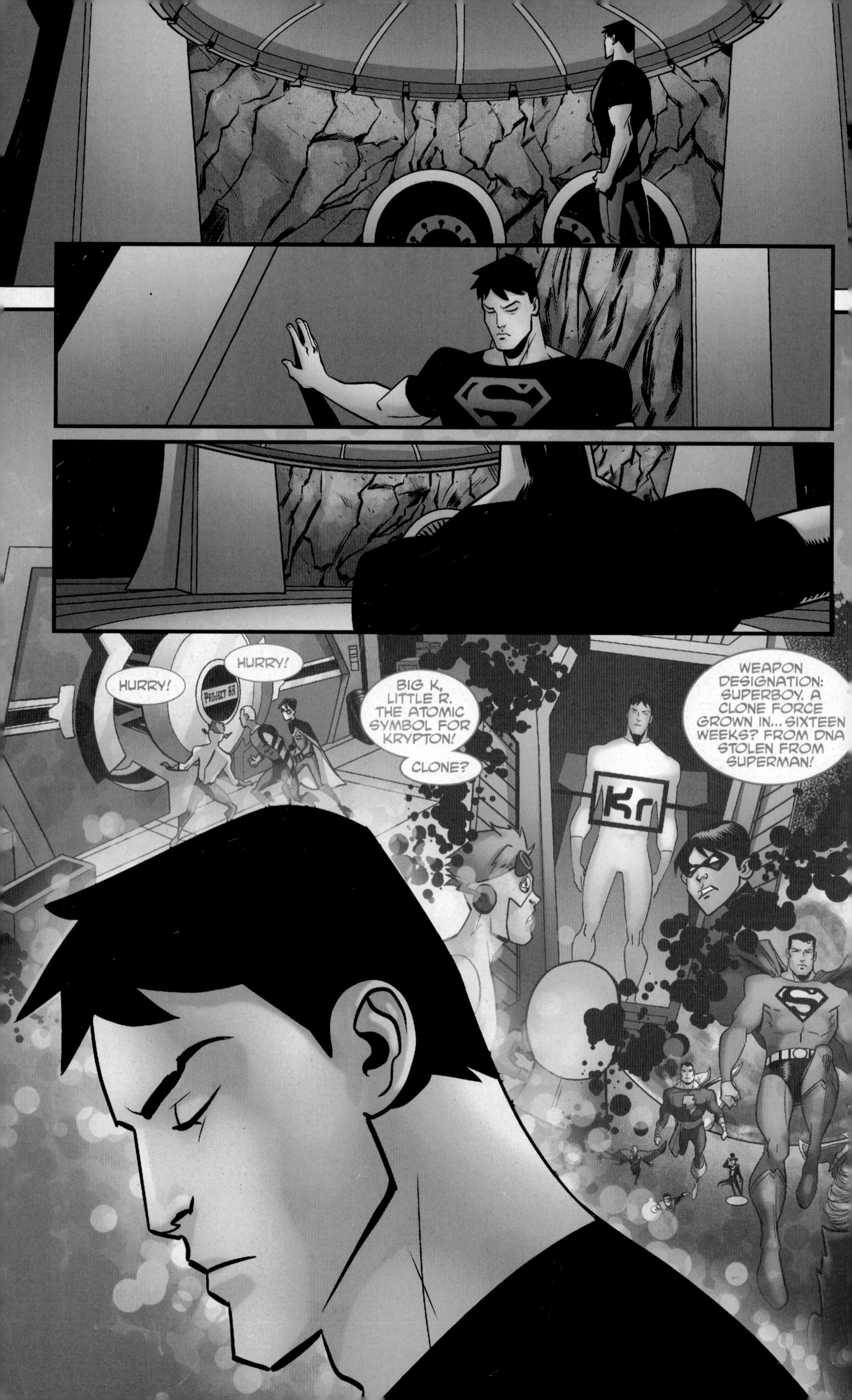
HURRY!
HURRY!
PROJECT KR
BIG K, LITTLE R. THE ATOMIC SYMBOL FOR KRYPTON!
CLONE?
WEAPON DESIGNATION: SUPERBOY. A CLONE FORCE GROWN IN... SIXTEEN WEEKS? FROM DNA STOLEN FROM SUPERMAN!
Kr

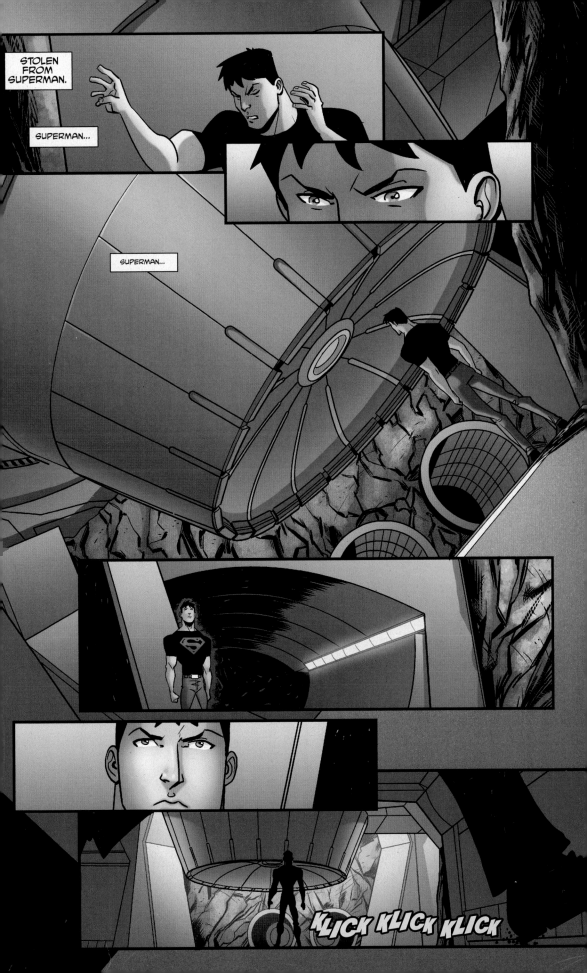

STOLEN FROM SUPERMAN.

SUPERMAN...

SUPERMAN...

KLICK KLICK KLICK

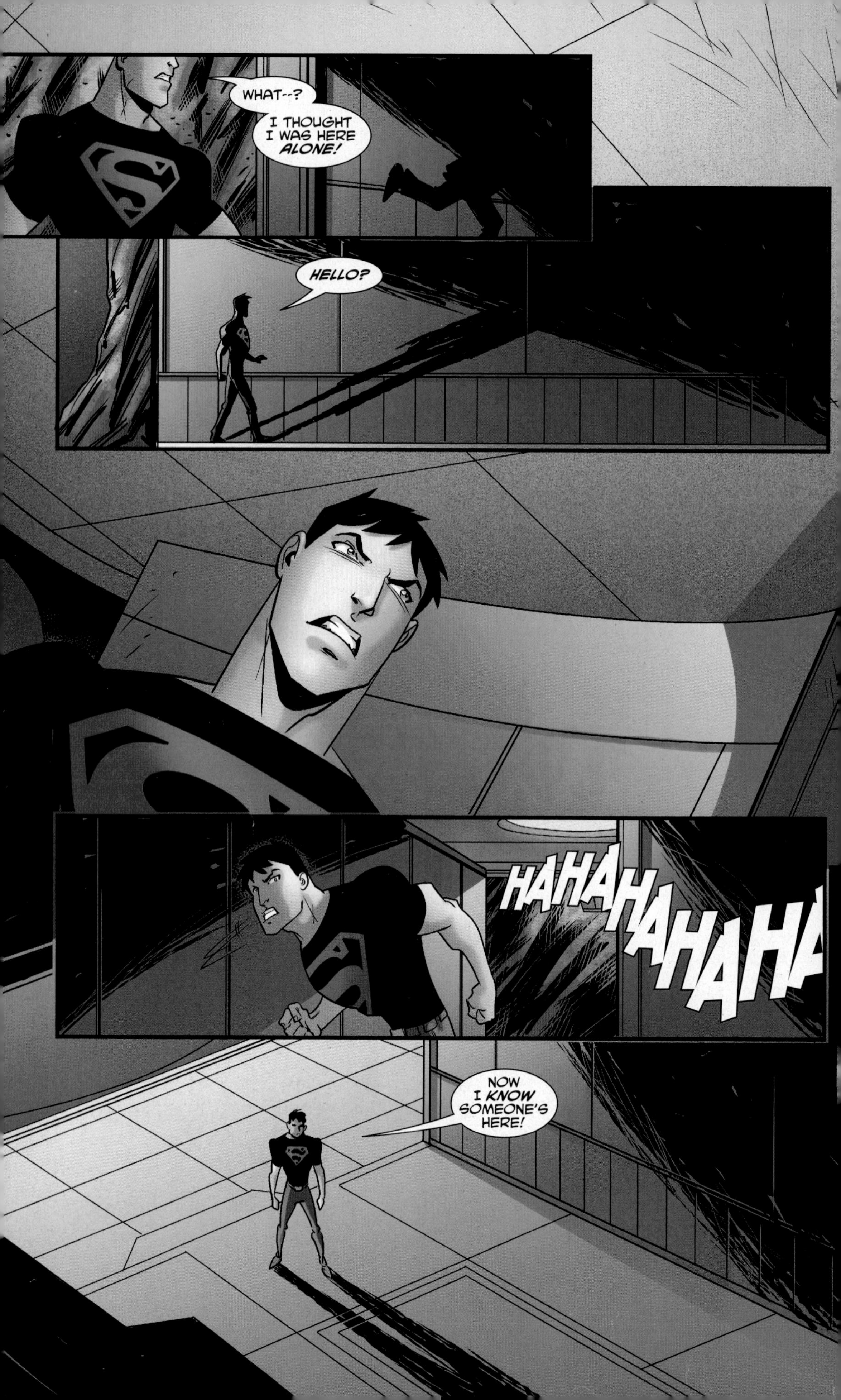
WHAT--?
I THOUGHT I WAS HERE *ALONE!*
HELLO?
HAHAHAHAHAHAHAHA
NOW I *KNOW* SOMEONE'S HERE!

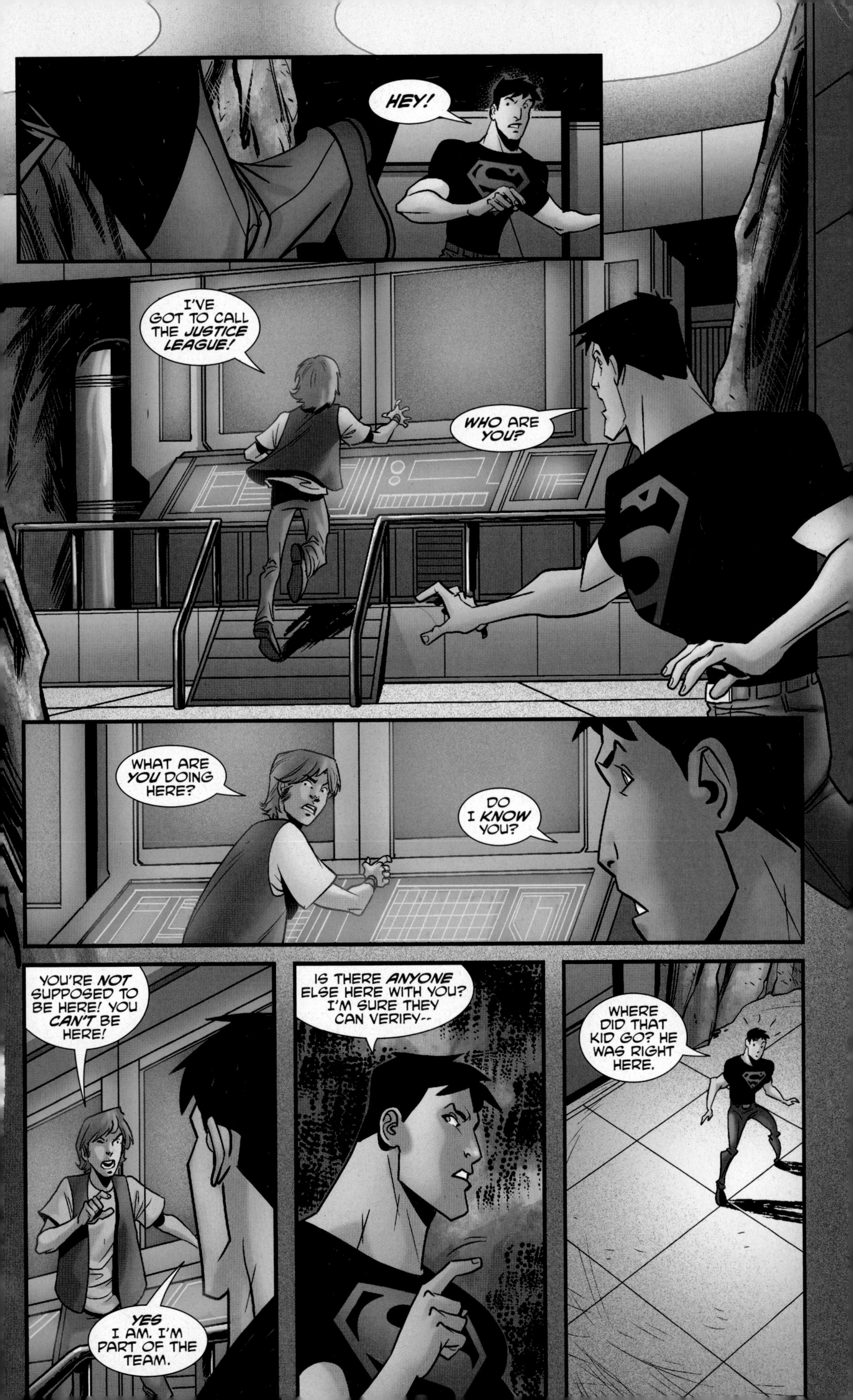
HEY!
I'VE GOT TO CALL THE JUSTICE LEAGUE!
WHO ARE YOU?
WHAT ARE YOU DOING HERE?
DO I KNOW YOU?
YOU'RE NOT SUPPOSED TO BE HERE! YOU CAN'T BE HERE!
YES I AM. I'M PART OF THE TEAM.
IS THERE ANYONE ELSE HERE WITH YOU? I'M SURE THEY CAN VERIFY--
WHERE DID THAT KID GO? HE WAS RIGHT HERE.

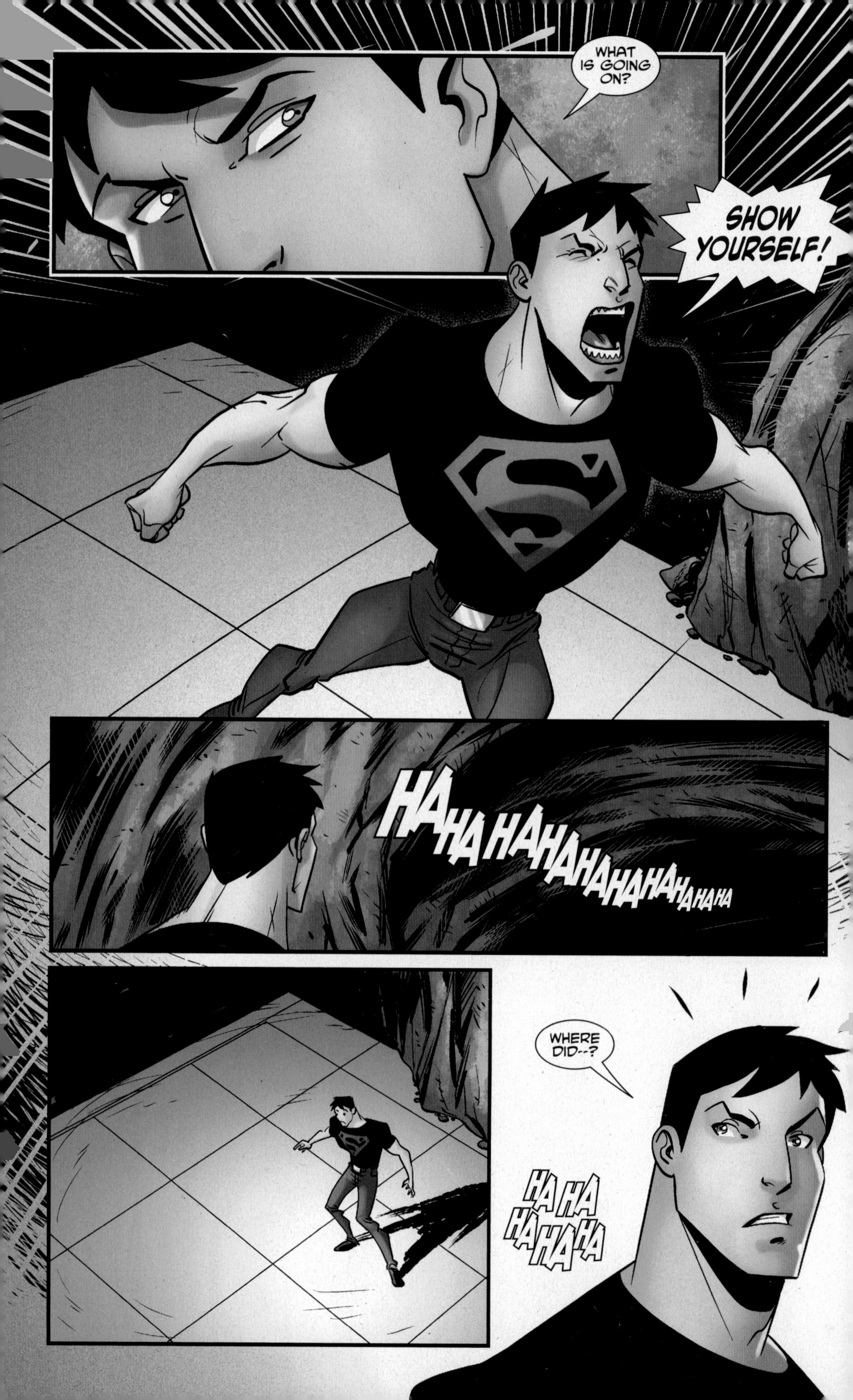
WHAT IS GOING ON?
SHOW YOURSELF!
HAHAHAHAHAHAHAHAHAHAHAHA
WHERE DID--?
HA HA HA HA HA HA

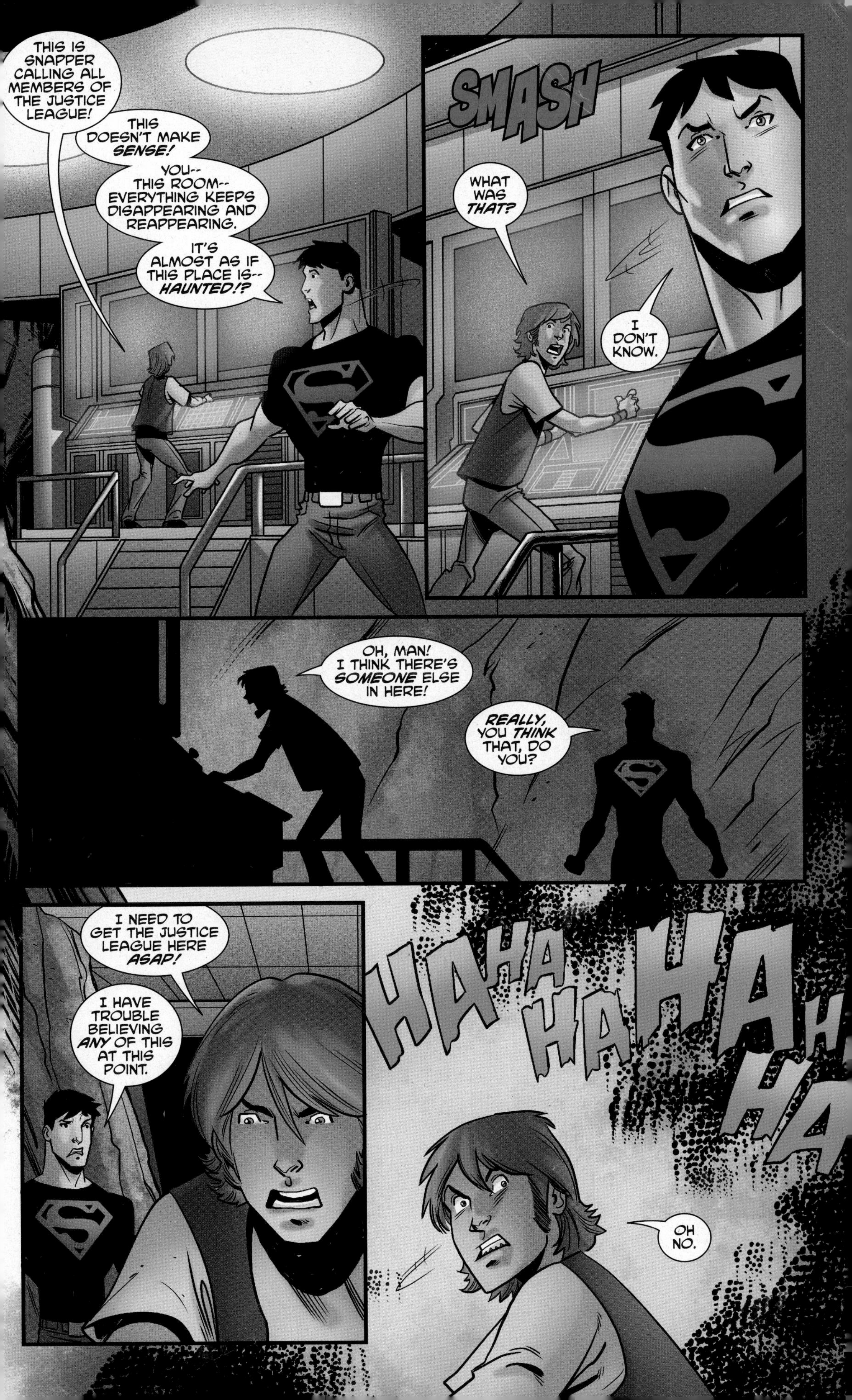
THIS IS SNAPPER CALLING ALL MEMBERS OF THE JUSTICE LEAGUE!
THIS DOESN'T MAKE *SENSE!*
YOU-- THIS ROOM-- EVERYTHING KEEPS DISAPPEARING AND REAPPEARING.
IT'S ALMOST AS IF THIS PLACE IS-- *HAUNTED!?*
SMASH
WHAT WAS *THAT?*
I DON'T KNOW.
OH, MAN! I THINK THERE'S *SOMEONE* ELSE IN HERE!
REALLY, YOU *THINK* THAT, DO YOU?
I NEED TO GET THE JUSTICE LEAGUE HERE *ASAP!*
I HAVE TROUBLE BELIEVING *ANY* OF THIS AT THIS POINT.
HAHA HAHA HAHA
OH NO.

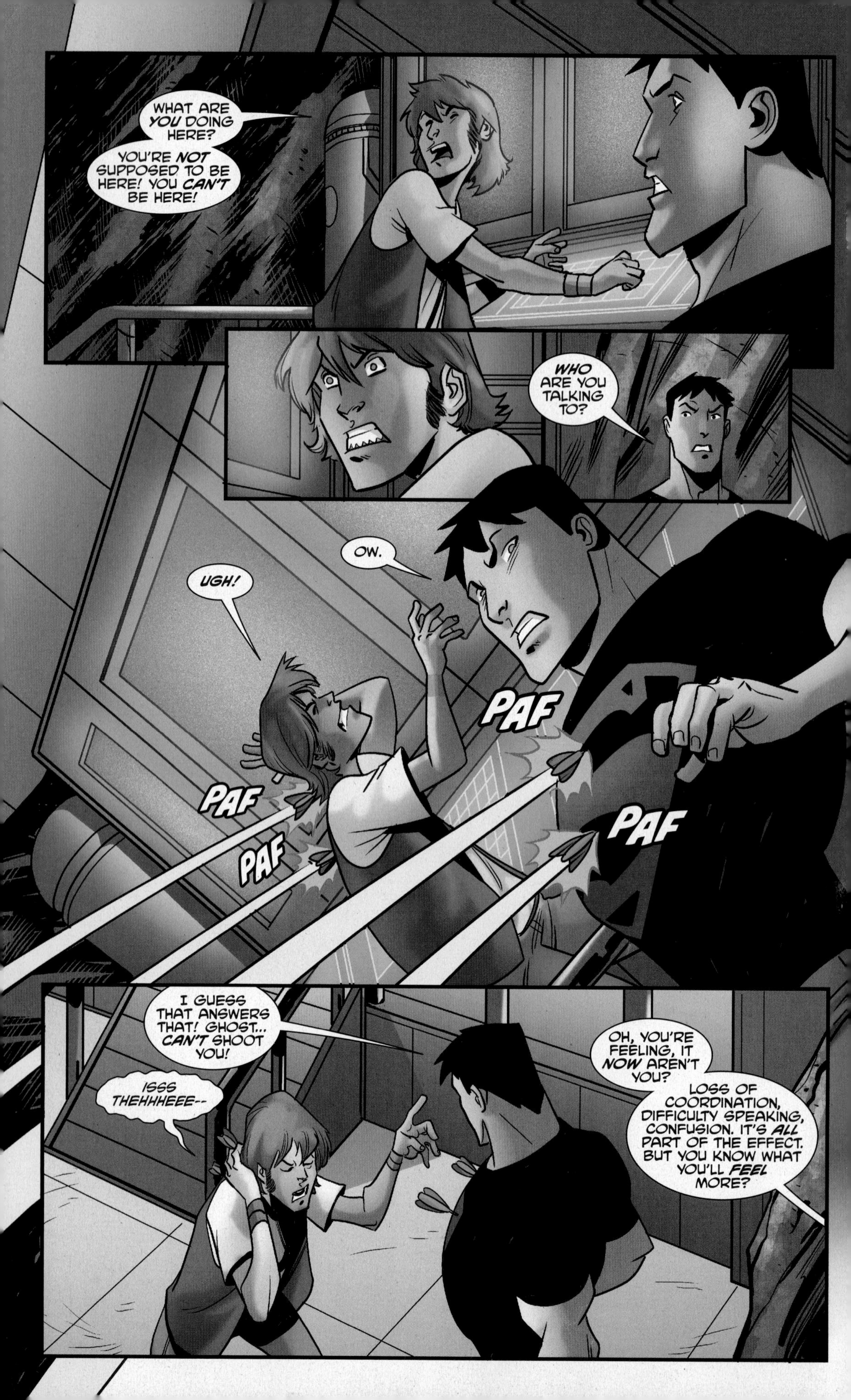
WHAT ARE *YOU* DOING HERE?
YOU'RE *NOT* SUPPOSED TO BE HERE! YOU *CAN'T* BE HERE!
WHO ARE YOU TALKING TO?
OW.
UGH!
PAF
PAF
PAF
PAF
I GUESS THAT ANSWERS THAT! GHOST... *CAN'T* SHOOT YOU!
ISSS THEHHHEEE--
OH, YOU'RE FEELING, IT *NOW* AREN'T YOU?
LOSS OF COORDINATION, DIFFICULTY SPEAKING, CONFUSION. IT'S *ALL* PART OF THE EFFECT. BUT YOU KNOW WHAT YOU'LL *FEEL* MORE?

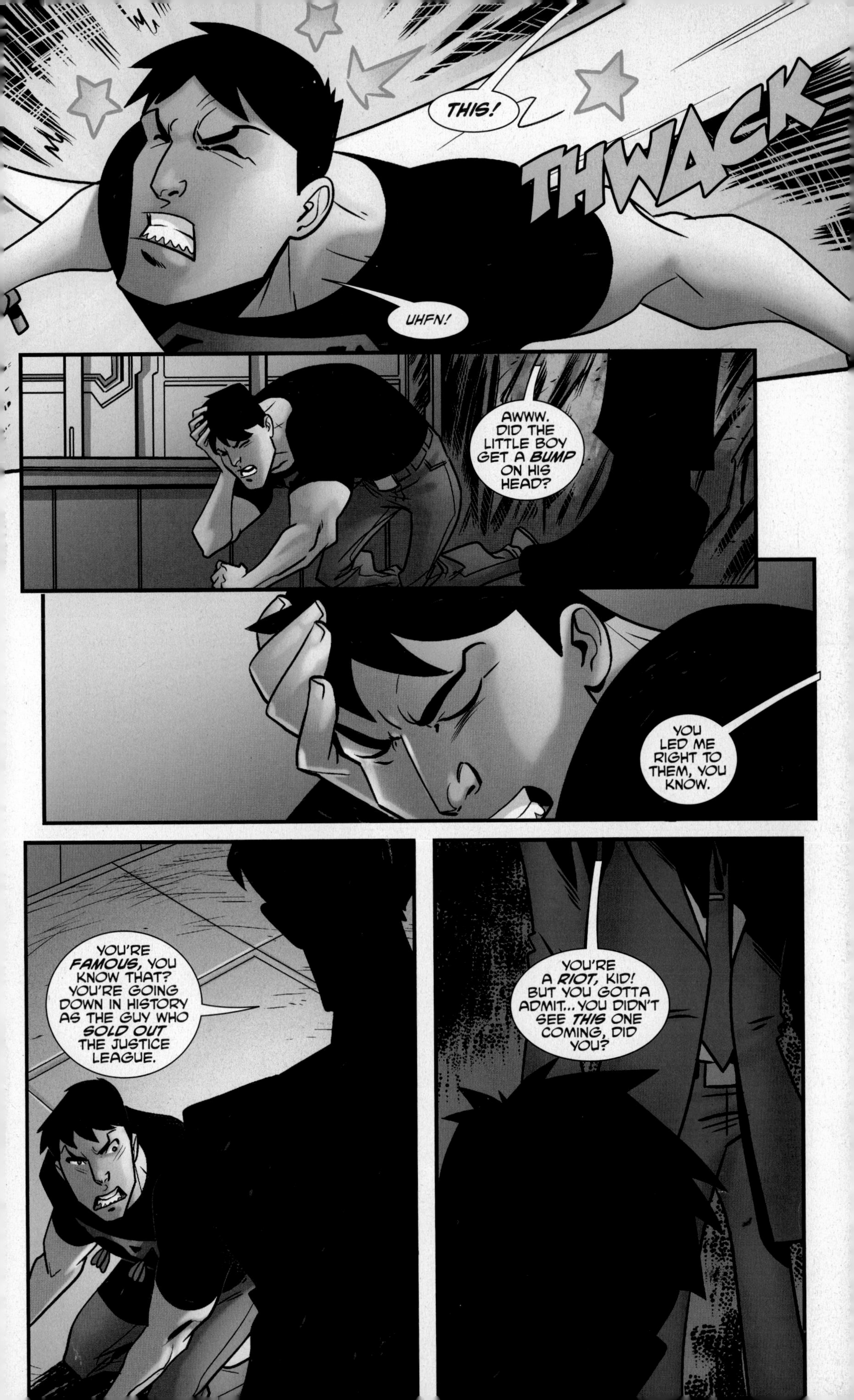
THIS!
THWACK
UHFN!
AWWW. DID THE LITTLE BOY GET A BUMP ON HIS HEAD?
YOU LED ME RIGHT TO THEM, YOU KNOW.
YOU'RE FAMOUS, YOU KNOW THAT? YOU'RE GOING DOWN IN HISTORY AS THE GUY WHO SOLD OUT THE JUSTICE LEAGUE.
YOU'RE A RIOT, KID! BUT YOU GOTTA ADMIT...YOU DIDN'T SEE THIS ONE COMING, DID YOU?

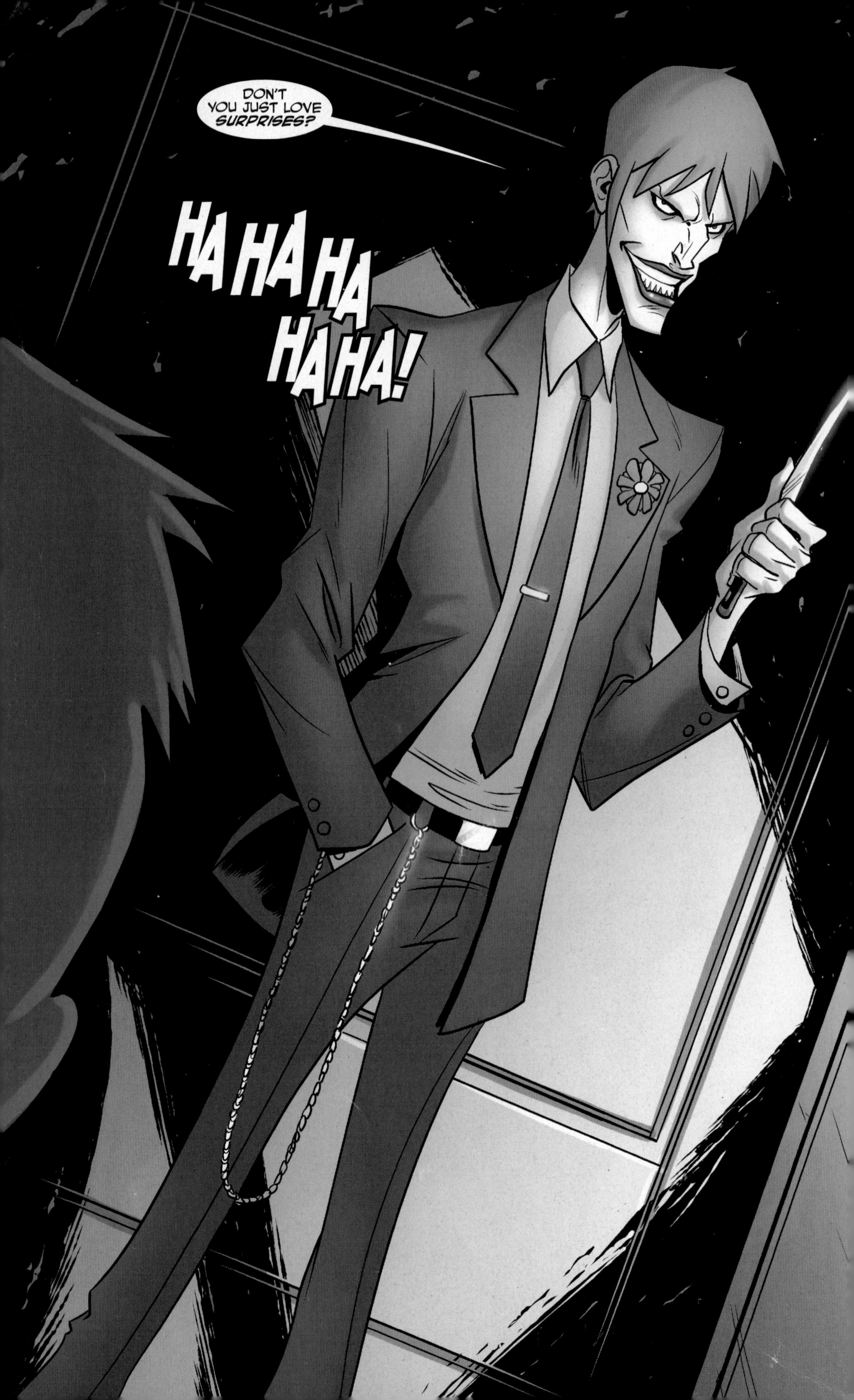
DON'T YOU JUST LOVE SURPRISES?
HA HA HA HA HA HA HA!

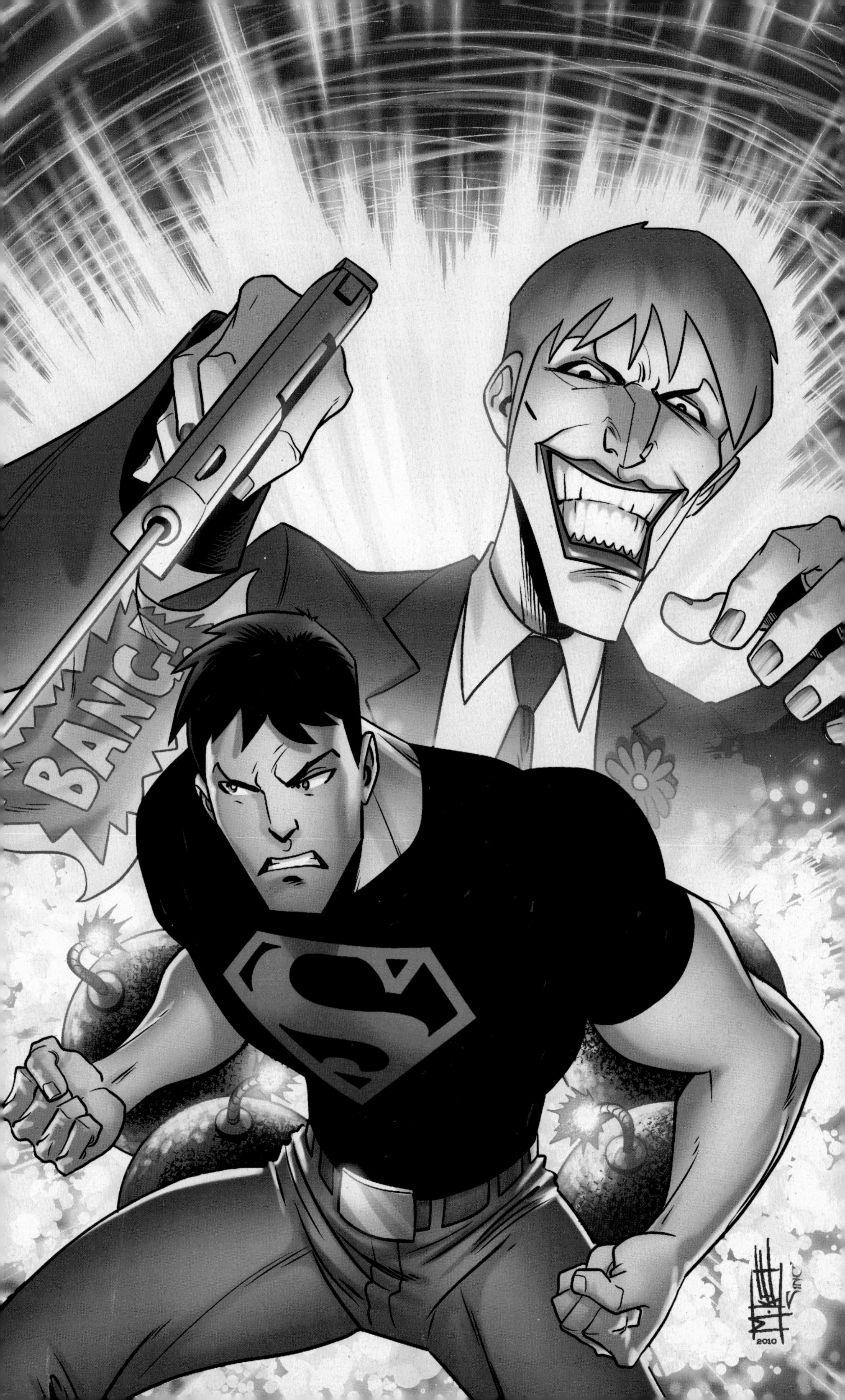
BANG!

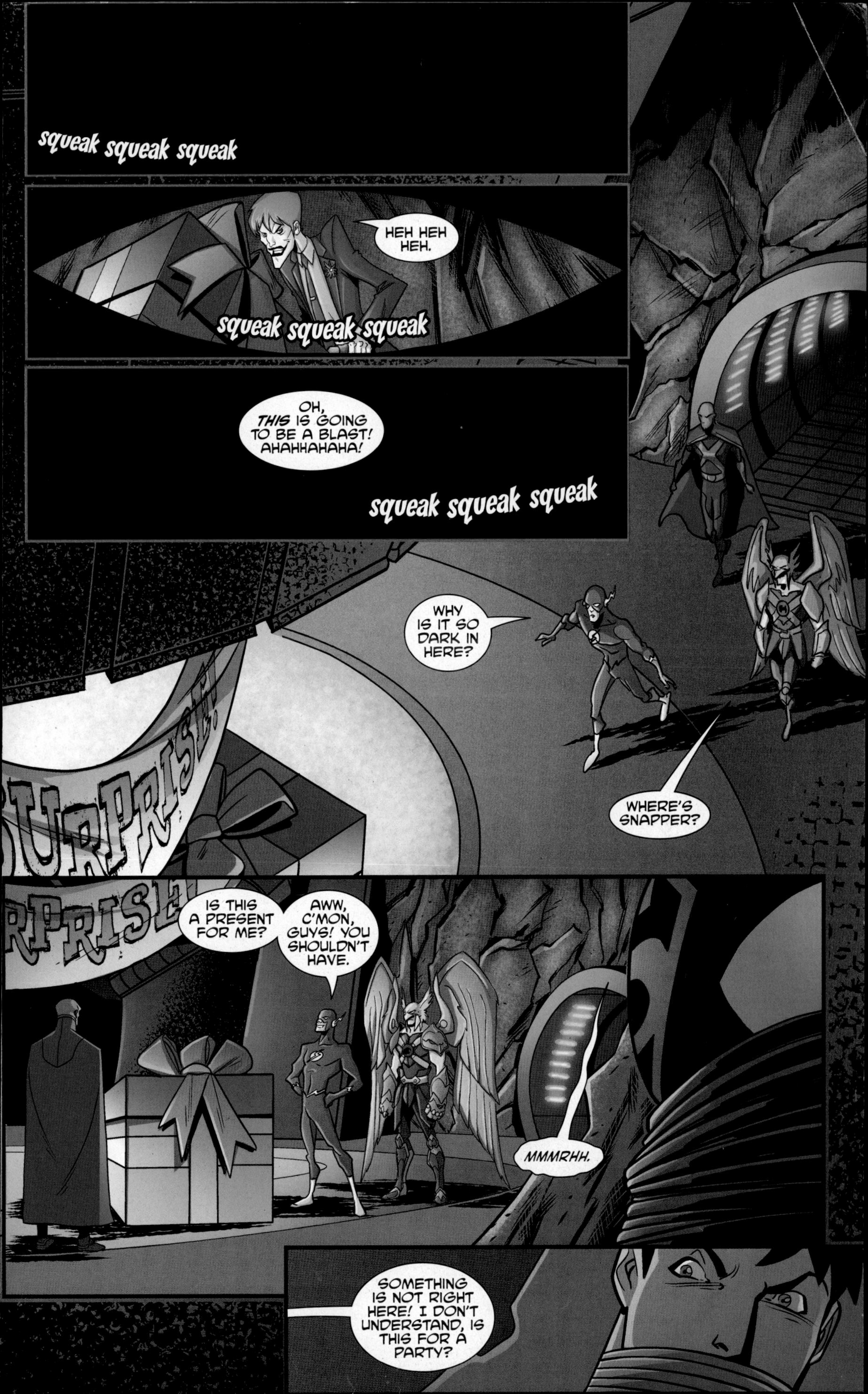
squeak squeak squeak
HEH HEH HEH.
squeak squeak squeak
OH, *THIS* IS GOING TO BE A BLAST! AHAHHAHAHA!
squeak squeak squeak
WHY IS IT SO DARK IN HERE?
WHERE'S SNAPPER?
SURPRISE!
IS THIS A PRESENT FOR ME?
AWW, C'MON, GUYS! YOU SHOULDN'T HAVE.
MMMRHH.
SOMETHING IS NOT RIGHT HERE! I DON'T UNDERSTAND, IS THIS FOR A PARTY?

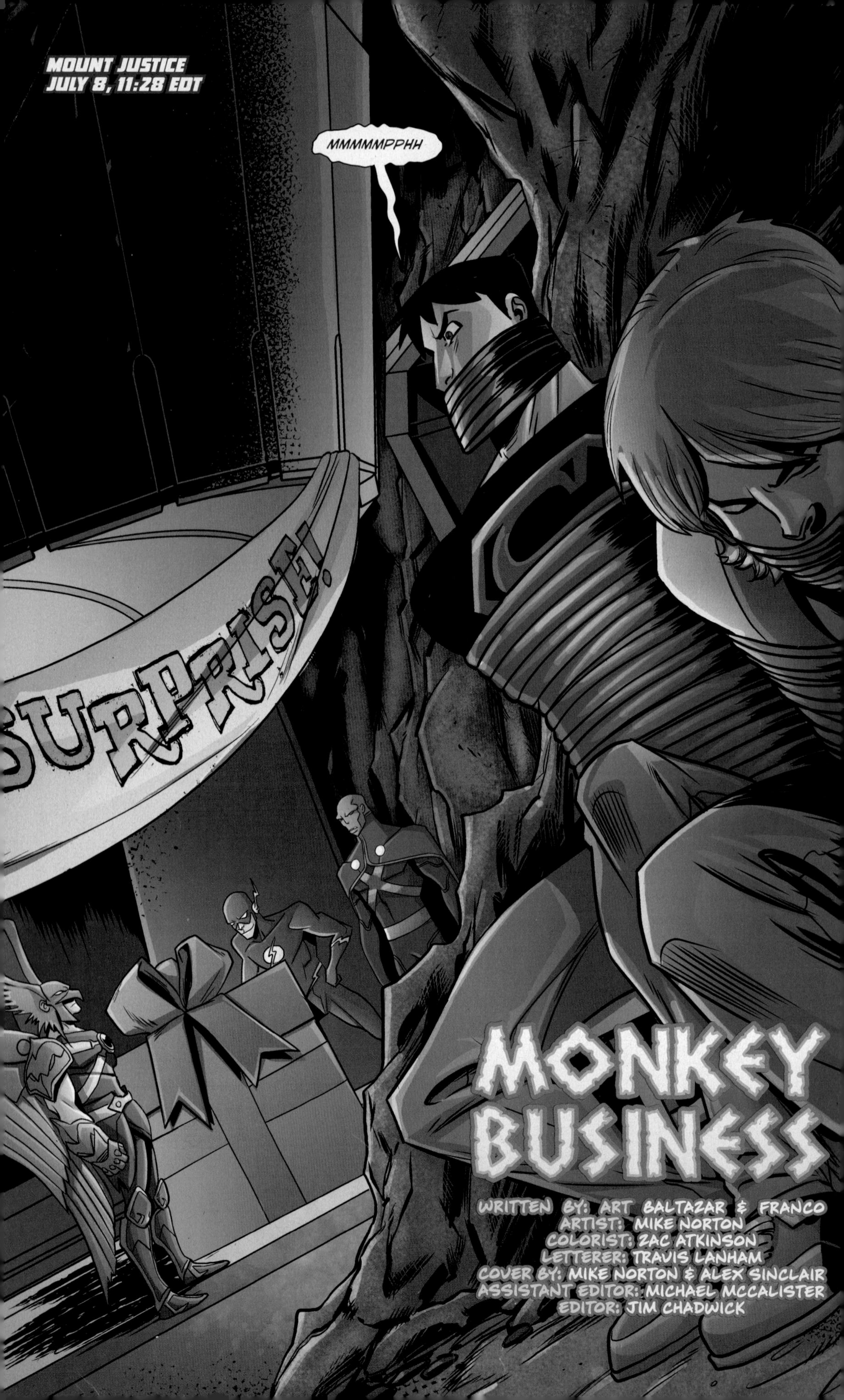
MOUNT JUSTICE
JULY 8, 11:28 EDT
MMMMMPPHH
SURPRISE!
MONKEY BUSINESS
WRITTEN BY: ART BALTAZAR & FRANCO
ARTIST: MIKE NORTON
COLORIST: ZAC ATKINSON
LETTERER: TRAVIS LANHAM
COVER BY: MIKE NORTON & ALEX SINCLAIR
ASSISTANT EDITOR: MICHAEL MCCALISTER
EDITOR: JIM CHADWICK

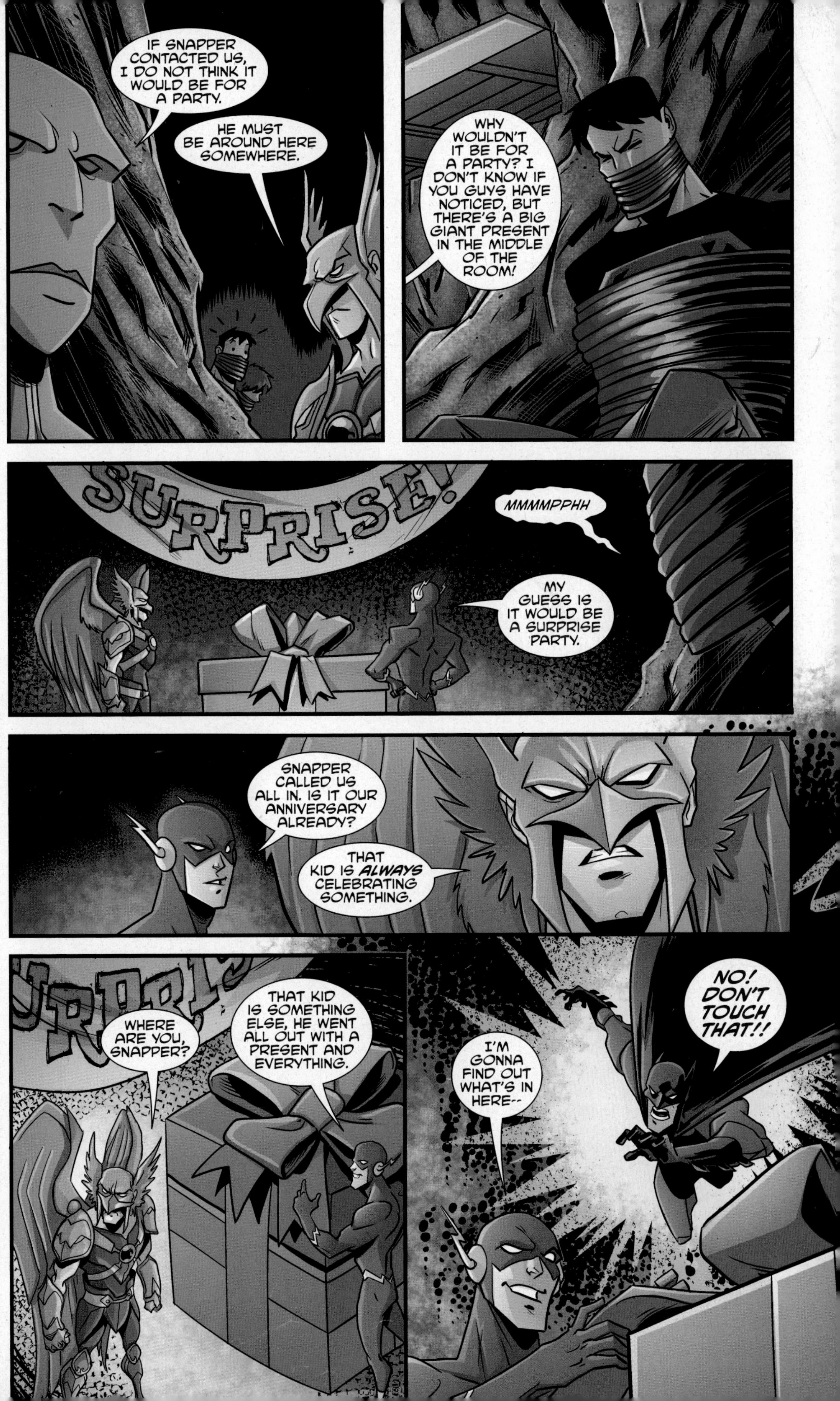
IF SNAPPER CONTACTED US, I DO NOT THINK IT WOULD BE FOR A PARTY.
HE MUST BE AROUND HERE SOMEWHERE.
WHY WOULDN'T IT BE FOR A PARTY? I DON'T KNOW IF YOU GUYS HAVE NOTICED, BUT THERE'S A BIG GIANT PRESENT IN THE MIDDLE OF THE ROOM!
SURPRISE!
MMMMPPHH
MY GUESS IS IT WOULD BE A SURPRISE PARTY.
SNAPPER CALLED US ALL IN. IS IT OUR ANNIVERSARY ALREADY?
THAT KID IS *ALWAYS* CELEBRATING SOMETHING.
WHERE ARE YOU, SNAPPER?
THAT KID IS SOMETHING ELSE, HE WENT ALL OUT WITH A PRESENT AND EVERYTHING.
I'M GONNA FIND OUT WHAT'S IN HERE--
NO! DON'T TOUCH THAT!!

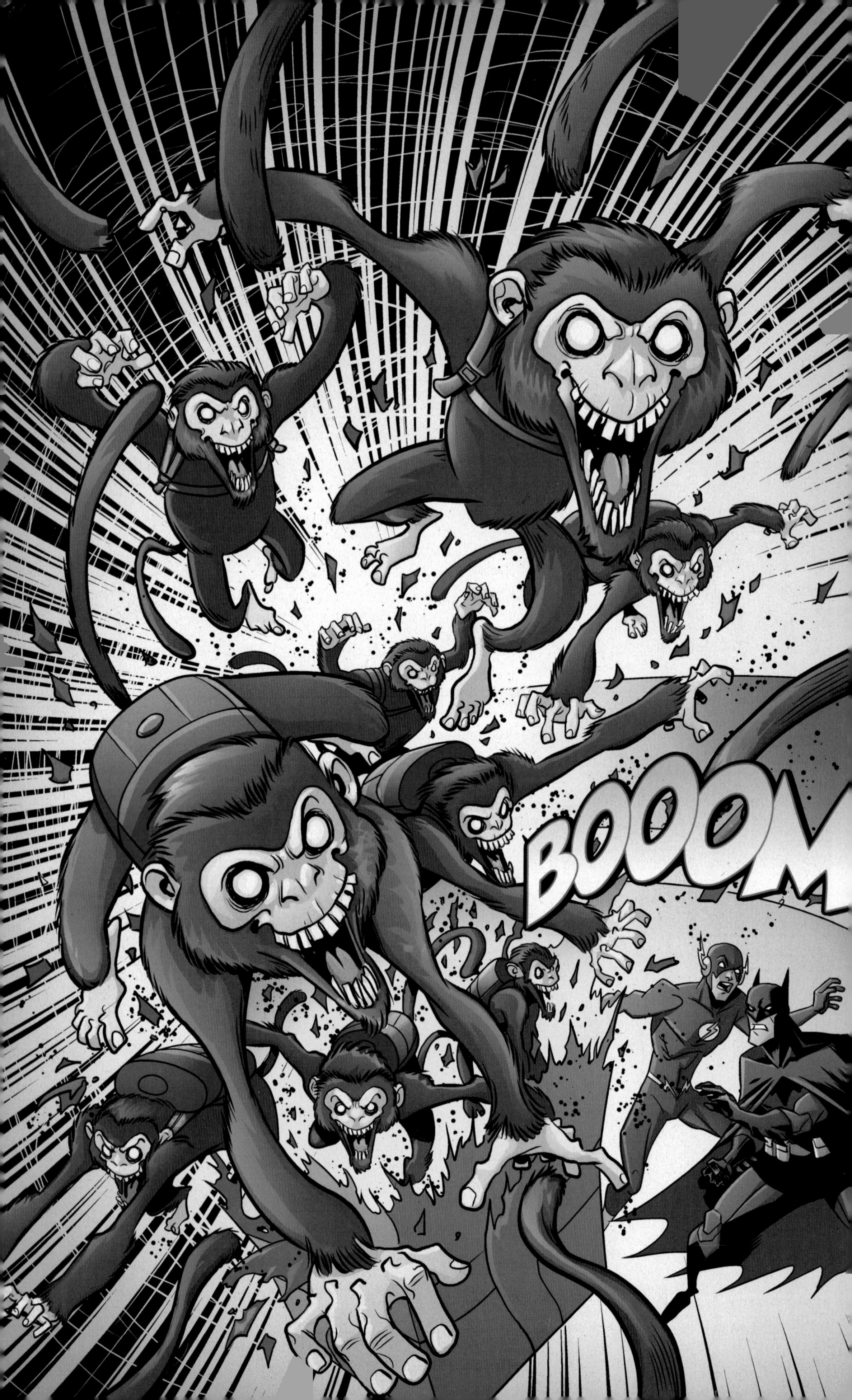
BOOOM

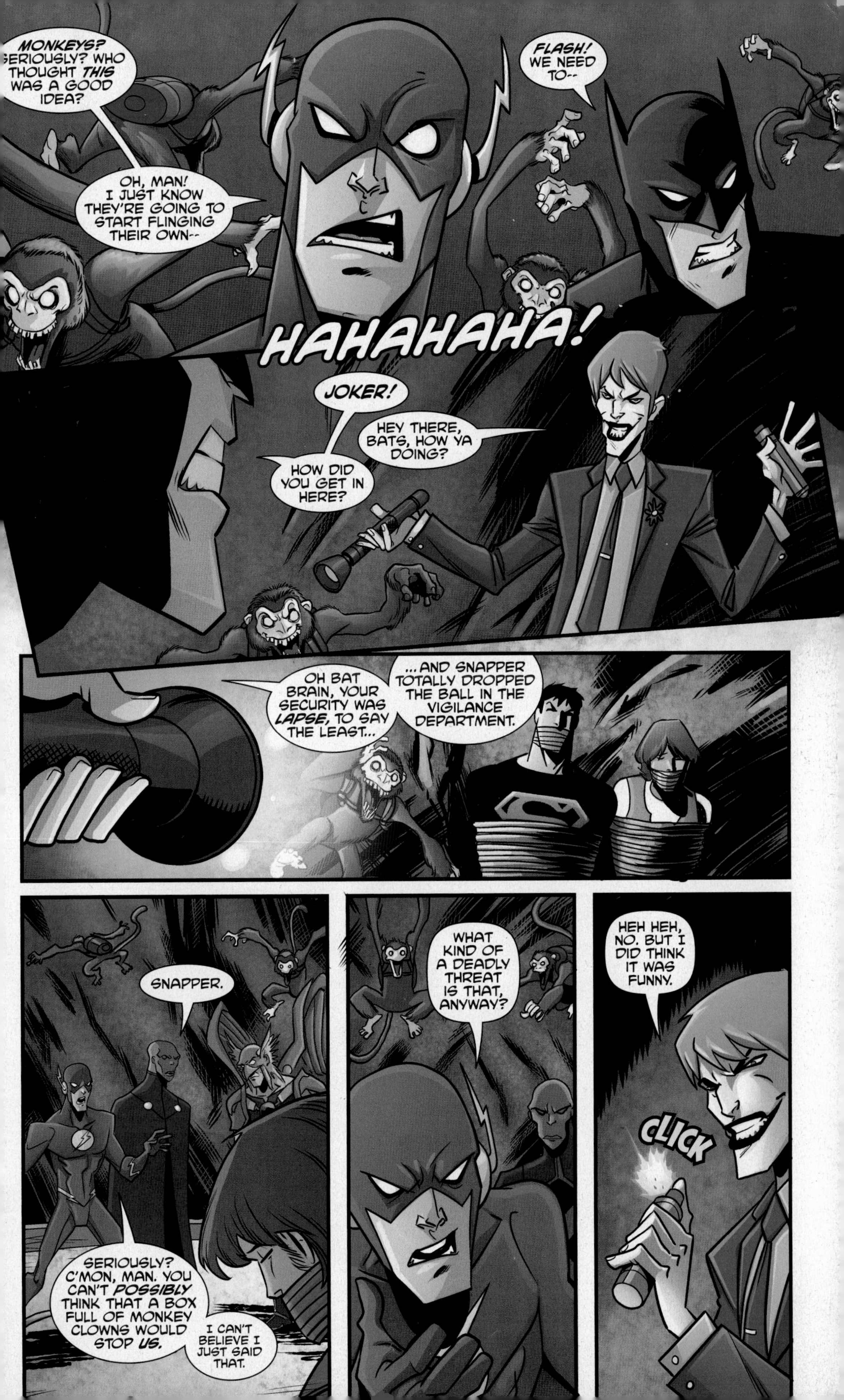
MONKEYS? SERIOUSLY? WHO THOUGHT THIS WAS A GOOD IDEA?
OH, MAN! I JUST KNOW THEY'RE GOING TO START FLINGING THEIR OWN--
FLASH! WE NEED TO--
HAHAHAHA!
JOKER!
HEY THERE, BATS, HOW YA DOING?
HOW DID YOU GET IN HERE?
OH BAT BRAIN, YOUR SECURITY WAS LAPSE, TO SAY THE LEAST...
...AND SNAPPER TOTALLY DROPPED THE BALL IN THE VIGILANCE DEPARTMENT.
SNAPPER.
SERIOUSLY? C'MON, MAN. YOU CAN'T POSSIBLY THINK THAT A BOX FULL OF MONKEY CLOWNS WOULD STOP US.
I CAN'T BELIEVE I JUST SAID THAT.
WHAT KIND OF A DEADLY THREAT IS THAT, ANYWAY?
HEH HEH, NO. BUT I DID THINK IT WAS FUNNY.
CLICK

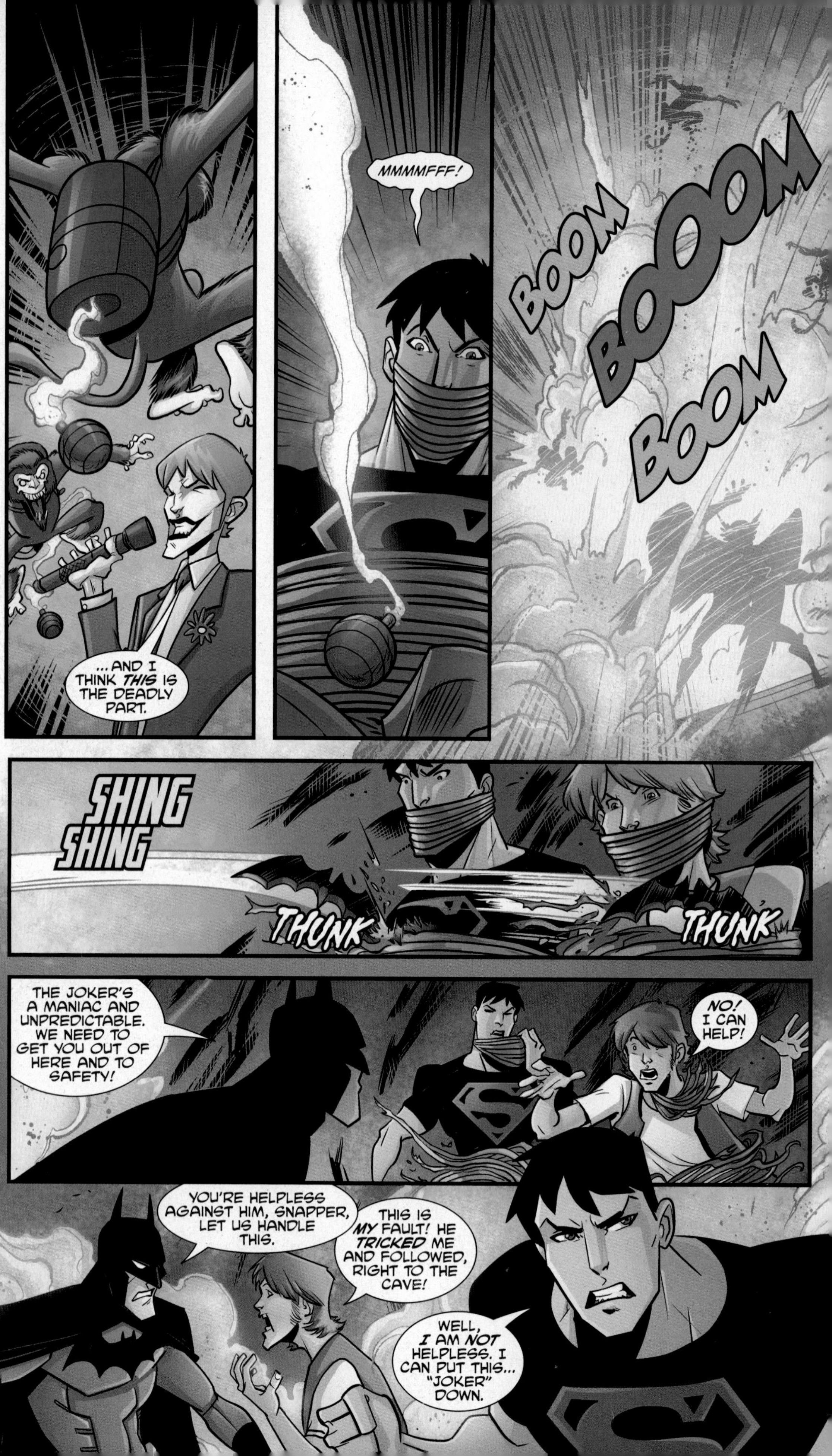
...AND I THINK *THIS* IS THE DEADLY PART.
MMMMFFF!
BOOM
BOOOOM
BOOM
SHING
SHING
THUNK
THUNK
THE JOKER'S A MANIAC AND UNPREDICTABLE. WE NEED TO GET YOU OUT OF HERE AND TO SAFETY!
NO! I CAN HELP!
YOU'RE HELPLESS AGAINST HIM, SNAPPER, LET US HANDLE THIS.
THIS IS *MY* FAULT! HE *TRICKED* ME AND FOLLOWED, RIGHT TO THE CAVE!
WELL, *I AM NOT* HELPLESS. I CAN PUT THIS... "JOKER" DOWN.

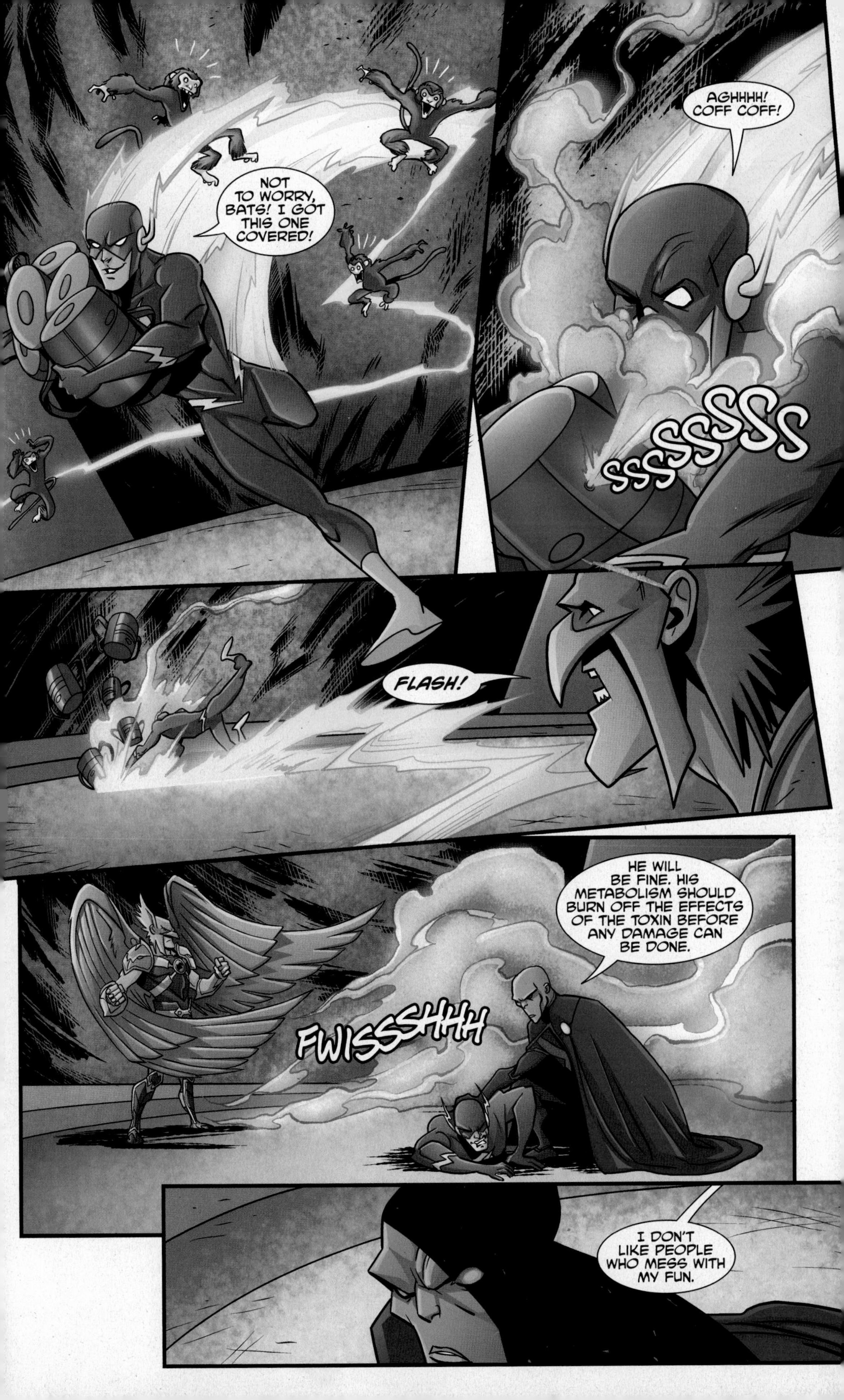
NOT TO WORRY, BATS! I GOT THIS ONE COVERED!
AGHHHH! COFF COFF!
SSSSSSSSS
FLASH!
HE WILL BE FINE. HIS METABOLISM SHOULD BURN OFF THE EFFECTS OF THE TOXIN BEFORE ANY DAMAGE CAN BE DONE.
FWISSSHHH
I DON'T LIKE PEOPLE WHO MESS WITH MY FUN.

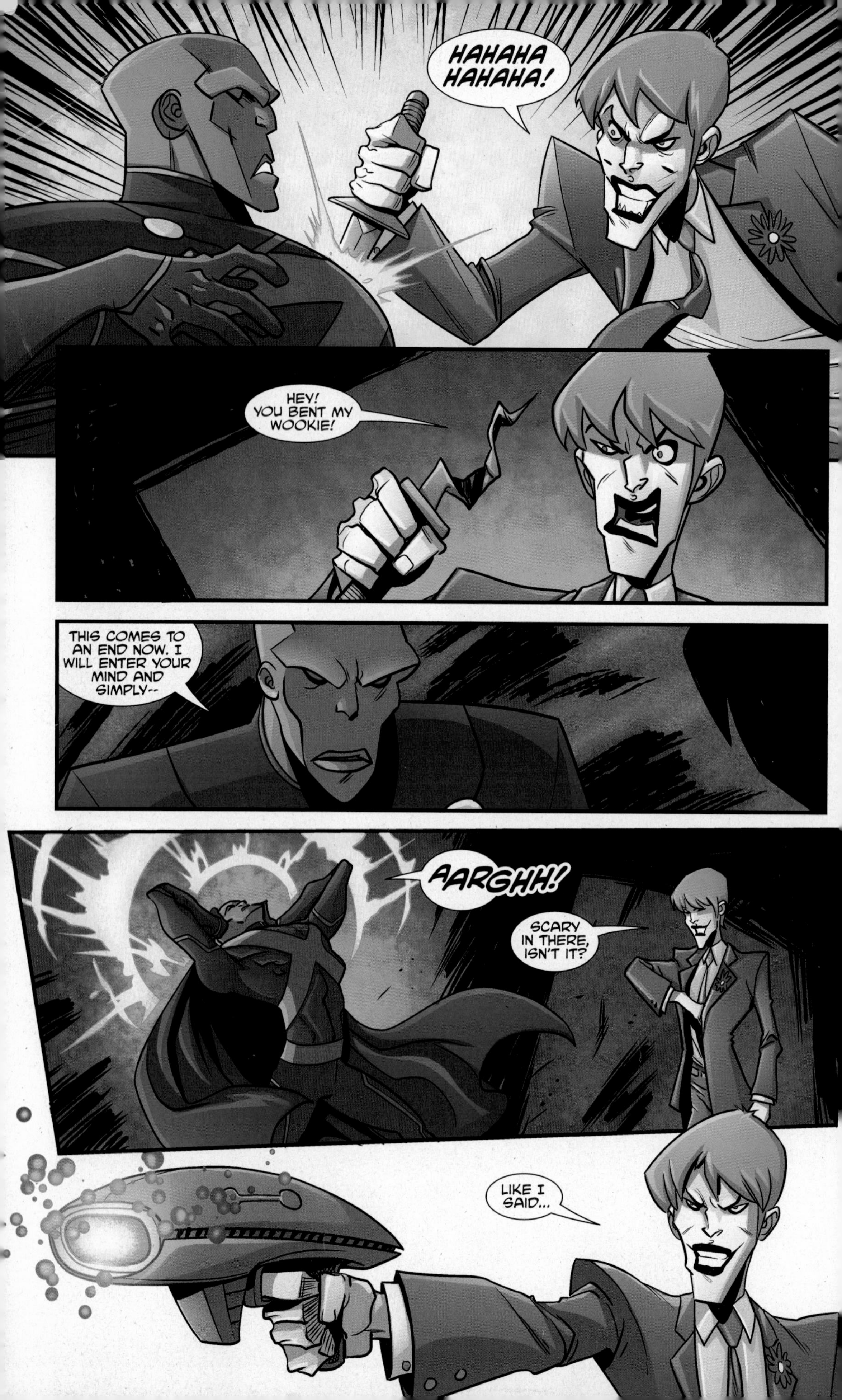
HAHAHA
HAHAHA!
HEY!
YOU BENT MY
WOOKIE!
THIS COMES TO
AN END NOW. I
WILL ENTER YOUR
MIND AND
SIMPLY--
AARGHH!
SCARY
IN THERE,
ISN'T IT?
LIKE I
SAID...

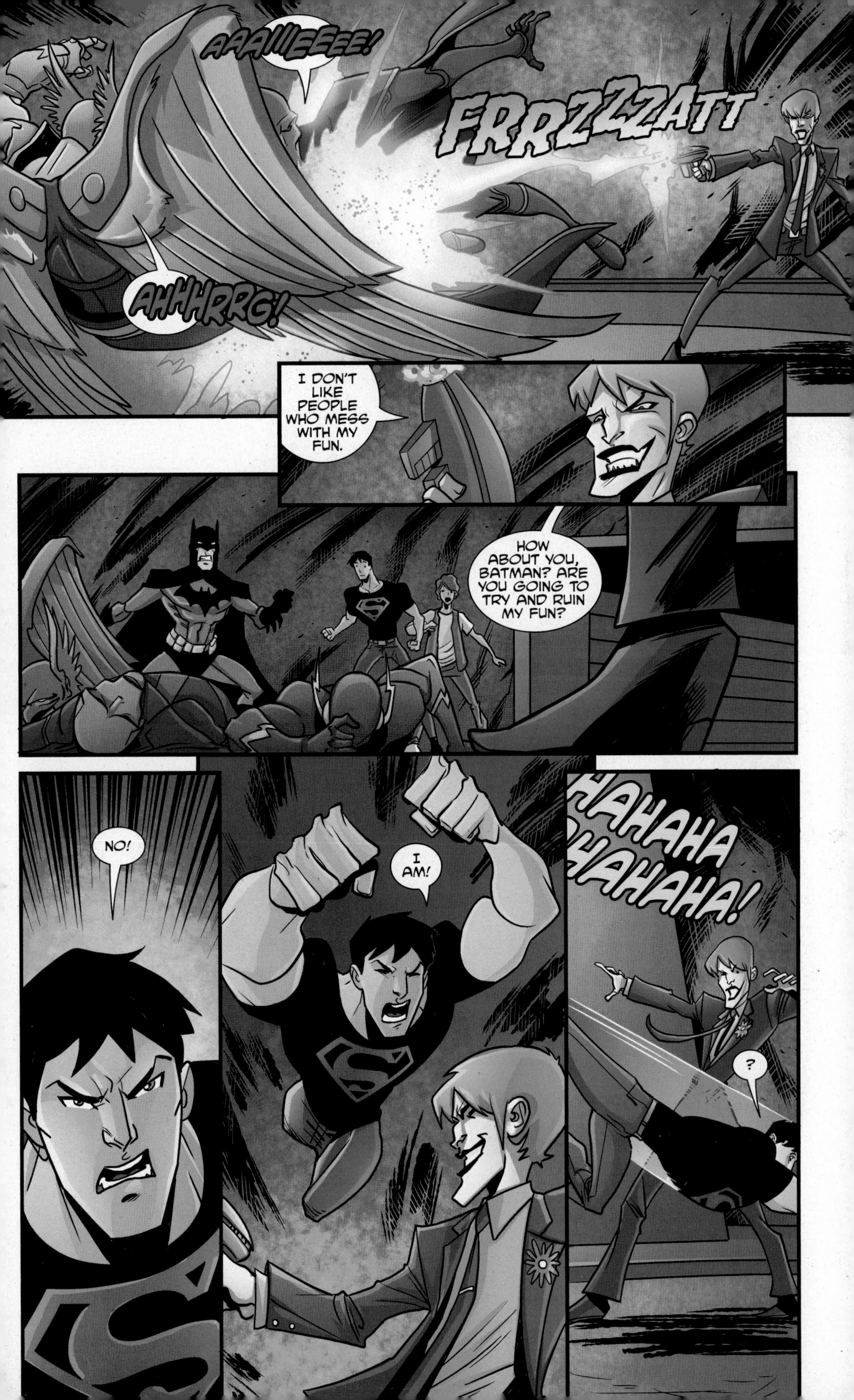
AAAIIIEEEEE!
FRRZZZATT
AHHHRRG!
I DON'T LIKE PEOPLE WHO MESS WITH MY FUN.
HOW ABOUT YOU, BATMAN? ARE YOU GOING TO TRY AND RUIN MY FUN?
NO!
I AM!
HAHAHA HAHAHAHA!
?

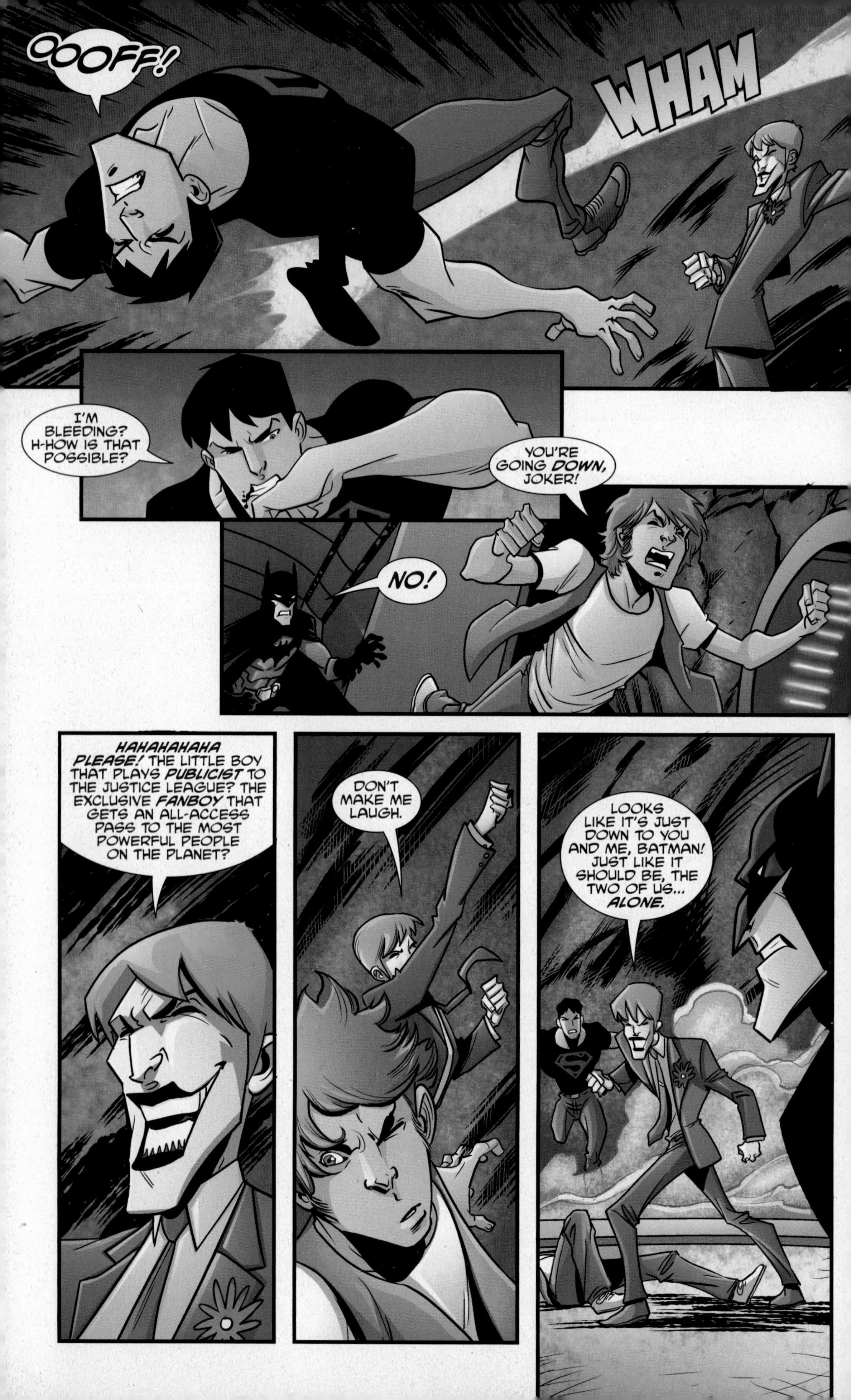
OOOFF!
WHAM
I'M BLEEDING? H-HOW IS THAT POSSIBLE?
YOU'RE GOING *DOWN,* JOKER!
NO!
HAHAHAHAHA PLEASE! THE LITTLE BOY THAT PLAYS *PUBLICIST* TO THE JUSTICE LEAGUE? THE EXCLUSIVE *FANBOY* THAT GETS AN ALL-ACCESS PASS TO THE MOST POWERFUL PEOPLE ON THE PLANET?
DON'T MAKE ME LAUGH.
LOOKS LIKE IT'S JUST DOWN TO YOU AND ME, BATMAN! JUST LIKE IT SHOULD BE, THE TWO OF US... *ALONE.*

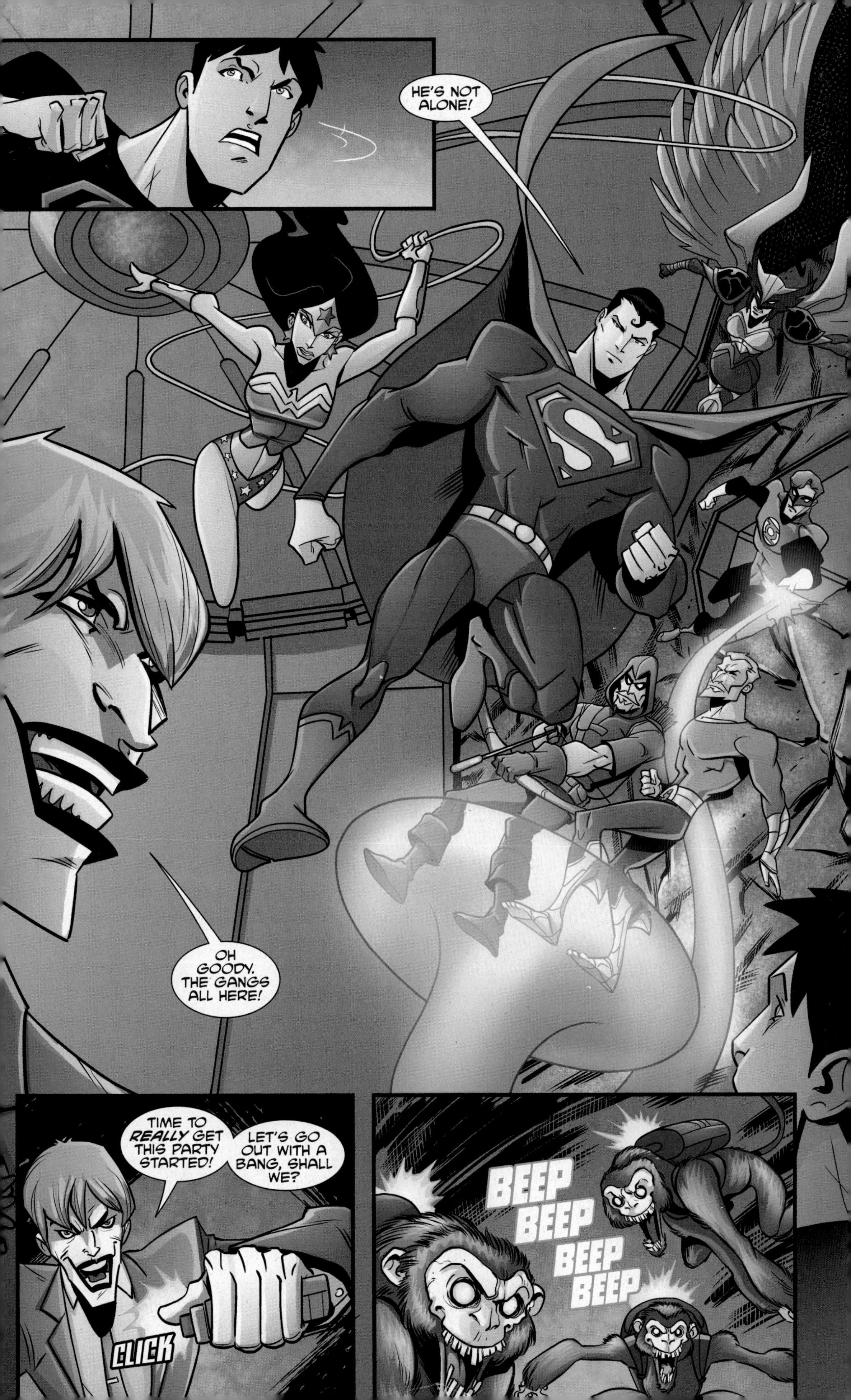
HE'S NOT ALONE!
OH GOODY. THE GANGS ALL HERE!
TIME TO *REALLY* GET THIS PARTY STARTED!
LET'S GO OUT WITH A BANG, SHALL WE?
CLICK
BEEP
BEEP
BEEP
BEEP

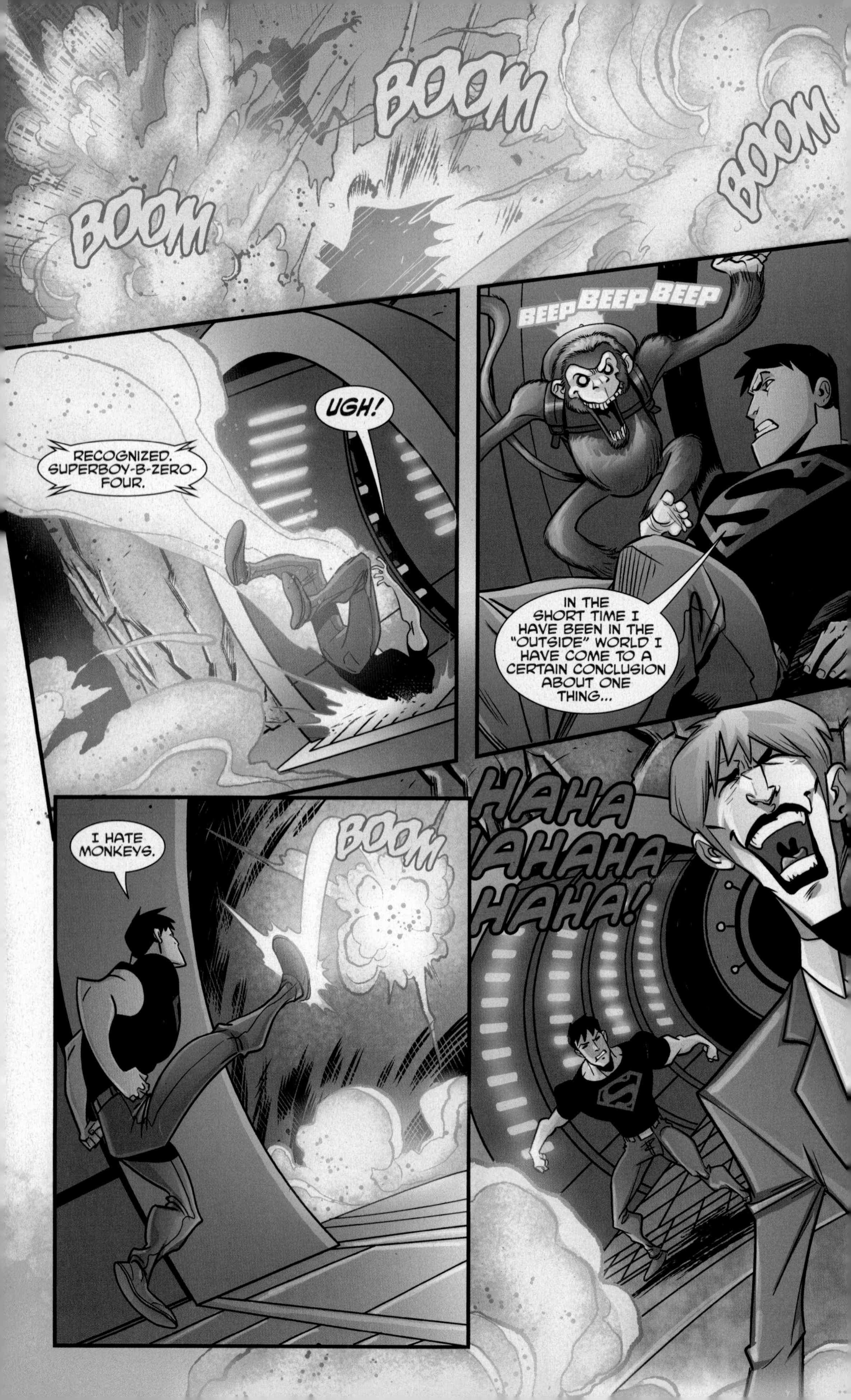

BOOM
BOOM
BOOM
RECOGNIZED. SUPERBOY-B-ZERO-FOUR.
UGH!
BEEP BEEP BEEP
IN THE SHORT TIME I HAVE BEEN IN THE "OUTSIDE" WORLD I HAVE COME TO A CERTAIN CONCLUSION ABOUT ONE THING...
I HATE MONKEYS.
BOOM
HAHA HAHAHA HAHA!

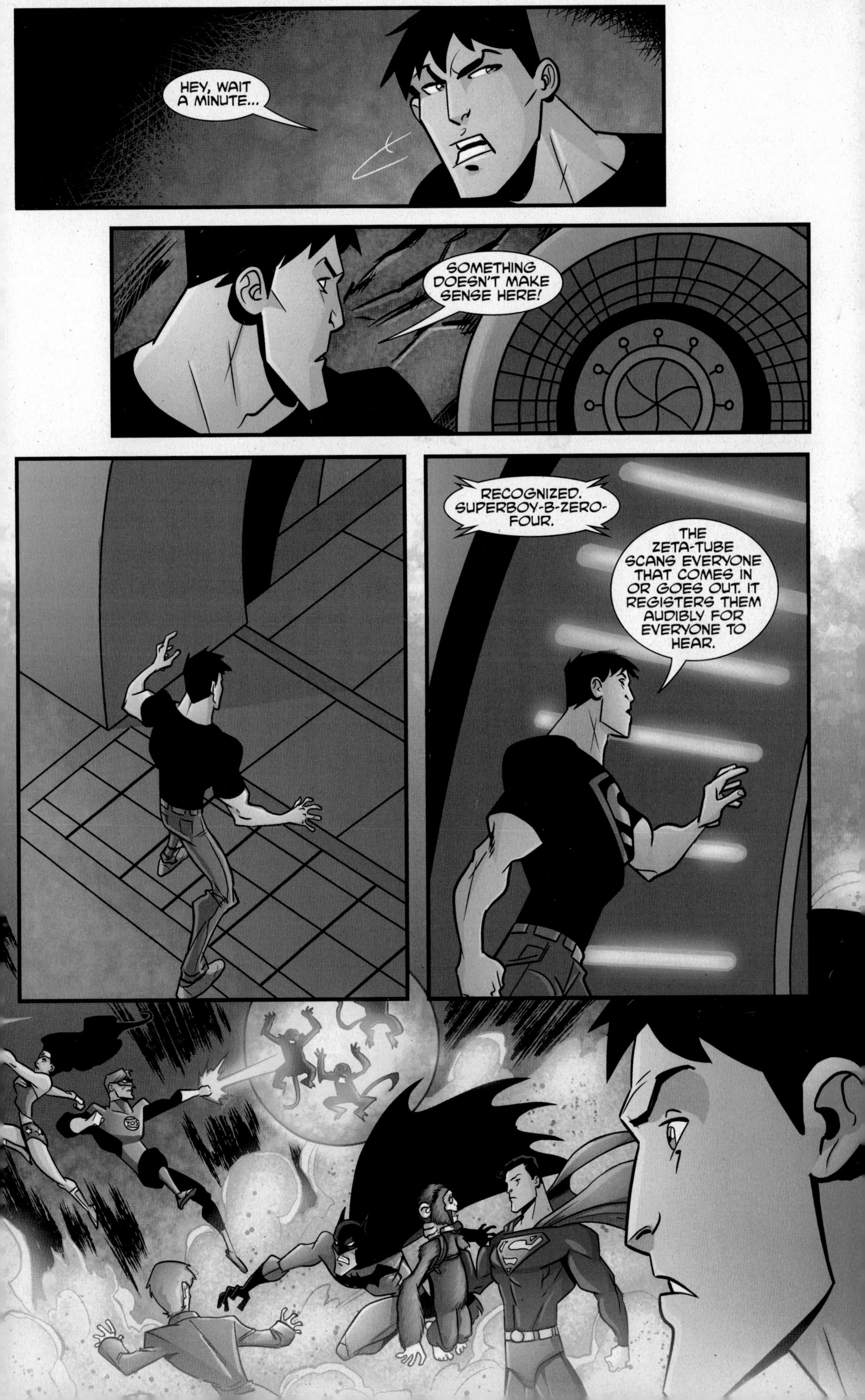
HEY, WAIT A MINUTE...
SOMETHING DOESN'T MAKE SENSE HERE!
RECOGNIZED. SUPERBOY-B-ZERO-FOUR.
THE ZETA-TUBE SCANS EVERYONE THAT COMES IN OR GOES OUT. IT REGISTERS THEM AUDIBLY FOR EVERYONE TO HEAR.

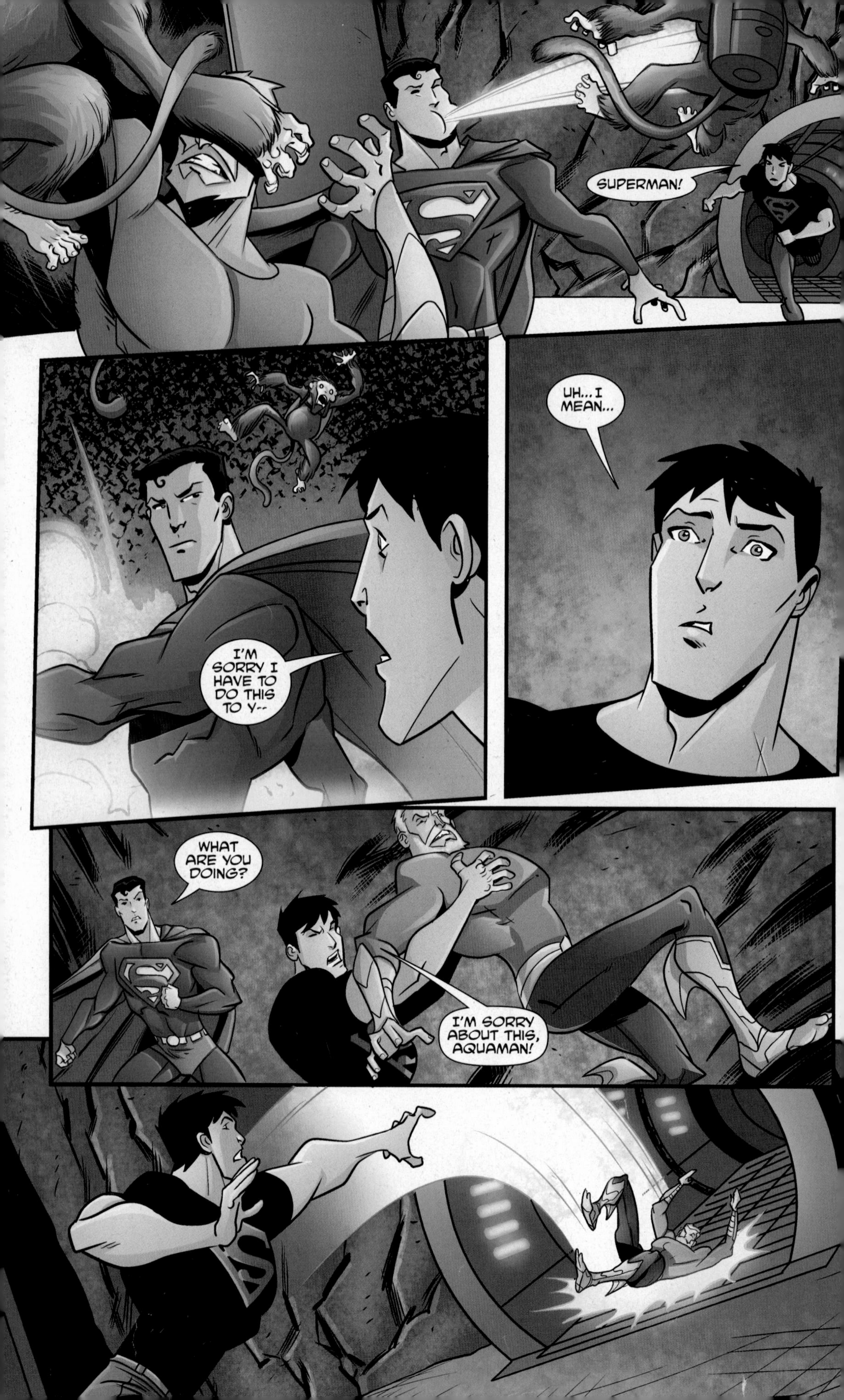
SUPERMAN!
UH... I MEAN...
I'M SORRY I HAVE TO DO THIS TO Y--
WHAT ARE YOU DOING?
I'M SORRY ABOUT THIS, AQUAMAN!

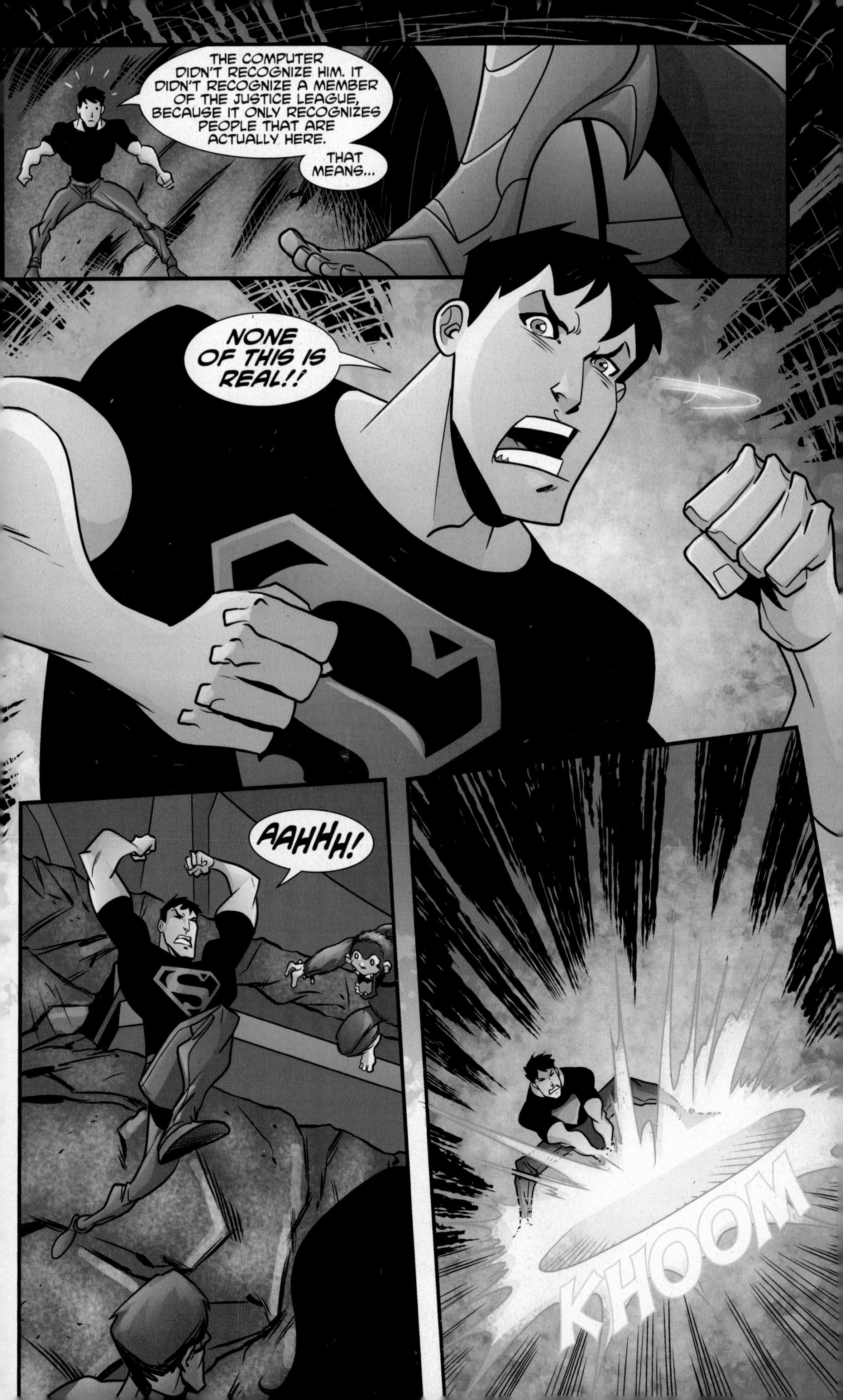
THE COMPUTER DIDN'T RECOGNIZE HIM. IT DIDN'T RECOGNIZE A MEMBER OF THE JUSTICE LEAGUE, BECAUSE IT ONLY RECOGNIZES PEOPLE THAT ARE ACTUALLY HERE.
THAT MEANS...
NONE OF THIS IS REAL!!
AAHHH!
KHOOM

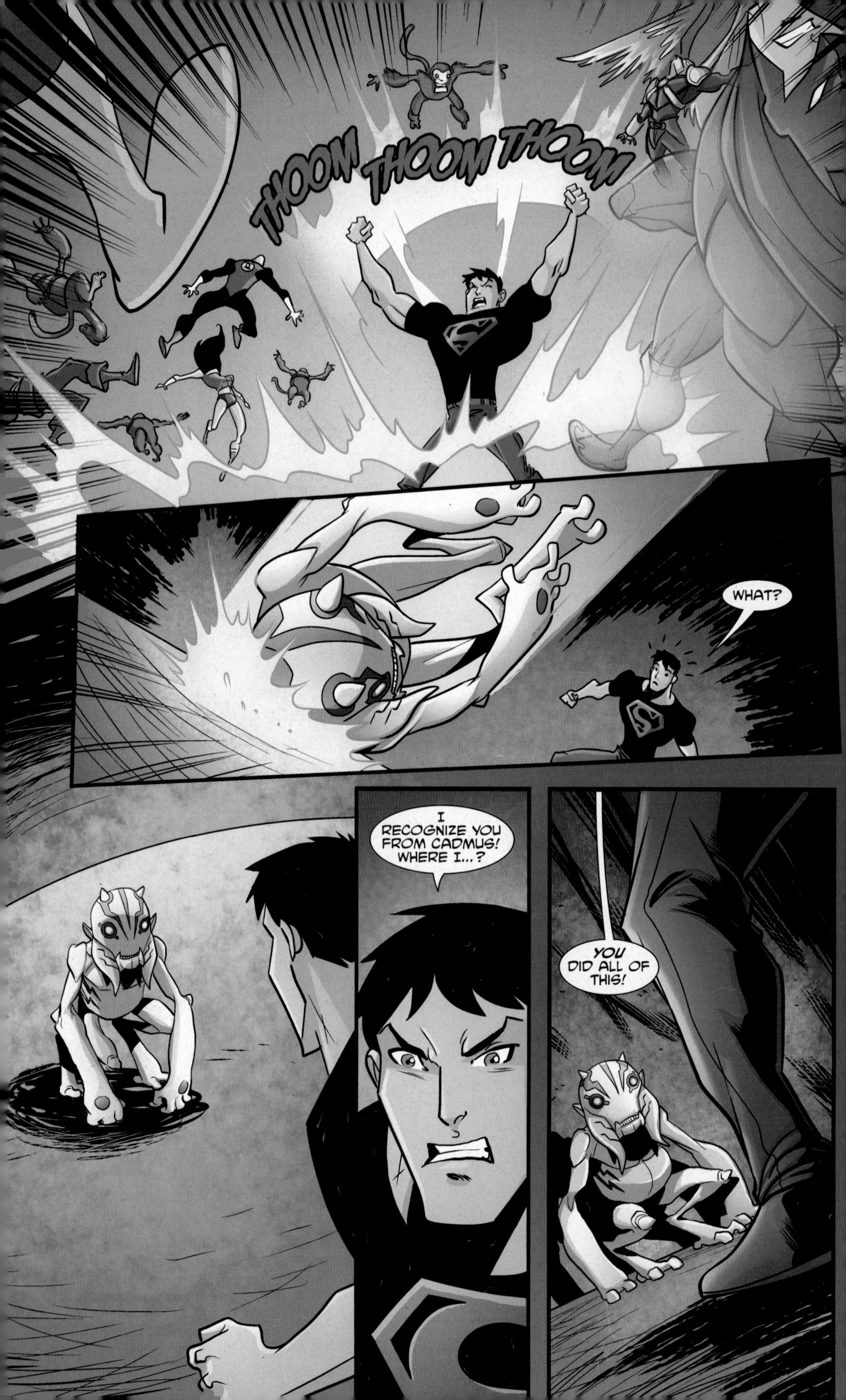
THOOM THOOM THOOM
WHAT?
I RECOGNIZE YOU FROM CADMUS! WHERE I...?
YOU DID ALL OF THIS!

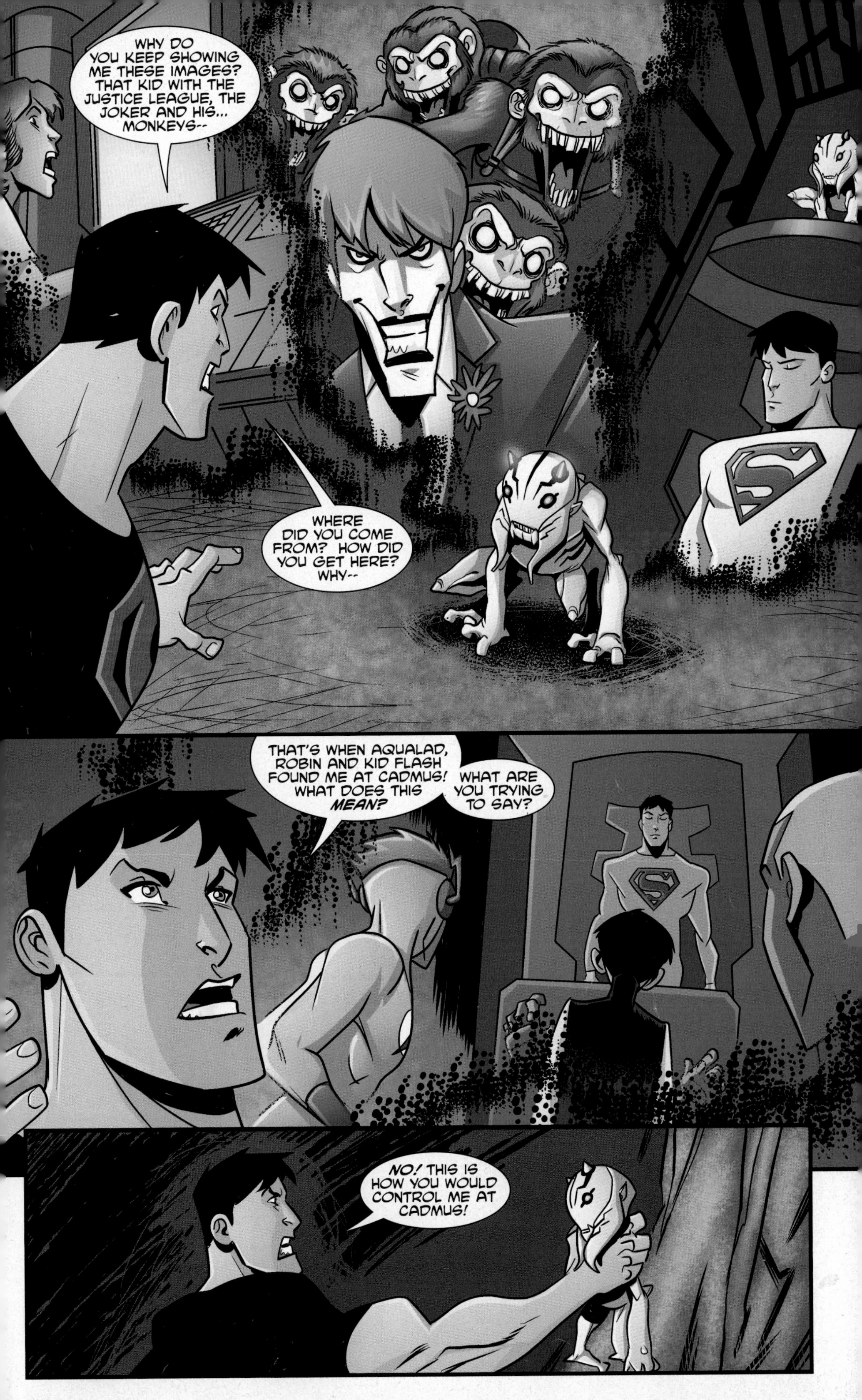
WHY DO YOU KEEP SHOWING ME THESE IMAGES? THAT KID WITH THE JUSTICE LEAGUE, THE JOKER AND HIS... MONKEYS--
WHERE DID YOU COME FROM? HOW DID YOU GET HERE? WHY--
THAT'S WHEN AQUALAD, ROBIN AND KID FLASH FOUND ME AT CADMUS! WHAT DOES THIS *MEAN?*
WHAT ARE YOU TRYING TO SAY?
NO! THIS IS HOW YOU WOULD CONTROL ME AT CADMUS!

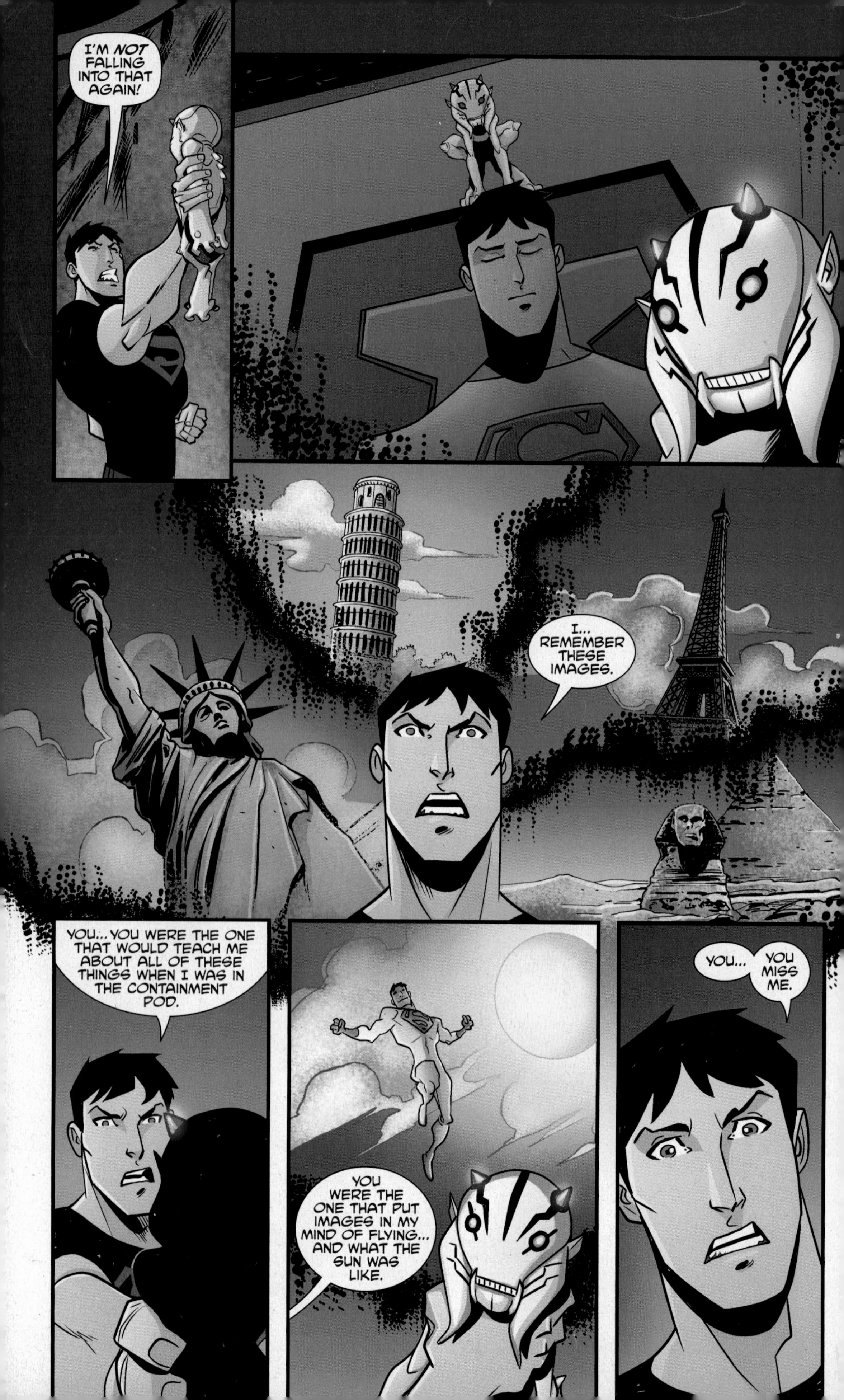
I'M NOT FALLING INTO THAT AGAIN!
I... REMEMBER THESE IMAGES.
YOU...YOU WERE THE ONE THAT WOULD TEACH ME ABOUT ALL OF THESE THINGS WHEN I WAS IN THE CONTAINMENT POD.
YOU WERE THE ONE THAT PUT IMAGES IN MY MIND OF FLYING... AND WHAT THE SUN WAS LIKE.
YOU...
YOU MISS ME.

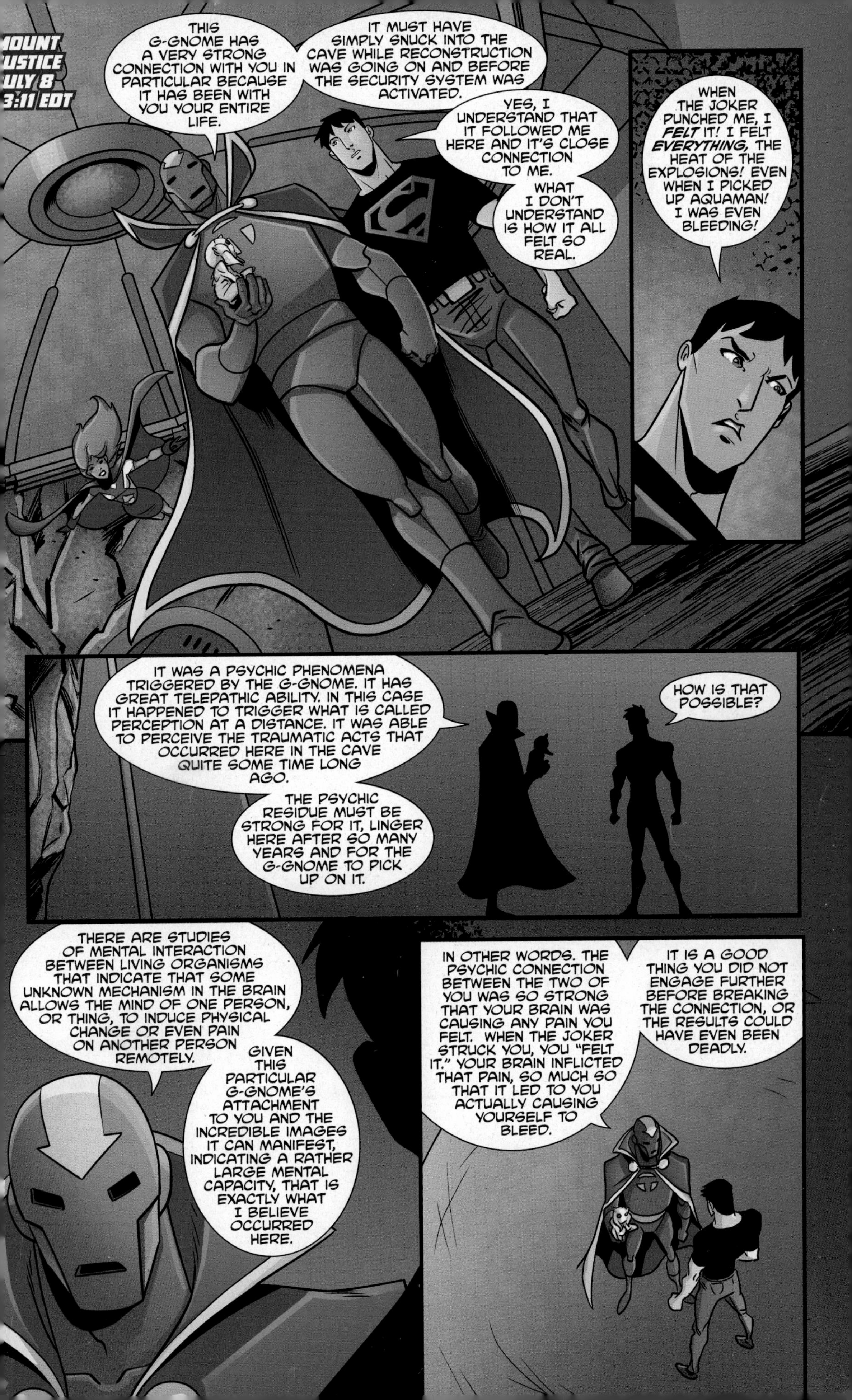
MOUNT JUSTICE JULY 8 3:11 EDT
THIS G-GNOME HAS A VERY STRONG CONNECTION WITH YOU IN PARTICULAR BECAUSE IT HAS BEEN WITH YOU YOUR ENTIRE LIFE.
IT MUST HAVE SIMPLY SNUCK INTO THE CAVE WHILE RECONSTRUCTION WAS GOING ON AND BEFORE THE SECURITY SYSTEM WAS ACTIVATED.
YES, I UNDERSTAND THAT IT FOLLOWED ME HERE AND IT'S CLOSE CONNECTION TO ME.
WHAT I DON'T UNDERSTAND IS HOW IT ALL FELT SO REAL.
WHEN THE JOKER PUNCHED ME, I FELT IT! I FELT EVERYTHING, THE HEAT OF THE EXPLOSIONS! EVEN WHEN I PICKED UP AQUAMAN! I WAS EVEN BLEEDING!
IT WAS A PSYCHIC PHENOMENA TRIGGERED BY THE G-GNOME. IT HAS GREAT TELEPATHIC ABILITY. IN THIS CASE IT HAPPENED TO TRIGGER WHAT IS CALLED PERCEPTION AT A DISTANCE. IT WAS ABLE TO PERCEIVE THE TRAUMATIC ACTS THAT OCCURRED HERE IN THE CAVE QUITE SOME TIME LONG AGO.
THE PSYCHIC RESIDUE MUST BE STRONG FOR IT, LINGER HERE AFTER SO MANY YEARS AND FOR THE G-GNOME TO PICK UP ON IT.
HOW IS THAT POSSIBLE?
THERE ARE STUDIES OF MENTAL INTERACTION BETWEEN LIVING ORGANISMS THAT INDICATE THAT SOME UNKNOWN MECHANISM IN THE BRAIN ALLOWS THE MIND OF ONE PERSON, OR THING, TO INDUCE PHYSICAL CHANGE OR EVEN PAIN ON ANOTHER PERSON REMOTELY.
GIVEN THIS PARTICULAR G-GNOME'S ATTACHMENT TO YOU AND THE INCREDIBLE IMAGES IT CAN MANIFEST, INDICATING A RATHER LARGE MENTAL CAPACITY, THAT IS EXACTLY WHAT I BELIEVE OCCURRED HERE.
IN OTHER WORDS. THE PSYCHIC CONNECTION BETWEEN THE TWO OF YOU WAS SO STRONG THAT YOUR BRAIN WAS CAUSING ANY PAIN YOU FELT. WHEN THE JOKER STRUCK YOU, YOU "FELT IT." YOUR BRAIN INFLICTED THAT PAIN, SO MUCH SO THAT IT LED TO YOU ACTUALLY CAUSING YOURSELF TO BLEED.
IT IS A GOOD THING YOU DID NOT ENGAGE FURTHER BEFORE BREAKING THE CONNECTION, OR THE RESULTS COULD HAVE EVEN BEEN DEADLY.

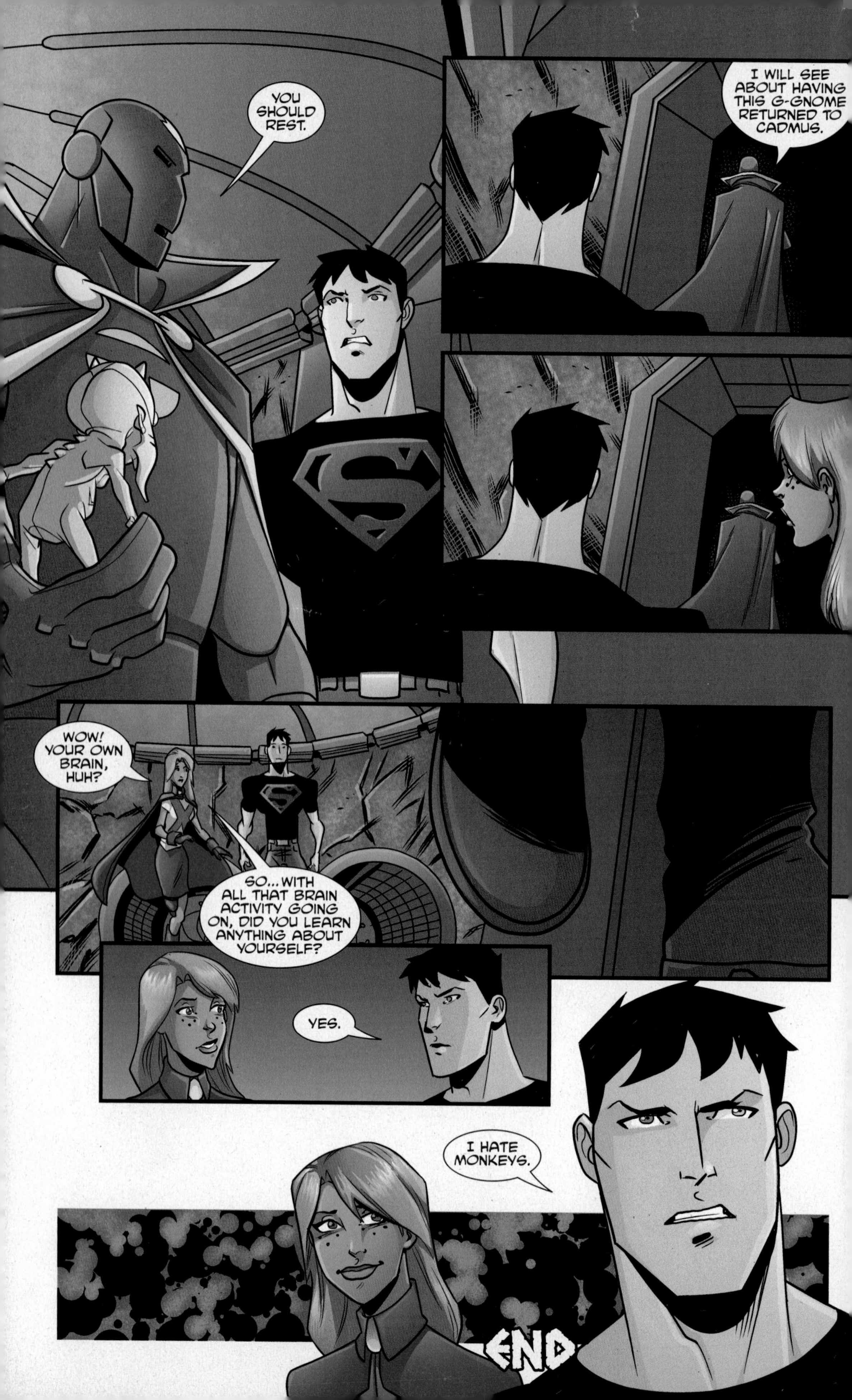
YOU SHOULD REST.
I WILL SEE ABOUT HAVING THIS G-GNOME RETURNED TO CADMUS.
WOW! YOUR OWN BRAIN, HUH?
SO... WITH ALL THAT BRAIN ACTIVITY GOING ON, DID YOU LEARN ANYTHING ABOUT YOURSELF?
YES.
I HATE MONKEYS.
END

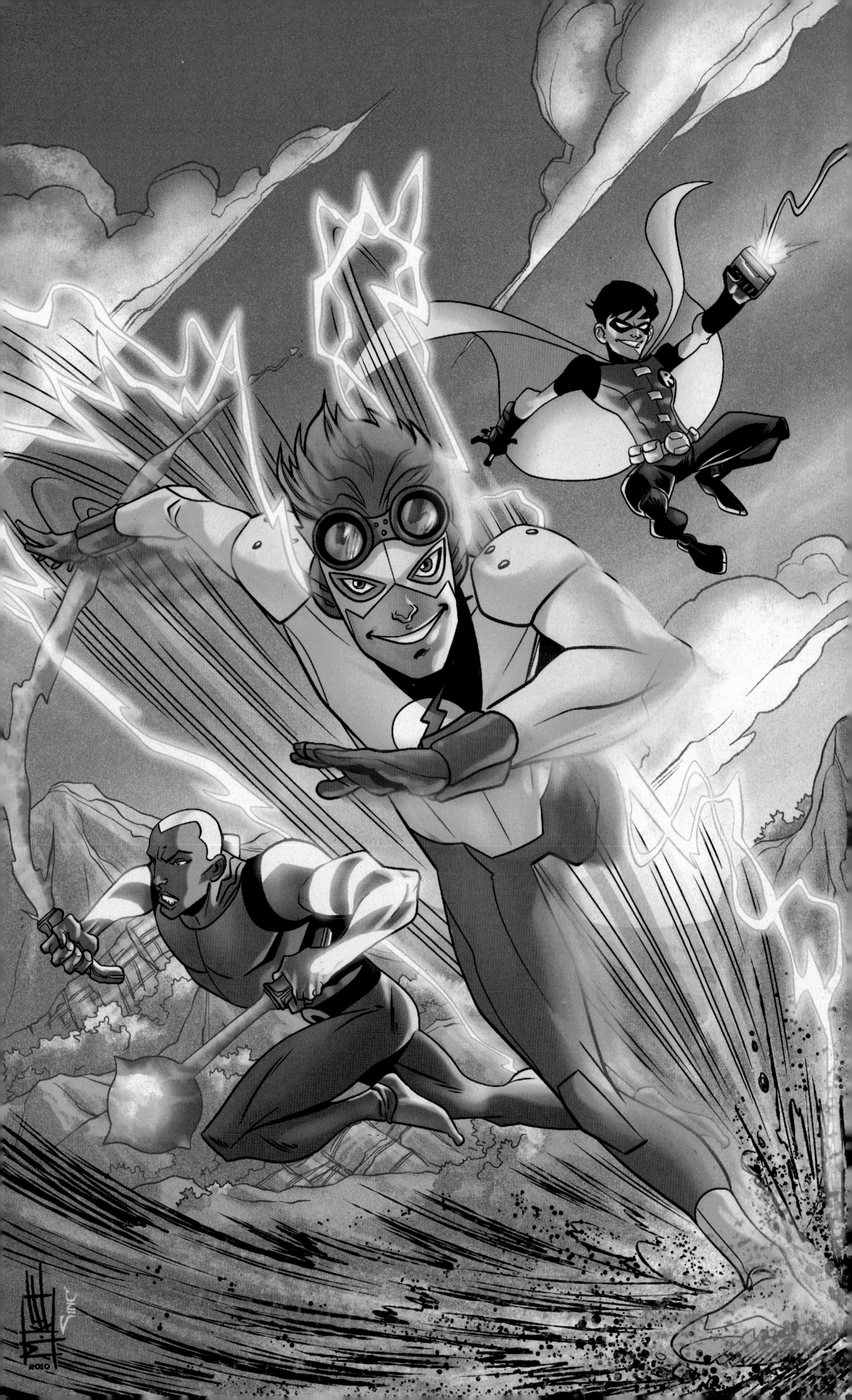

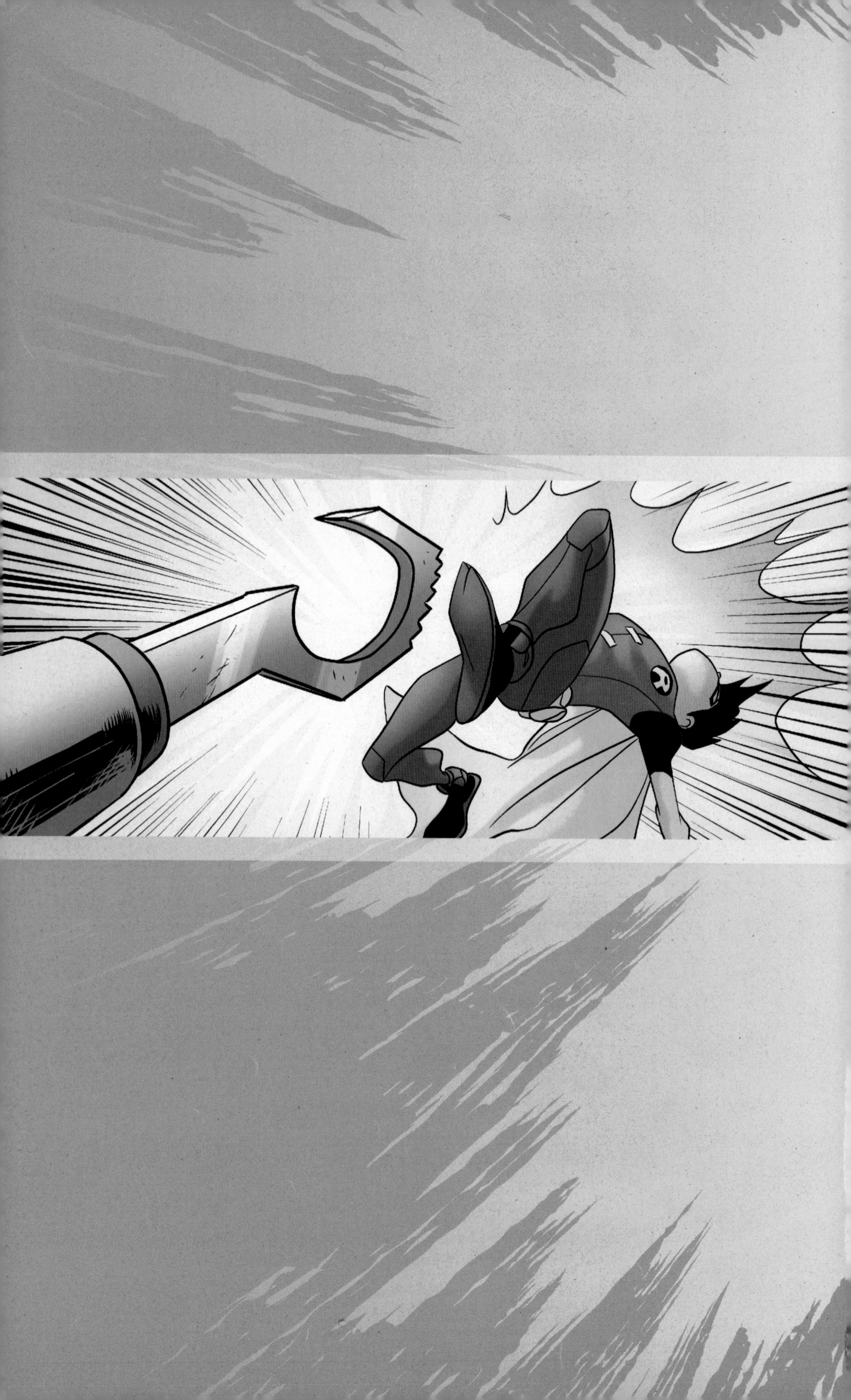

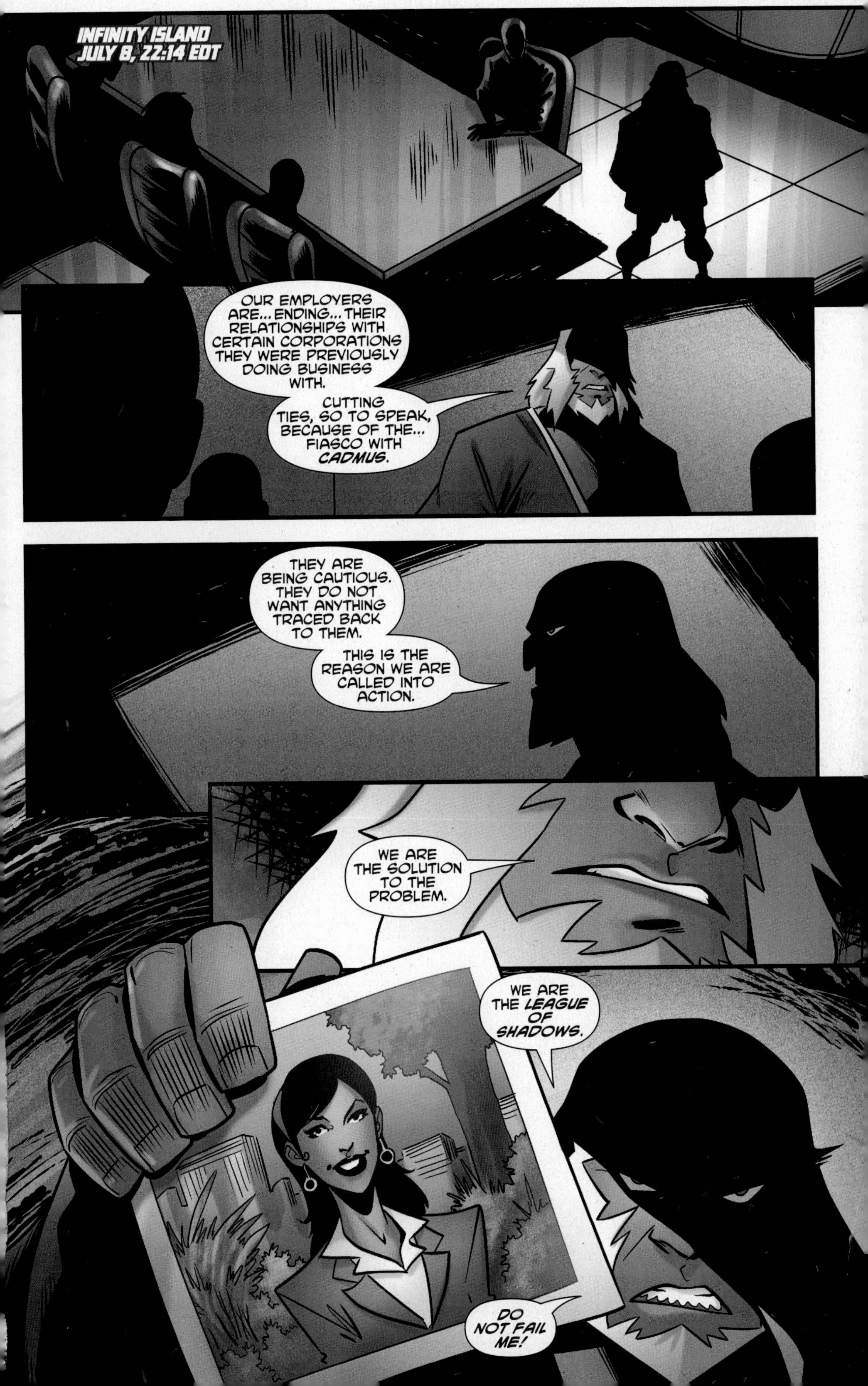
INFINITY ISLAND
JULY 8, 22:14 EDT
OUR EMPLOYERS ARE... ENDING... THEIR RELATIONSHIPS WITH CERTAIN CORPORATIONS THEY WERE PREVIOUSLY DOING BUSINESS WITH.
CUTTING TIES, SO TO SPEAK, BECAUSE OF THE... FIASCO WITH CADMUS.
THEY ARE BEING CAUTIOUS. THEY DO NOT WANT ANYTHING TRACED BACK TO THEM.
THIS IS THE REASON WE ARE CALLED INTO ACTION.
WE ARE THE SOLUTION TO THE PROBLEM.
WE ARE THE LEAGUE OF SHADOWS.
DO NOT FAIL ME!

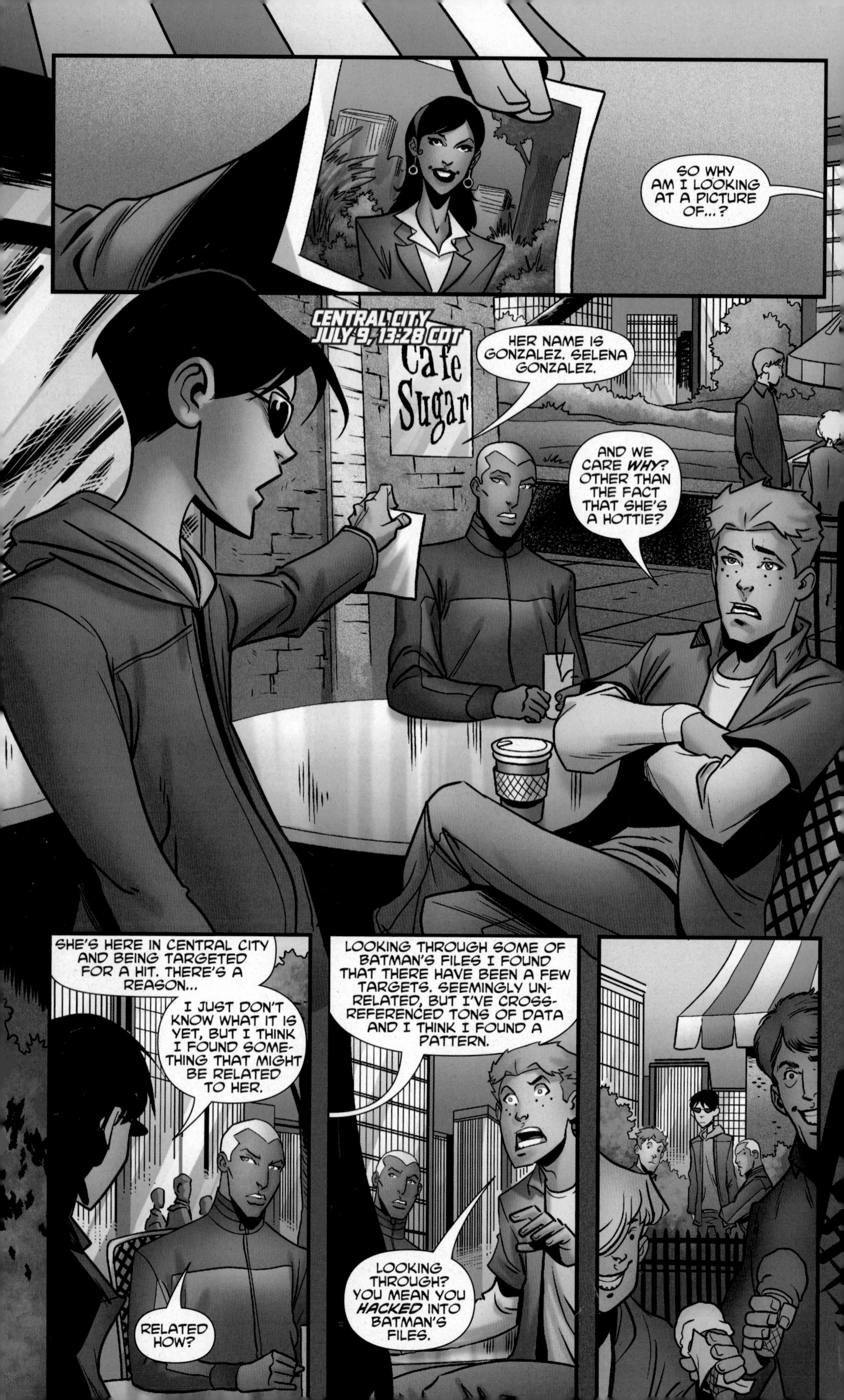
SO WHY AM I LOOKING AT A PICTURE OF...?
CENTRAL CITY JULY 9, 13:28 CDT
Cafe Sugar
HER NAME IS GONZALEZ. SELENA GONZALEZ.
AND WE CARE WHY? OTHER THAN THE FACT THAT SHE'S A HOTTIE?
SHE'S HERE IN CENTRAL CITY AND BEING TARGETED FOR A HIT. THERE'S A REASON...
I JUST DON'T KNOW WHAT IT IS YET, BUT I THINK I FOUND SOMETHING THAT MIGHT BE RELATED TO HER.
RELATED HOW?
LOOKING THROUGH SOME OF BATMAN'S FILES I FOUND THAT THERE HAVE BEEN A FEW TARGETS. SEEMINGLY UNRELATED, BUT I'VE CROSS-REFERENCED TONS OF DATA AND I THINK I FOUND A PATTERN.
LOOKING THROUGH? YOU MEAN YOU HACKED INTO BATMAN'S FILES.

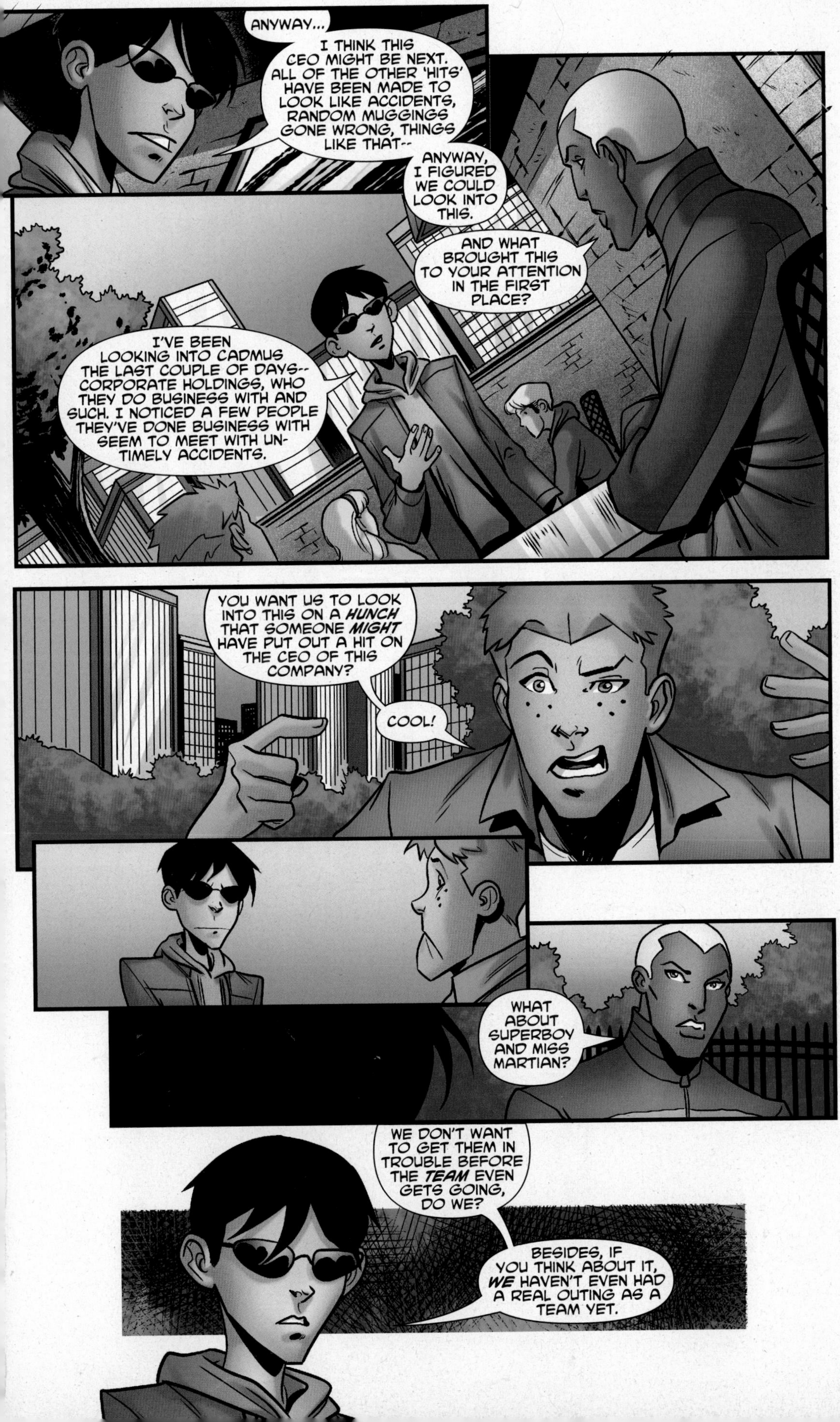
ANYWAY...
I THINK THIS CEO MIGHT BE NEXT. ALL OF THE OTHER 'HITS' HAVE BEEN MADE TO LOOK LIKE ACCIDENTS, RANDOM MUGGINGS GONE WRONG, THINGS LIKE THAT--
ANYWAY, I FIGURED WE COULD LOOK INTO THIS.
AND WHAT BROUGHT THIS TO YOUR ATTENTION IN THE FIRST PLACE?
I'VE BEEN LOOKING INTO CADMUS THE LAST COUPLE OF DAYS--CORPORATE HOLDINGS, WHO THEY DO BUSINESS WITH AND SUCH. I NOTICED A FEW PEOPLE THEY'VE DONE BUSINESS WITH SEEM TO MEET WITH UNTIMELY ACCIDENTS.
YOU WANT US TO LOOK INTO THIS ON A *HUNCH* THAT SOMEONE *MIGHT* HAVE PUT OUT A HIT ON THE CEO OF THIS COMPANY?
COOL!
WHAT ABOUT SUPERBOY AND MISS MARTIAN?
WE DON'T WANT TO GET THEM IN TROUBLE BEFORE THE *TEAM* EVEN GETS GOING, DO WE?
BESIDES, IF YOU THINK ABOUT IT, *WE* HAVEN'T EVEN HAD A REAL OUTING AS A TEAM YET.

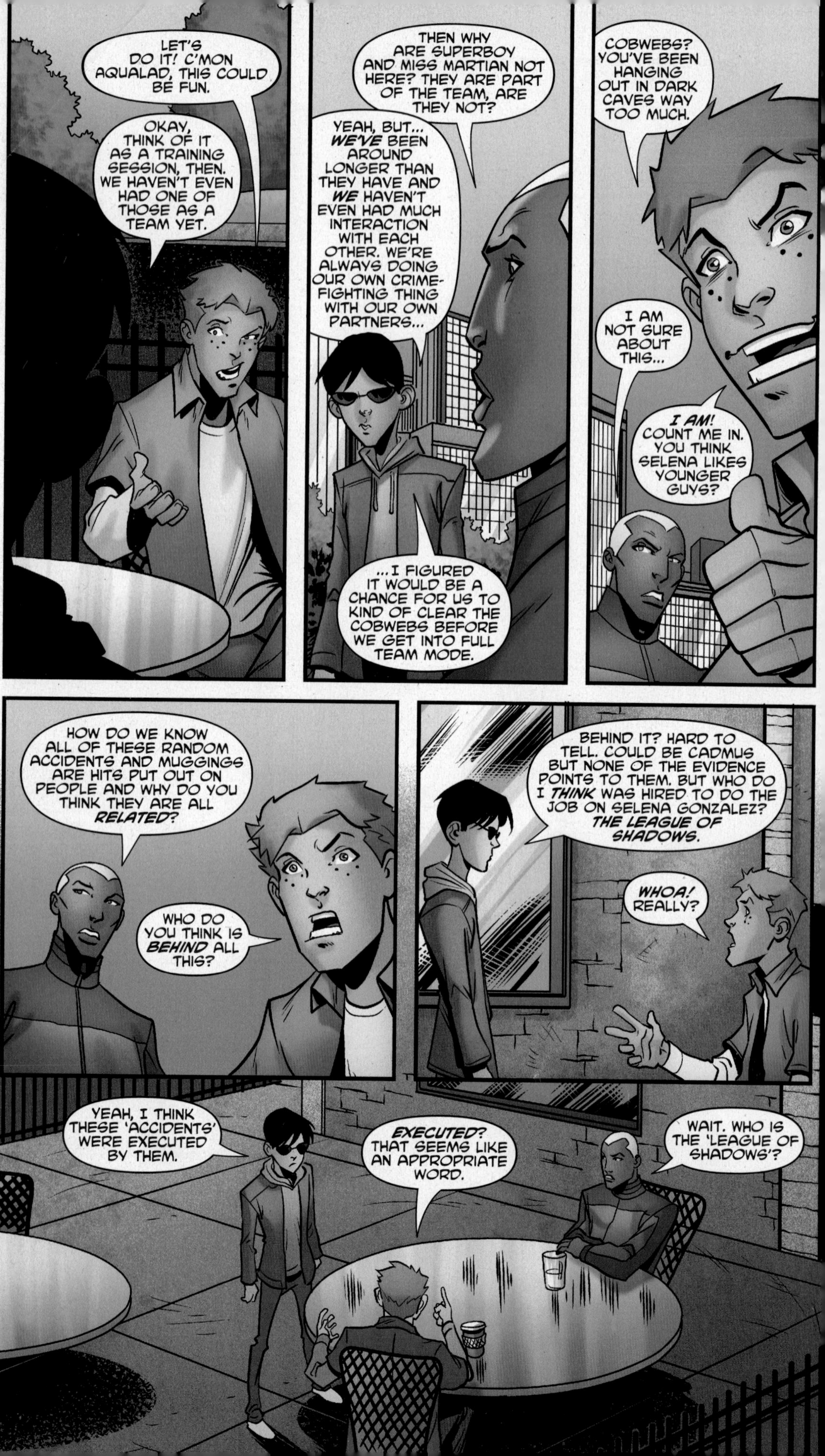
LET'S DO IT! C'MON AQUALAD, THIS COULD BE FUN.
OKAY, THINK OF IT AS A TRAINING SESSION, THEN. WE HAVEN'T EVEN HAD ONE OF THOSE AS A TEAM YET.
THEN WHY ARE SUPERBOY AND MISS MARTIAN NOT HERE? THEY ARE PART OF THE TEAM, ARE THEY NOT?
YEAH, BUT... WE'VE BEEN AROUND LONGER THAN THEY HAVE AND WE HAVEN'T EVEN HAD MUCH INTERACTION WITH EACH OTHER. WE'RE ALWAYS DOING OUR OWN CRIME-FIGHTING THING WITH OUR OWN PARTNERS...
...I FIGURED IT WOULD BE A CHANCE FOR US TO KIND OF CLEAR THE COBWEBS BEFORE WE GET INTO FULL TEAM MODE.
COBWEBS? YOU'VE BEEN HANGING OUT IN DARK CAVES WAY TOO MUCH.
I AM NOT SURE ABOUT THIS...
I AM! COUNT ME IN. YOU THINK SELENA LIKES YOUNGER GUYS?
HOW DO WE KNOW ALL OF THESE RANDOM ACCIDENTS AND MUGGINGS ARE HITS PUT OUT ON PEOPLE AND WHY DO YOU THINK THEY ARE ALL RELATED?
WHO DO YOU THINK IS BEHIND ALL THIS?
BEHIND IT? HARD TO TELL. COULD BE CADMUS BUT NONE OF THE EVIDENCE POINTS TO THEM. BUT WHO DO I THINK WAS HIRED TO DO THE JOB ON SELENA GONZALEZ? THE LEAGUE OF SHADOWS.
WHOA! REALLY?
YEAH, I THINK THESE 'ACCIDENTS' WERE EXECUTED BY THEM.
EXECUTED? THAT SEEMS LIKE AN APPROPRIATE WORD.
WAIT. WHO IS THE 'LEAGUE OF SHADOWS'?

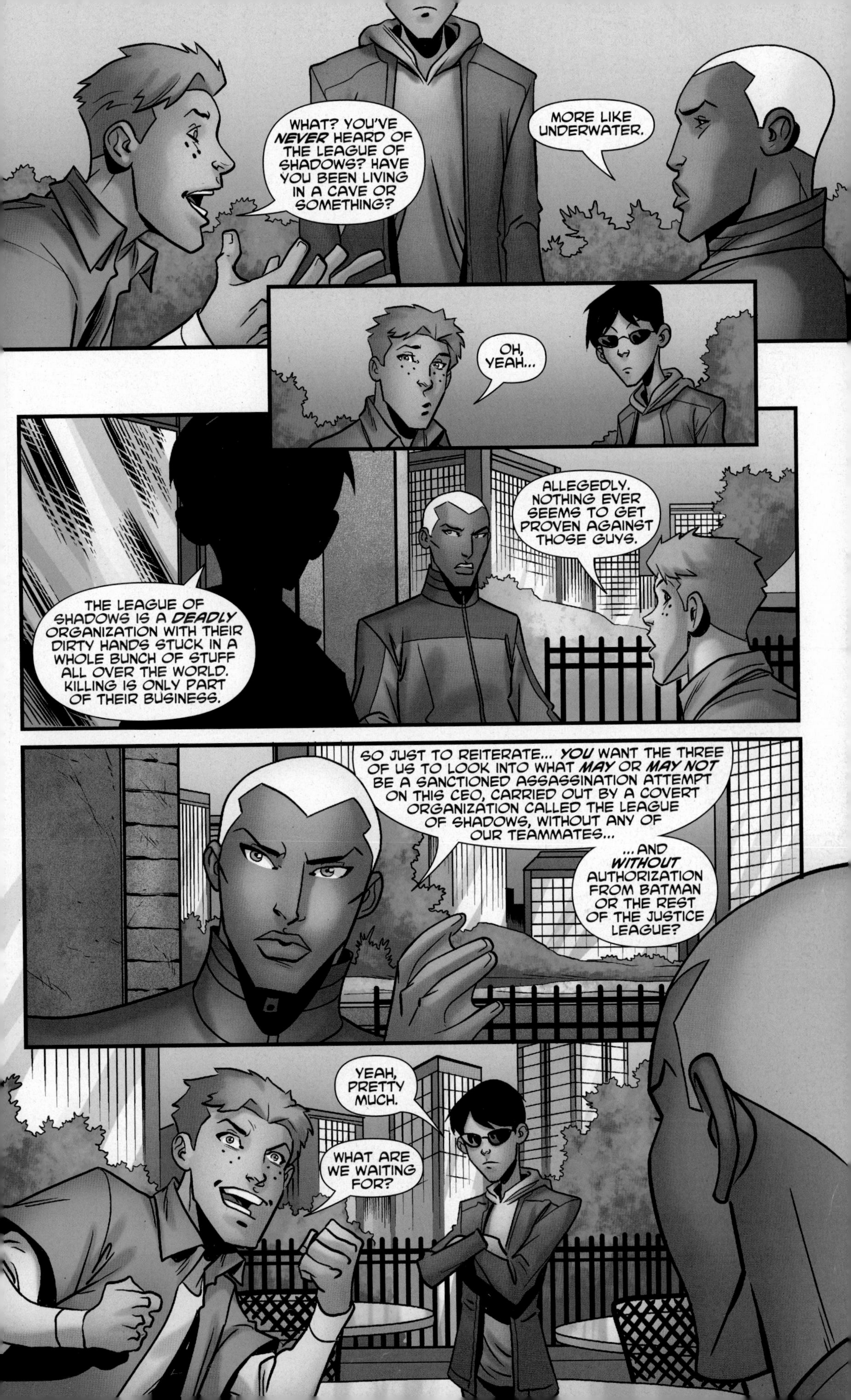
WHAT? YOU'VE NEVER HEARD OF THE LEAGUE OF SHADOWS? HAVE YOU BEEN LIVING IN A CAVE OR SOMETHING?
MORE LIKE UNDERWATER.
OH, YEAH...
THE LEAGUE OF SHADOWS IS A DEADLY ORGANIZATION WITH THEIR DIRTY HANDS STUCK IN A WHOLE BUNCH OF STUFF ALL OVER THE WORLD. KILLING IS ONLY PART OF THEIR BUSINESS.
ALLEGEDLY. NOTHING SEEMS TO GET PROVEN AGAINST THOSE GUYS.
SO JUST TO REITERATE... YOU WANT THE THREE OF US TO LOOK INTO WHAT MAY OR MAY NOT BE A SANCTIONED ASSASSINATION ATTEMPT ON THIS CEO, CARRIED OUT BY A COVERT ORGANIZATION CALLED THE LEAGUE OF SHADOWS, WITHOUT ANY OF OUR TEAMMATES...
...AND WITHOUT AUTHORIZATION FROM BATMAN OR THE REST OF THE JUSTICE LEAGUE?
YEAH, PRETTY MUCH.
WHAT ARE WE WAITING FOR?

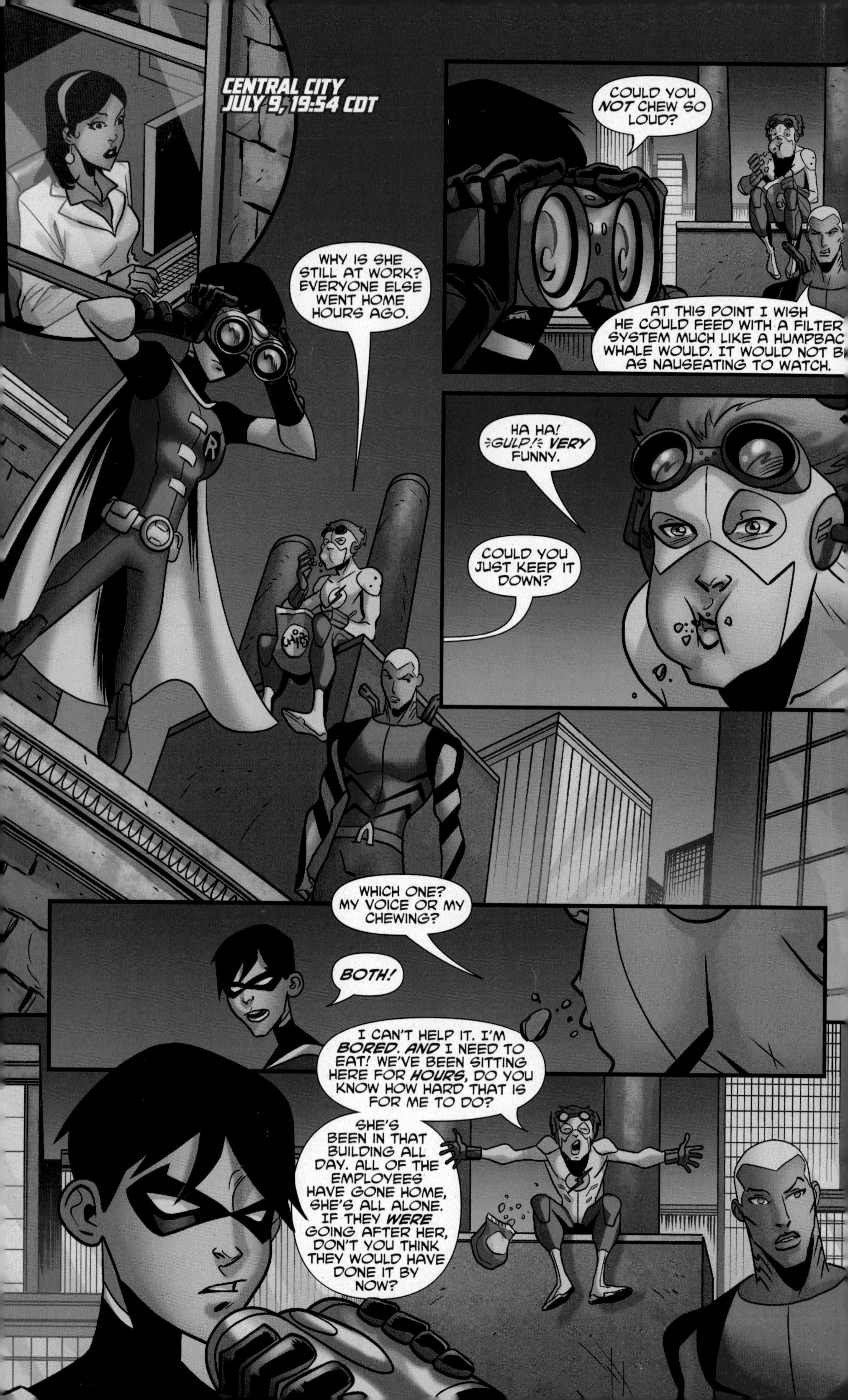
CENTRAL CITY
JULY 9, 19:54 CDT
WHY IS SHE STILL AT WORK? EVERYONE ELSE WENT HOME HOURS AGO.
COULD YOU NOT CHEW SO LOUD?
AT THIS POINT I WISH HE COULD FEED WITH A FILTER SYSTEM MUCH LIKE A HUMPBAC WHALE WOULD. IT WOULD NOT B AS NAUSEATING TO WATCH.
HA HA! GULP! VERY FUNNY.
COULD YOU JUST KEEP IT DOWN?
WHICH ONE? MY VOICE OR MY CHEWING?
BOTH!
I CAN'T HELP IT. I'M BORED. AND I NEED TO EAT! WE'VE BEEN SITTING HERE FOR HOURS, DO YOU KNOW HOW HARD THAT IS FOR ME TO DO?
SHE'S BEEN IN THAT BUILDING ALL DAY. ALL OF THE EMPLOYEES HAVE GONE HOME, SHE'S ALL ALONE. IF THEY WERE GOING AFTER HER, DON'T YOU THINK THEY WOULD HAVE DONE IT BY NOW?

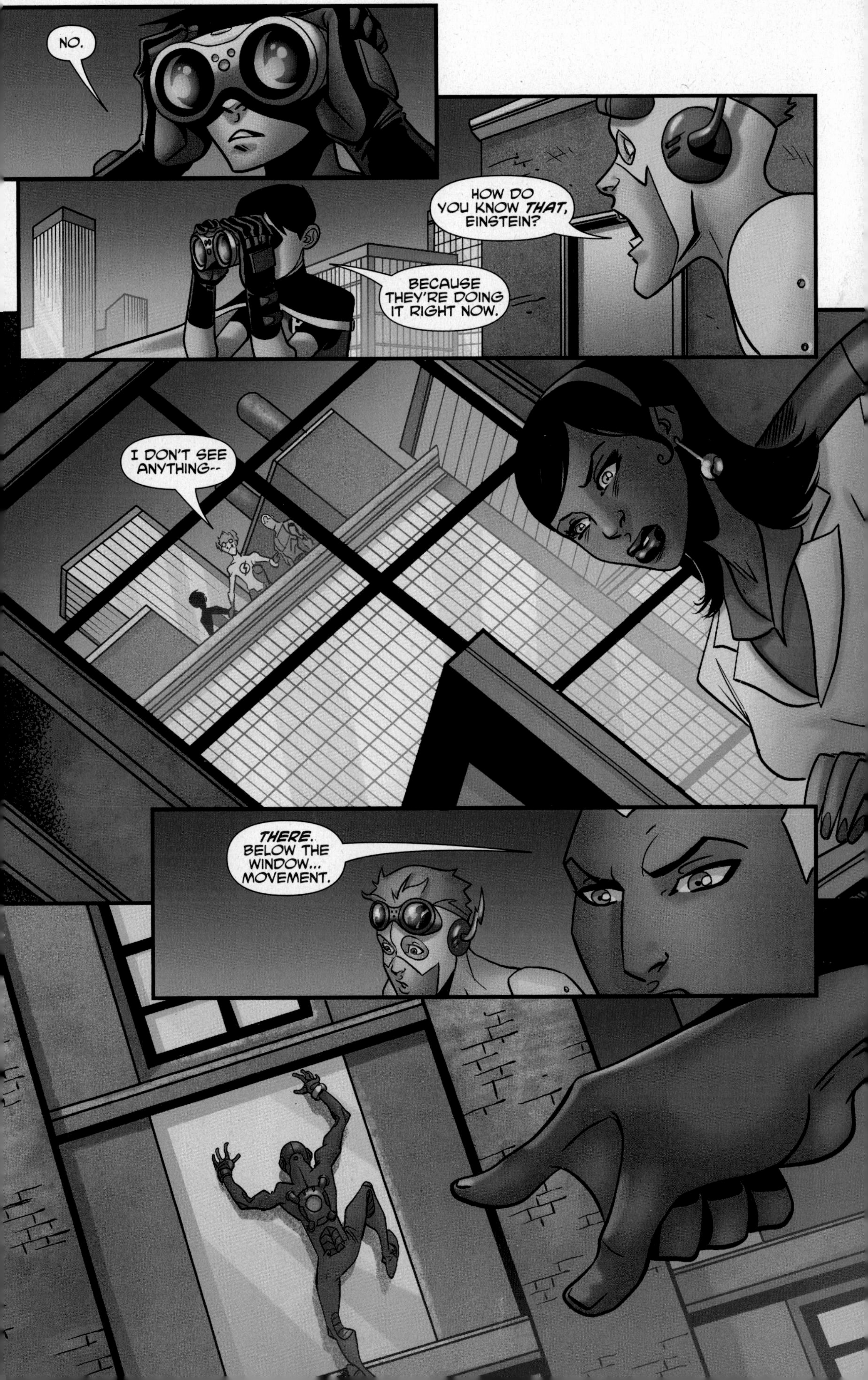
NO.
HOW DO YOU KNOW *THAT*, EINSTEIN?
BECAUSE THEY'RE DOING IT RIGHT NOW.
I DON'T SEE ANYTHING--
THERE. BELOW THE WINDOW... MOVEMENT.

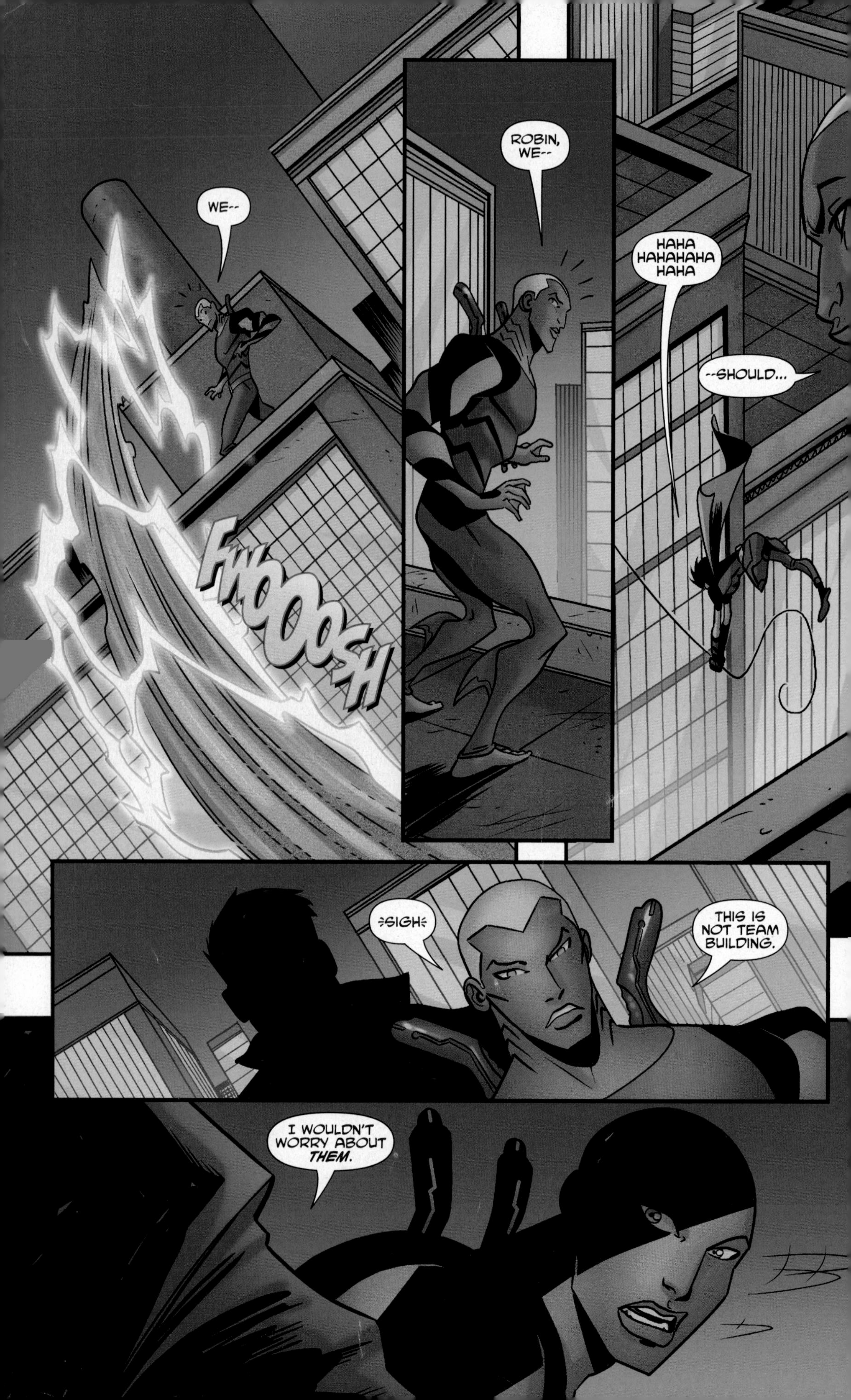
WE--
FWOOOSH
ROBIN, WE--
HAHA HAHAHAHA HAHA
--SHOULD...
SIGH
THIS IS NOT TEAM BUILDING.
I WOULDN'T WORRY ABOUT *THEM*.

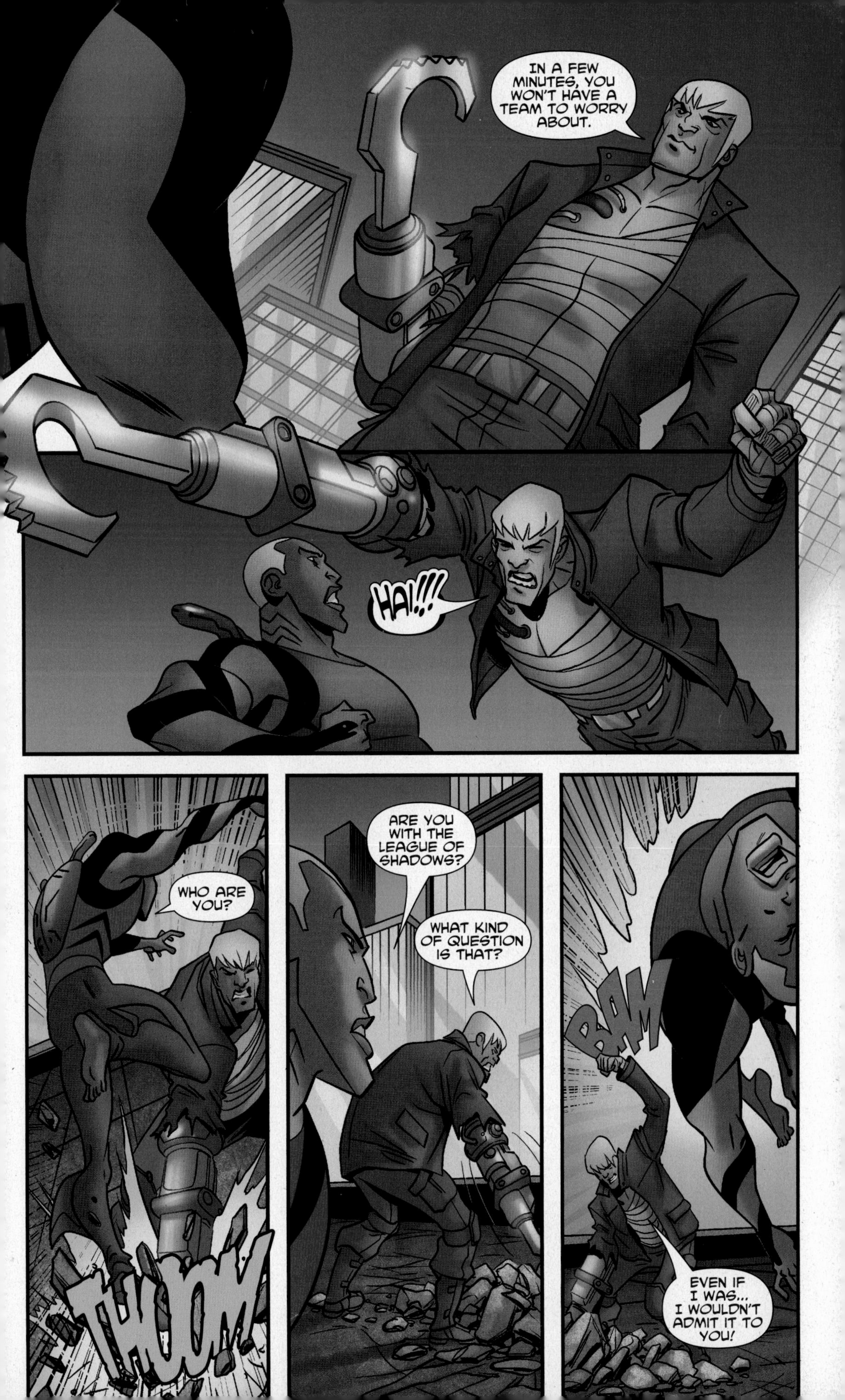

IN A FEW MINUTES, YOU WON'T HAVE A TEAM TO WORRY ABOUT.
HA!!!!
WHO ARE YOU?
THOOM
ARE YOU WITH THE LEAGUE OF SHADOWS?
WHAT KIND OF QUESTION IS THAT?
BAM
EVEN IF I WAS... I WOULDN'T ADMIT IT TO YOU!

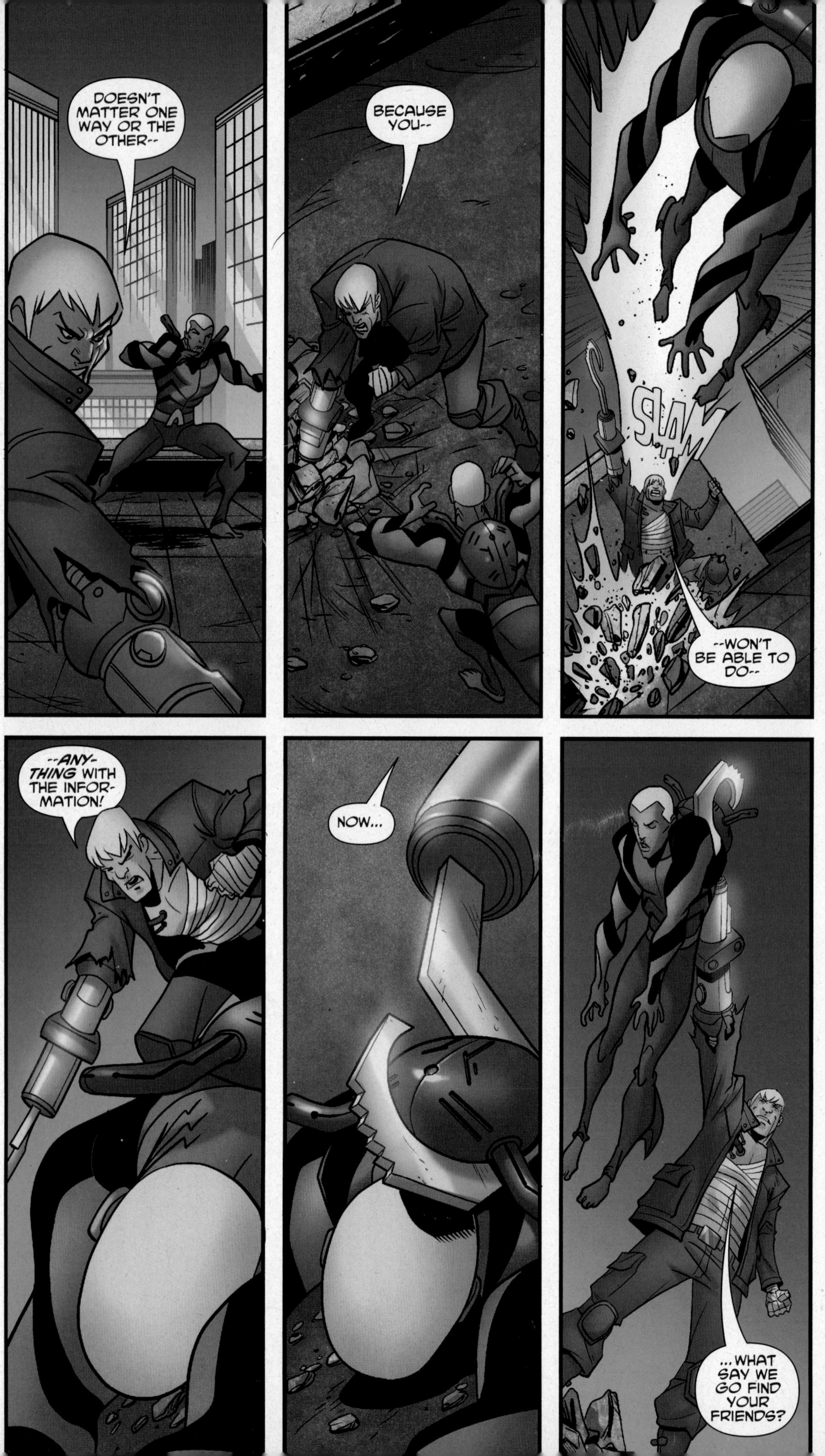
DOESN'T MATTER ONE WAY OR THE OTHER--
BECAUSE YOU--
SLAM
--WON'T BE ABLE TO DO--
--*ANY-THING* WITH THE INFOR-MATION!
NOW...
...WHAT SAY WE GO FIND YOUR FRIENDS?

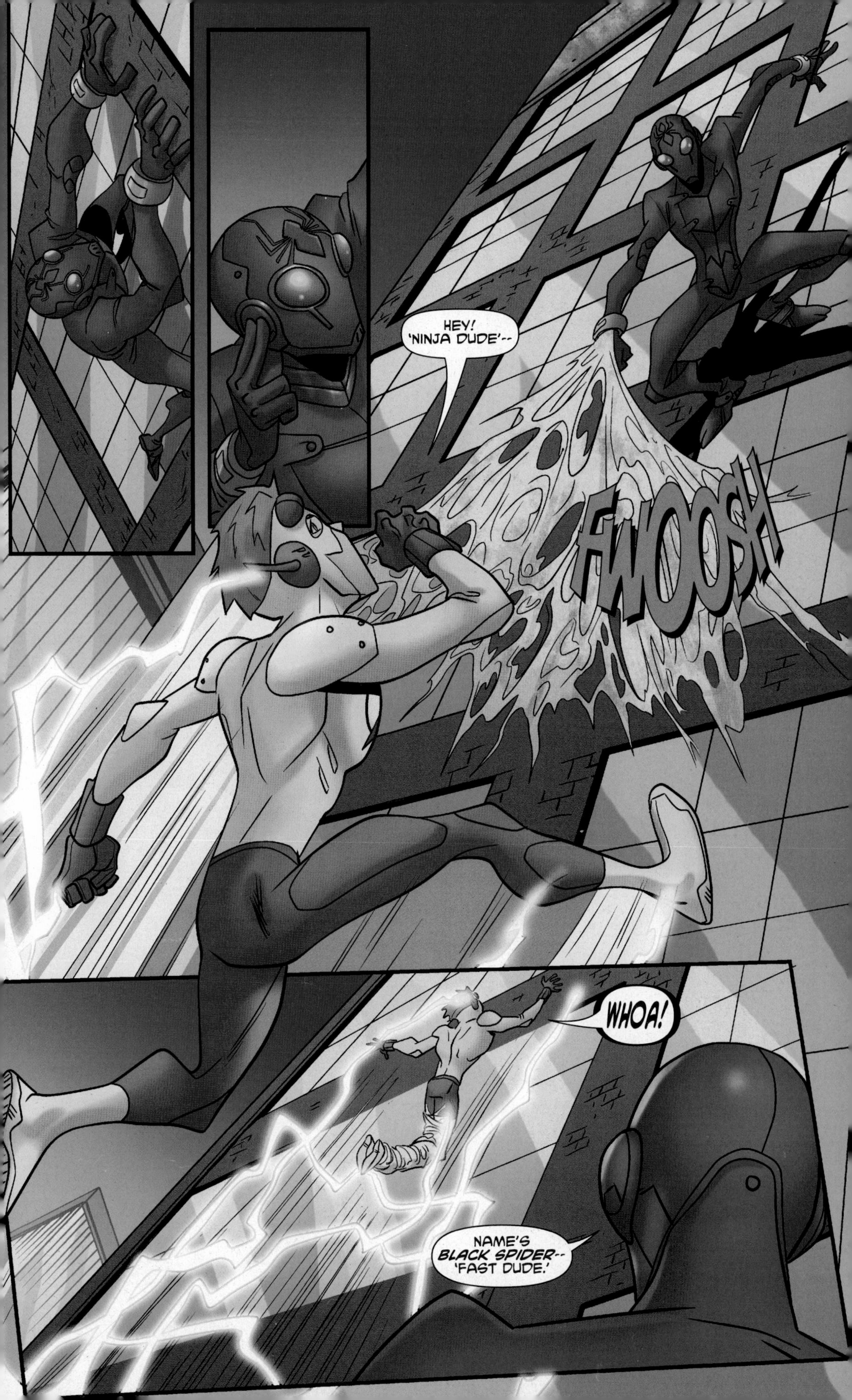
HEY! 'NINJA DUDE'--
FWOOSH
WHOA!
NAME'S BLACK SPIDER-- 'FAST DUDE.'

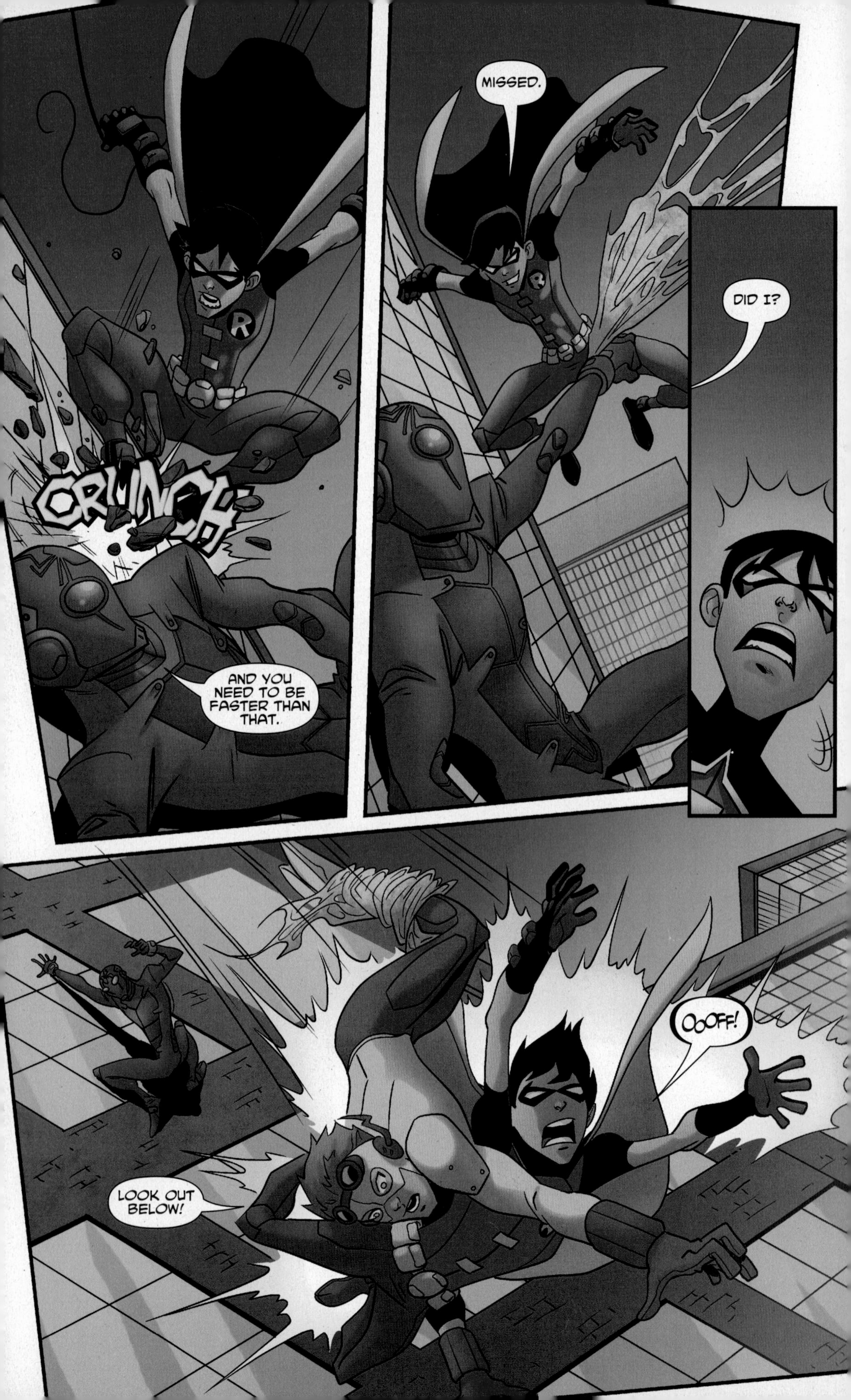
CRUNCH
AND YOU NEED TO BE FASTER THAN THAT.
MISSED.
DID I?
OOOFF!
LOOK OUT BELOW!

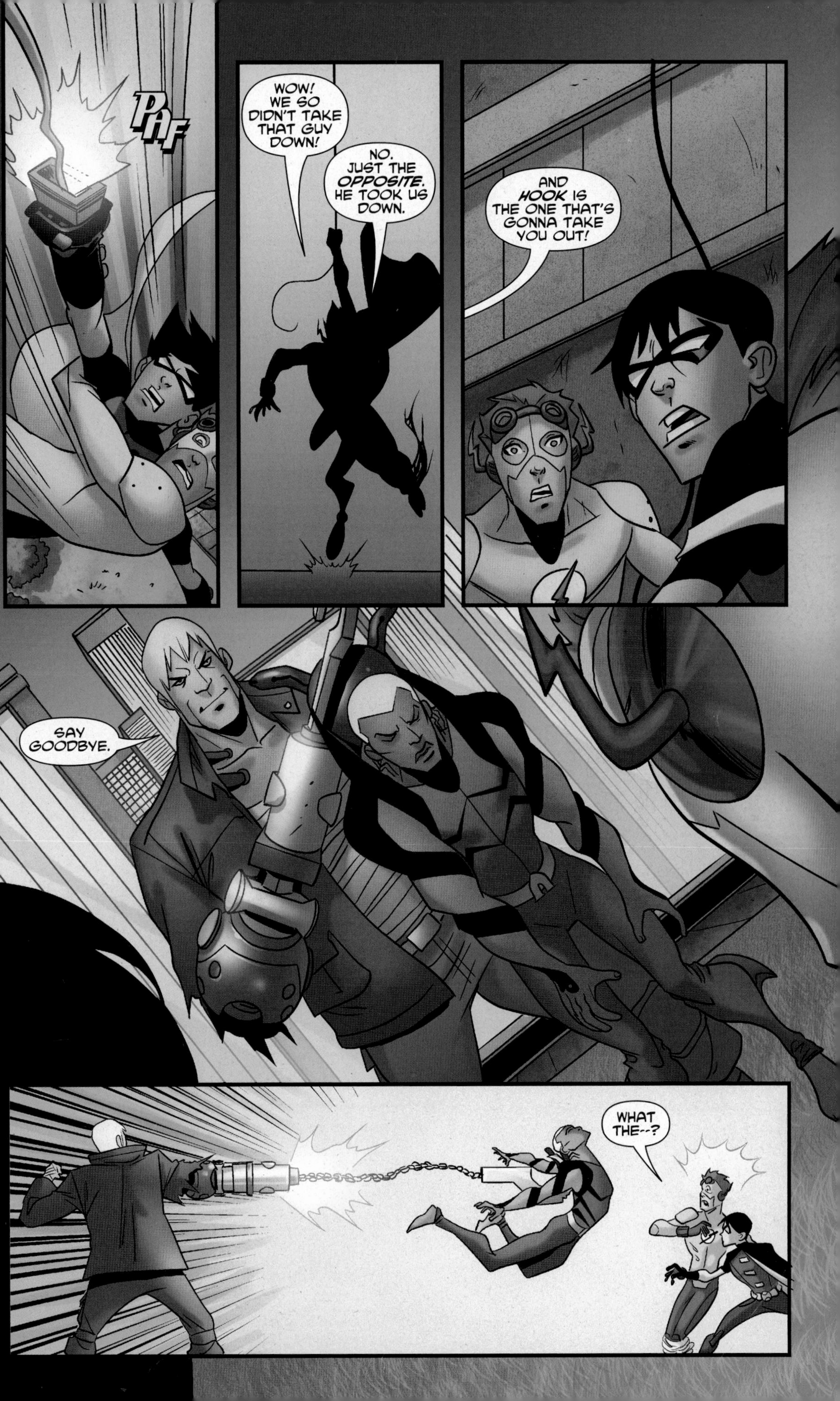
PAF
WOW! WE SO DIDN'T TAKE THAT GUY DOWN!
NO. JUST THE OPPOSITE. HE TOOK US DOWN.
AND HOOK IS THE ONE THAT'S GONNA TAKE YOU OUT!
SAY GOODBYE.
WHAT THE--?

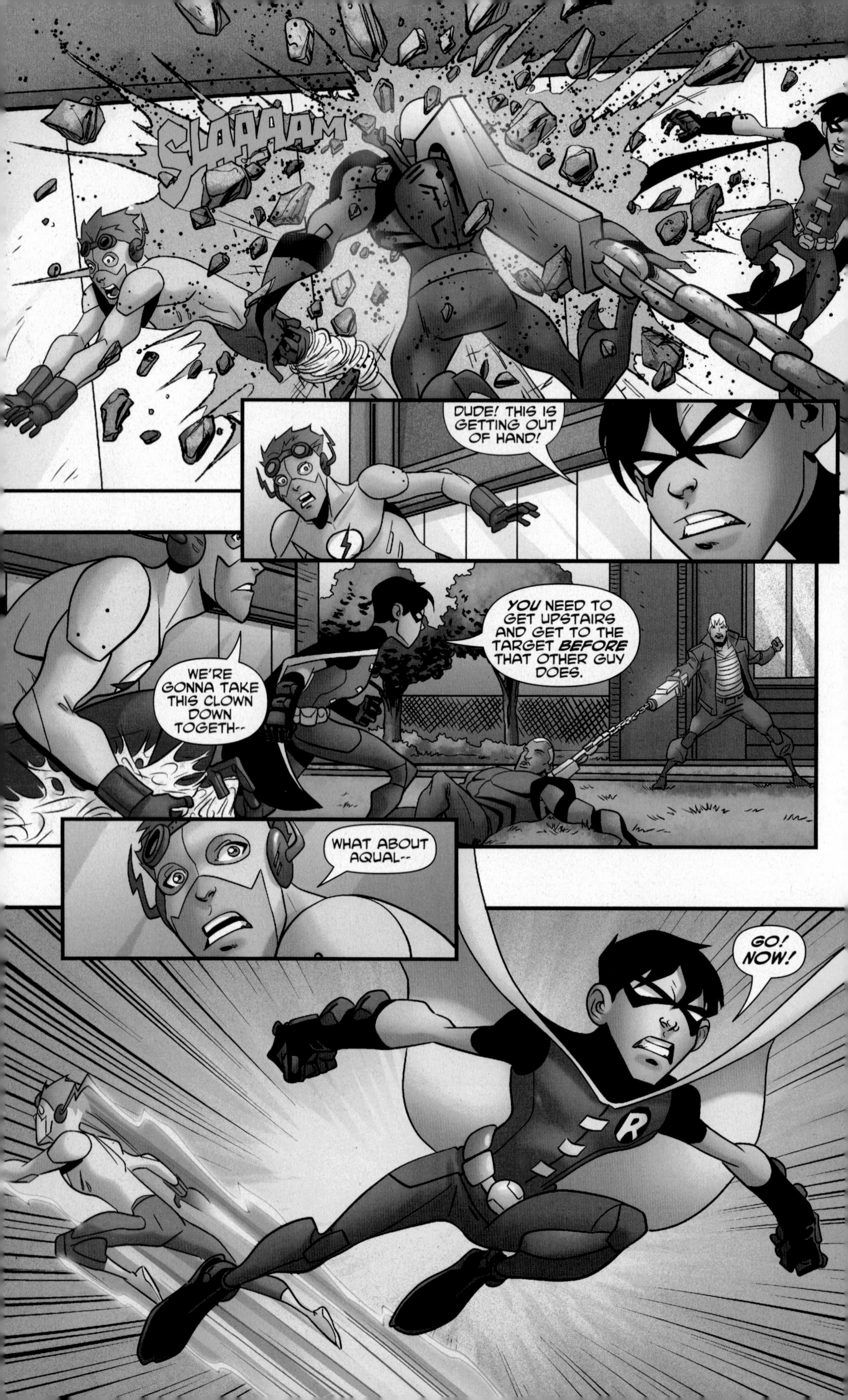
SLAAAAM
DUDE! THIS IS GETTING OUT OF HAND!
YOU NEED TO GET UPSTAIRS AND GET TO THE TARGET BEFORE THAT OTHER GUY DOES.
WE'RE GONNA TAKE THIS CLOWN DOWN TOGETH--
WHAT ABOUT AQUAL--
GO! NOW!

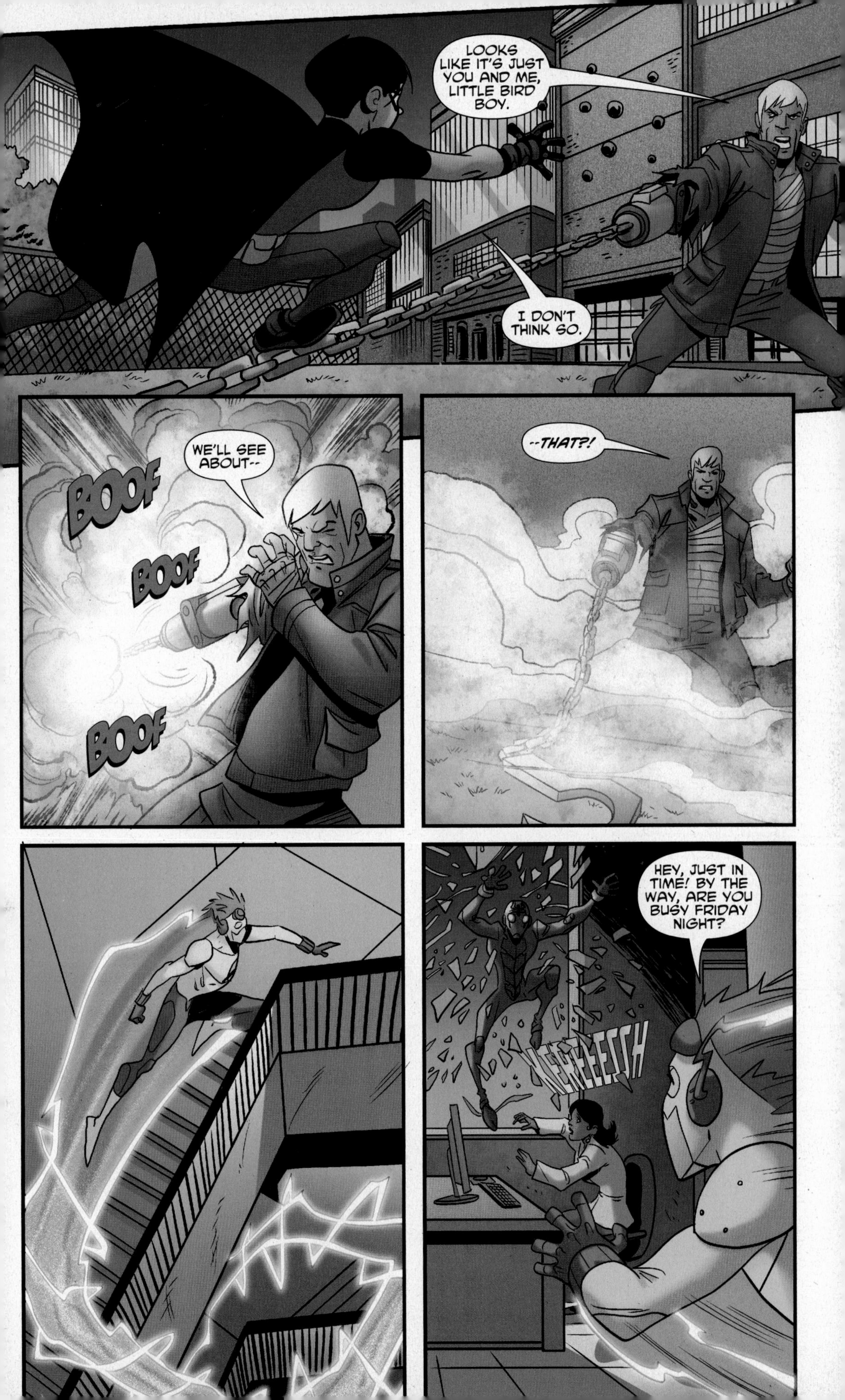
LOOKS LIKE IT'S JUST YOU AND ME, LITTLE BIRD BOY.
I DON'T THINK SO.
BOOF
BOOF
BOOF
WE'LL SEE ABOUT--
--THAT?!
HEY, JUST IN TIME! BY THE WAY, ARE YOU BUSY FRIDAY NIGHT?

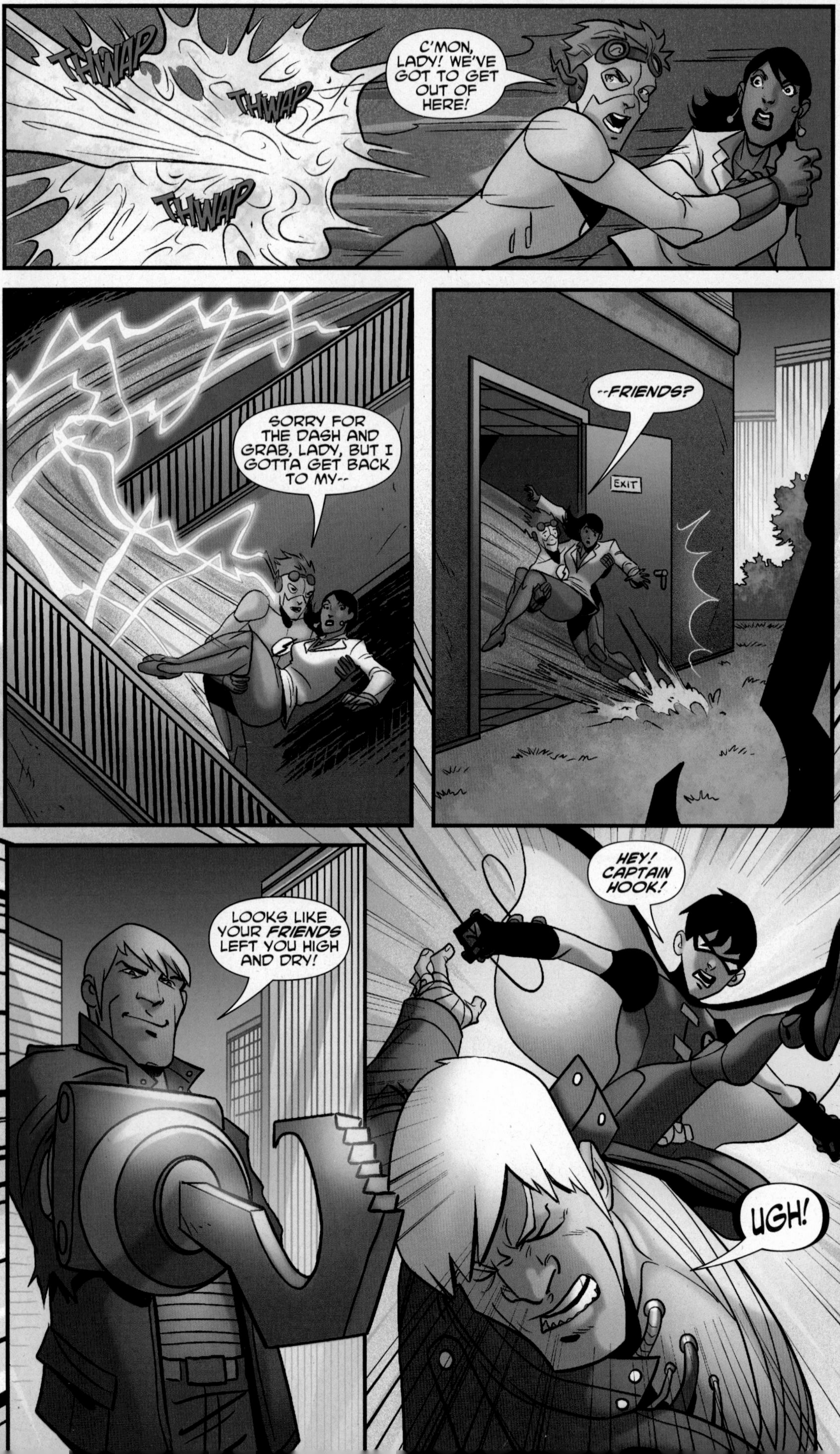
THWAP
THWAP
THWAP
C'MON, LADY! WE'VE GOT TO GET OUT OF HERE!
SORRY FOR THE DASH AND GRAB, LADY, BUT I GOTTA GET BACK TO MY--
--FRIENDS?
EXIT
LOOKS LIKE YOUR FRIENDS LEFT YOU HIGH AND DRY!
HEY! CAPTAIN HOOK!
UGH!

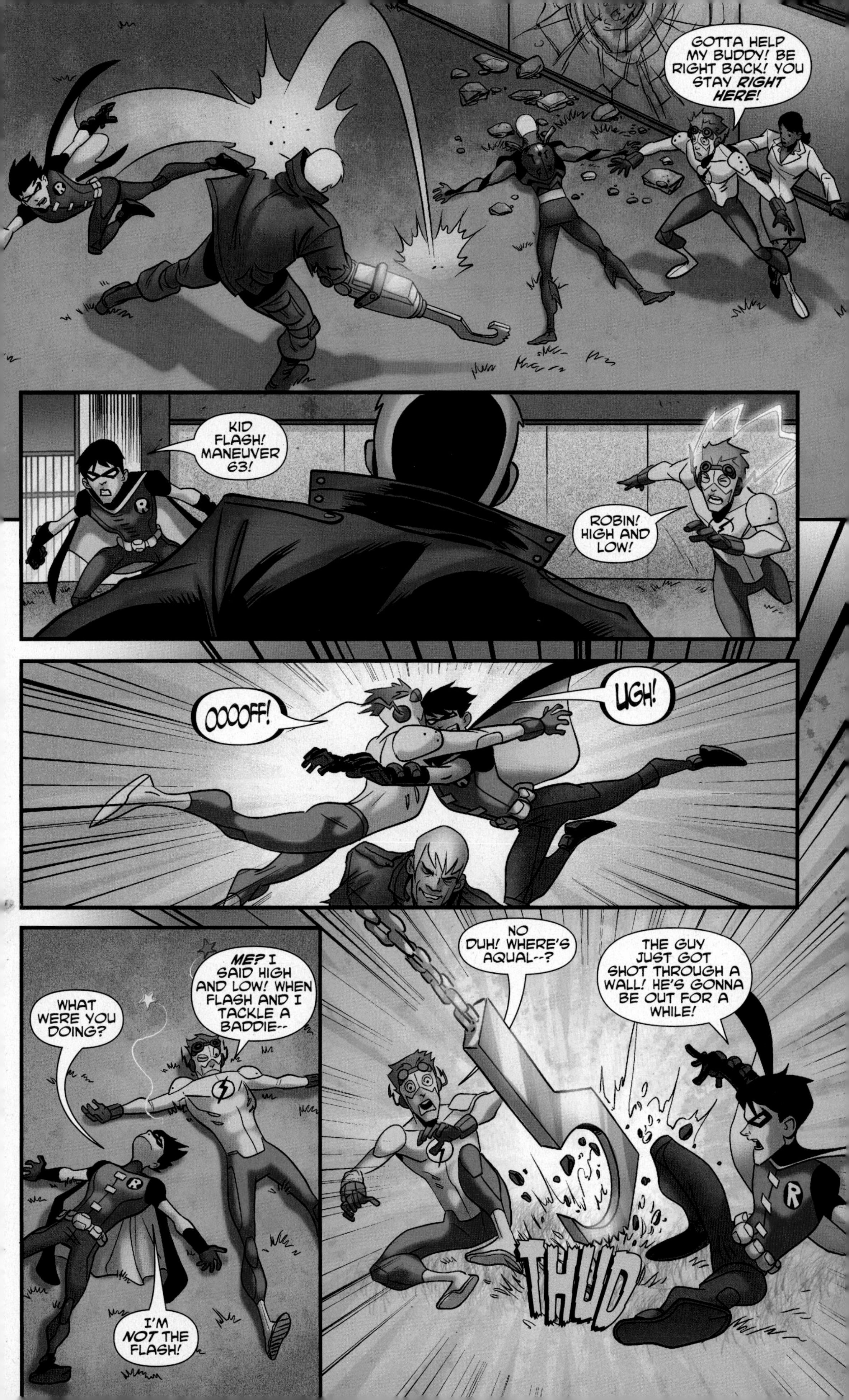
GOTTA HELP MY BUDDY! BE RIGHT BACK! YOU STAY *RIGHT HERE*!
KID FLASH! MANEUVER 63!
ROBIN! HIGH AND LOW!
OOOOFF!
UGH!
WHAT WERE YOU DOING?
ME? I SAID HIGH AND LOW! WHEN FLASH AND I TACKLE A BADDIE--
I'M *NOT* THE FLASH!
NO DUH! WHERE'S AQUAL--?
THE GUY JUST GOT SHOT THROUGH A WALL! HE'S GONNA BE OUT FOR A WHILE!
THUD

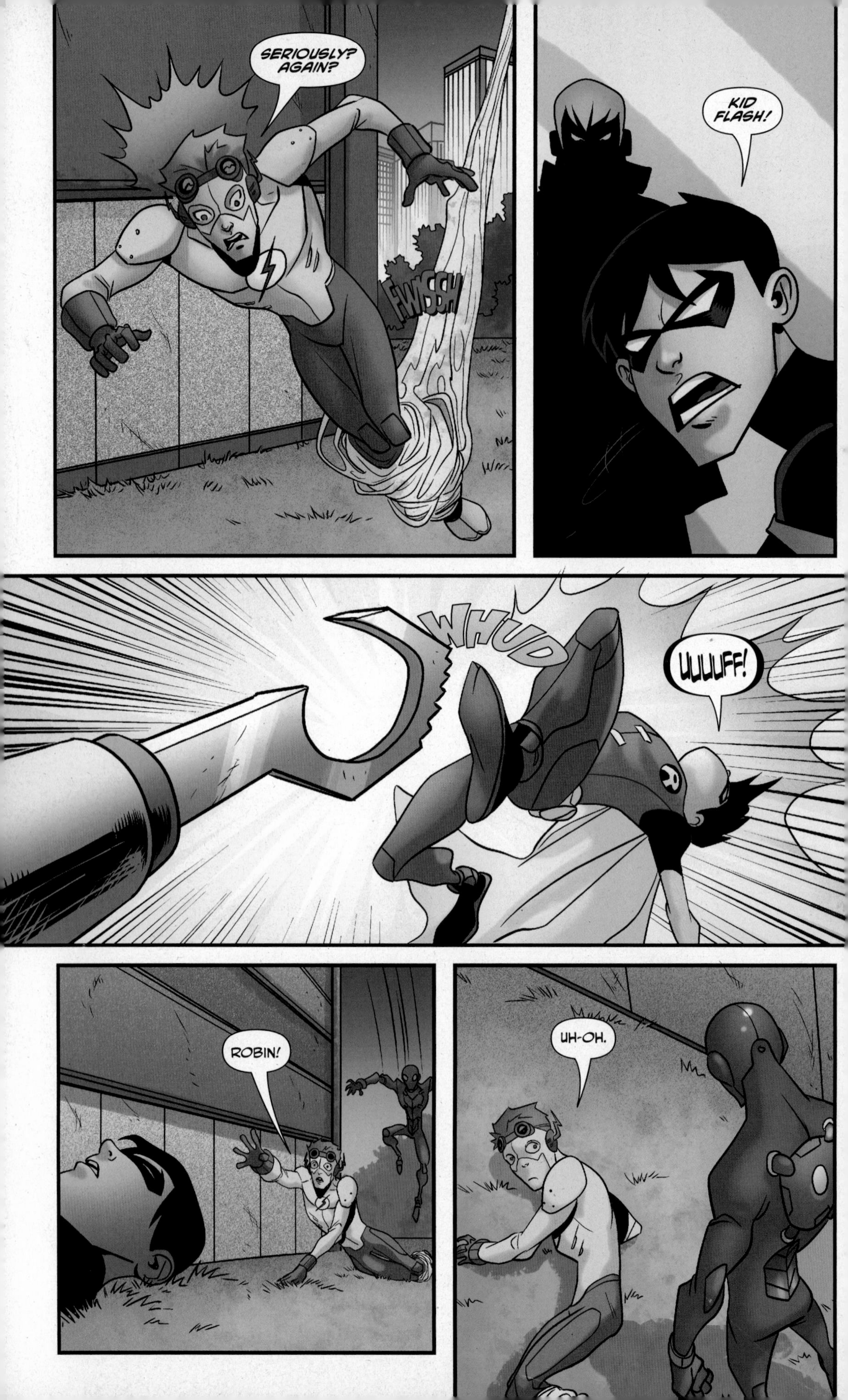
SERIOUSLY? AGAIN?
FWISSH
KID FLASH!
WHUD
UUUUFF!
ROBIN!
UH-OH.

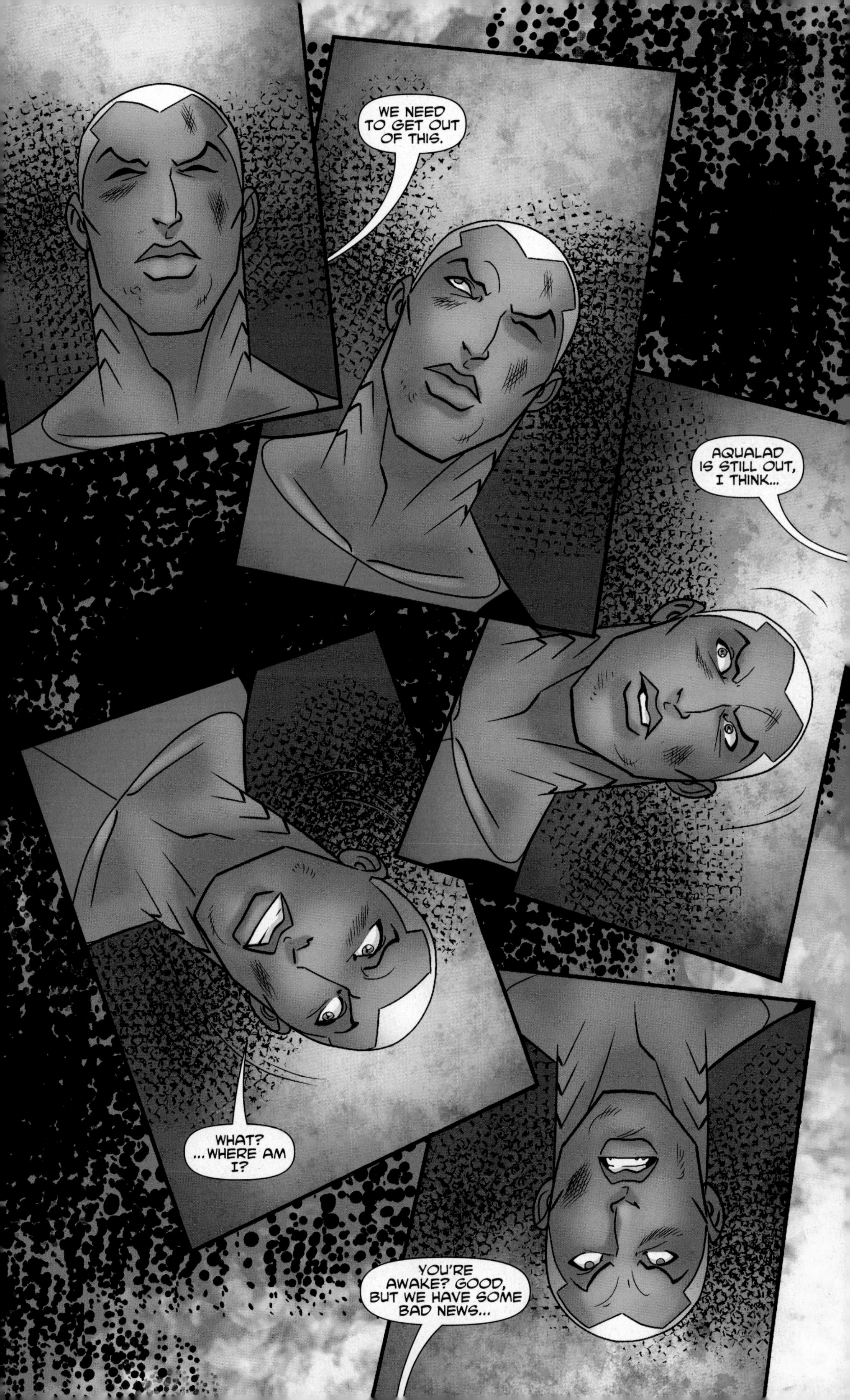
WE NEED TO GET OUT OF THIS.
AQUALAD IS STILL OUT, I THINK...
WHAT? ...WHERE AM I?
YOU'RE AWAKE? GOOD, BUT WE HAVE SOME BAD NEWS...

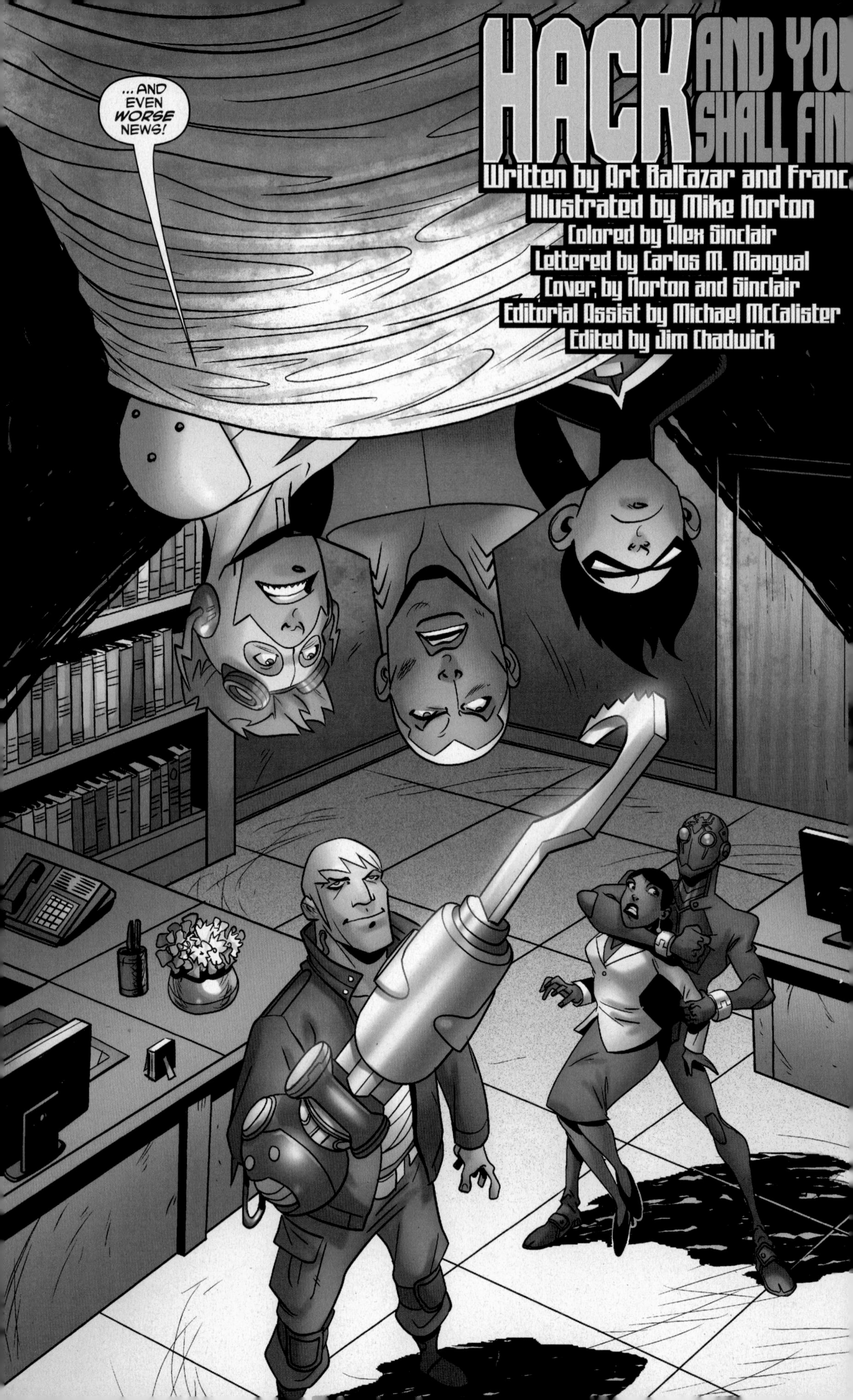

...AND EVEN WORSE NEWS!
HACK AND YOU SHALL FIN
Written by Art Baltazar and Franc
Illustrated by Mike Norton
Colored by Alex Sinclair
Lettered by Carlos M. Mangual
Cover by Norton and Sinclair
Editorial Assist by Michael McCalister
Edited by Jim Chadwick

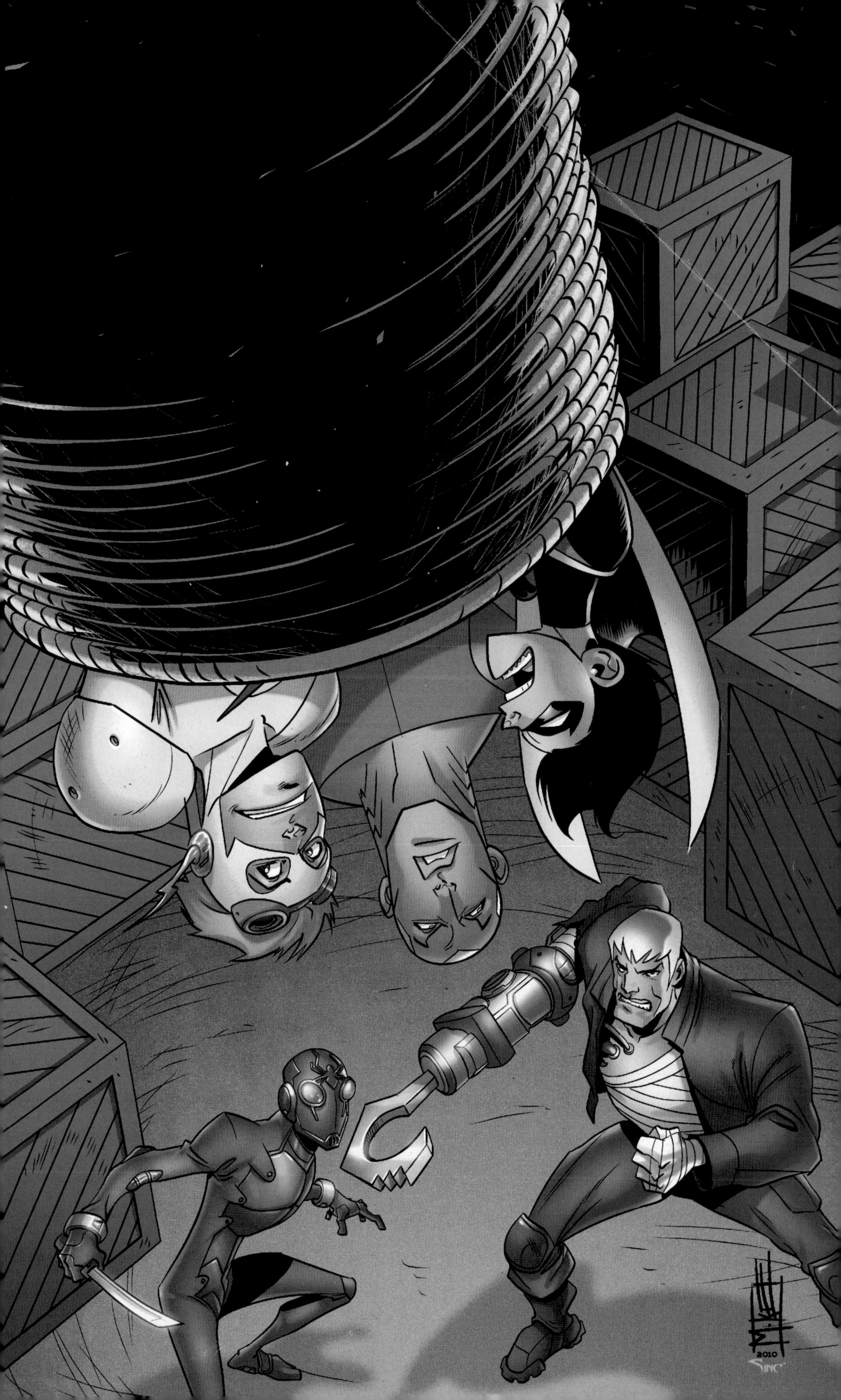
2010

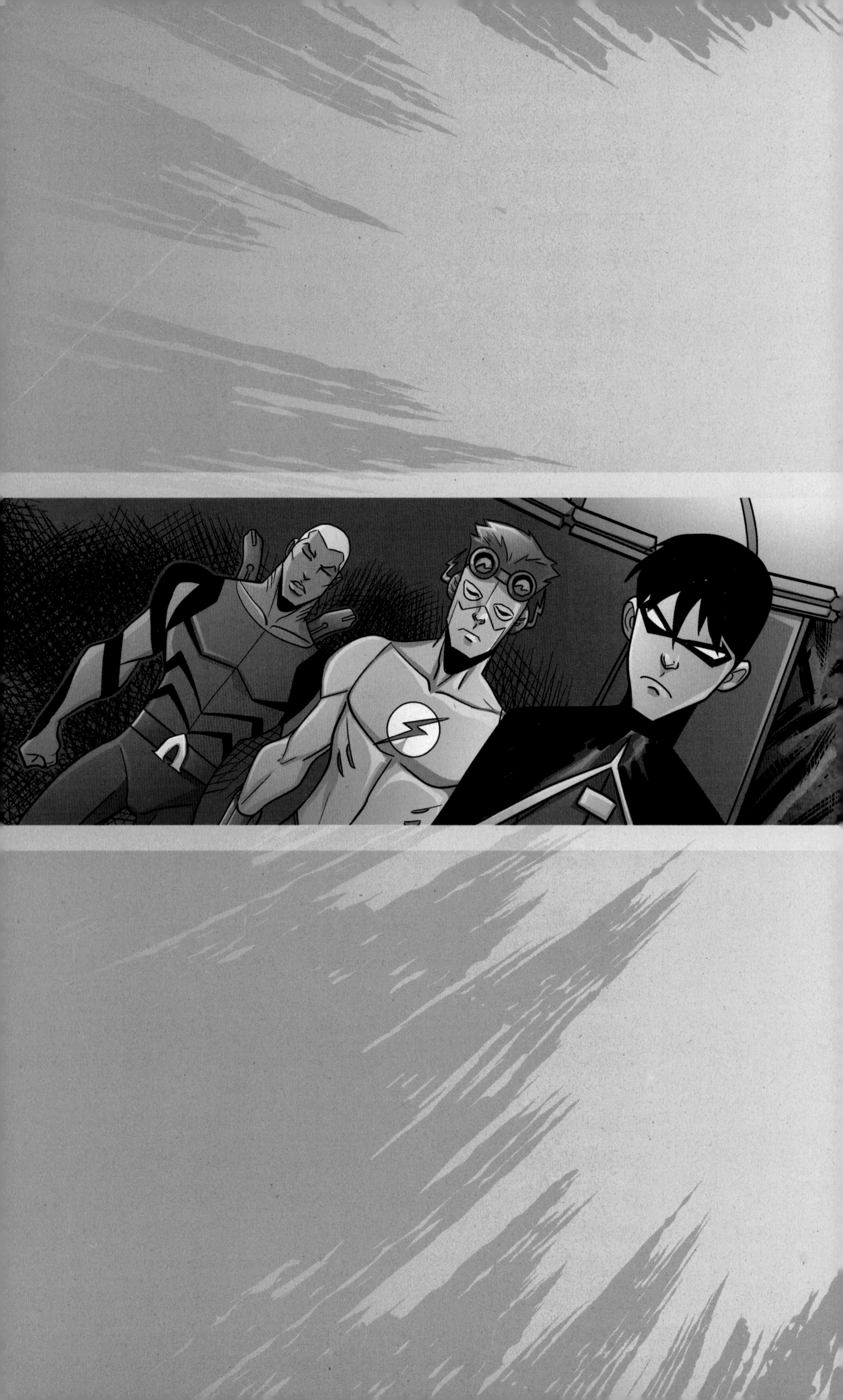

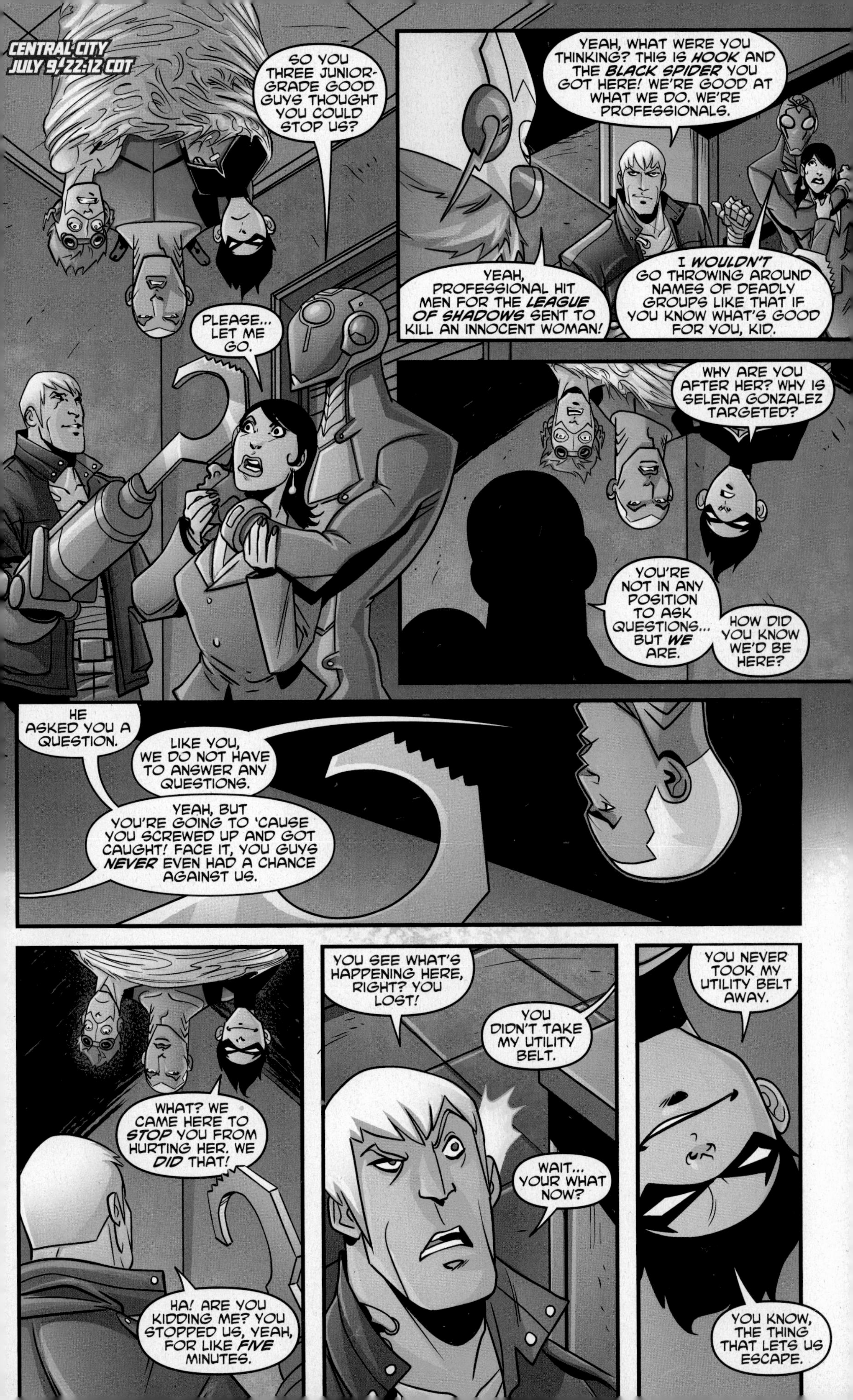
CENTRAL CITY
JULY 9, 22:12 CDT
SO YOU THREE JUNIOR-GRADE GOOD GUYS THOUGHT YOU COULD STOP US?
PLEASE... LET ME GO.
YEAH, WHAT WERE YOU THINKING? THIS IS HOOK AND THE BLACK SPIDER YOU GOT HERE! WE'RE GOOD AT WHAT WE DO. WE'RE PROFESSIONALS.
YEAH, PROFESSIONAL HIT MEN FOR THE LEAGUE OF SHADOWS SENT TO KILL AN INNOCENT WOMAN!
I WOULDN'T GO THROWING AROUND NAMES OF DEADLY GROUPS LIKE THAT IF YOU KNOW WHAT'S GOOD FOR YOU, KID.
WHY ARE YOU AFTER HER? WHY IS SELENA GONZALEZ TARGETED?
YOU'RE NOT IN ANY POSITION TO ASK QUESTIONS... BUT WE ARE.
HOW DID YOU KNOW WE'D BE HERE?
HE ASKED YOU A QUESTION.
LIKE YOU, WE DO NOT HAVE TO ANSWER ANY QUESTIONS.
YEAH, BUT YOU'RE GOING TO 'CAUSE YOU SCREWED UP AND GOT CAUGHT! FACE IT, YOU GUYS NEVER EVEN HAD A CHANCE AGAINST US.
WHAT? WE CAME HERE TO STOP YOU FROM HURTING HER. WE DID THAT!
HA! ARE YOU KIDDING ME? YOU STOPPED US, YEAH, FOR LIKE FIVE MINUTES.
YOU SEE WHAT'S HAPPENING HERE, RIGHT? YOU LOST!
YOU DIDN'T TAKE MY UTILITY BELT.
WAIT... YOUR WHAT NOW?
YOU NEVER TOOK MY UTILITY BELT AWAY.
YOU KNOW, THE THING THAT LETS US ESCAPE.

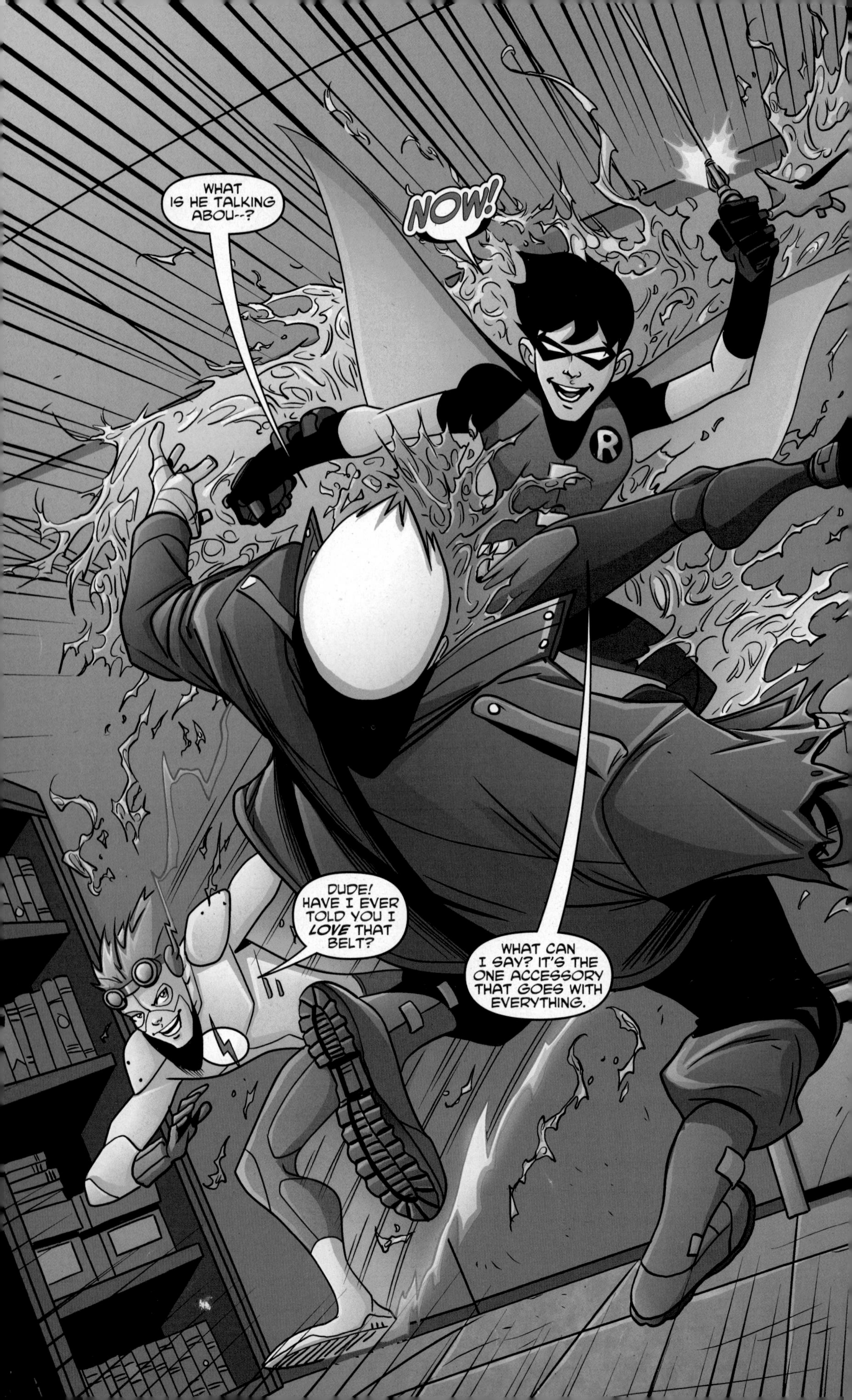
WHAT IS HE TALKING ABOU--?
NOW!
DUDE! HAVE I EVER TOLD YOU I *LOVE* THAT BELT?
WHAT CAN I SAY? IT'S THE ONE ACCESSORY THAT GOES WITH EVERYTHING.

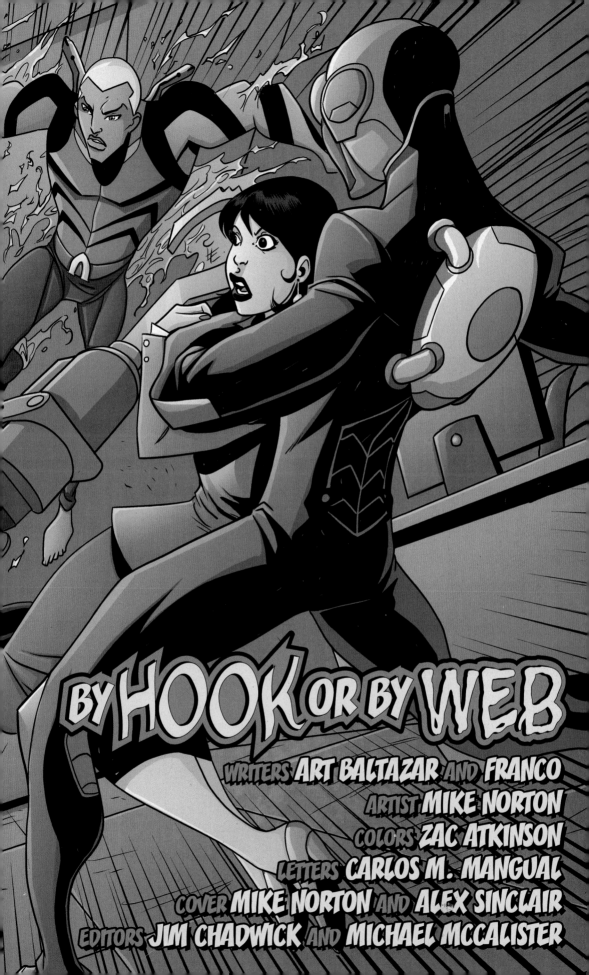

BY HOOK OR BY WEB

WRITERS: **ART BALTAZAR** AND **FRANCO**
ARTIST: **MIKE NORTON**
COLORS: **ZAC ATKINSON**
LETTERS: **CARLOS M. MANGUAL**
COVER: **MIKE NORTON** AND **ALEX SINCLAIR**
EDITORS: **JIM CHADWICK** AND **MICHAEL MCCALISTER**

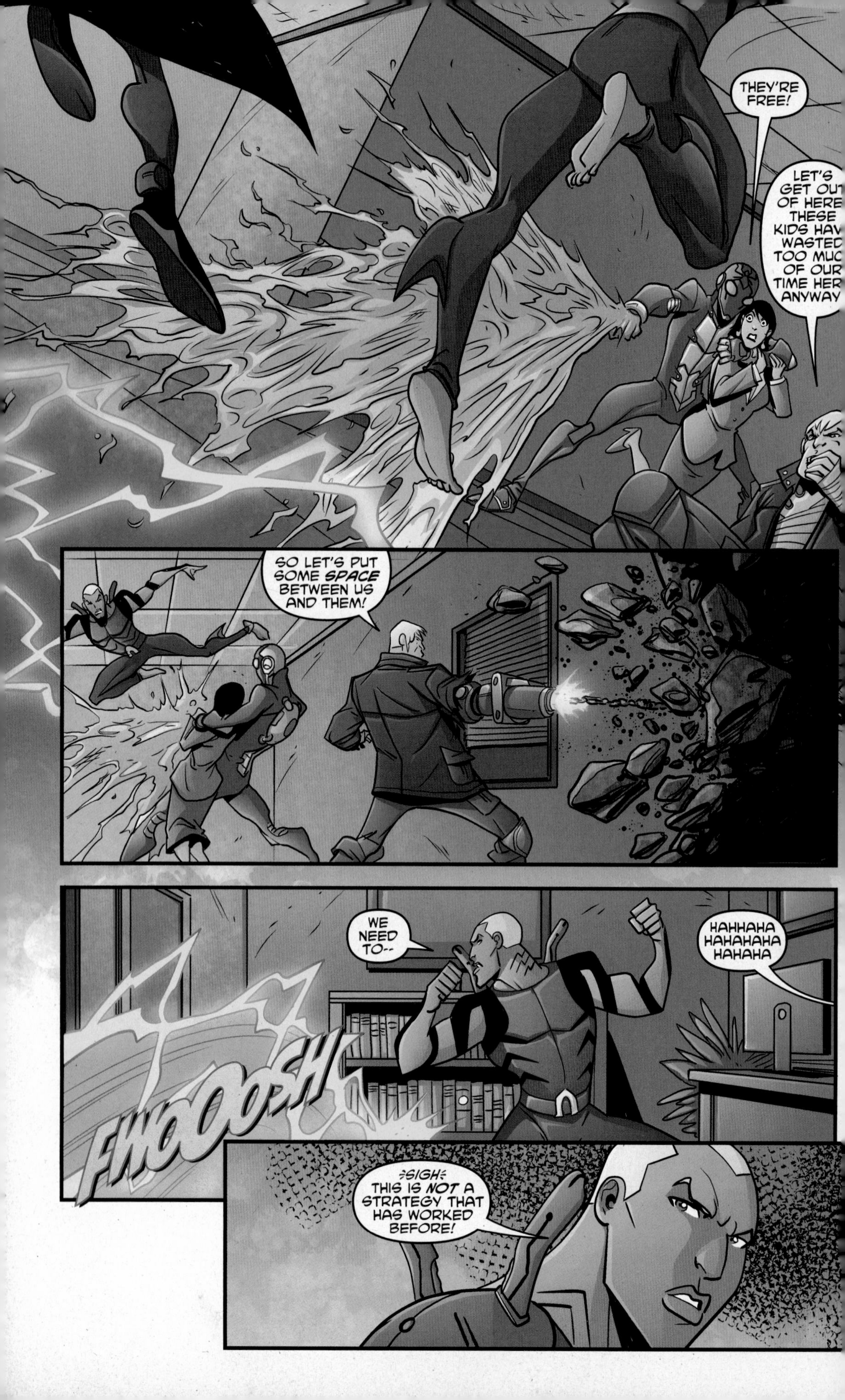
THEY'RE FREE!
LET'S GET OUT OF HERE THESE KIDS HAV WASTED TOO MUC OF OUR TIME HER ANYWAY
SO LET'S PUT SOME SPACE BETWEEN US AND THEM!
WE NEED TO--
HAHHAHA HAHAHAHA HAHAHA
FWOOOSH
SIGH
THIS IS NOT A STRATEGY THAT HAS WORKED BEFORE!

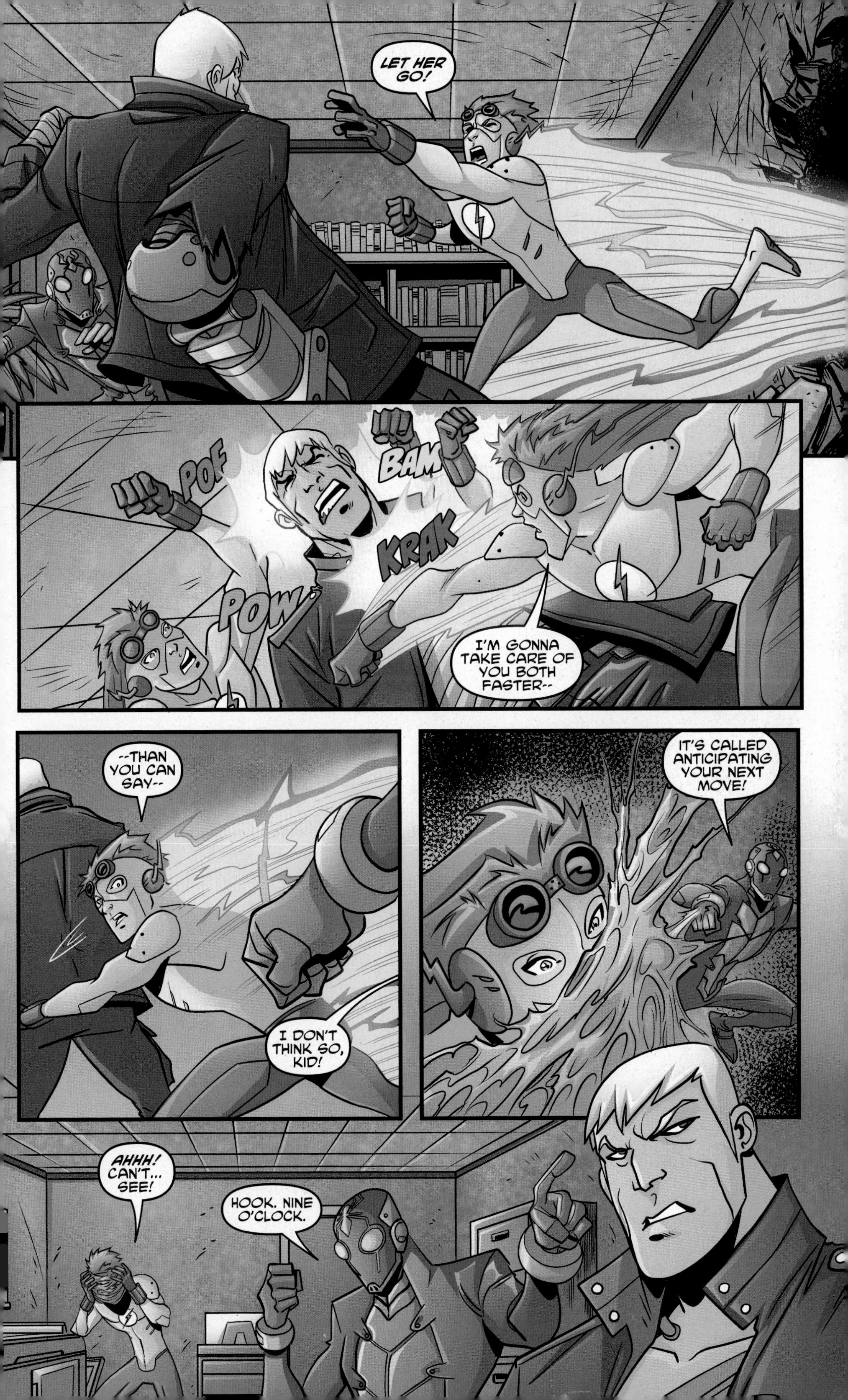
LET HER GO!
POF
BAM
KRAK
POW
I'M GONNA TAKE CARE OF YOU BOTH FASTER--
--THAN YOU CAN SAY--
I DON'T THINK SO, KID!
IT'S CALLED ANTICIPATING YOUR NEXT MOVE!
AHHH! CAN'T... SEE!
HOOK. NINE O'CLOCK.

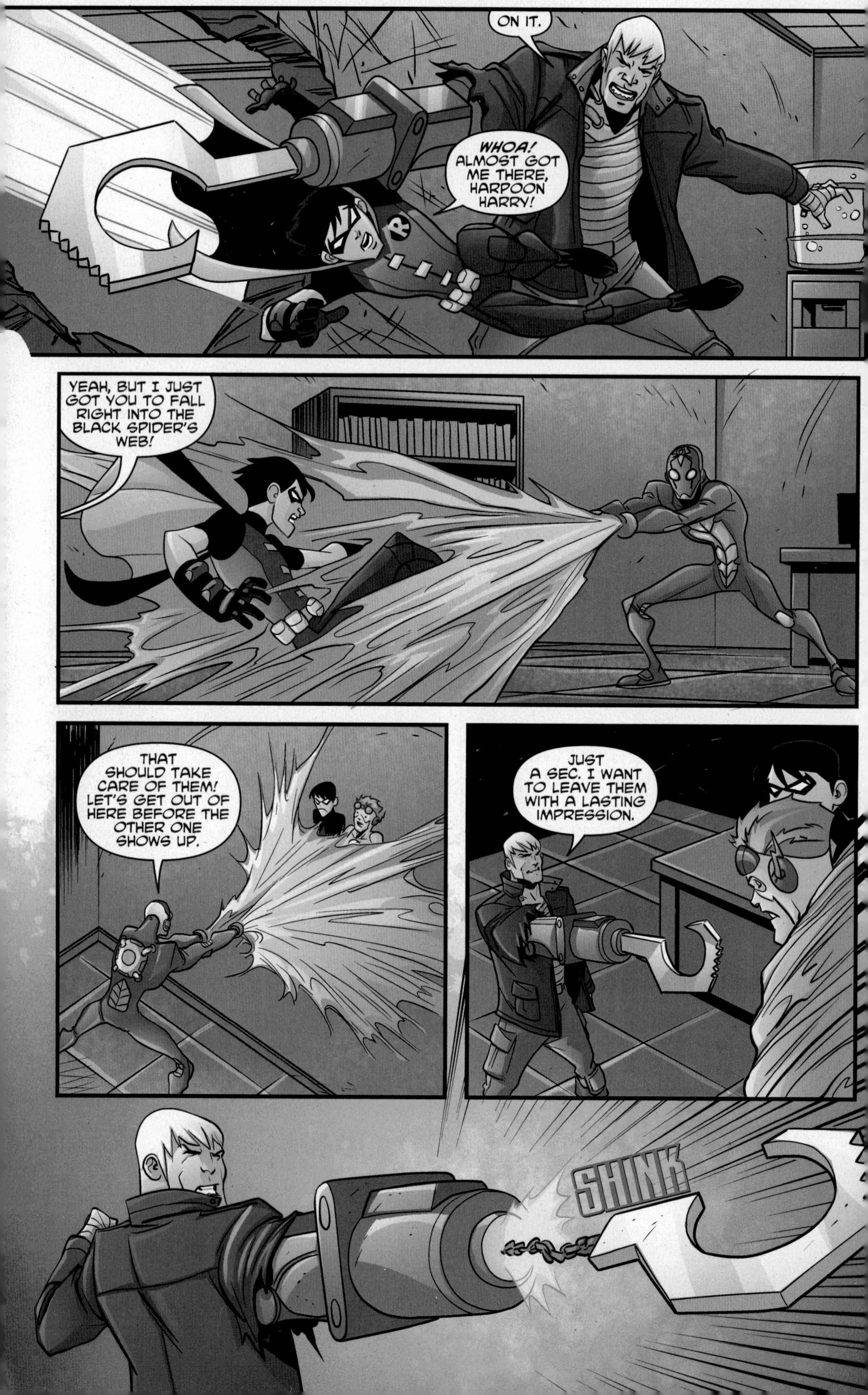
ON IT.
WHOA! ALMOST GOT ME THERE, HARPOON HARRY!
YEAH, BUT I JUST GOT YOU TO FALL RIGHT INTO THE BLACK SPIDER'S WEB!
THAT SHOULD TAKE CARE OF THEM! LET'S GET OUT OF HERE BEFORE THE OTHER ONE SHOWS UP.
JUST A SEC. I WANT TO LEAVE THEM WITH A LASTING IMPRESSION.
SHINK

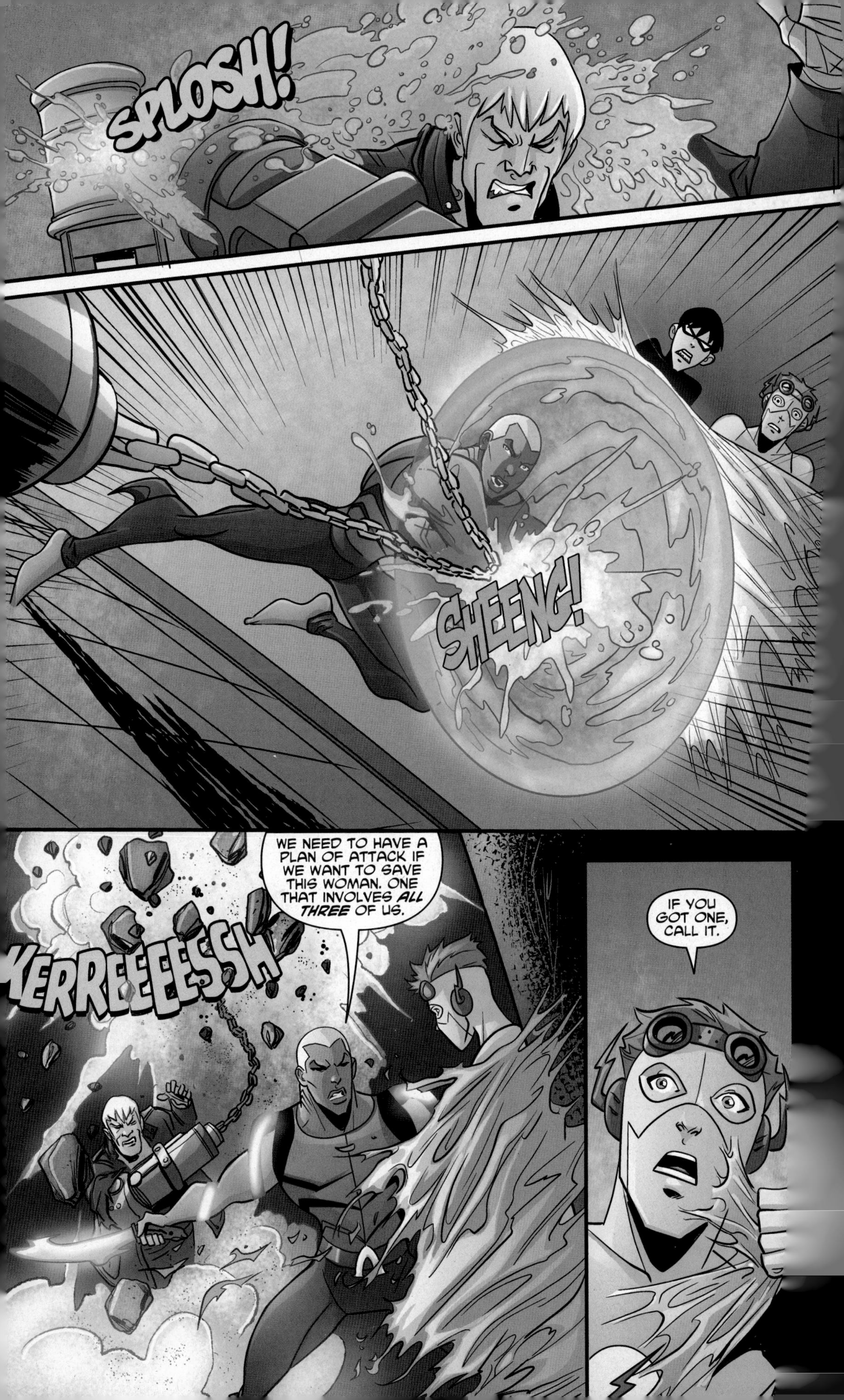
SPLOSH!
SHEENG!
KERREEEEESSH
WE NEED TO HAVE A PLAN OF ATTACK IF WE WANT TO SAVE THIS WOMAN. ONE THAT INVOLVES ALL THREE OF US.
IF YOU GOT ONE, CALL IT.

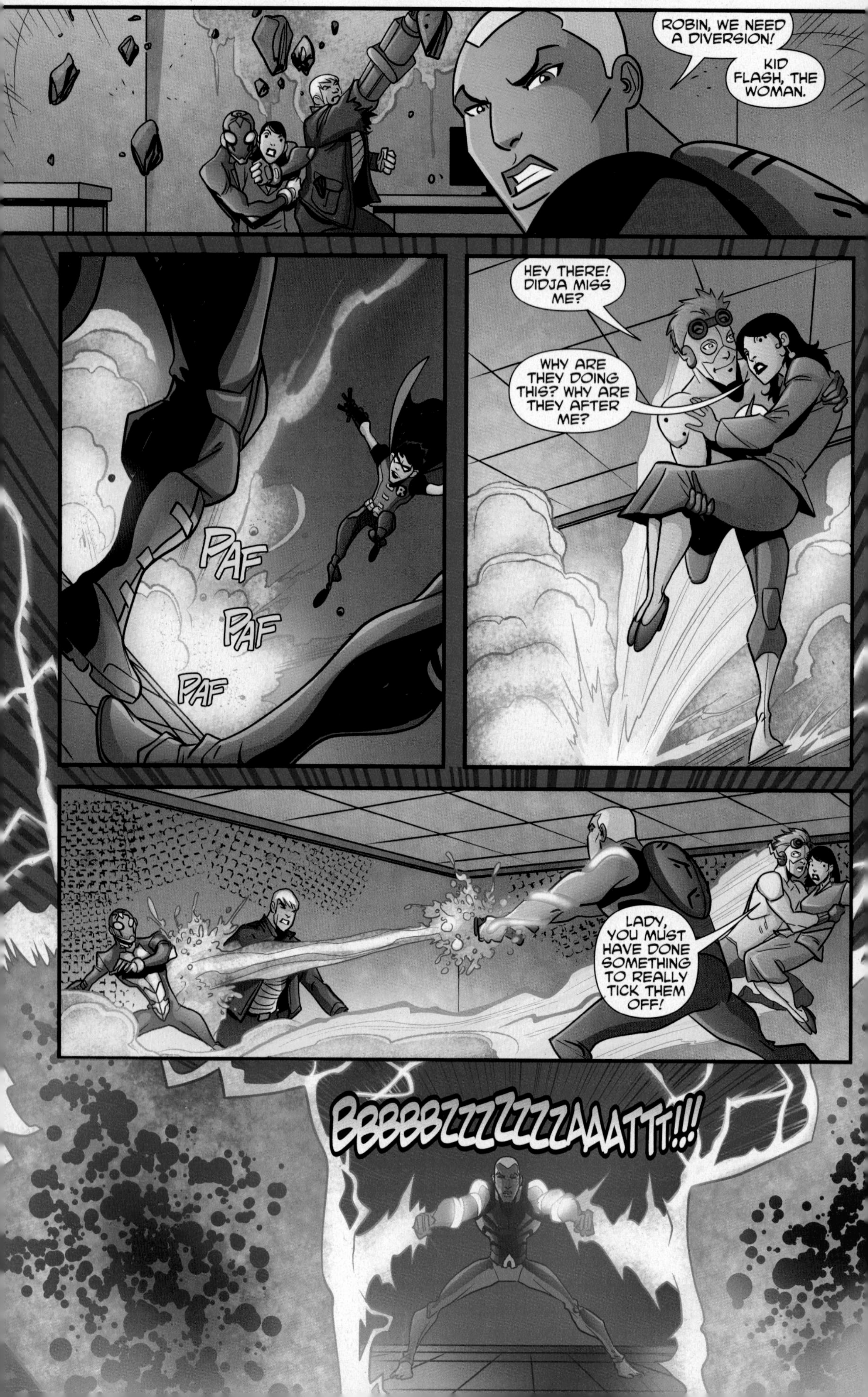
ROBIN, WE NEED A DIVERSION!
KID FLASH, THE WOMAN.
PAF
PAF
PAF
HEY THERE! DIDJA MISS ME?
WHY ARE THEY DOING THIS? WHY ARE THEY AFTER ME?
LADY, YOU MUST HAVE DONE SOMETHING TO REALLY TICK THEM OFF!
BBBBBZZZZZZZAAATTT!!!

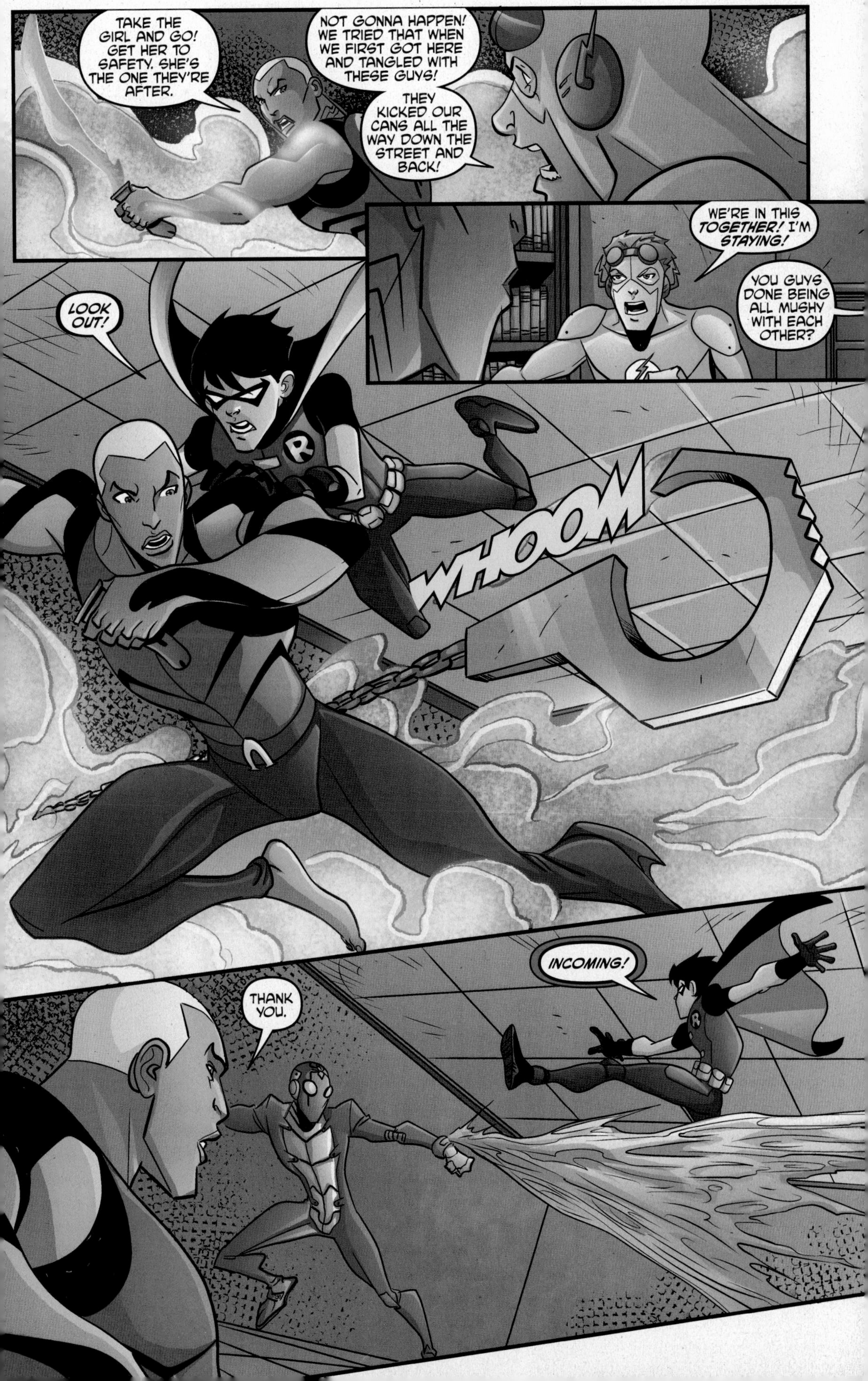

TAKE THE GIRL AND GO! GET HER TO SAFETY. SHE'S THE ONE THEY'RE AFTER.
NOT GONNA HAPPEN! WE TRIED THAT WHEN WE FIRST GOT HERE AND TANGLED WITH THESE GUYS!
THEY KICKED OUR CANS ALL THE WAY DOWN THE STREET AND BACK!
WE'RE IN THIS TOGETHER! I'M STAYING!
YOU GUYS DONE BEING ALL MUSHY WITH EACH OTHER?
LOOK OUT!
WHOOM
INCOMING!
THANK YOU.

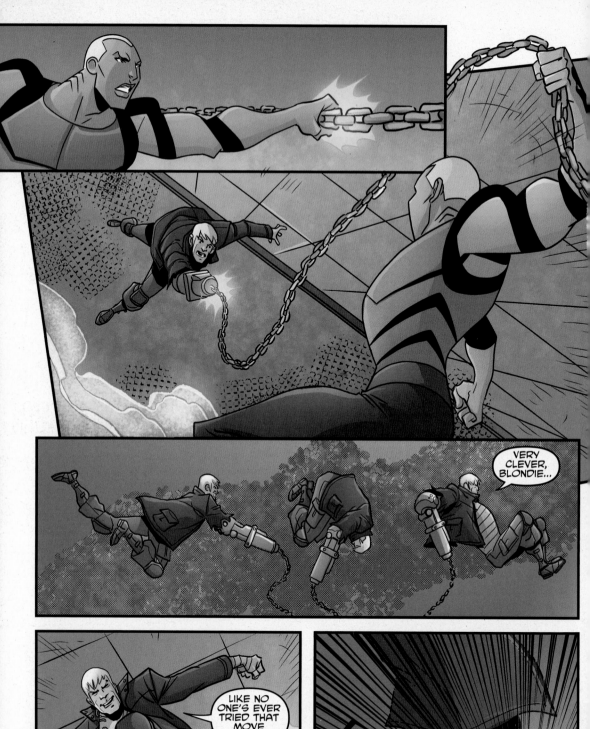

VERY CLEVER, BLONDIE...

LIKE NO ONE'S EVER TRIED THAT MOVE BEFORE.

BAW

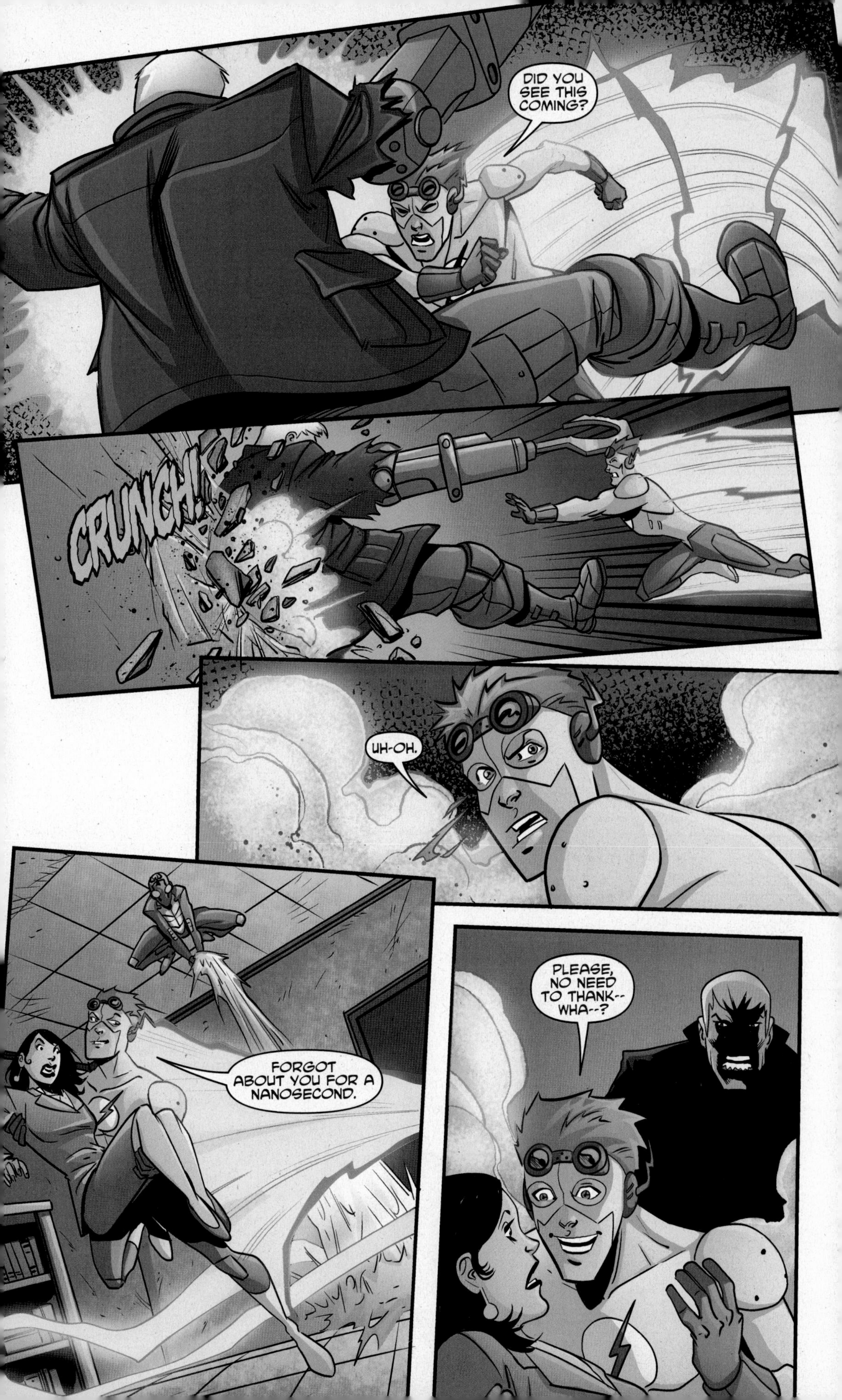
DID YOU SEE THIS COMING?
CRUNCH!
UH-OH.
FORGOT ABOUT YOU FOR A NANOSECOND.
PLEASE, NO NEED TO THANK-- WHA--?

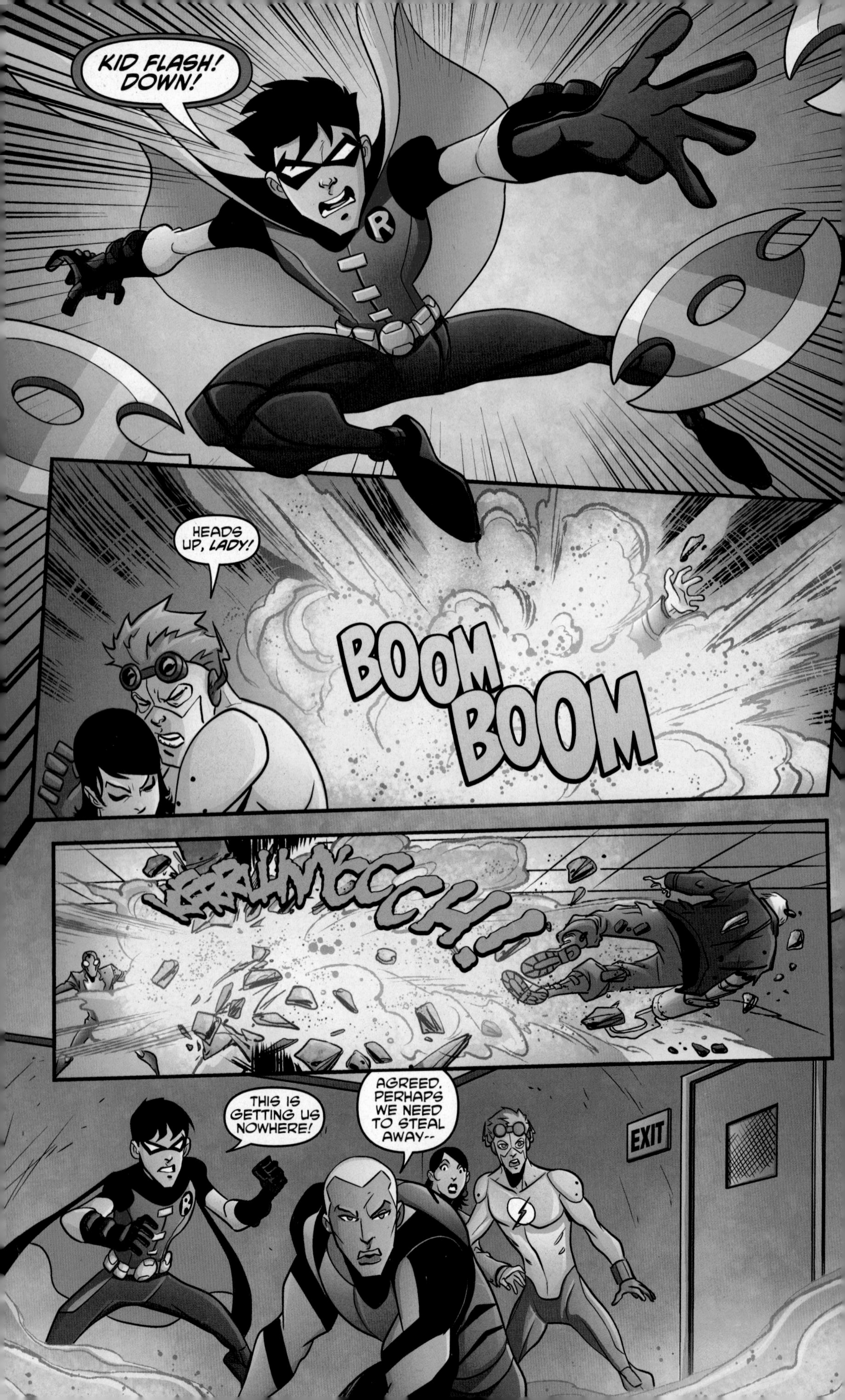
KID FLASH! DOWN!
HEADS UP, LADY!
BOOM
BOOM
KRRUNCCH!!
THIS IS GETTING US NOWHERE!
AGREED. PERHAPS WE NEED TO STEAL AWAY--
EXIT

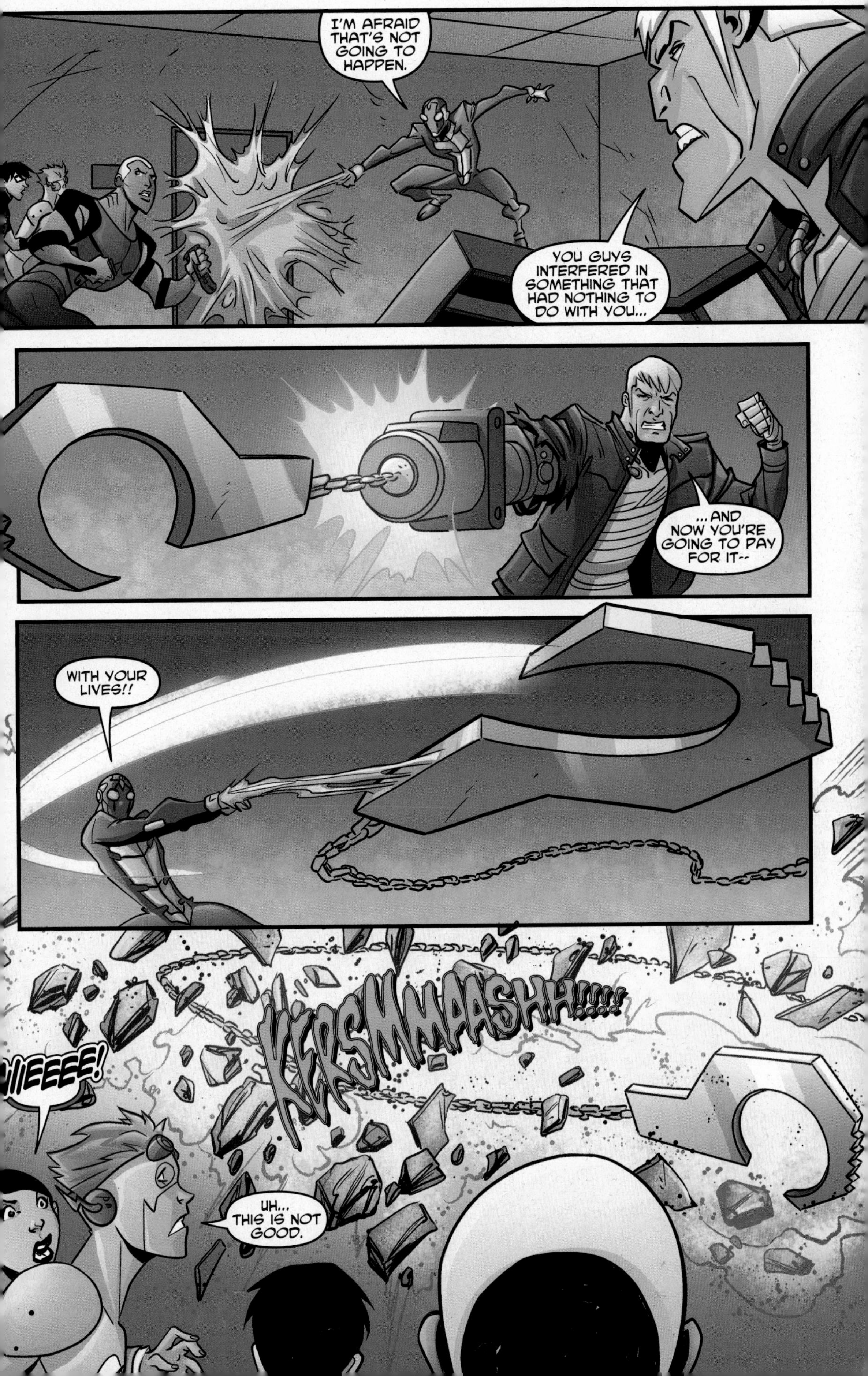
I'M AFRAID THAT'S NOT GOING TO HAPPEN.
YOU GUYS INTERFERED IN SOMETHING THAT HAD NOTHING TO DO WITH YOU...
...AND NOW YOU'RE GOING TO PAY FOR IT--
WITH YOUR LIVES!!
KERSMMAASHH!!!!!
IIEEEEE!
UH... THIS IS NOT GOOD.

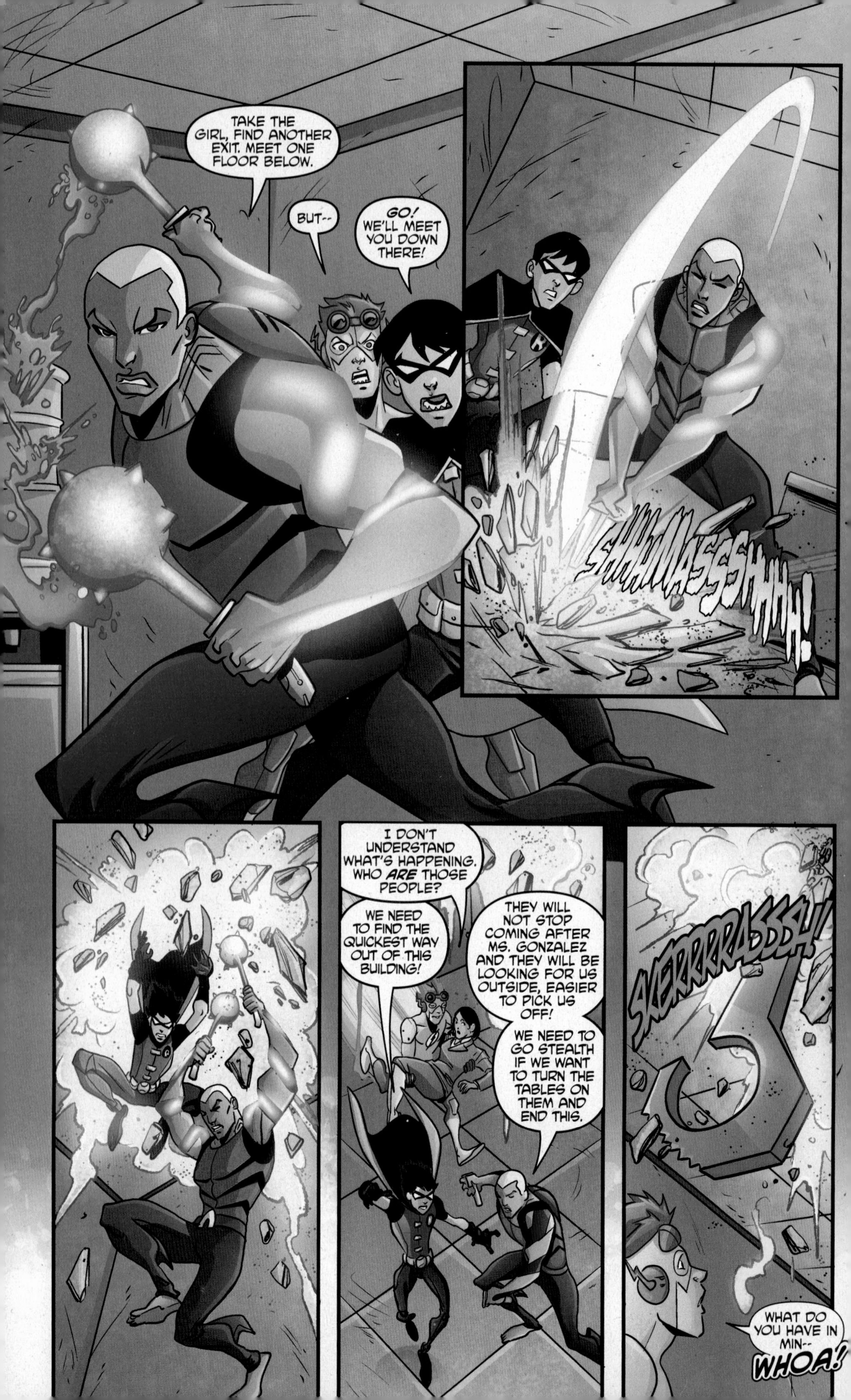
TAKE THE GIRL, FIND ANOTHER EXIT. MEET ONE FLOOR BELOW.
BUT--
GO! WE'LL MEET YOU DOWN THERE!
SHHHMASSSHHHH!
I DON'T UNDERSTAND WHAT'S HAPPENING. WHO ARE THOSE PEOPLE?
WE NEED TO FIND THE QUICKEST WAY OUT OF THIS BUILDING!
THEY WILL NOT STOP COMING AFTER MS. GONZALEZ AND THEY WILL BE LOOKING FOR US OUTSIDE, EASIER TO PICK US OFF!
WE NEED TO GO STEALTH IF WE WANT TO TURN THE TABLES ON THEM AND END THIS.
SKERRRRASSSH!
WHAT DO YOU HAVE IN MIN-- WHOA!

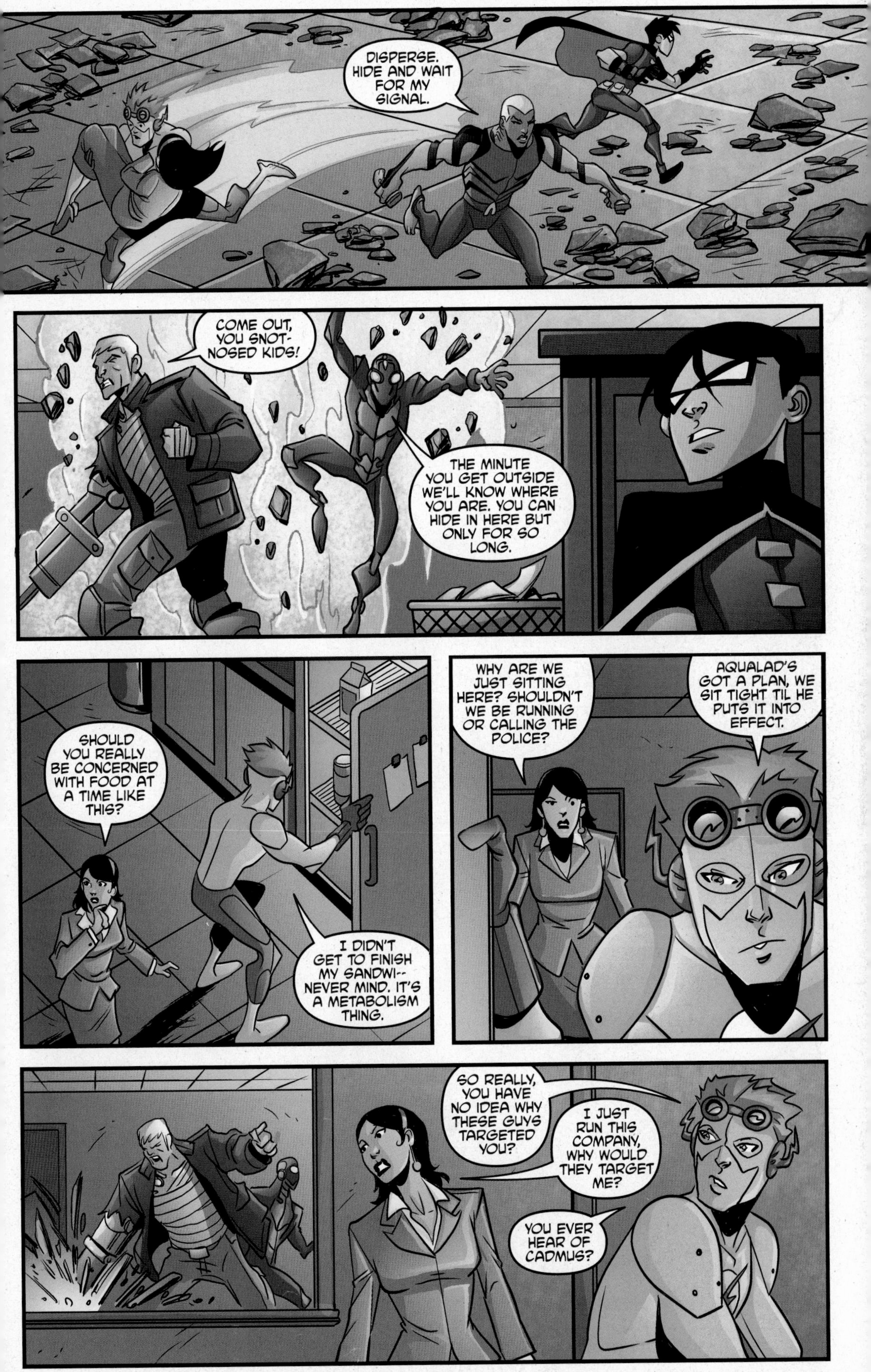
DISPERSE. HIDE AND WAIT FOR MY SIGNAL.
COME OUT, YOU SNOT-NOSED KIDS!
THE MINUTE YOU GET OUTSIDE WE'LL KNOW WHERE YOU ARE. YOU CAN HIDE IN HERE BUT ONLY FOR SO LONG.
SHOULD YOU REALLY BE CONCERNED WITH FOOD AT A TIME LIKE THIS?
I DIDN'T GET TO FINISH MY SANDWI-- NEVER MIND. IT'S A METABOLISM THING.
WHY ARE WE JUST SITTING HERE? SHOULDN'T WE BE RUNNING OR CALLING THE POLICE?
AQUALAD'S GOT A PLAN, WE SIT TIGHT TIL HE PUTS IT INTO EFFECT.
SO REALLY, YOU HAVE NO IDEA WHY THESE GUYS TARGETED YOU?
I JUST RUN THIS COMPANY, WHY WOULD THEY TARGET ME?
YOU EVER HEAR OF CADMUS?

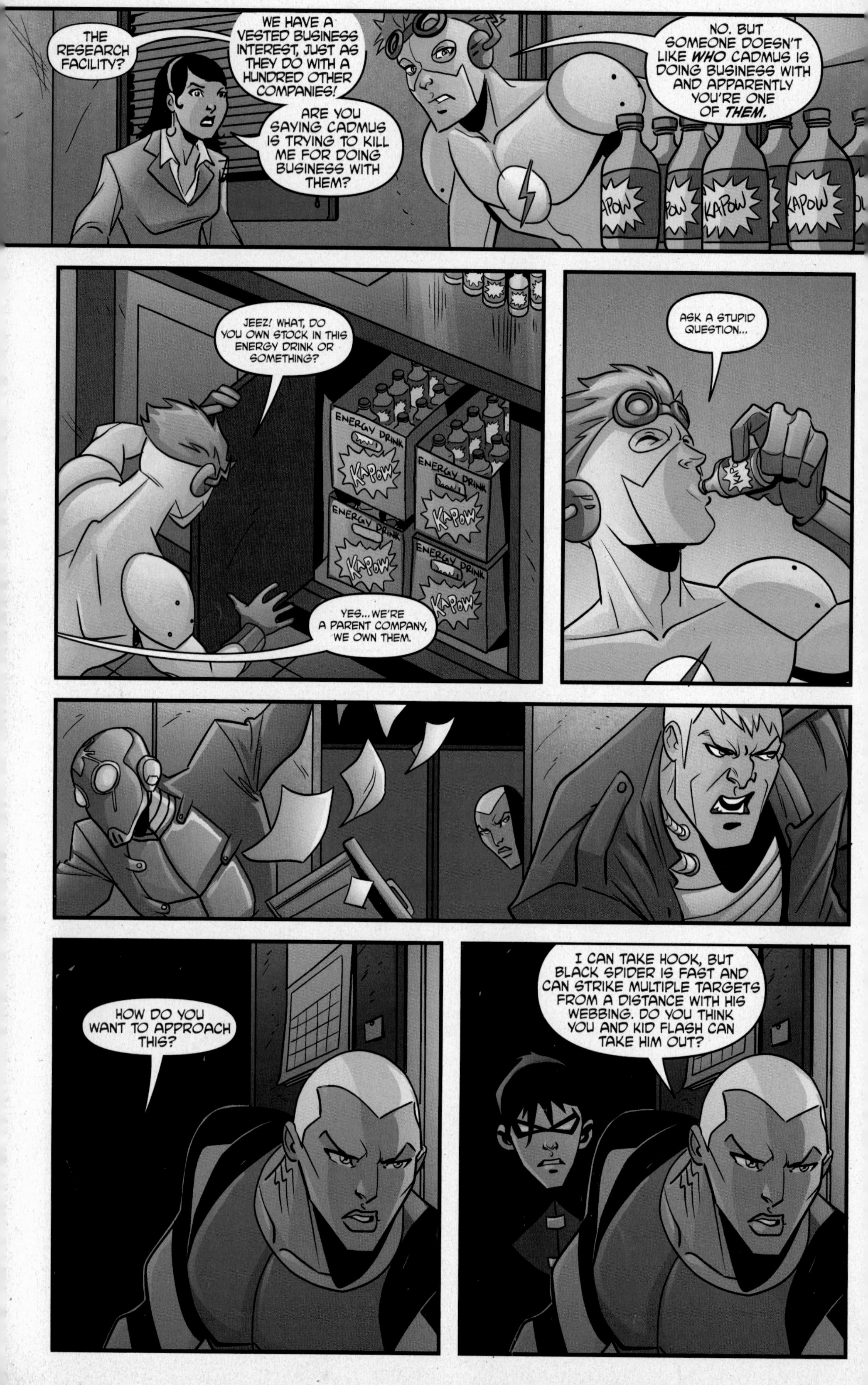
THE RESEARCH FACILITY?
WE HAVE A VESTED BUSINESS INTEREST, JUST AS THEY DO WITH A HUNDRED OTHER COMPANIES!
ARE YOU SAYING CADMUS IS TRYING TO KILL ME FOR DOING BUSINESS WITH THEM?
NO. BUT SOMEONE DOESN'T LIKE WHO CADMUS IS DOING BUSINESS WITH AND APPARENTLY YOU'RE ONE OF THEM.
KAPOW
JEEZ! WHAT, DO YOU OWN STOCK IN THIS ENERGY DRINK OR SOMETHING?
ENERGY DRINK
KAPOW
YES...WE'RE A PARENT COMPANY, WE OWN THEM.
ASK A STUPID QUESTION...
HOW DO YOU WANT TO APPROACH THIS?
I CAN TAKE HOOK, BUT BLACK SPIDER IS FAST AND CAN STRIKE MULTIPLE TARGETS FROM A DISTANCE WITH HIS WEBBING. DO YOU THINK YOU AND KID FLASH CAN TAKE HIM OUT?

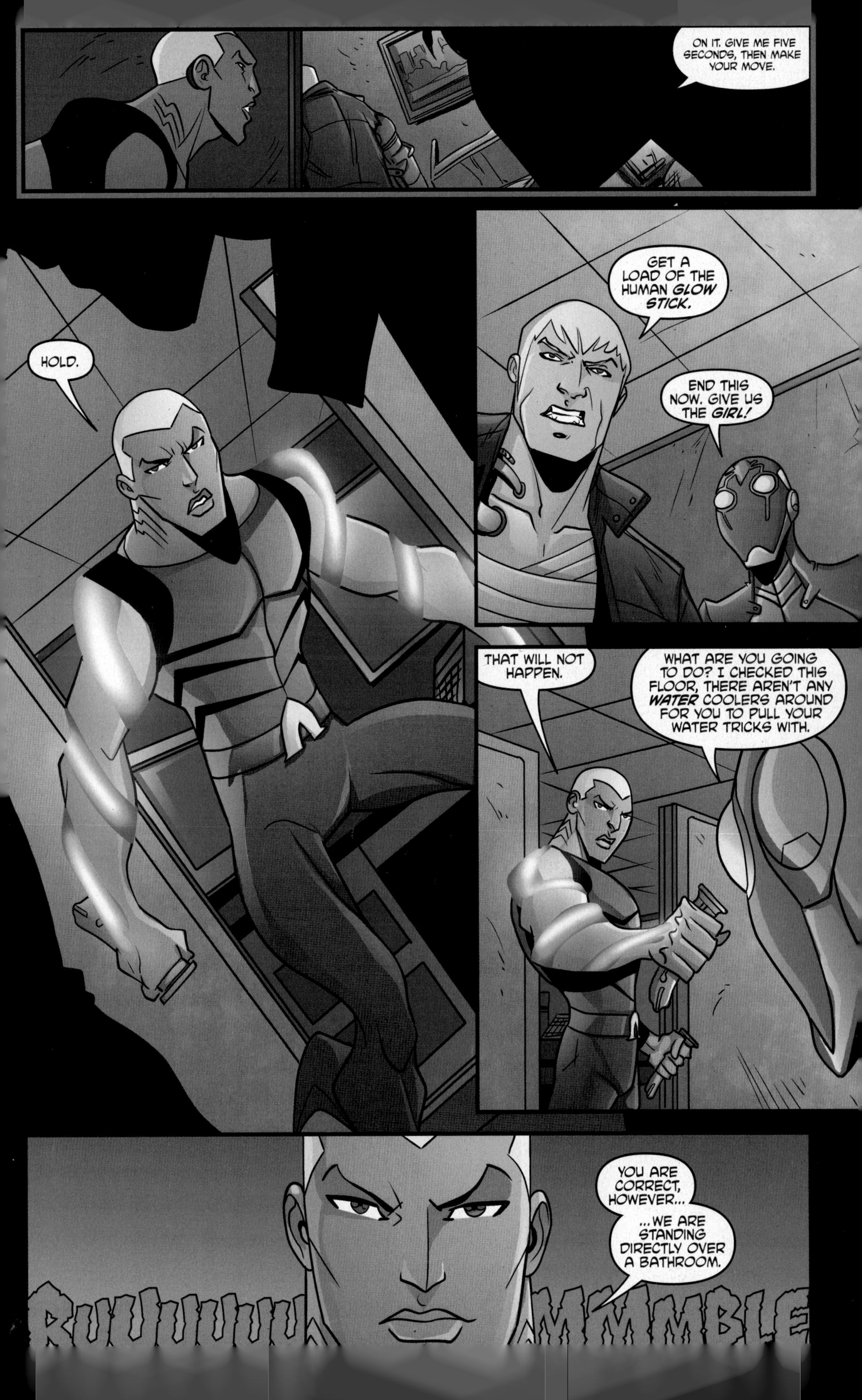
ON IT. GIVE ME FIVE SECONDS, THEN MAKE YOUR MOVE.
HOLD.
GET A LOAD OF THE HUMAN GLOW STICK.
END THIS NOW. GIVE US THE GIRL!
THAT WILL NOT HAPPEN.
WHAT ARE YOU GOING TO DO? I CHECKED THIS FLOOR, THERE AREN'T ANY WATER COOLERS AROUND FOR YOU TO PULL YOUR WATER TRICKS WITH.
YOU ARE CORRECT, HOWEVER...
...WE ARE STANDING DIRECTLY OVER A BATHROOM.
RUUUUUU MMMBLE

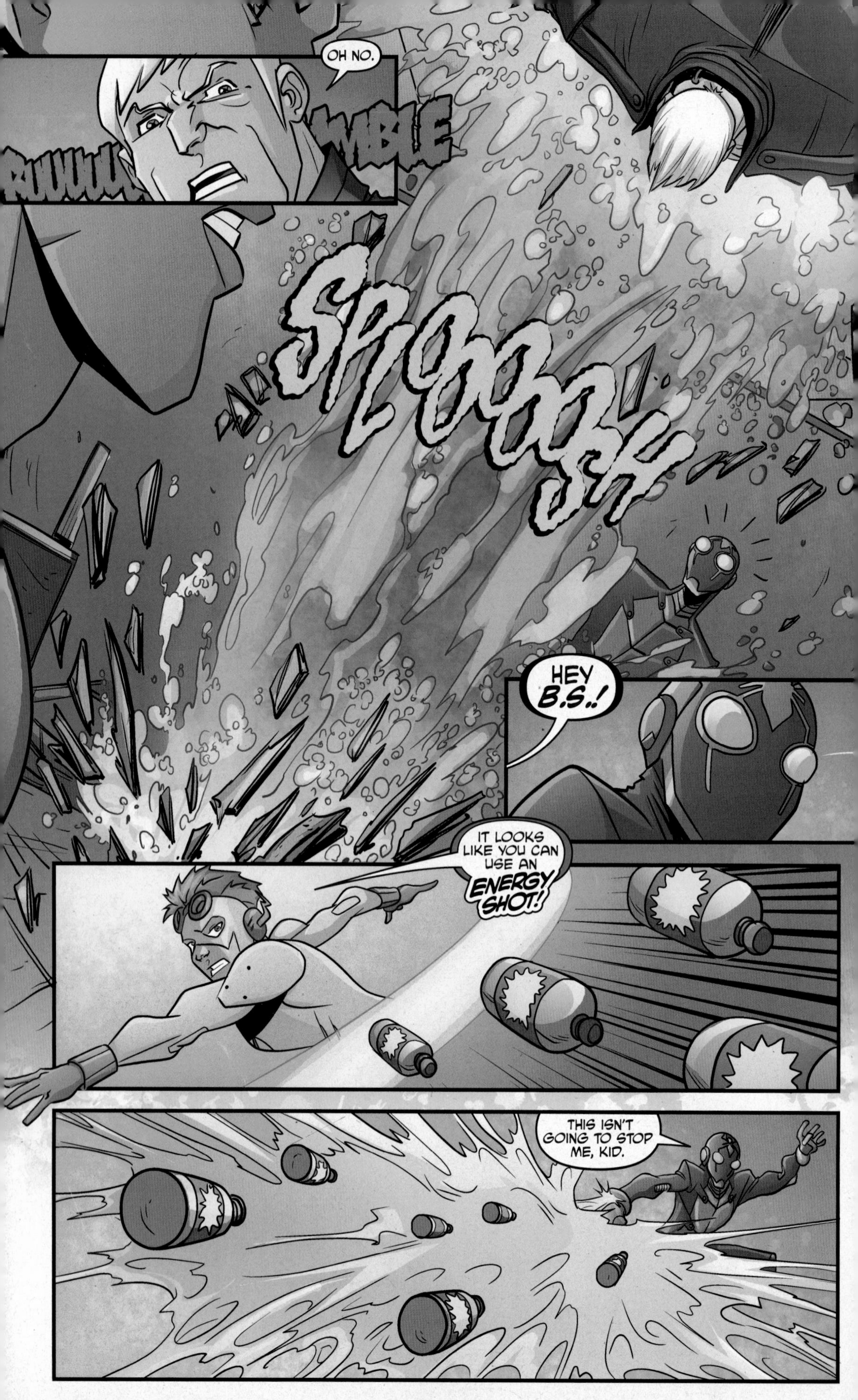
OH NO.
RUUUUUMBLE
SPLOOOOSH
HEY B.S.!
IT LOOKS LIKE YOU CAN USE AN ENERGY SHOT!
THIS ISN'T GOING TO STOP ME, KID.

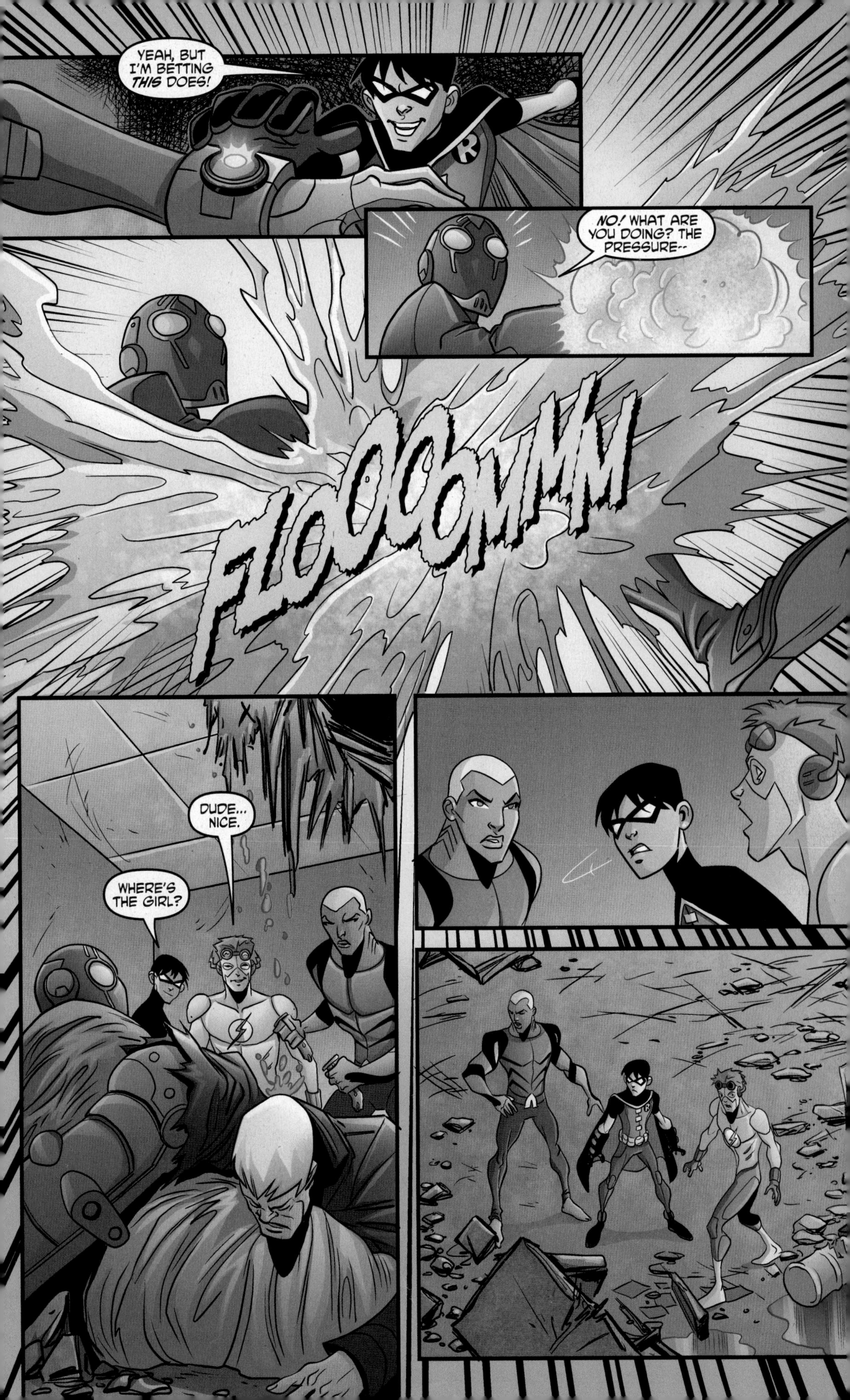
YEAH, BUT I'M BETTING *THIS* DOES!
NO! WHAT ARE YOU DOING? THE PRESSURE--
FLOOOOMMM
DUDE... NICE.
WHERE'S THE GIRL?

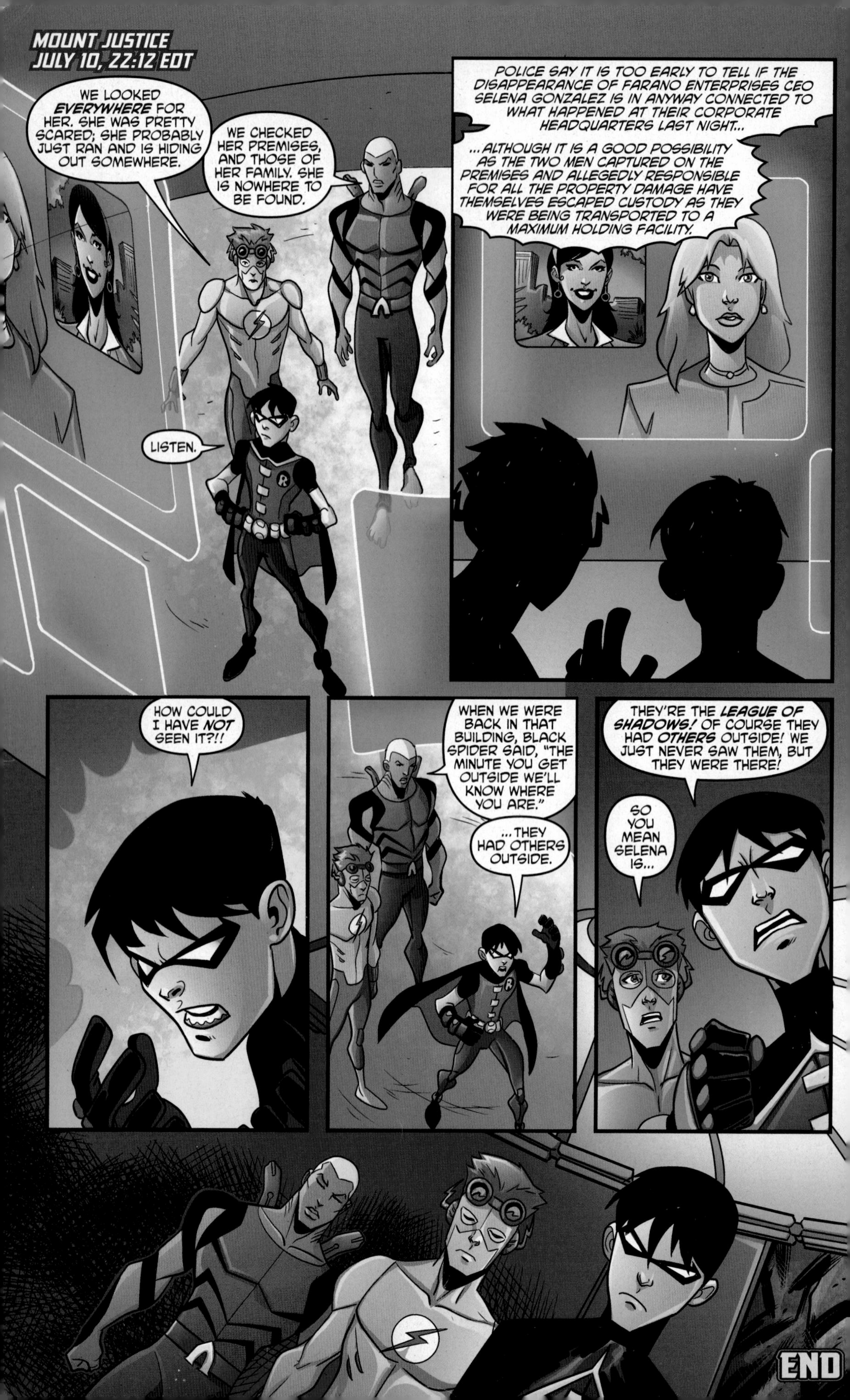
MOUNT JUSTICE
JULY 10, 22:12 EDT
WE LOOKED EVERYWHERE FOR HER. SHE WAS PRETTY SCARED; SHE PROBABLY JUST RAN AND IS HIDING OUT SOMEWHERE.
WE CHECKED HER PREMISES, AND THOSE OF HER FAMILY. SHE IS NOWHERE TO BE FOUND.
LISTEN.
POLICE SAY IT IS TOO EARLY TO TELL IF THE DISAPPEARANCE OF FARANO ENTERPRISES CEO SELENA GONZALEZ IS IN ANYWAY CONNECTED TO WHAT HAPPENED AT THEIR CORPORATE HEADQUARTERS LAST NIGHT...
...ALTHOUGH IT IS A GOOD POSSIBILITY AS THE TWO MEN CAPTURED ON THE PREMISES AND ALLEGEDLY RESPONSIBLE FOR ALL THE PROPERTY DAMAGE HAVE THEMSELVES ESCAPED CUSTODY AS THEY WERE BEING TRANSPORTED TO A MAXIMUM HOLDING FACILITY.
HOW COULD I HAVE NOT SEEN IT?!!
WHEN WE WERE BACK IN THAT BUILDING, BLACK SPIDER SAID, "THE MINUTE YOU GET OUTSIDE WE'LL KNOW WHERE YOU ARE."
...THEY HAD OTHERS OUTSIDE.
THEY'RE THE LEAGUE OF SHADOWS! OF COURSE THEY HAD OTHERS OUTSIDE! WE JUST NEVER SAW THEM, BUT THEY WERE THERE!
SO YOU MEAN SELENA IS...
END

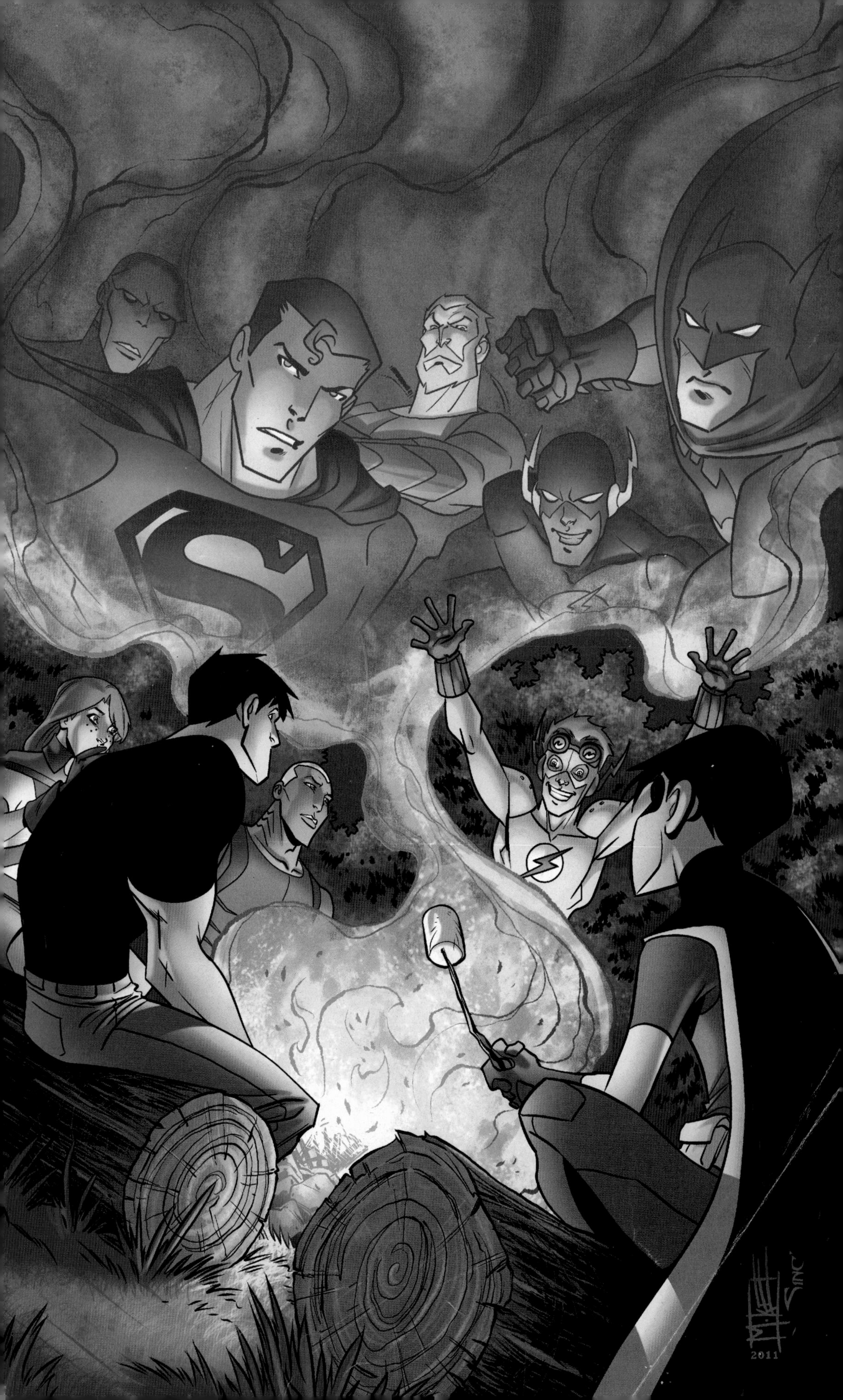
2011

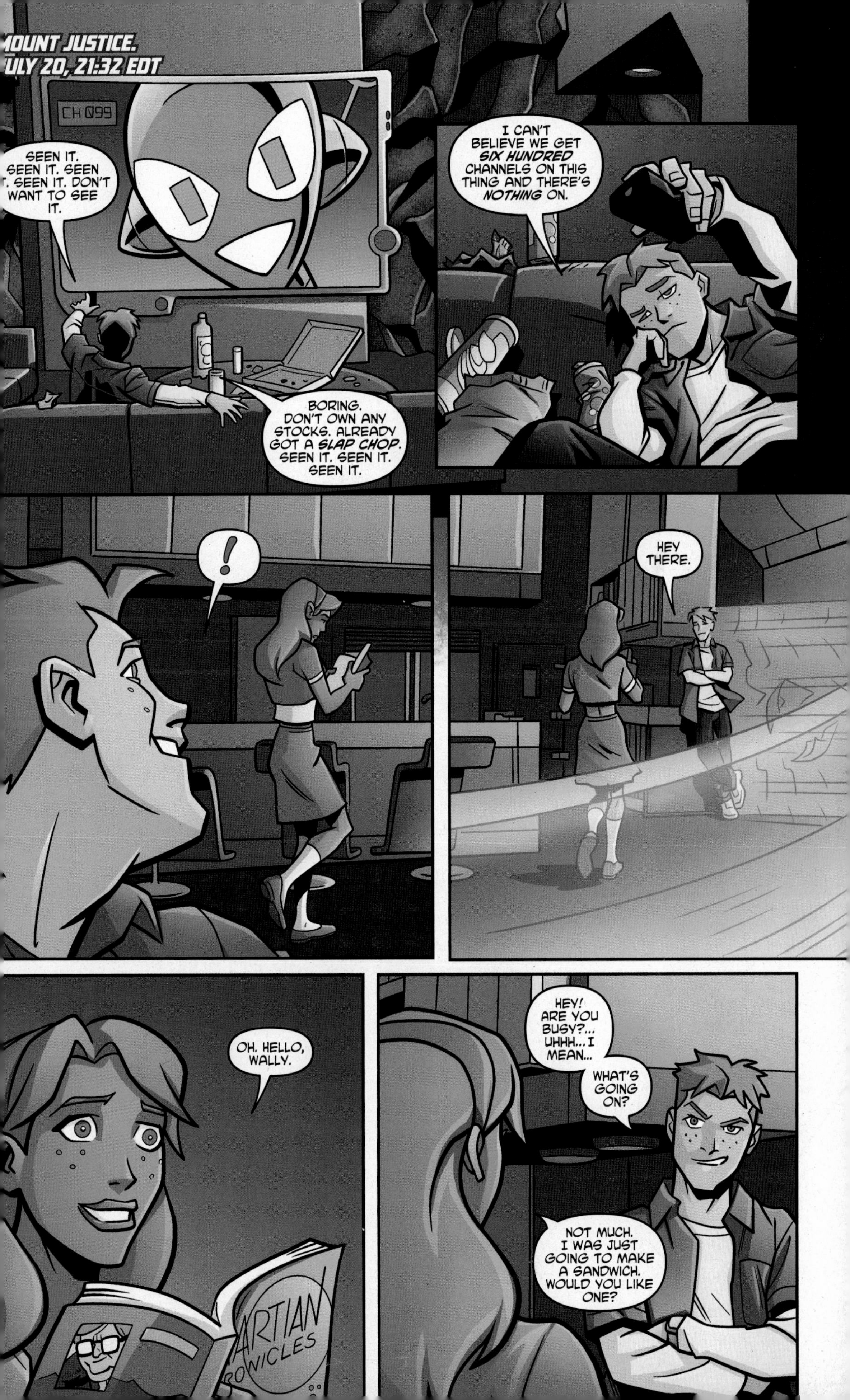
MOUNT JUSTICE.
ULY 20, 21:32 EDT
CH 099
SEEN IT. SEEN IT. SEEN IT. SEEN IT. DON'T WANT TO SEE IT.
BORING. DON'T OWN ANY STOCKS. ALREADY GOT A SLAP CHOP. SEEN IT. SEEN IT. SEEN IT.
I CAN'T BELIEVE WE GET SIX HUNDRED CHANNELS ON THIS THING AND THERE'S NOTHING ON.
!
HEY THERE.
OH. HELLO, WALLY.
HEY! ARE YOU BUSY?... UHHH... I MEAN...
WHAT'S GOING ON?
NOT MUCH. I WAS JUST GOING TO MAKE A SANDWICH. WOULD YOU LIKE ONE?
ARTIAN
RONICLES

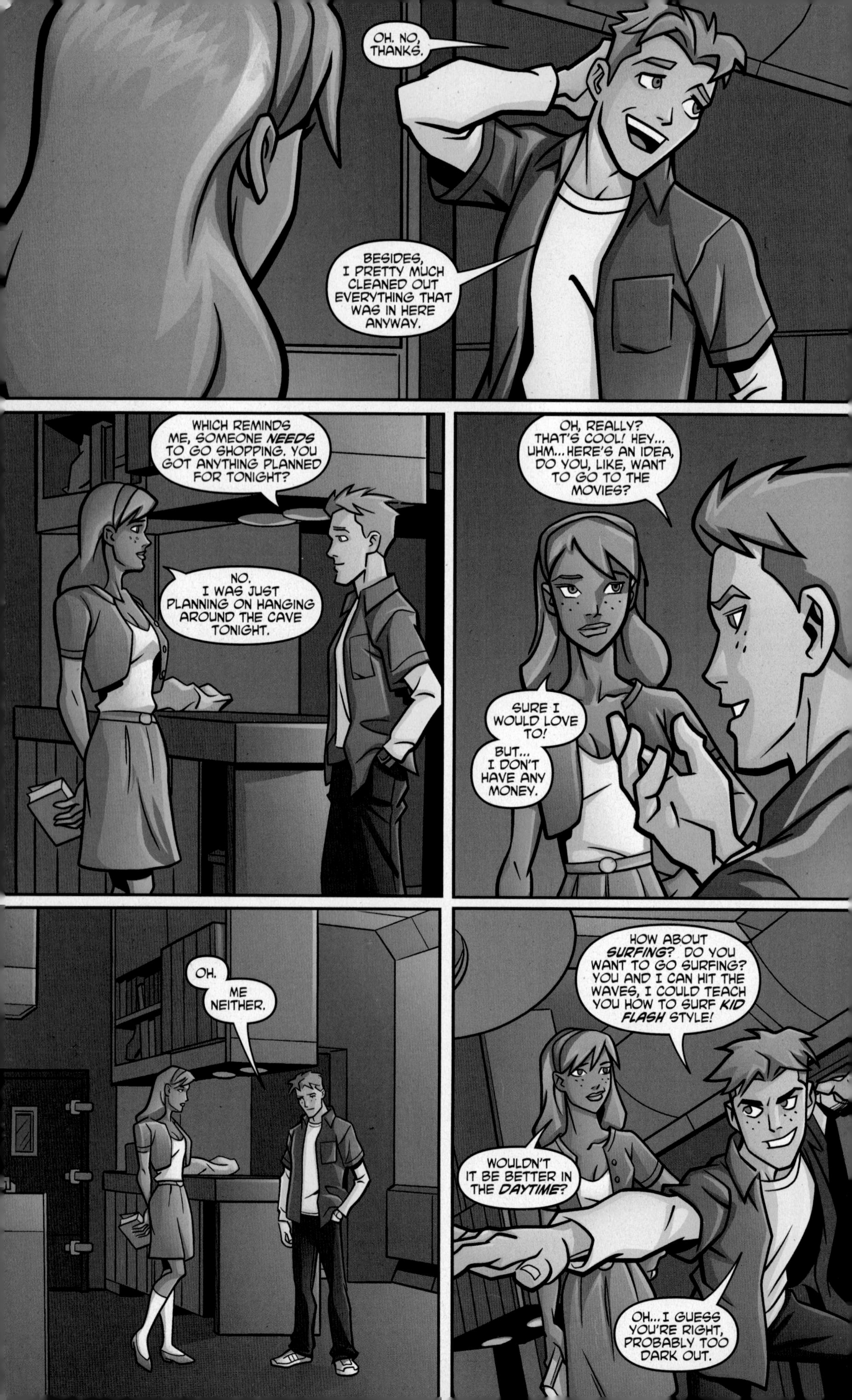

OH. NO, THANKS.
BESIDES, I PRETTY MUCH CLEANED OUT EVERYTHING THAT WAS IN HERE ANYWAY.
WHICH REMINDS ME, SOMEONE NEEDS TO GO SHOPPING. YOU GOT ANYTHING PLANNED FOR TONIGHT?
NO. I WAS JUST PLANNING ON HANGING AROUND THE CAVE TONIGHT.
OH, REALLY? THAT'S COOL! HEY... UHM...HERE'S AN IDEA, DO YOU, LIKE, WANT TO GO TO THE MOVIES?
SURE I WOULD LOVE TO!
BUT... I DON'T HAVE ANY MONEY.
OH.
ME NEITHER.
HOW ABOUT SURFING? DO YOU WANT TO GO SURFING? YOU AND I CAN HIT THE WAVES, I COULD TEACH YOU HOW TO SURF KID FLASH STYLE!
WOULDN'T IT BE BETTER IN THE DAYTIME?
OH...I GUESS YOU'RE RIGHT, PROBABLY TOO DARK OUT.

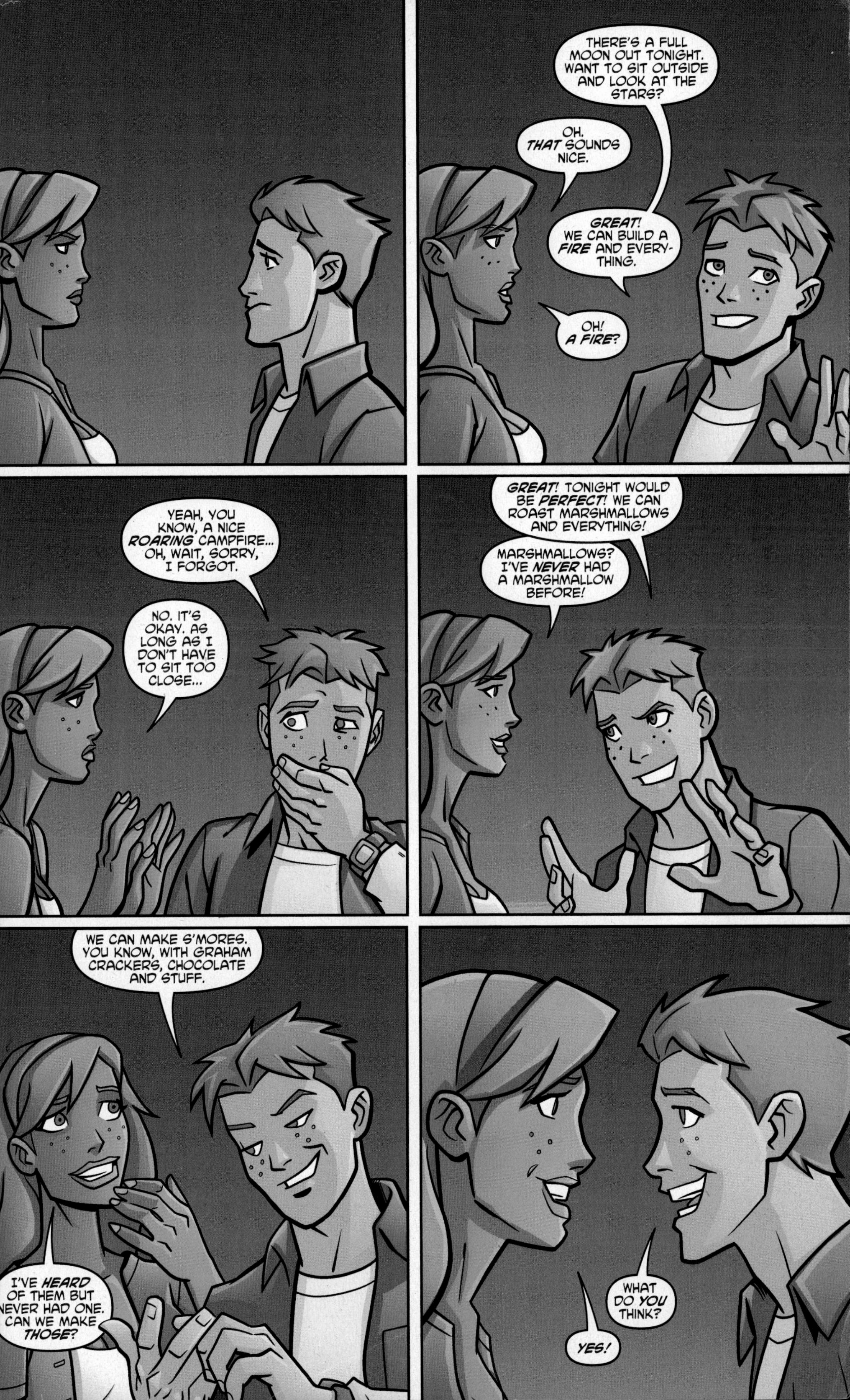
THERE'S A FULL MOON OUT TONIGHT. WANT TO SIT OUTSIDE AND LOOK AT THE STARS?
OH. THAT SOUNDS NICE.
GREAT! WE CAN BUILD A FIRE AND EVERY-THING.
OH! A FIRE?
YEAH, YOU KNOW, A NICE ROARING CAMPFIRE... OH, WAIT, SORRY, I FORGOT.
NO. IT'S OKAY. AS LONG AS I DON'T HAVE TO SIT TOO CLOSE...
GREAT! TONIGHT WOULD BE PERFECT! WE CAN ROAST MARSHMALLOWS AND EVERYTHING!
MARSHMALLOWS? I'VE NEVER HAD A MARSHMALLOW BEFORE!
WE CAN MAKE S'MORES. YOU KNOW, WITH GRAHAM CRACKERS, CHOCOLATE AND STUFF.
I'VE HEARD OF THEM BUT NEVER HAD ONE. CAN WE MAKE THOSE?
WHAT DO YOU THINK?
YES!

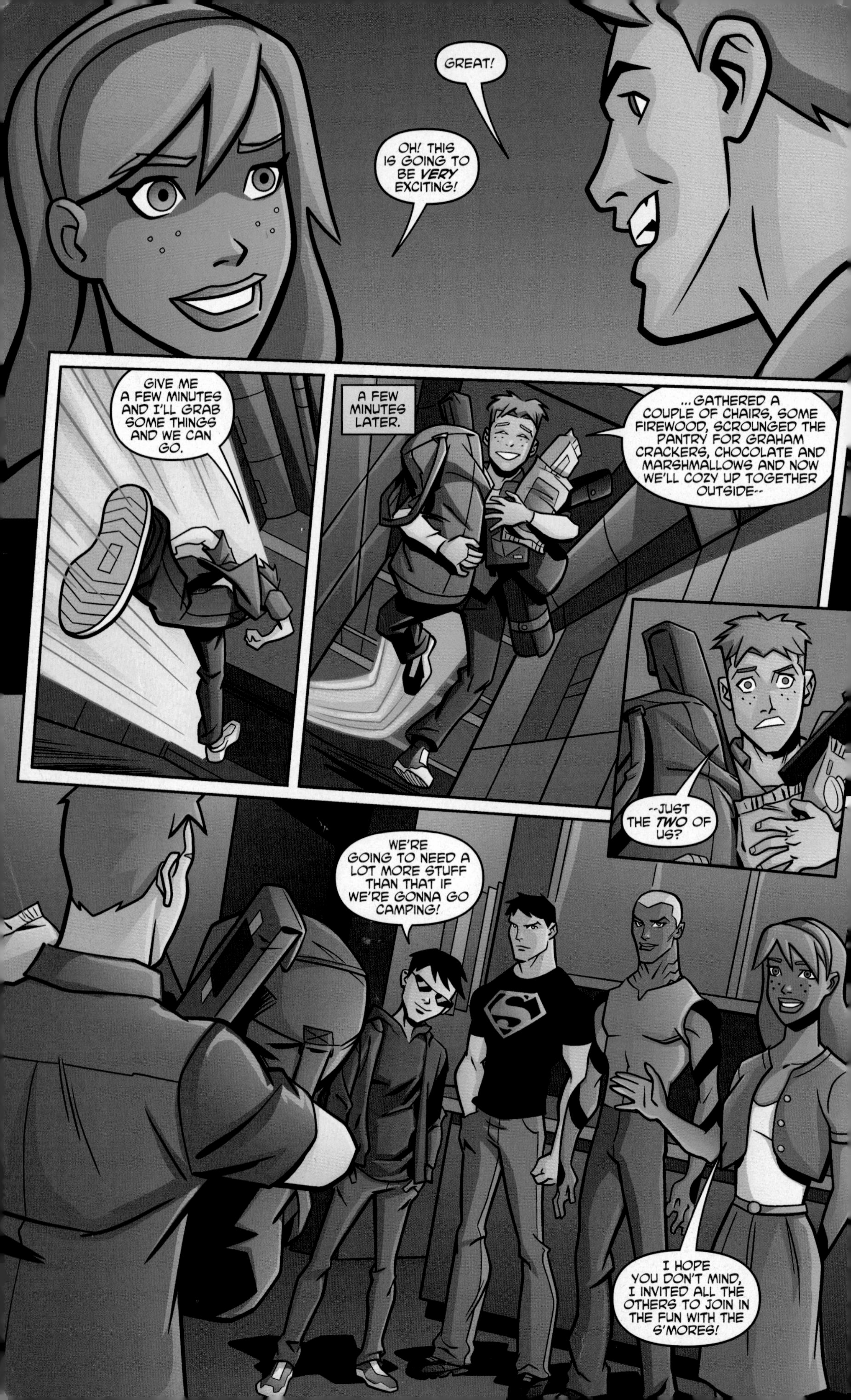
GREAT!
OH! THIS IS GOING TO BE *VERY* EXCITING!
GIVE ME A FEW MINUTES AND I'LL GRAB SOME THINGS AND WE CAN GO.
A FEW MINUTES LATER.
...GATHERED A COUPLE OF CHAIRS, SOME FIREWOOD, SCROUNGED THE PANTRY FOR GRAHAM CRACKERS, CHOCOLATE AND MARSHMALLOWS AND NOW WE'LL COZY UP TOGETHER OUTSIDE--
--JUST THE *TWO* OF US?
WE'RE GOING TO NEED A LOT MORE STUFF THAN THAT IF WE'RE GONNA GO CAMPING!
I HOPE YOU DON'T MIND, I INVITED ALL THE OTHERS TO JOIN IN THE FUN WITH THE S'MORES!

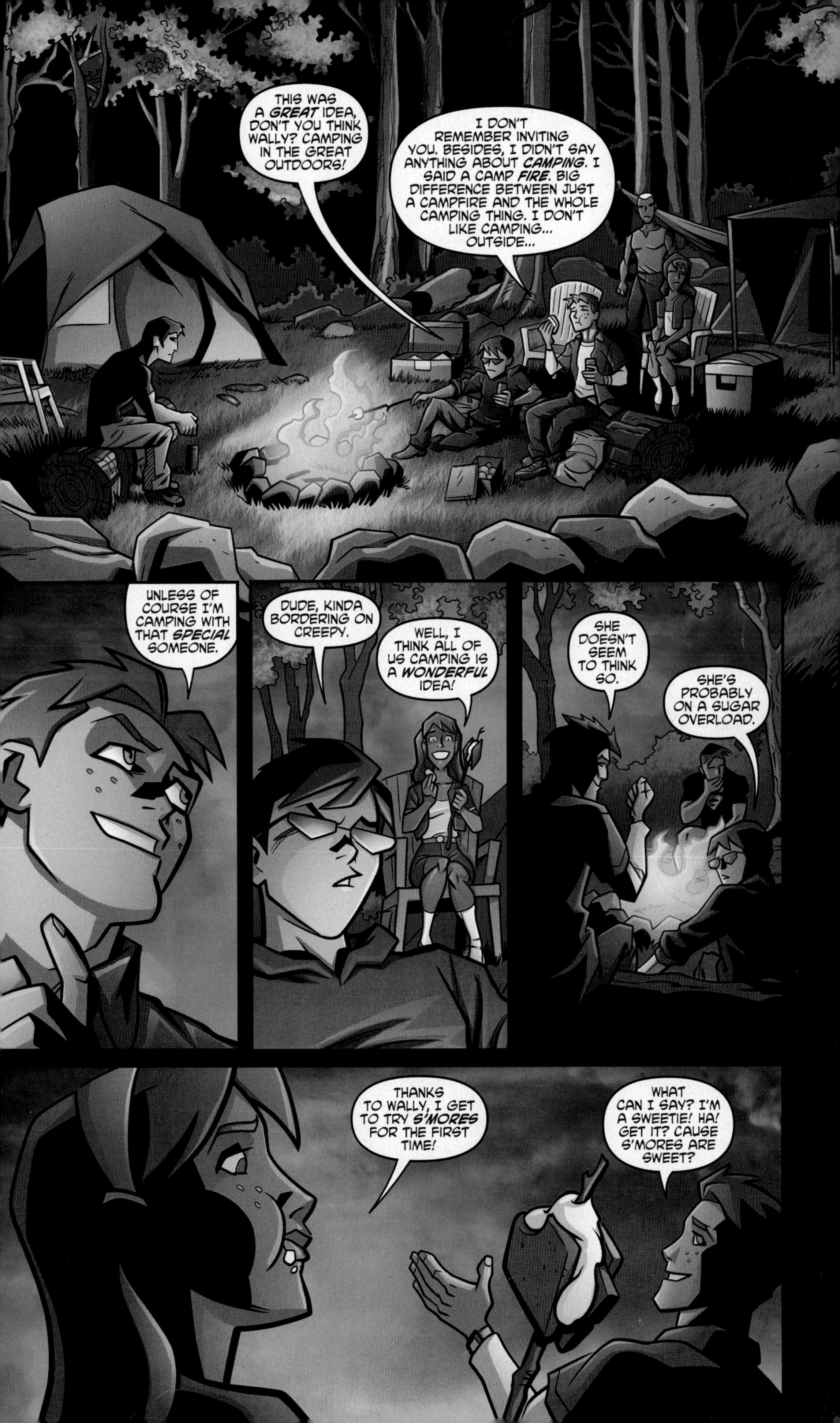
THIS WAS A GREAT IDEA, DON'T YOU THINK WALLY? CAMPING IN THE GREAT OUTDOORS!
I DON'T REMEMBER INVITING YOU. BESIDES, I DIDN'T SAY ANYTHING ABOUT CAMPING. I SAID A CAMP FIRE. BIG DIFFERENCE BETWEEN JUST A CAMPFIRE AND THE WHOLE CAMPING THING. I DON'T LIKE CAMPING... OUTSIDE...
UNLESS OF COURSE I'M CAMPING WITH THAT SPECIAL SOMEONE.
DUDE, KINDA BORDERING ON CREEPY.
WELL, I THINK ALL OF US CAMPING IS A WONDERFUL IDEA!
SHE DOESN'T SEEM TO THINK SO.
SHE'S PROBABLY ON A SUGAR OVERLOAD.
THANKS TO WALLY, I GET TO TRY S'MORES FOR THE FIRST TIME!
WHAT CAN I SAY? I'M A SWEETIE! HA! GET IT? CAUSE S'MORES ARE SWEET?

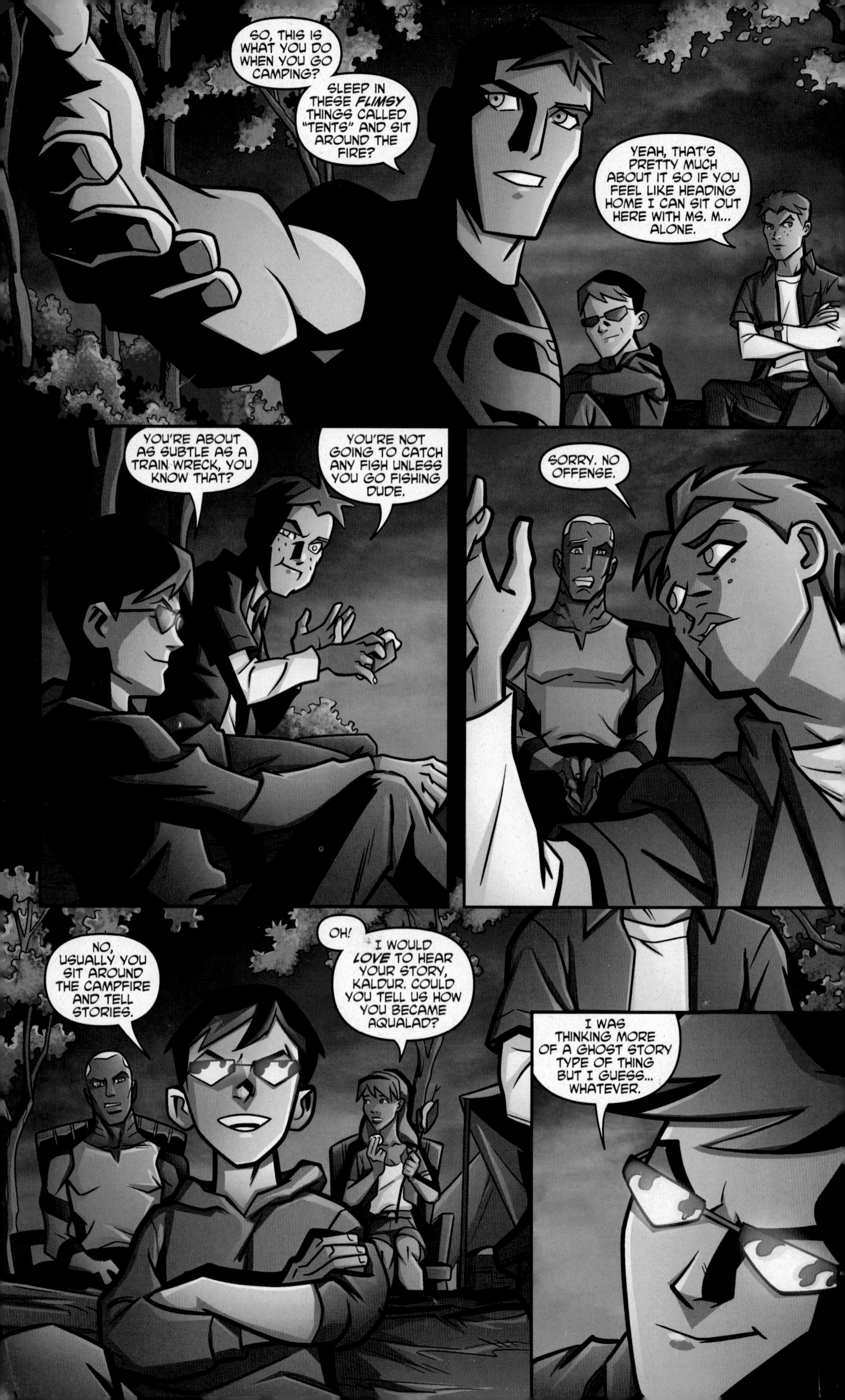
SO, THIS IS WHAT YOU DO WHEN YOU GO CAMPING?
SLEEP IN THESE *FLIMSY* THINGS CALLED "TENTS" AND SIT AROUND THE FIRE?
YEAH, THAT'S PRETTY MUCH ABOUT IT SO IF YOU FEEL LIKE HEADING HOME I CAN SIT OUT HERE WITH MS. M... ALONE.
YOU'RE ABOUT AS SUBTLE AS A TRAIN WRECK, YOU KNOW THAT?
YOU'RE NOT GOING TO CATCH ANY FISH UNLESS YOU GO FISHING DUDE.
SORRY. NO OFFENSE.
NO, USUALLY YOU SIT AROUND THE CAMPFIRE AND TELL STORIES.
OH!
I WOULD *LOVE* TO HEAR YOUR STORY, KALDUR. COULD YOU TELL US HOW YOU BECAME AQUALAD?
I WAS THINKING MORE OF A GHOST STORY TYPE OF THING BUT I GUESS... WHATEVER.

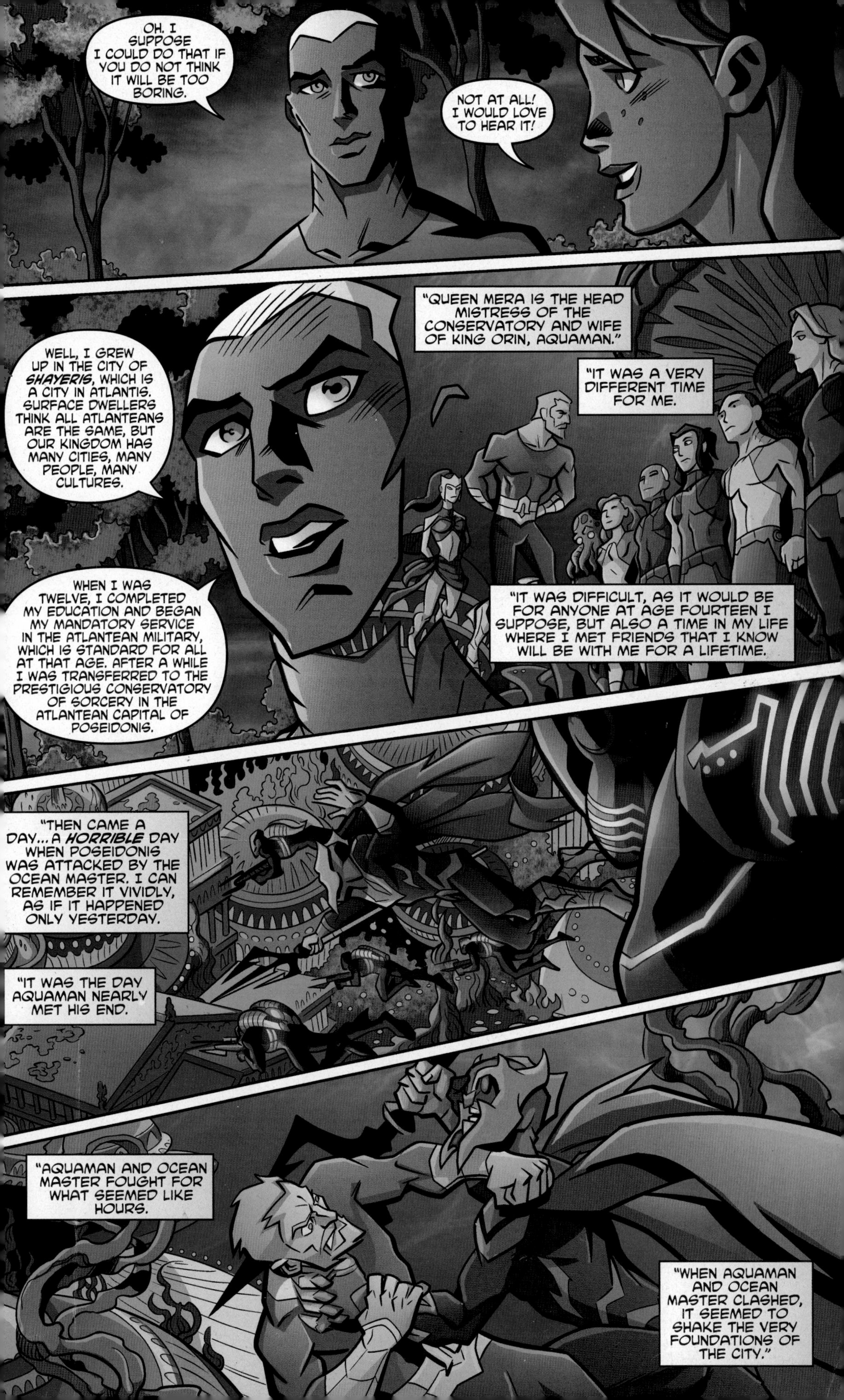
OH. I SUPPOSE I COULD DO THAT IF YOU DO NOT THINK IT WILL BE TOO BORING.
NOT AT ALL! I WOULD LOVE TO HEAR IT!
WELL, I GREW UP IN THE CITY OF SHAYERIS, WHICH IS A CITY IN ATLANTIS. SURFACE DWELLERS THINK ALL ATLANTEANS ARE THE SAME, BUT OUR KINGDOM HAS MANY CITIES, MANY PEOPLE, MANY CULTURES.
WHEN I WAS TWELVE, I COMPLETED MY EDUCATION AND BEGAN MY MANDATORY SERVICE IN THE ATLANTEAN MILITARY, WHICH IS STANDARD FOR ALL AT THAT AGE. AFTER A WHILE I WAS TRANSFERRED TO THE PRESTIGIOUS CONSERVATORY OF SORCERY IN THE ATLANTEAN CAPITAL OF POSEIDONIS.
"QUEEN MERA IS THE HEAD MISTRESS OF THE CONSERVATORY AND WIFE OF KING ORIN, AQUAMAN."
"IT WAS A VERY DIFFERENT TIME FOR ME.
"IT WAS DIFFICULT, AS IT WOULD BE FOR ANYONE AT AGE FOURTEEN I SUPPOSE, BUT ALSO A TIME IN MY LIFE WHERE I MET FRIENDS THAT I KNOW WILL BE WITH ME FOR A LIFETIME.
"THEN CAME A DAY... A HORRIBLE DAY WHEN POSEIDONIS WAS ATTACKED BY THE OCEAN MASTER. I CAN REMEMBER IT VIVIDLY, AS IF IT HAPPENED ONLY YESTERDAY.
"IT WAS THE DAY AQUAMAN NEARLY MET HIS END.
"AQUAMAN AND OCEAN MASTER FOUGHT FOR WHAT SEEMED LIKE HOURS.
"WHEN AQUAMAN AND OCEAN MASTER CLASHED, IT SEEMED TO SHAKE THE VERY FOUNDATIONS OF THE CITY."

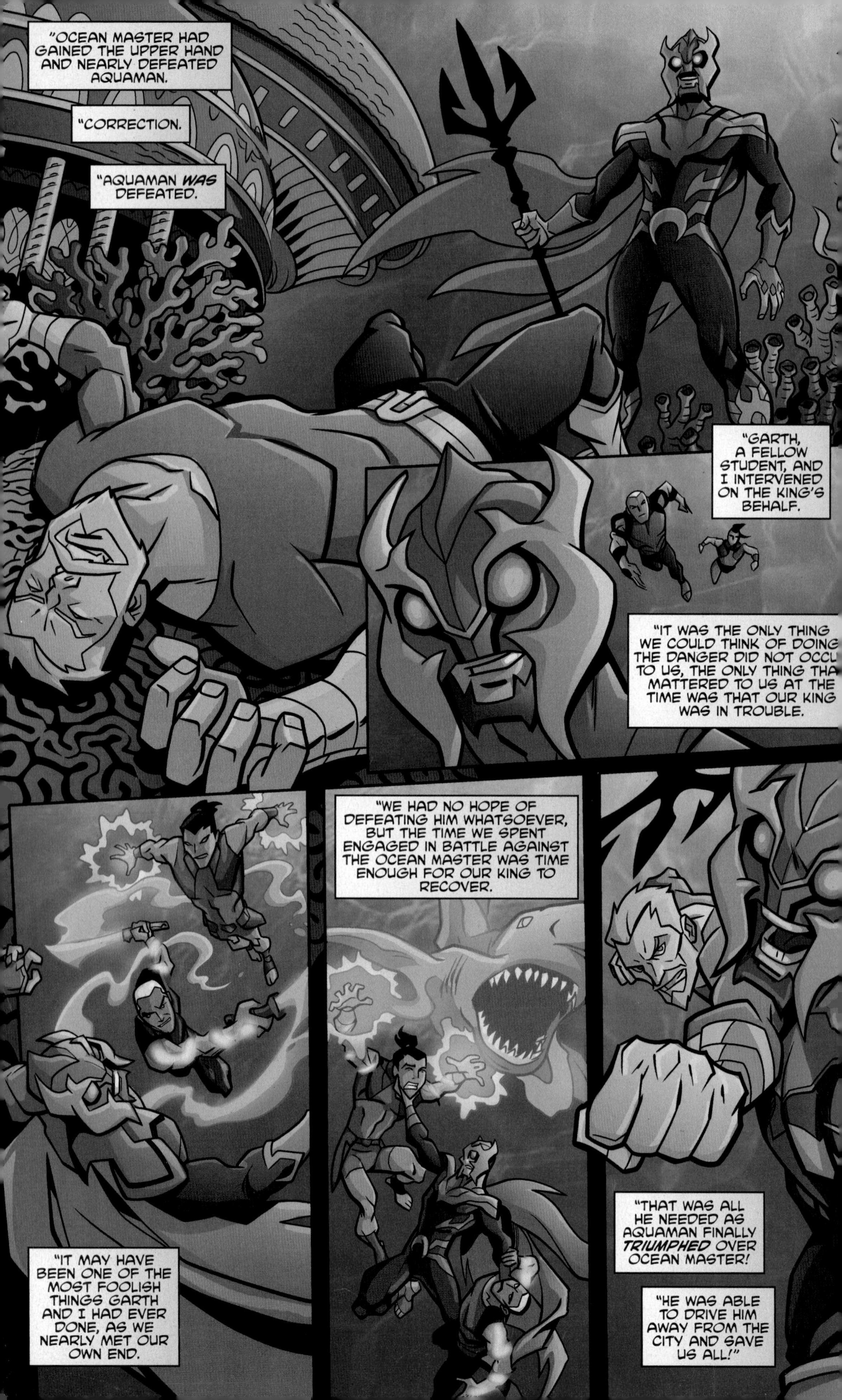
"OCEAN MASTER HAD GAINED THE UPPER HAND AND NEARLY DEFEATED AQUAMAN.
"CORRECTION.
"AQUAMAN *WAS* DEFEATED.
"GARTH, A FELLOW STUDENT, AND I INTERVENED ON THE KING'S BEHALF.
"IT WAS THE ONLY THING WE COULD THINK OF DOING THE DANGER DID NOT OCCU TO US, THE ONLY THING THA MATTERED TO US AT THE TIME WAS THAT OUR KING WAS IN TROUBLE.
"IT MAY HAVE BEEN ONE OF THE MOST FOOLISH THINGS GARTH AND I HAD EVER DONE, AS WE NEARLY MET OUR OWN END.
"WE HAD NO HOPE OF DEFEATING HIM WHATSOEVER, BUT THE TIME WE SPENT ENGAGED IN BATTLE AGAINST THE OCEAN MASTER WAS TIME ENOUGH FOR OUR KING TO RECOVER.
"THAT WAS ALL HE NEEDED AS AQUAMAN FINALLY *TRIUMPHED* OVER OCEAN MASTER!
"HE WAS ABLE TO DRIVE HIM AWAY FROM THE CITY AND SAVE US ALL!"

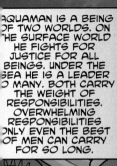

AQUAMAN IS A BEING OF TWO WORLDS. ON THE SURFACE WORLD HE FIGHTS FOR JUSTICE FOR ALL BEINGS. UNDER THE SEA HE IS A LEADER TO MANY. BOTH CARRY THE WEIGHT OF RESPONSIBILITIES. OVERWHELMING RESPONSIBILITIES ONLY EVEN THE BEST OF MEN CAN CARRY FOR SO LONG.

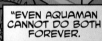

"EVEN AQUAMAN CANNOT DO BOTH FOREVER.

"REALIZING THAT ON THE SURFACE BOTH BATMAN AND GREEN ARROW HAD TAKEN ON *APPRENTICES* THAT COULD ONE DAY TAKE OVER THEIR RESPECTIVE MANTELS, KING ORIN HAD BEEN CONTEMPLATING THE SAME IDEA.

"WITH THIS IN MIND, HE APPROACHED BOTH GARTH AND MYSELF WITH THE POSSIBILITY OF BECOMING HIS PROTÉGÉS.

"I MUST ADMIT THE POSSIBILITY INTRIGUED ME IMMEDIATELY.

"I HAD NEVER BEEN TO THE SURFACE WORLD. AND I AM THE FIRST TO ADMIT THAT I AM A BIT OF AN ADVENTURER. MANY IS THE DAY IN CLASS THAT I WOULD DREAM OF VISITING DISTANT OCEANS AND POSSIBLY ONE DAY EVEN THE SURFACE WORLD.

"BOTH GARTH AND I *SERIOUSLY* CONSIDERED THE KING'S OFFER.

"GARTH ULTIMATELY CHOSE TO CONTINUE HIS STUDIES WITH QUEEN MERA AT THE CONSERVATORY OF SORCERY.

"FOR ME, HOWEVER, THE CHANCE TO VISIT THE SURFACE WORLD WAS A DREAM COME TRUE."

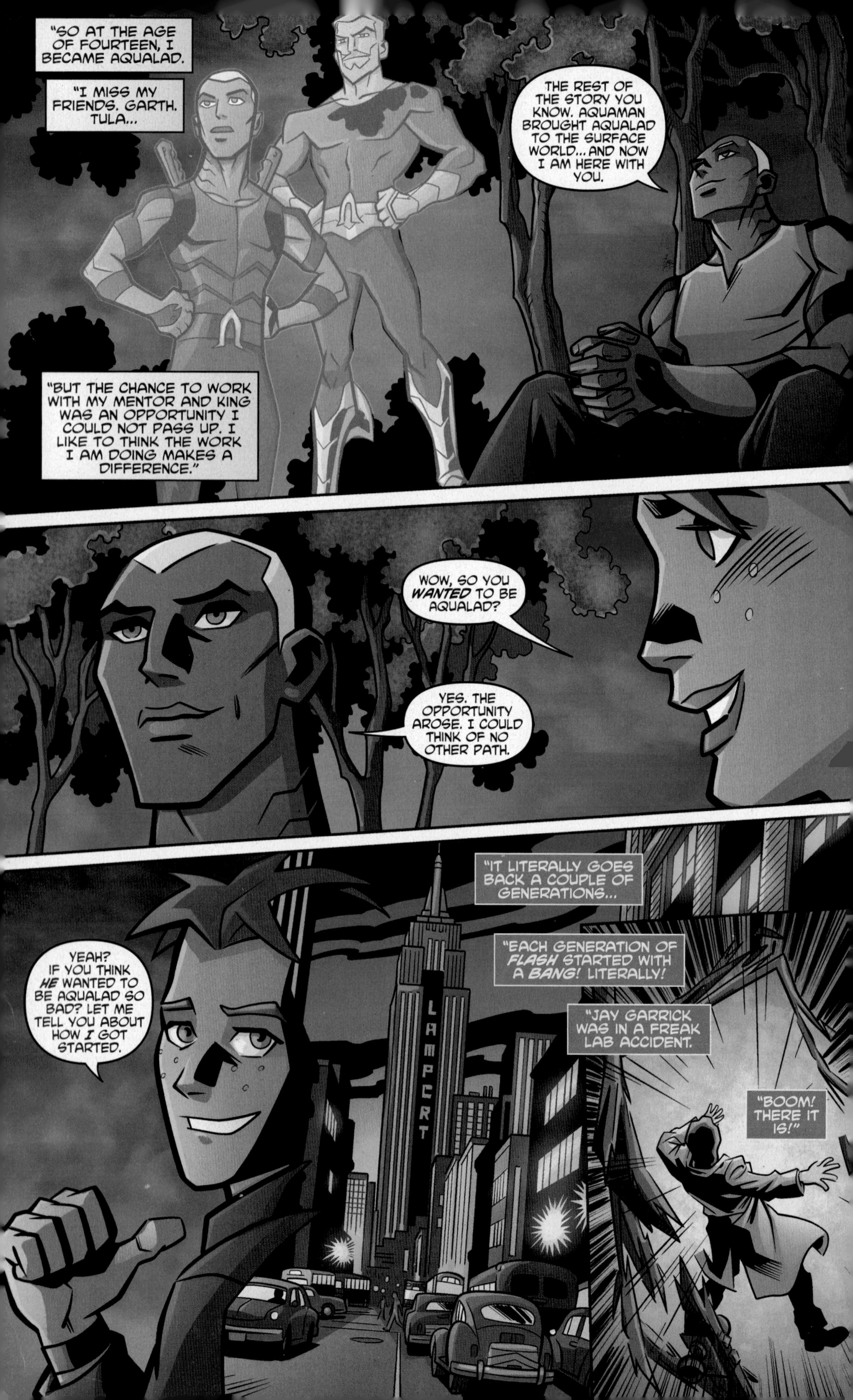
"SO AT THE AGE OF FOURTEEN, I BECAME AQUALAD.
"I MISS MY FRIENDS. GARTH. TULA...
"BUT THE CHANCE TO WORK WITH MY MENTOR AND KING WAS AN OPPORTUNITY I COULD NOT PASS UP. I LIKE TO THINK THE WORK I AM DOING MAKES A DIFFERENCE."
THE REST OF THE STORY YOU KNOW. AQUAMAN BROUGHT AQUALAD TO THE SURFACE WORLD... AND NOW I AM HERE WITH YOU.
WOW, SO YOU *WANTED* TO BE AQUALAD?
YES. THE OPPORTUNITY AROSE. I COULD THINK OF NO OTHER PATH.
YEAH? IF YOU THINK *HE* WANTED TO BE AQUALAD SO BAD? LET ME TELL YOU ABOUT HOW *I* GOT STARTED.
"IT LITERALLY GOES BACK A COUPLE OF GENERATIONS...
"EACH GENERATION OF *FLASH* STARTED WITH A *BANG*! LITERALLY!
"JAY GARRICK WAS IN A FREAK LAB ACCIDENT.
"BOOM! THERE IT IS!"
LAMPCRT

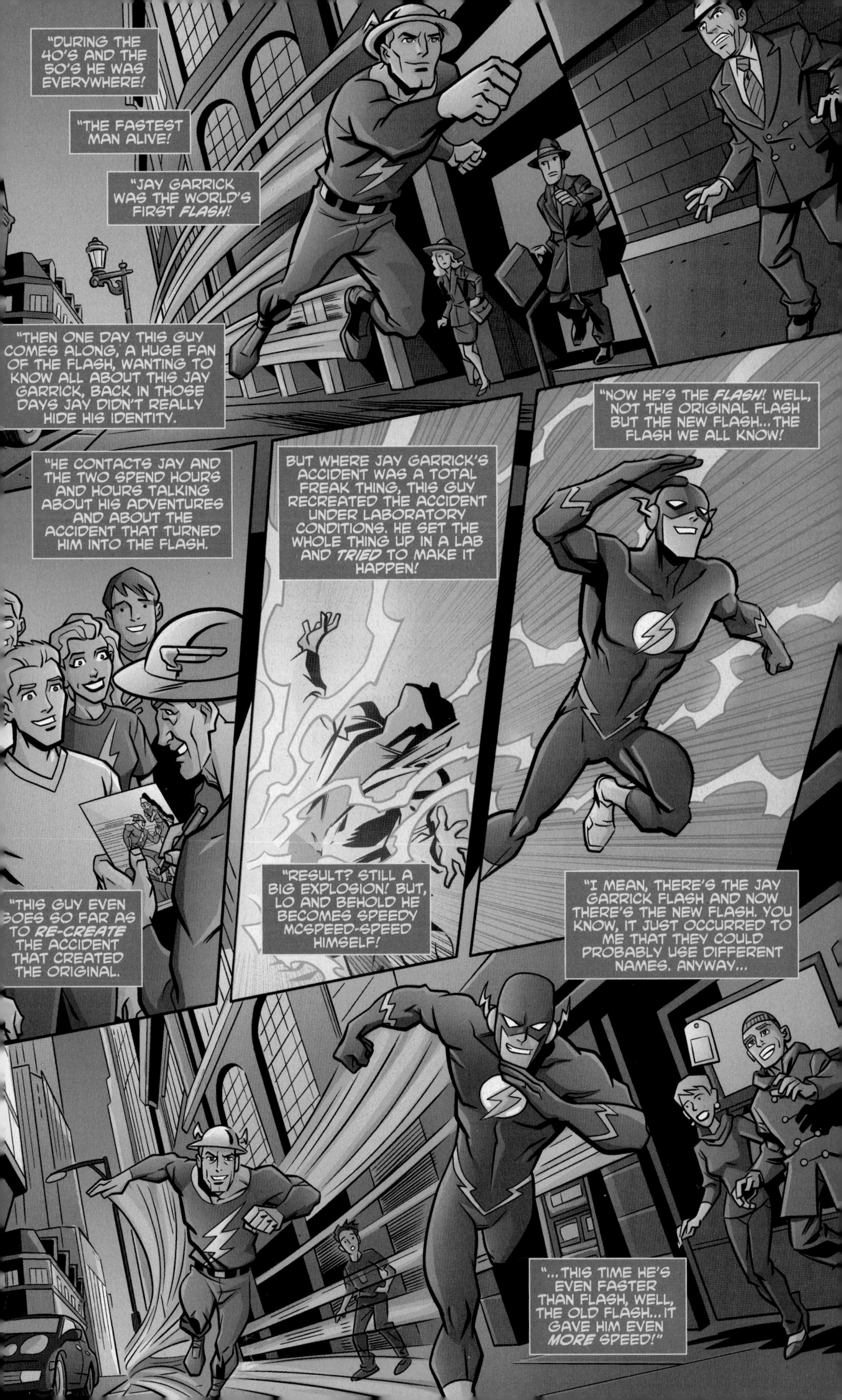
"DURING THE 40'S AND THE 50'S HE WAS EVERYWHERE!
"THE FASTEST MAN ALIVE!
"JAY GARRICK WAS THE WORLD'S FIRST FLASH!
"THEN ONE DAY THIS GUY COMES ALONG, A HUGE FAN OF THE FLASH, WANTING TO KNOW ALL ABOUT THIS JAY GARRICK, BACK IN THOSE DAYS JAY DIDN'T REALLY HIDE HIS IDENTITY.
"HE CONTACTS JAY AND THE TWO SPEND HOURS AND HOURS TALKING ABOUT HIS ADVENTURES AND ABOUT THE ACCIDENT THAT TURNED HIM INTO THE FLASH.
"THIS GUY EVEN GOES SO FAR AS TO RE-CREATE THE ACCIDENT THAT CREATED THE ORIGINAL.
BUT WHERE JAY GARRICK'S ACCIDENT WAS A TOTAL FREAK THING, THIS GUY RECREATED THE ACCIDENT UNDER LABORATORY CONDITIONS. HE SET THE WHOLE THING UP IN A LAB AND TRIED TO MAKE IT HAPPEN!
"RESULT? STILL A BIG EXPLOSION! BUT, LO AND BEHOLD HE BECOMES SPEEDY MCSPEED-SPEED HIMSELF!
"NOW HE'S THE FLASH! WELL, NOT THE ORIGINAL FLASH BUT THE NEW FLASH...THE FLASH WE ALL KNOW!
"I MEAN, THERE'S THE JAY GARRICK FLASH AND NOW THERE'S THE NEW FLASH. YOU KNOW, IT JUST OCCURRED TO ME THAT THEY COULD PROBABLY USE DIFFERENT NAMES. ANYWAY...
"...THIS TIME HE'S EVEN FASTER THAN FLASH, WELL, THE OLD FLASH...IT GAVE HIM EVEN MORE SPEED!"

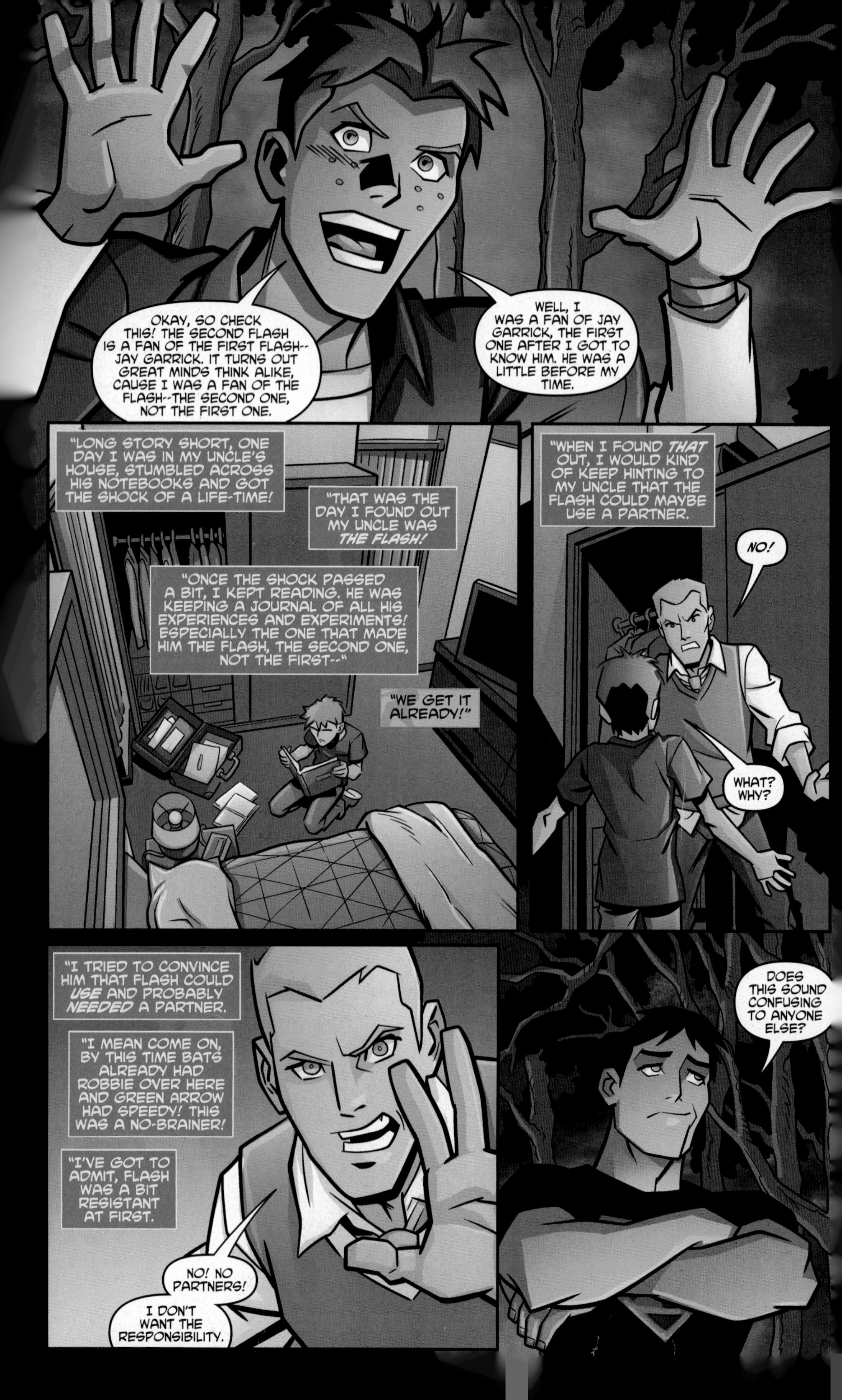
OKAY, SO CHECK THIS! THE SECOND FLASH IS A FAN OF THE FIRST FLASH--JAY GARRICK. IT TURNS OUT GREAT MINDS THINK ALIKE, CAUSE I WAS A FAN OF THE FLASH--THE SECOND ONE, NOT THE FIRST ONE.
WELL, I WAS A FAN OF JAY GARRICK, THE FIRST ONE AFTER I GOT TO KNOW HIM. HE WAS A LITTLE BEFORE MY TIME.
"LONG STORY SHORT, ONE DAY I WAS IN MY UNCLE'S HOUSE, STUMBLED ACROSS HIS NOTEBOOKS AND GOT THE SHOCK OF A LIFE-TIME!
"THAT WAS THE DAY I FOUND OUT MY UNCLE WAS *THE FLASH!*
"ONCE THE SHOCK PASSED A BIT, I KEPT READING. HE WAS KEEPING A JOURNAL OF ALL HIS EXPERIENCES AND EXPERIMENTS! ESPECIALLY THE ONE THAT MADE HIM THE FLASH, THE SECOND ONE, NOT THE FIRST--"
"WE GET IT ALREADY!"
"WHEN I FOUND *THAT* OUT, I WOULD KIND OF KEEP HINTING TO MY UNCLE THAT THE FLASH COULD MAYBE USE A PARTNER.
NO!
WHAT? WHY?
"I TRIED TO CONVINCE HIM THAT FLASH COULD *USE* AND PROBABLY *NEEDED* A PARTNER.
"I MEAN COME ON, BY THIS TIME BATS ALREADY HAD ROBBIE OVER HERE AND GREEN ARROW HAD SPEEDY! THIS WAS A NO-BRAINER!
"I'VE GOT TO ADMIT, FLASH WAS A BIT RESISTANT AT FIRST.
NO! NO PARTNERS!
I DON'T WANT THE RESPONSIBILITY.
DOES THIS SOUND CONFUSING TO ANYONE ELSE?

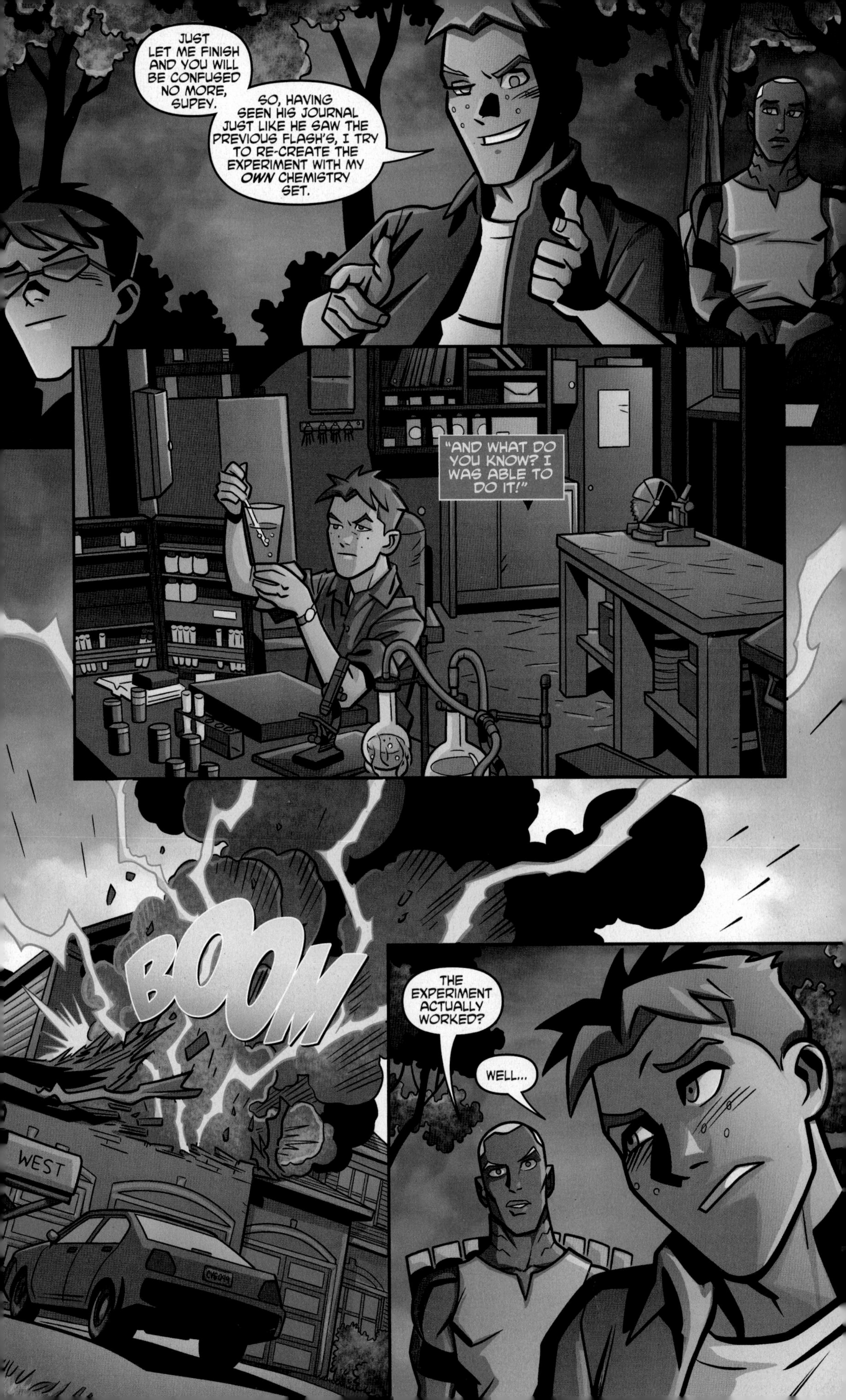
JUST LET ME FINISH AND YOU WILL BE CONFUSED NO MORE, SUPEY.
SO, HAVING SEEN HIS JOURNAL JUST LIKE HE SAW THE PREVIOUS FLASH'S, I TRY TO RE-CREATE THE EXPERIMENT WITH MY *OWN* CHEMISTRY SET.
"AND WHAT DO YOU KNOW? I WAS ABLE TO DO IT!"
BOOM
WEST
THE EXPERIMENT ACTUALLY WORKED?
WELL...

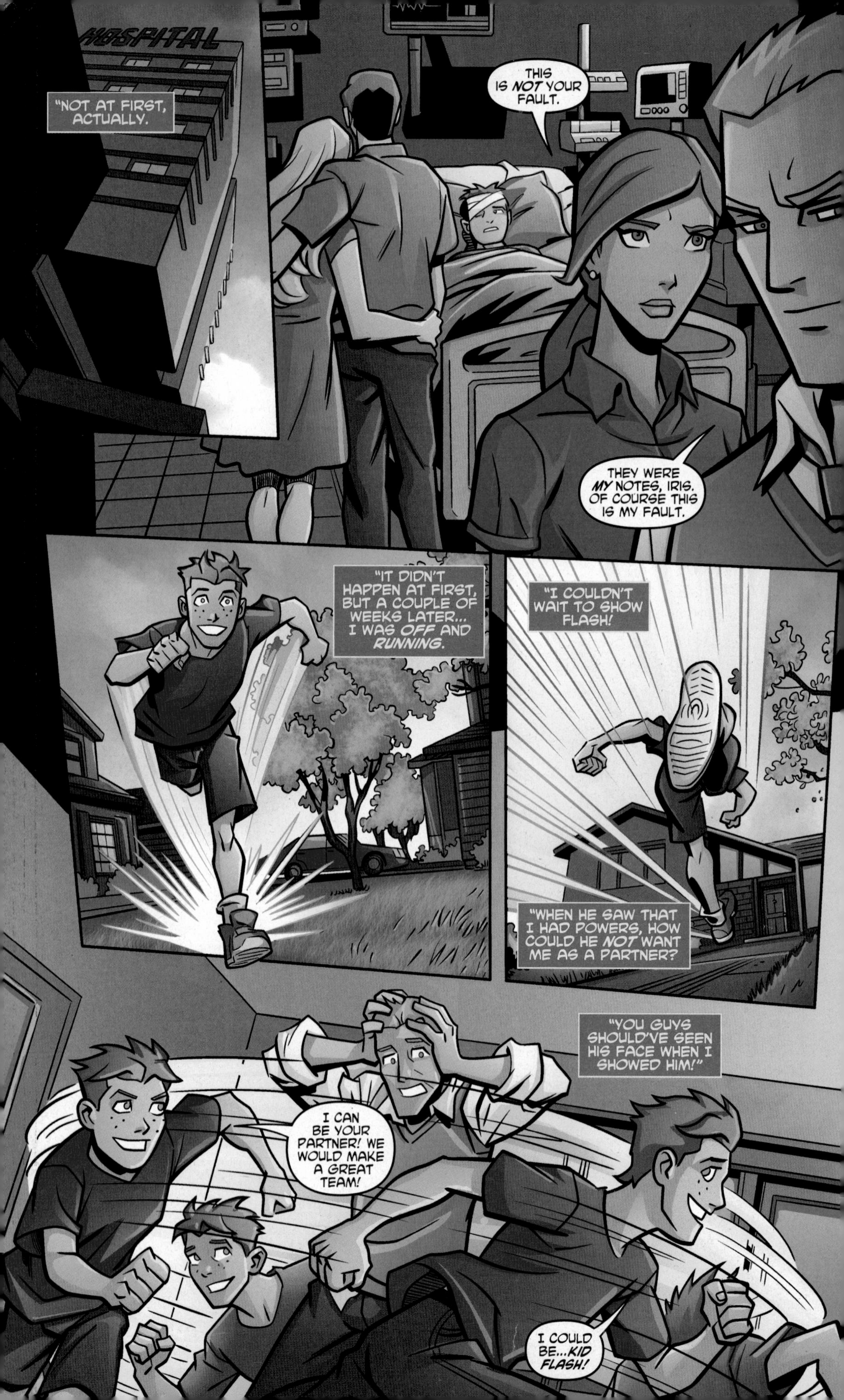
HOSPITAL
"NOT AT FIRST, ACTUALLY.
THIS IS *NOT* YOUR FAULT.
THEY WERE *MY* NOTES, IRIS. OF COURSE THIS IS MY FAULT.
"IT DIDN'T HAPPEN AT FIRST, BUT A COUPLE OF WEEKS LATER... I WAS *OFF* AND *RUNNING*.
"I COULDN'T WAIT TO SHOW FLASH!
"WHEN HE SAW THAT I HAD POWERS, HOW COULD HE *NOT* WANT ME AS A PARTNER?
"YOU GUYS SHOULD'VE SEEN HIS FACE WHEN I SHOWED HIM!"
I CAN BE YOUR PARTNER! WE WOULD MAKE A GREAT TEAM!
I COULD BE...*KID FLASH!*

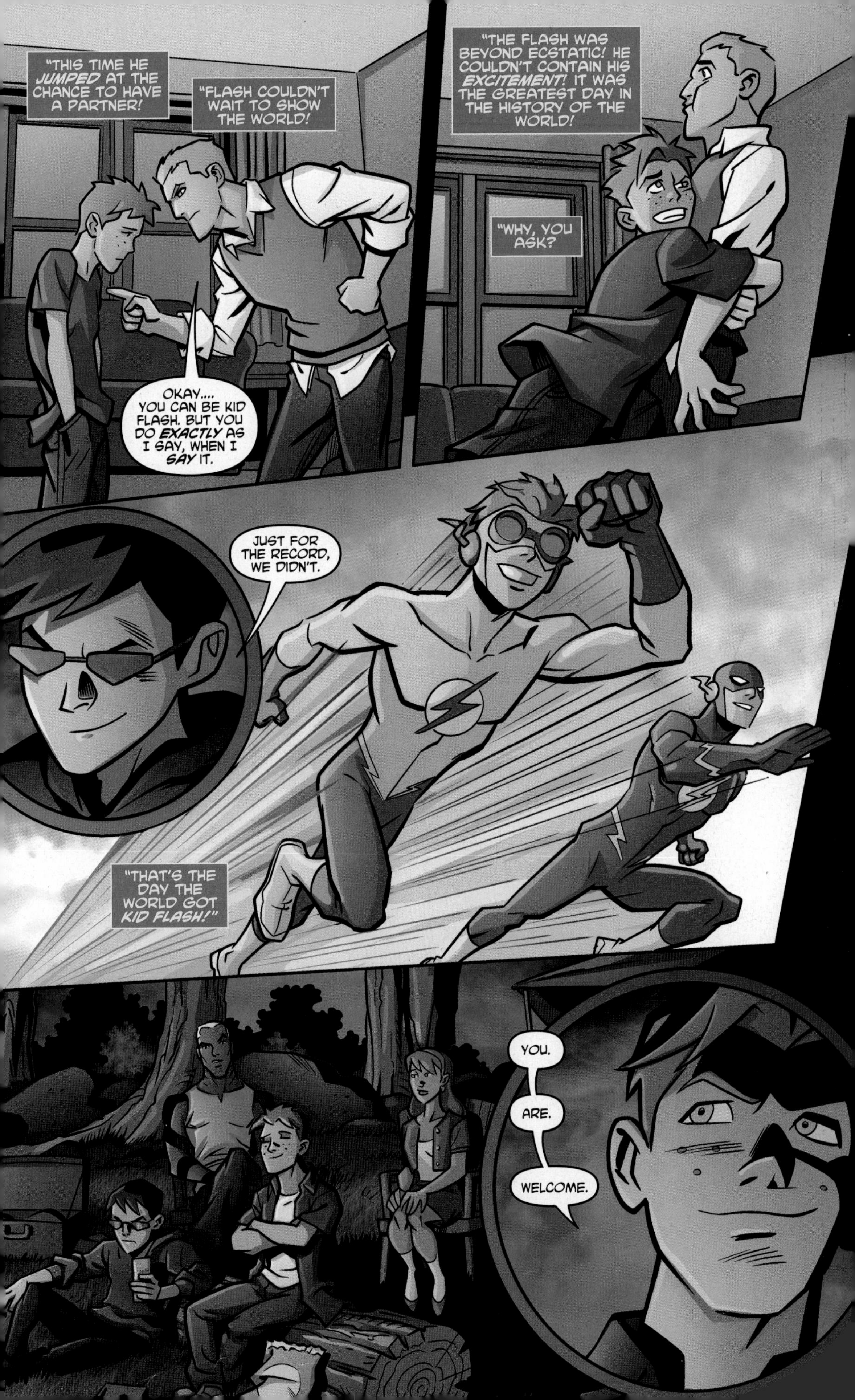
"THIS TIME HE JUMPED AT THE CHANCE TO HAVE A PARTNER!
"FLASH COULDN'T WAIT TO SHOW THE WORLD!
OKAY.... YOU CAN BE KID FLASH. BUT YOU DO EXACTLY AS I SAY, WHEN I SAY IT.
"THE FLASH WAS BEYOND ECSTATIC! HE COULDN'T CONTAIN HIS EXCITEMENT! IT WAS THE GREATEST DAY IN THE HISTORY OF THE WORLD!
"WHY, YOU ASK?
JUST FOR THE RECORD, WE DIDN'T.
"THAT'S THE DAY THE WORLD GOT KID FLASH!"
YOU.
ARE.
WELCOME.

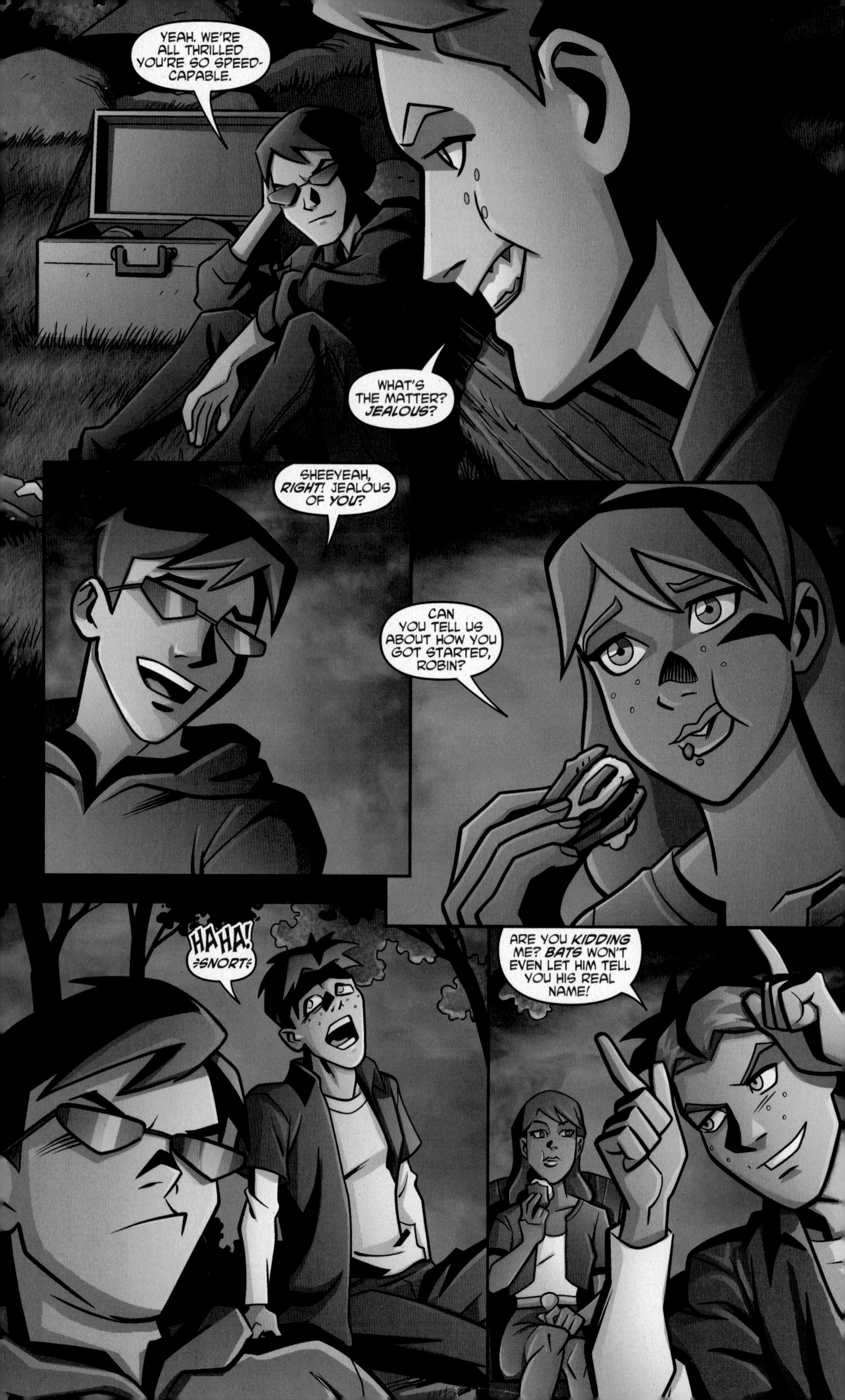
YEAH. WE'RE ALL THRILLED YOU'RE SO SPEED-CAPABLE.
WHAT'S THE MATTER? *JEALOUS?*
SHEEYEAH, *RIGHT!* JEALOUS OF *YOU?*
CAN YOU TELL US ABOUT HOW YOU GOT STARTED, ROBIN?
HAHA! *SNORT*
ARE YOU *KIDDING* ME? *BATS* WON'T EVEN LET HIM TELL YOU HIS REAL NAME!

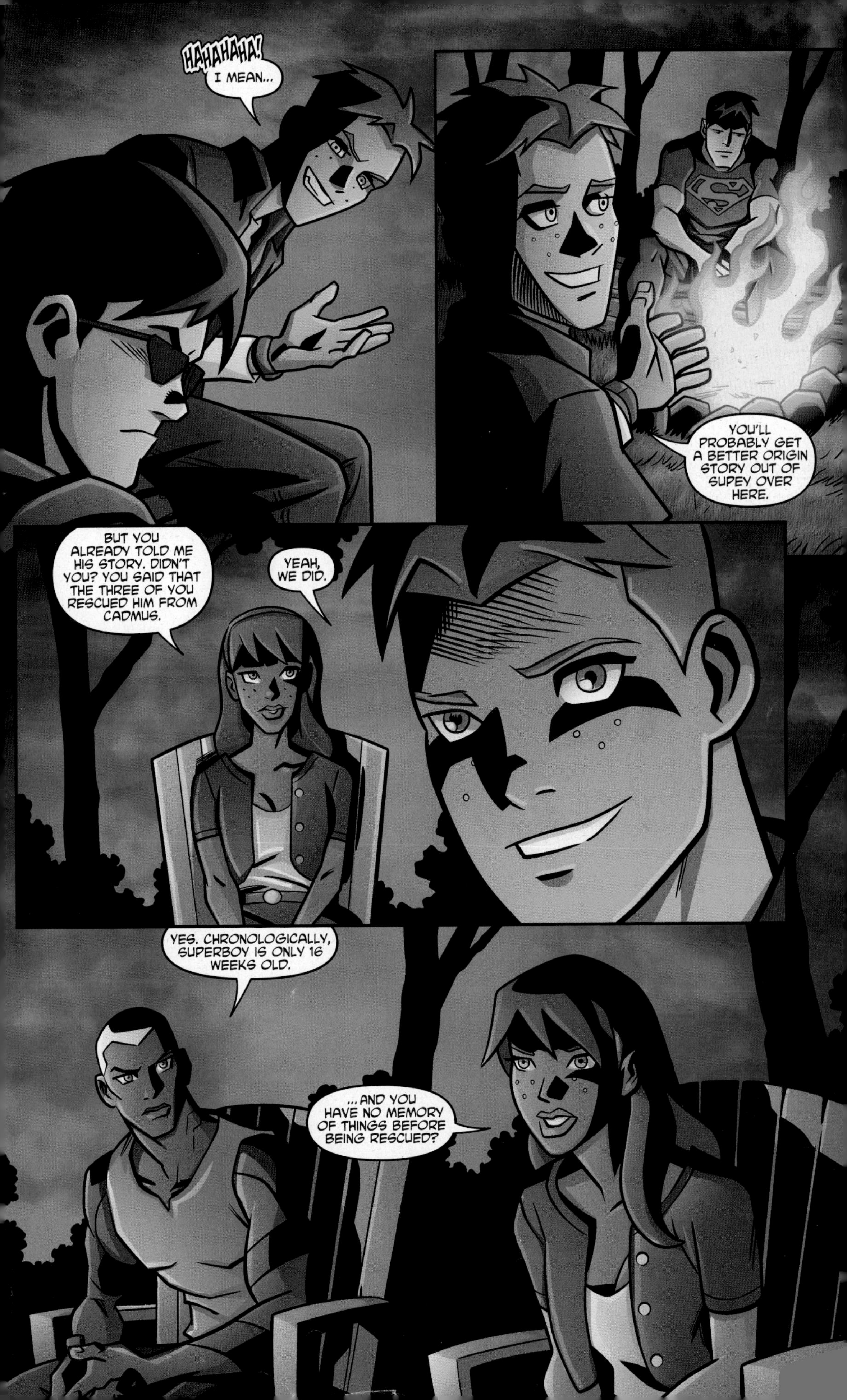
HAHAHAHA!
I MEAN...
YOU'LL PROBABLY GET A BETTER ORIGIN STORY OUT OF SUPEY OVER HERE.
BUT YOU ALREADY TOLD ME HIS STORY. DIDN'T YOU? YOU SAID THAT THE THREE OF YOU RESCUED HIM FROM CADMUS.
YEAH, WE DID.
YES. CHRONOLOGICALLY, SUPERBOY IS ONLY 16 WEEKS OLD.
...AND YOU HAVE NO MEMORY OF THINGS BEFORE BEING RESCUED?

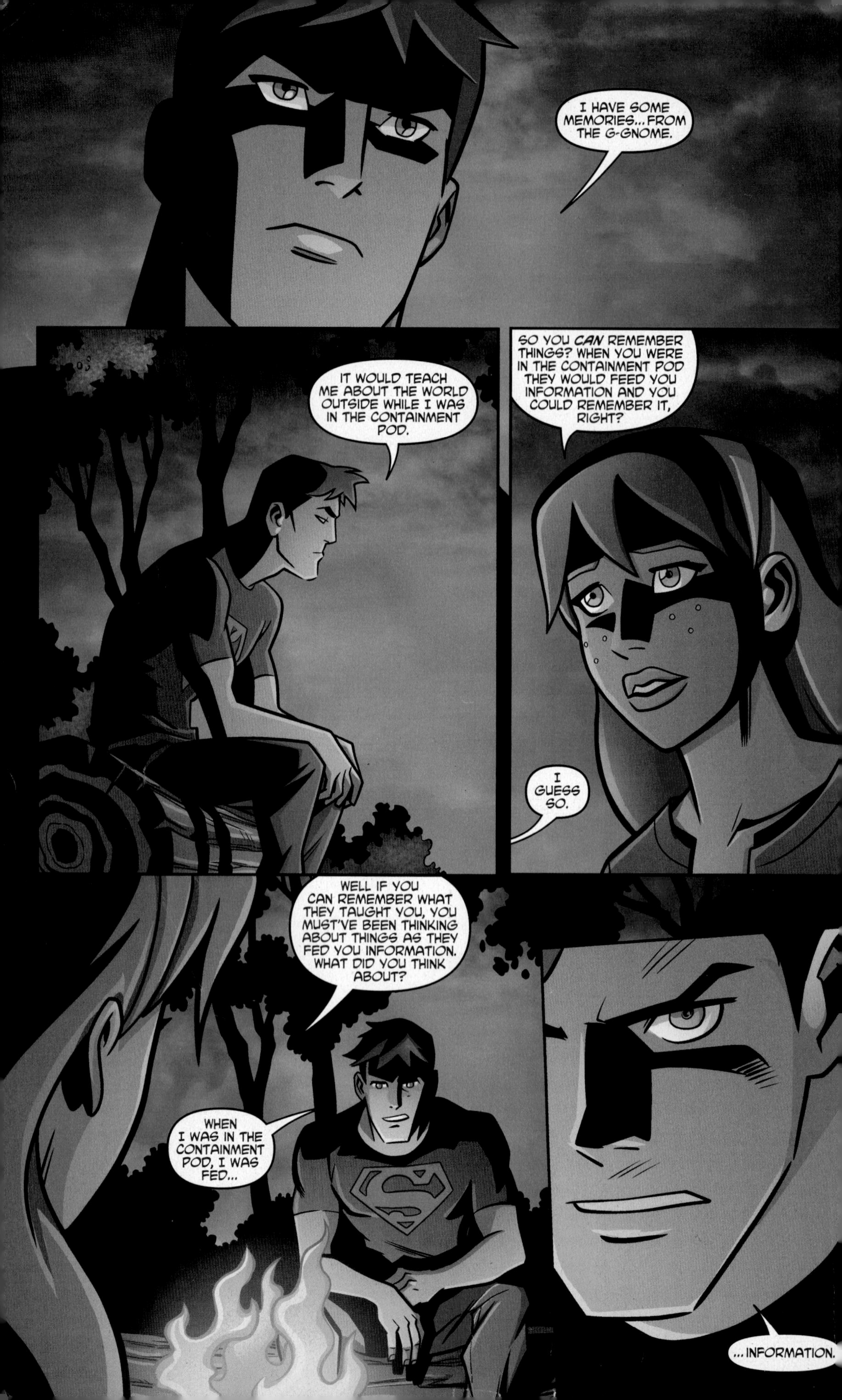

I HAVE SOME MEMORIES...FROM THE G-GNOME.
IT WOULD TEACH ME ABOUT THE WORLD OUTSIDE WHILE I WAS IN THE CONTAINMENT POD.
SO YOU CAN REMEMBER THINGS? WHEN YOU WERE IN THE CONTAINMENT POD THEY WOULD FEED YOU INFORMATION AND YOU COULD REMEMBER IT, RIGHT?
I GUESS SO.
WELL IF YOU CAN REMEMBER WHAT THEY TAUGHT YOU, YOU MUST'VE BEEN THINKING ABOUT THINGS AS THEY FED YOU INFORMATION. WHAT DID YOU THINK ABOUT?
WHEN I WAS IN THE CONTAINMENT POD, I WAS FED...
...INFORMATION.

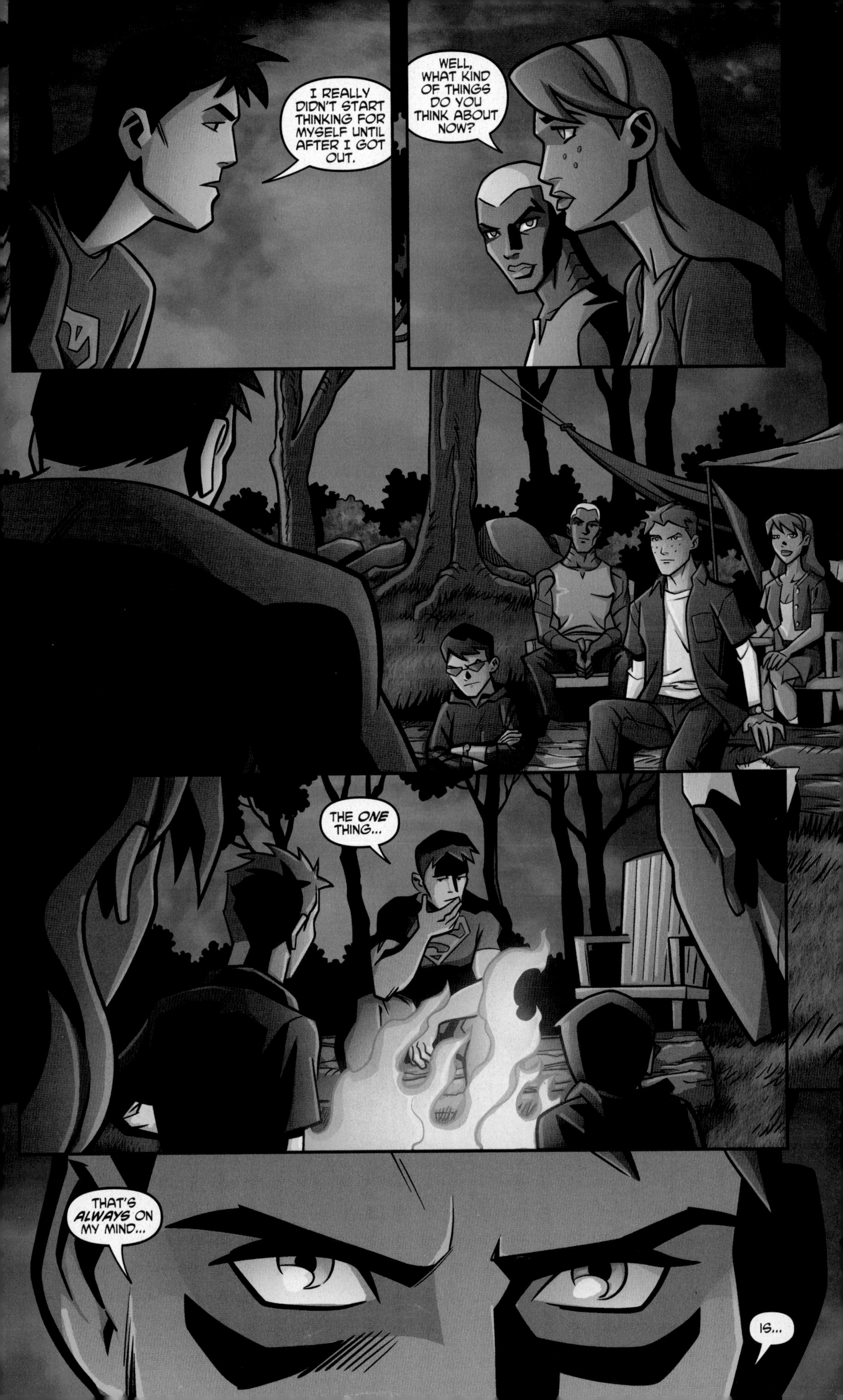
I REALLY DIDN'T START THINKING FOR MYSELF UNTIL AFTER I GOT OUT.
WELL, WHAT KIND OF THINGS DO YOU THINK ABOUT NOW?
THE *ONE* THING...
THAT'S ***ALWAYS*** ON MY MIND...
IS...

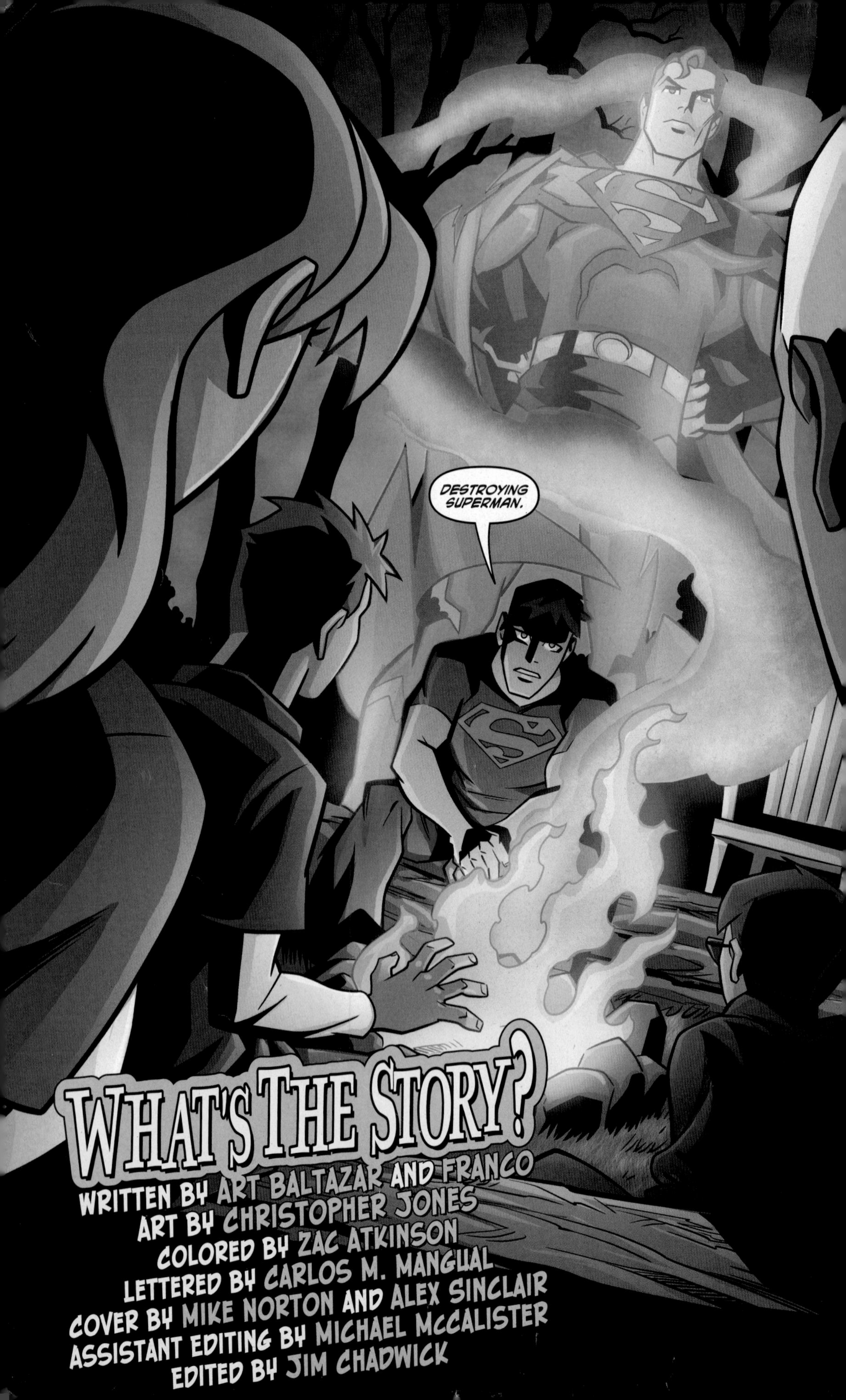
DESTROYING SUPERMAN.
WHAT'S THE STORY?
WRITTEN BY ART BALTAZAR AND FRANCO
ART BY CHRISTOPHER JONES
COLORED BY ZAC ATKINSON
LETTERED BY CARLOS M. MANGUAL
COVER BY MIKE NORTON AND ALEX SINCLAIR
ASSISTANT EDITING BY MICHAEL McCALISTER
EDITED BY JIM CHADWICK

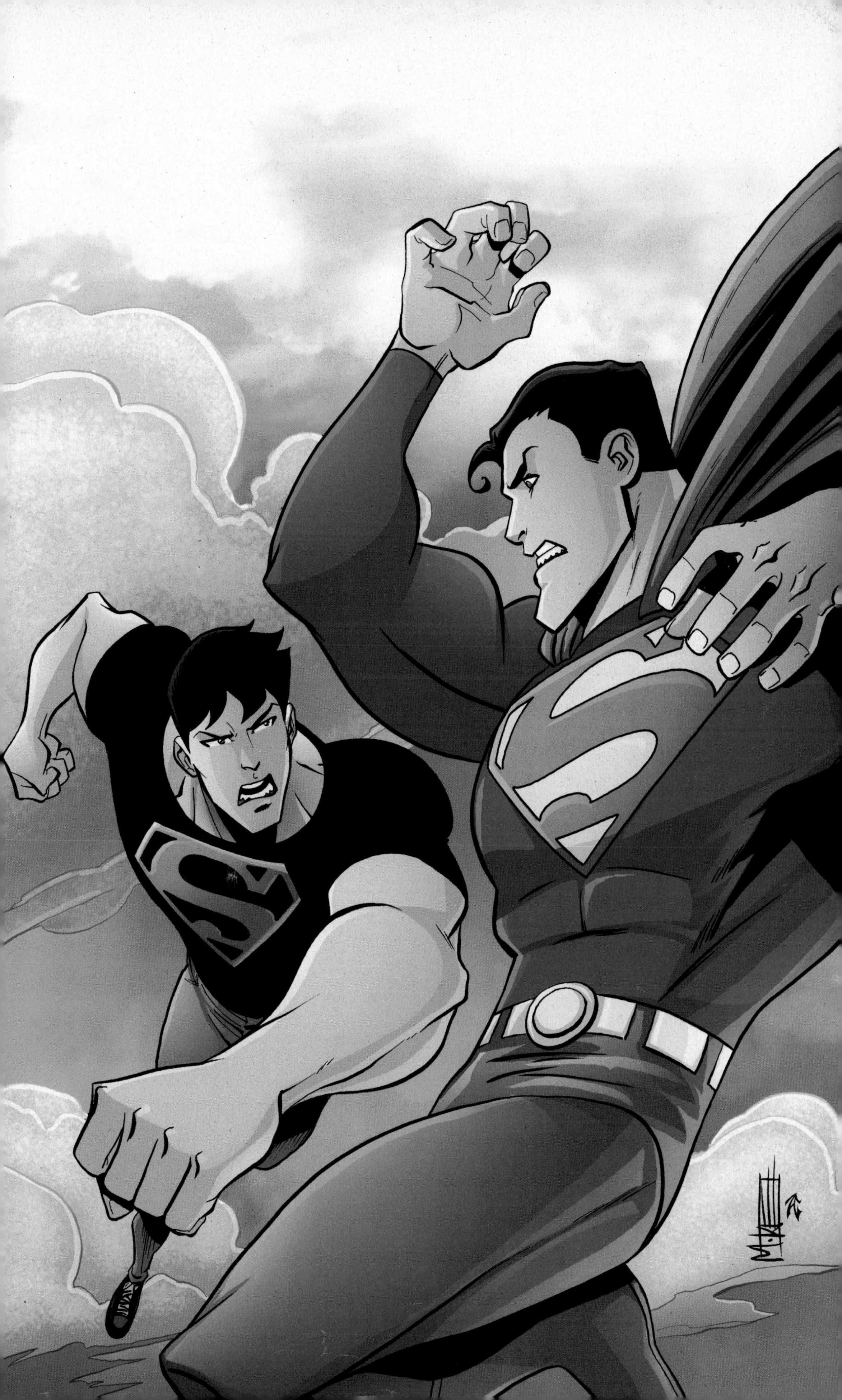

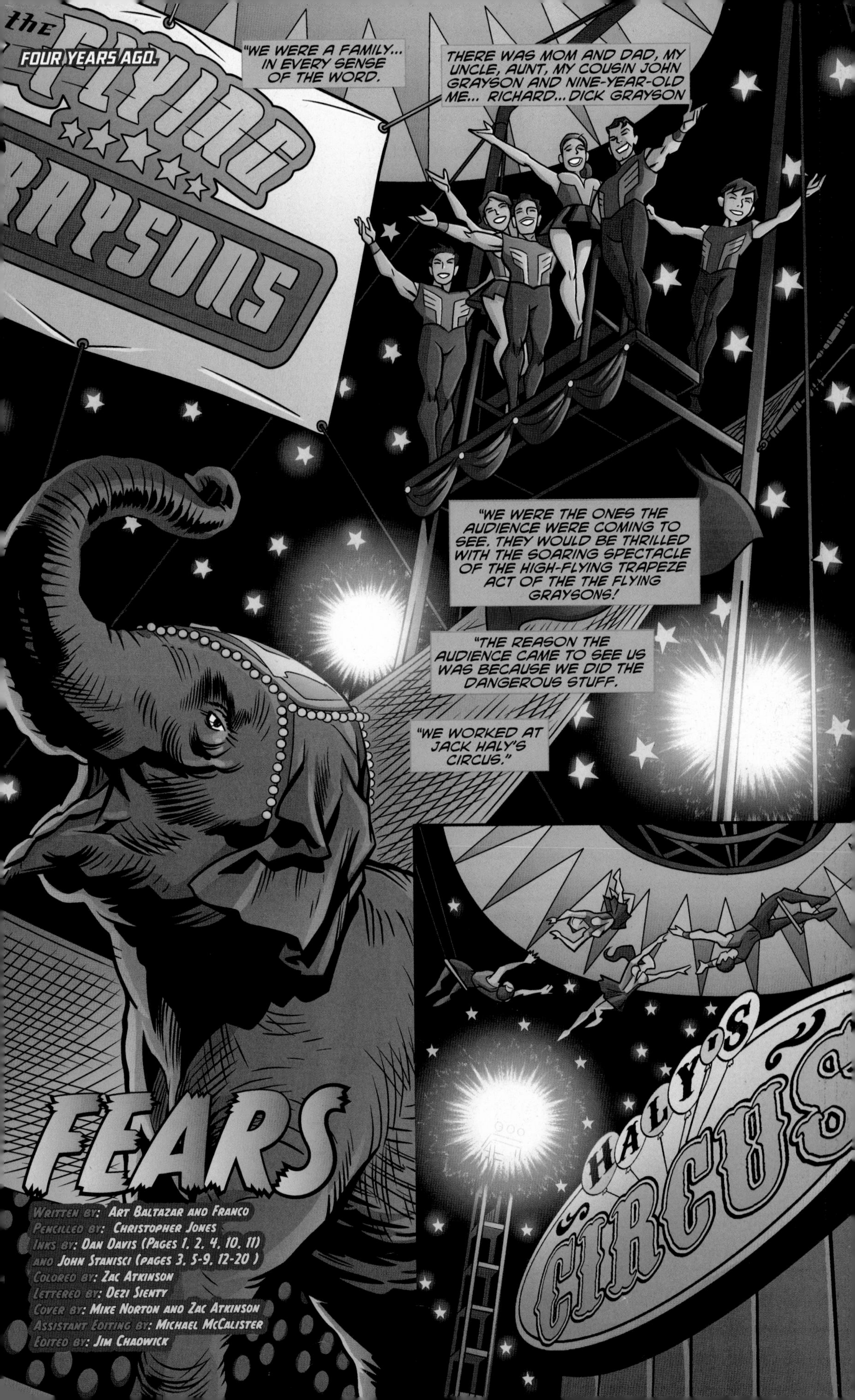
the FLYING GRAYSONS
FOUR YEARS AGO.
"WE WERE A FAMILY... IN EVERY SENSE OF THE WORD.
THERE WAS MOM AND DAD, MY UNCLE, AUNT, MY COUSIN JOHN GRAYSON AND NINE-YEAR-OLD ME... RICHARD... DICK GRAYSON
"WE WERE THE ONES THE AUDIENCE WERE COMING TO SEE. THEY WOULD BE THRILLED WITH THE SOARING SPECTACLE OF THE HIGH-FLYING TRAPEZE ACT OF THE THE FLYING GRAYSONS!
"THE REASON THE AUDIENCE CAME TO SEE US WAS BECAUSE WE DID THE DANGEROUS STUFF.
"WE WORKED AT JACK HALY'S CIRCUS."
FEARS
WRITTEN BY: ART BALTAZAR AND FRANCO
PENCILLED BY: CHRISTOPHER JONES
INKS BY: DAN DAVIS (PAGES 1, 2, 4, 10, 11)
AND JOHN STANISCI (PAGES 3, 5-9, 12-20)
COLORED BY: ZAC ATKINSON
LETTERED BY: DEZI SIENTY
COVER BY: MIKE NORTON AND ZAC ATKINSON
ASSISTANT EDITING BY: MICHAEL MCCALISTER
EDITED BY: JIM CHADWICK
HALY'S CIRCUS

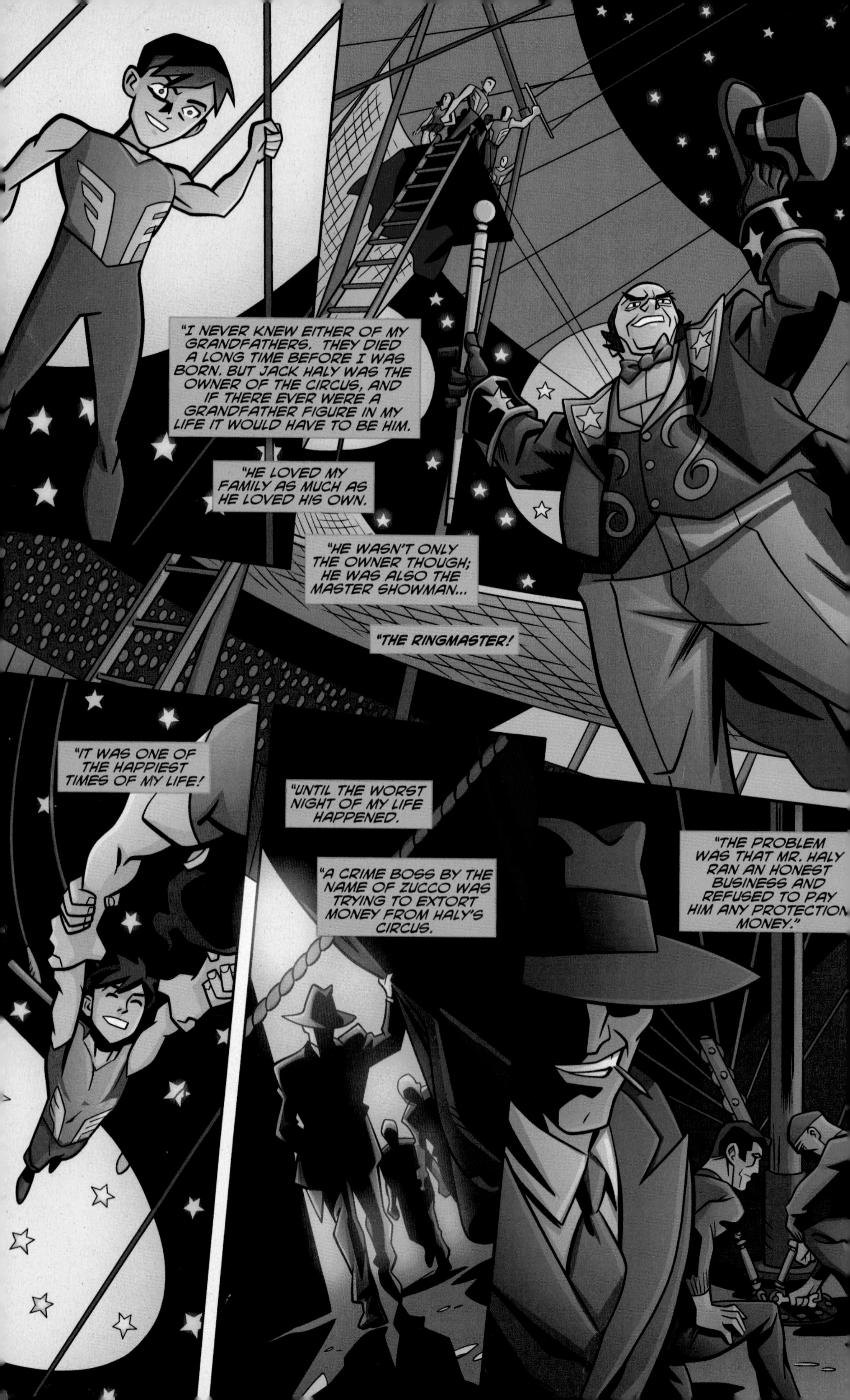
"I NEVER KNEW EITHER OF MY GRANDFATHERS. THEY DIED A LONG TIME BEFORE I WAS BORN. BUT JACK HALY WAS THE OWNER OF THE CIRCUS, AND IF THERE EVER WERE A GRANDFATHER FIGURE IN MY LIFE IT WOULD HAVE TO BE HIM.
"HE LOVED MY FAMILY AS MUCH AS HE LOVED HIS OWN.
"HE WASN'T ONLY THE OWNER THOUGH; HE WAS ALSO THE MASTER SHOWMAN...
"THE RINGMASTER!
"IT WAS ONE OF THE HAPPIEST TIMES OF MY LIFE!
"UNTIL THE WORST NIGHT OF MY LIFE HAPPENED.
"A CRIME BOSS BY THE NAME OF ZUCCO WAS TRYING TO EXTORT MONEY FROM HALY'S CIRCUS.
"THE PROBLEM WAS THAT MR. HALY RAN AN HONEST BUSINESS AND REFUSED TO PAY HIM ANY PROTECTION MONEY."

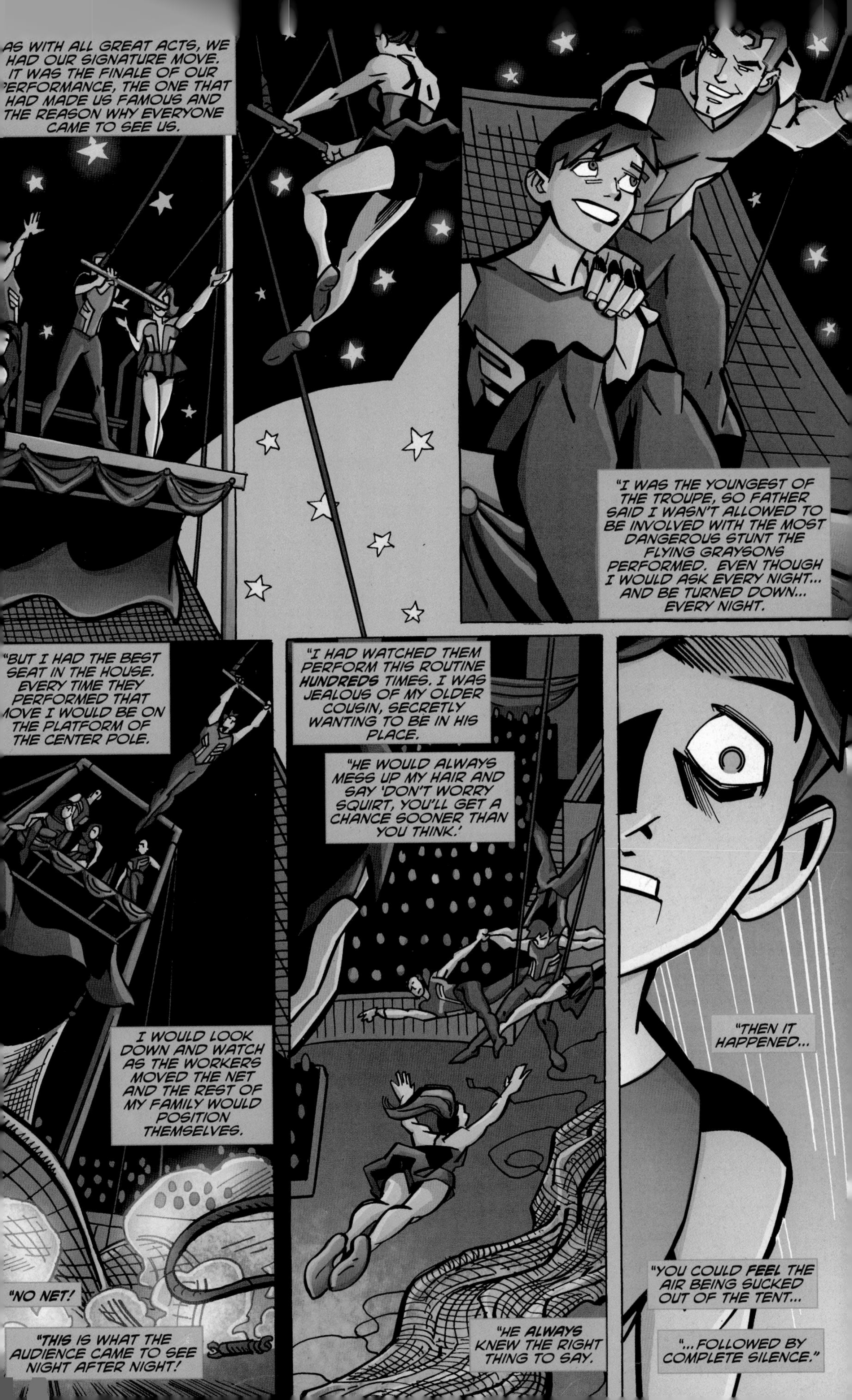

AS WITH ALL GREAT ACTS, WE HAD OUR SIGNATURE MOVE. IT WAS THE FINALE OF OUR PERFORMANCE, THE ONE THAT HAD MADE US FAMOUS AND THE REASON WHY EVERYONE CAME TO SEE US.
"I WAS THE YOUNGEST OF THE TROUPE, SO FATHER SAID I WASN'T ALLOWED TO BE INVOLVED WITH THE MOST DANGEROUS STUNT THE FLYING GRAYSONS PERFORMED. EVEN THOUGH I WOULD ASK EVERY NIGHT... AND BE TURNED DOWN... EVERY NIGHT.
"BUT I HAD THE BEST SEAT IN THE HOUSE. EVERY TIME THEY PERFORMED THAT MOVE I WOULD BE ON THE PLATFORM OF THE CENTER POLE.
I WOULD LOOK DOWN AND WATCH AS THE WORKERS MOVED THE NET AND THE REST OF MY FAMILY WOULD POSITION THEMSELVES.
"NO NET!
"THIS IS WHAT THE AUDIENCE CAME TO SEE NIGHT AFTER NIGHT!
"I HAD WATCHED THEM PERFORM THIS ROUTINE HUNDREDS TIMES. I WAS JEALOUS OF MY OLDER COUSIN, SECRETLY WANTING TO BE IN HIS PLACE.
"HE WOULD ALWAYS MESS UP MY HAIR AND SAY 'DON'T WORRY SQUIRT, YOU'LL GET A CHANCE SOONER THAN YOU THINK.'
"HE ALWAYS KNEW THE RIGHT THING TO SAY.
"THEN IT HAPPENED...
"YOU COULD FEEL THE AIR BEING SUCKED OUT OF THE TENT...
"...FOLLOWED BY COMPLETE SILENCE."

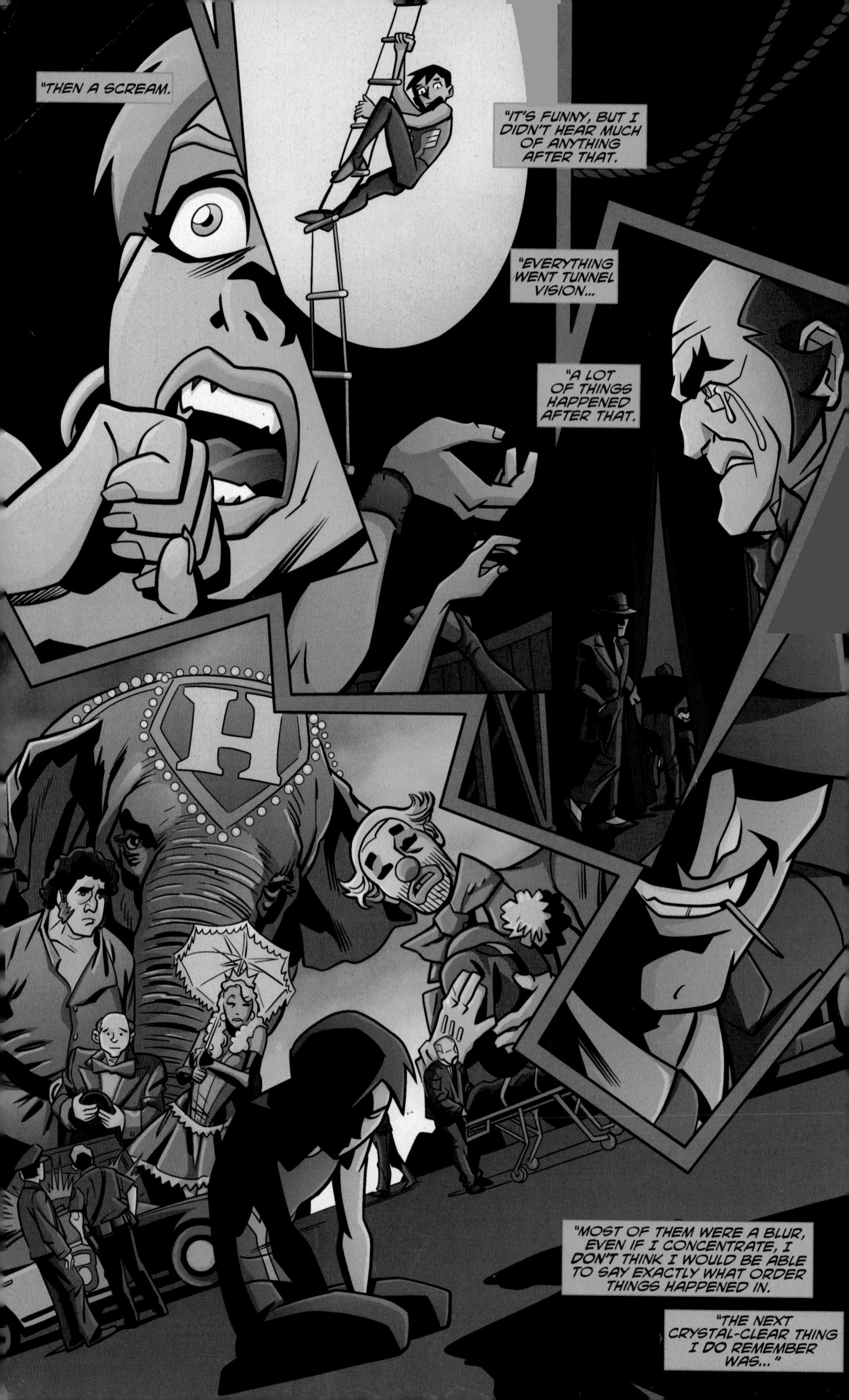
"THEN A SCREAM.
"IT'S FUNNY, BUT I DIDN'T HEAR MUCH OF ANYTHING AFTER THAT.
"EVERYTHING WENT TUNNEL VISION...
"A LOT OF THINGS HAPPENED AFTER THAT.
"MOST OF THEM WERE A BLUR, EVEN IF I CONCENTRATE, I DON'T THINK I WOULD BE ABLE TO SAY EXACTLY WHAT ORDER THINGS HAPPENED IN.
"THE NEXT CRYSTAL-CLEAR THING I DO REMEMBER WAS..."

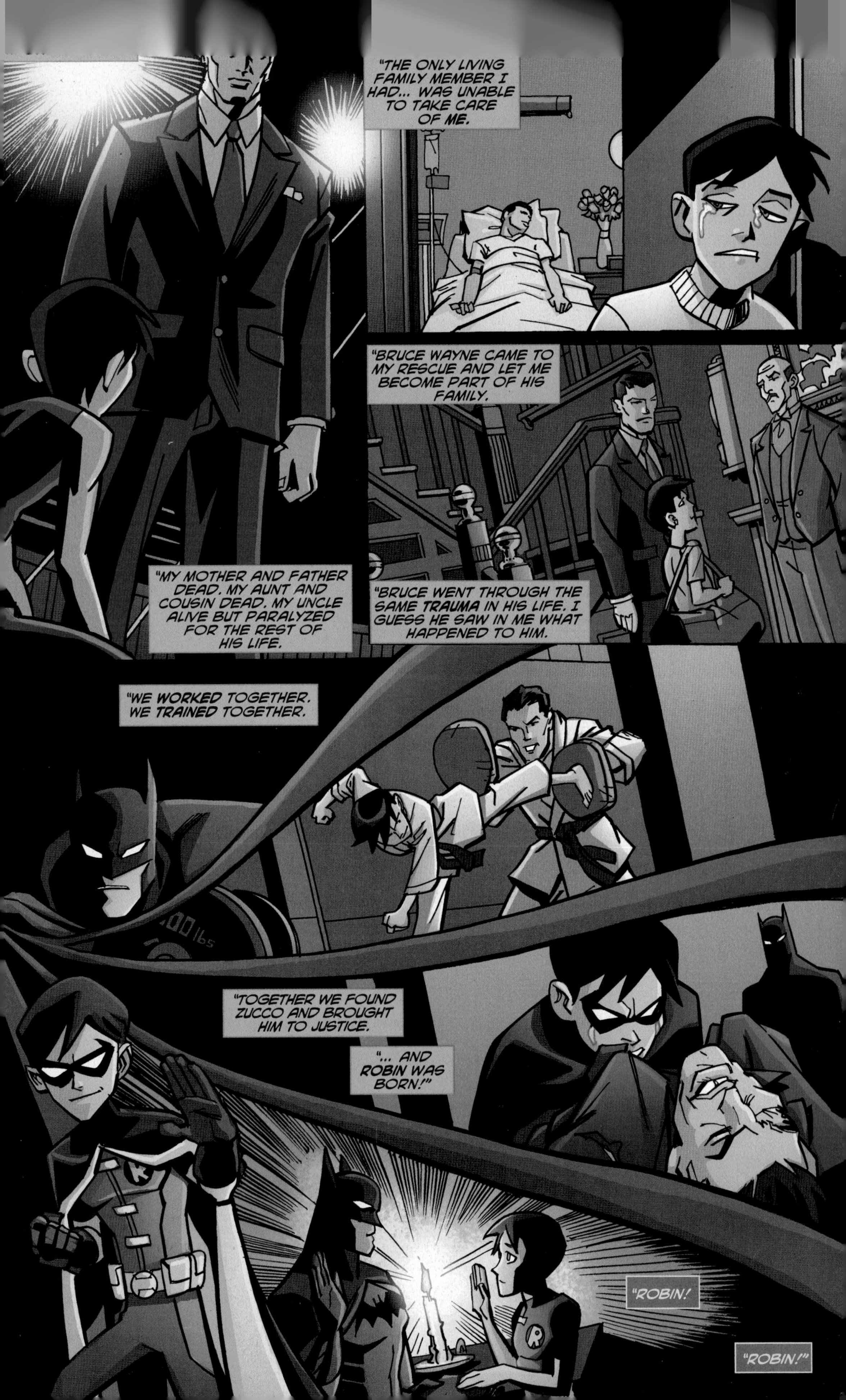
"THE ONLY LIVING FAMILY MEMBER I HAD... WAS UNABLE TO TAKE CARE OF ME.
"MY MOTHER AND FATHER DEAD. MY AUNT AND COUSIN DEAD. MY UNCLE ALIVE BUT PARALYZED FOR THE REST OF HIS LIFE.
"BRUCE WAYNE CAME TO MY RESCUE AND LET ME BECOME PART OF HIS FAMILY.
"BRUCE WENT THROUGH THE SAME TRAUMA IN HIS LIFE. I GUESS HE SAW IN ME WHAT HAPPENED TO HIM.
"WE WORKED TOGETHER. WE TRAINED TOGETHER.
"TOGETHER WE FOUND ZUCCO AND BROUGHT HIM TO JUSTICE.
"... AND ROBIN WAS BORN!"
"ROBIN!
"ROBIN!"

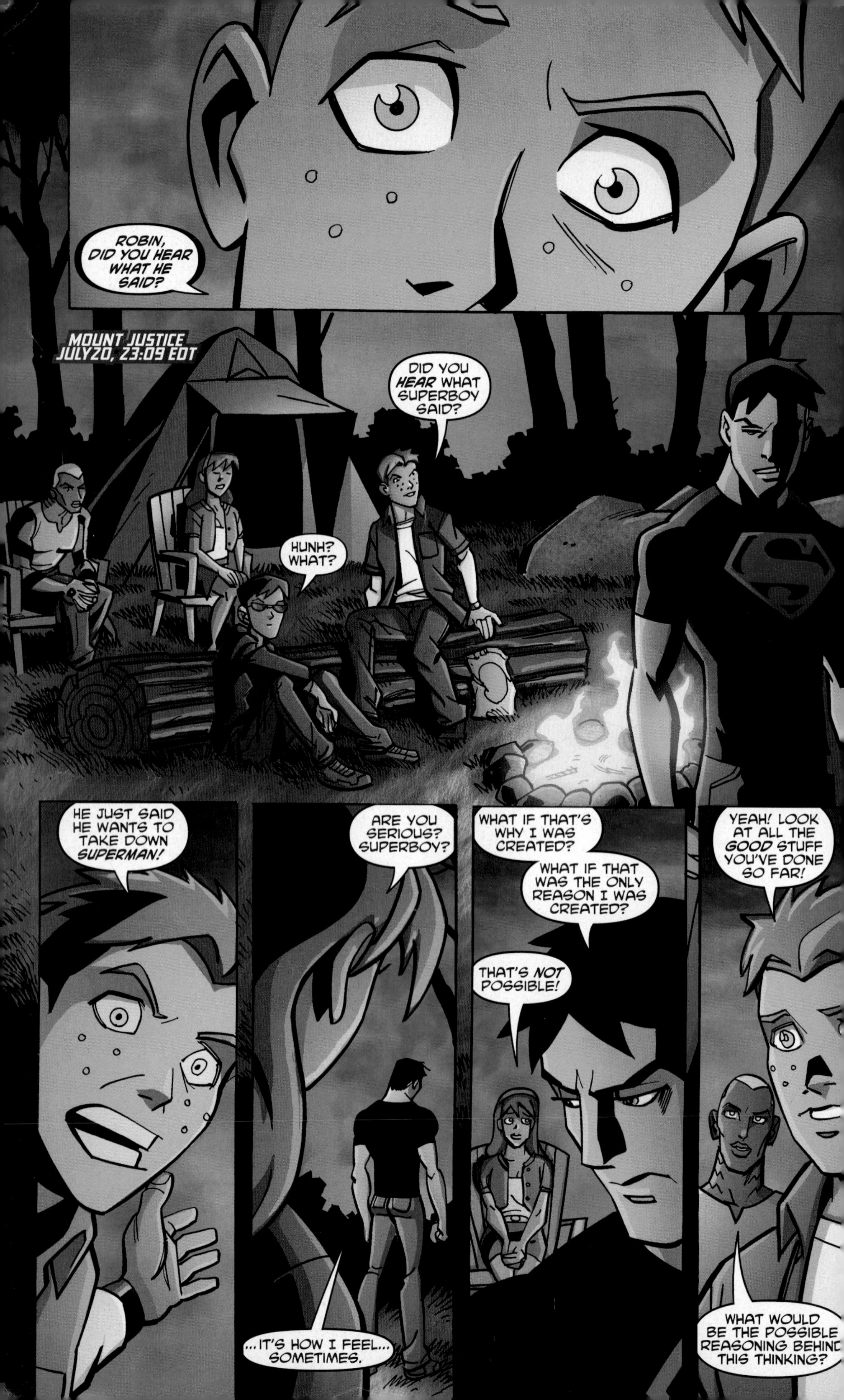
ROBIN, DID YOU HEAR WHAT HE SAID?
MOUNT JUSTICE JULY20, 23:09 EDT
DID YOU HEAR WHAT SUPERBOY SAID?
HUNH? WHAT?
HE JUST SAID HE WANTS TO TAKE DOWN SUPERMAN!
ARE YOU SERIOUS? SUPERBOY?
...IT'S HOW I FEEL... SOMETIMES.
WHAT IF THAT'S WHY I WAS CREATED?
WHAT IF THAT WAS THE ONLY REASON I WAS CREATED?
THAT'S NOT POSSIBLE!
YEAH! LOOK AT ALL THE GOOD STUFF YOU'VE DONE SO FAR!
WHAT WOULD BE THE POSSIBLE REASONING BEHIND THIS THINKING?

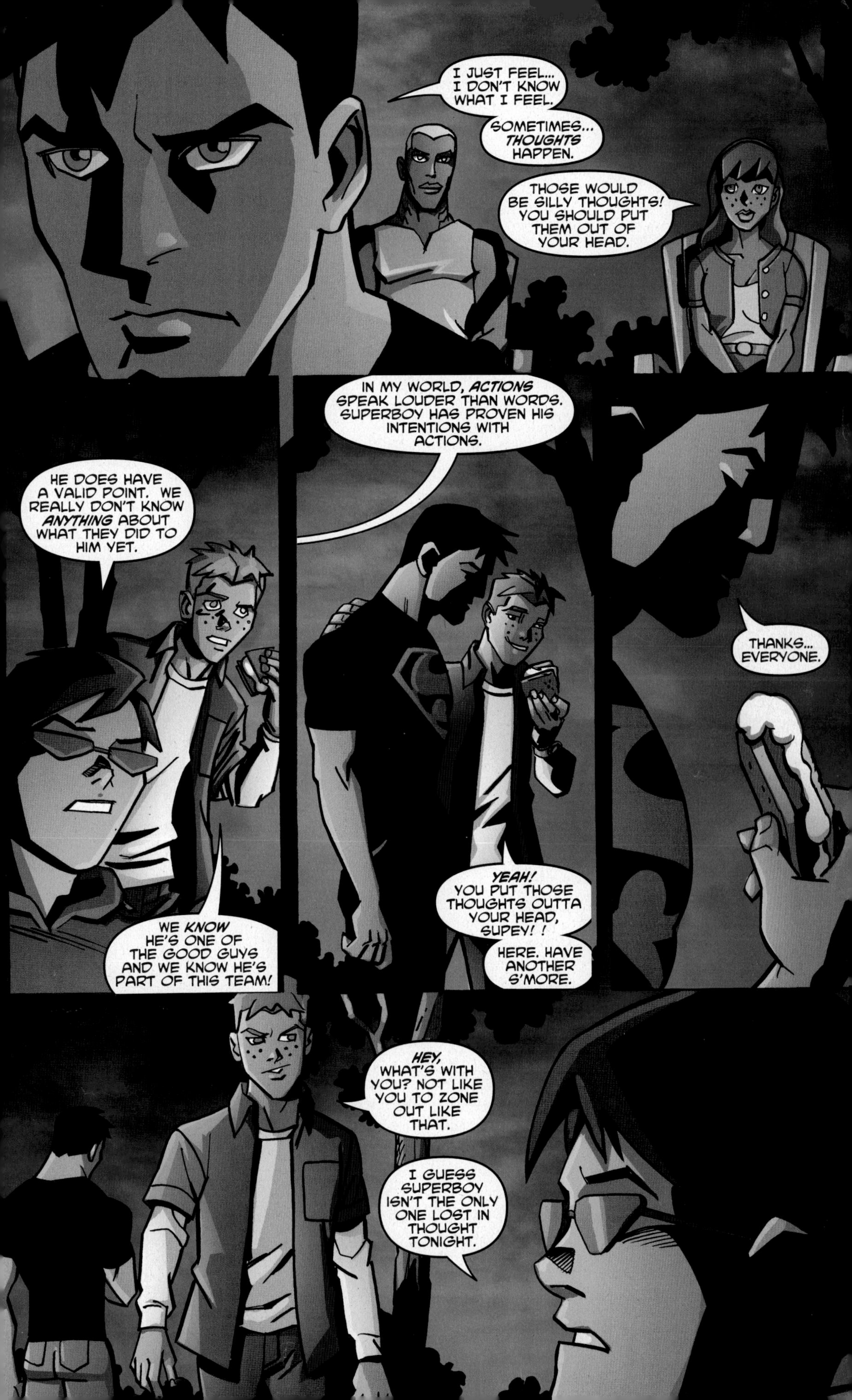

I JUST FEEL... I DON'T KNOW WHAT I FEEL.
SOMETIMES... THOUGHTS HAPPEN.
THOSE WOULD BE SILLY THOUGHTS! YOU SHOULD PUT THEM OUT OF YOUR HEAD.
HE DOES HAVE A VALID POINT. WE REALLY DON'T KNOW ANYTHING ABOUT WHAT THEY DID TO HIM YET.
WE KNOW HE'S ONE OF THE GOOD GUYS AND WE KNOW HE'S PART OF THIS TEAM!
IN MY WORLD, ACTIONS SPEAK LOUDER THAN WORDS. SUPERBOY HAS PROVEN HIS INTENTIONS WITH ACTIONS.
YEAH! YOU PUT THOSE THOUGHTS OUTTA YOUR HEAD, SUPEY! !
HERE. HAVE ANOTHER S'MORE.
THANKS... EVERYONE.
HEY, WHAT'S WITH YOU? NOT LIKE YOU TO ZONE OUT LIKE THAT.
I GUESS SUPERBOY ISN'T THE ONLY ONE LOST IN THOUGHT TONIGHT.

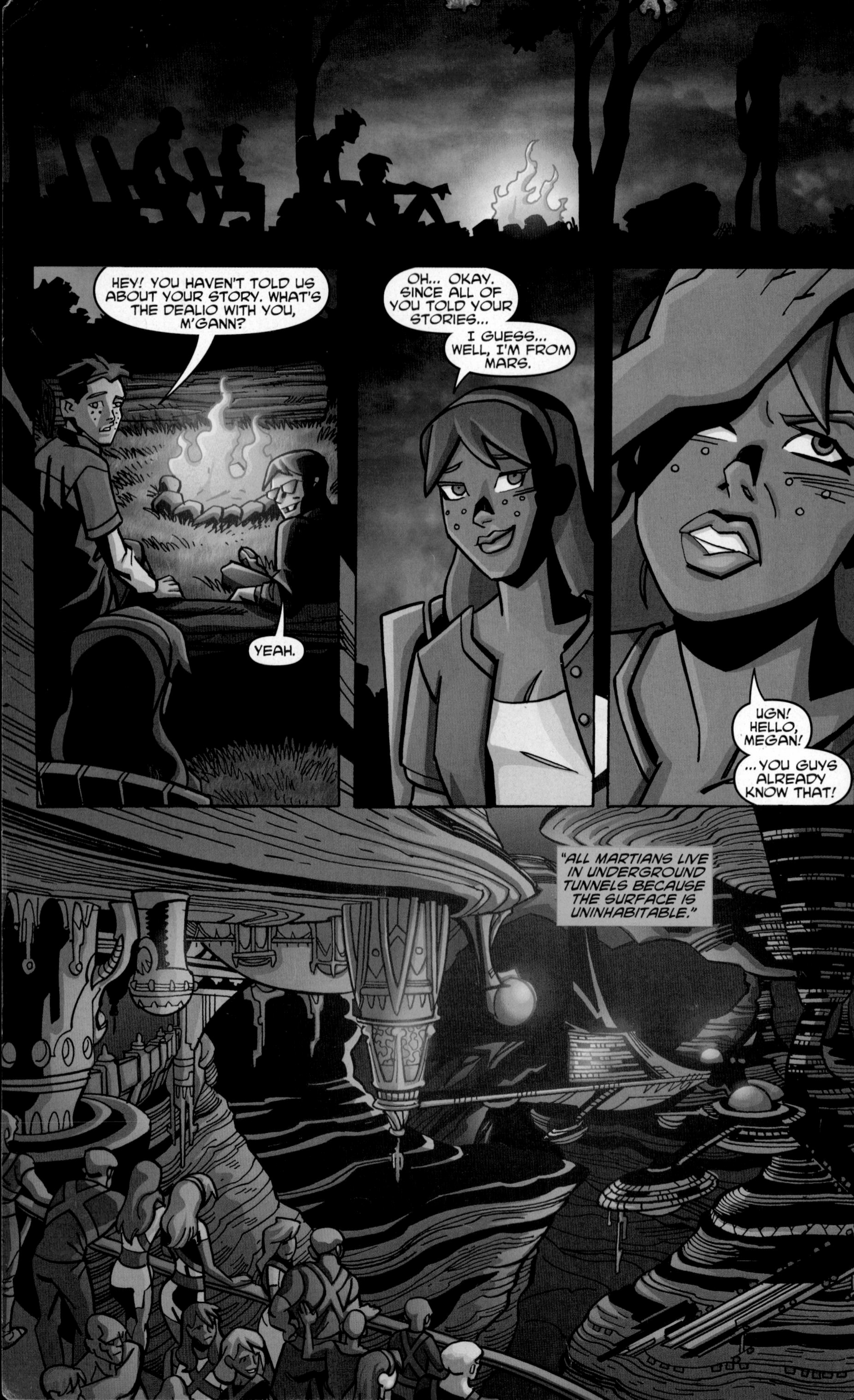
HEY! YOU HAVEN'T TOLD US ABOUT YOUR STORY. WHAT'S THE DEALIO WITH YOU, M'GANN?
YEAH.
OH... OKAY. SINCE ALL OF YOU TOLD YOUR STORIES...
I GUESS... WELL, I'M FROM MARS.
UGN! HELLO, MEGAN!
...YOU GUYS ALREADY KNOW THAT!
"ALL MARTIANS LIVE IN UNDERGROUND TUNNELS BECAUSE THE SURFACE IS UNINHABITABLE."

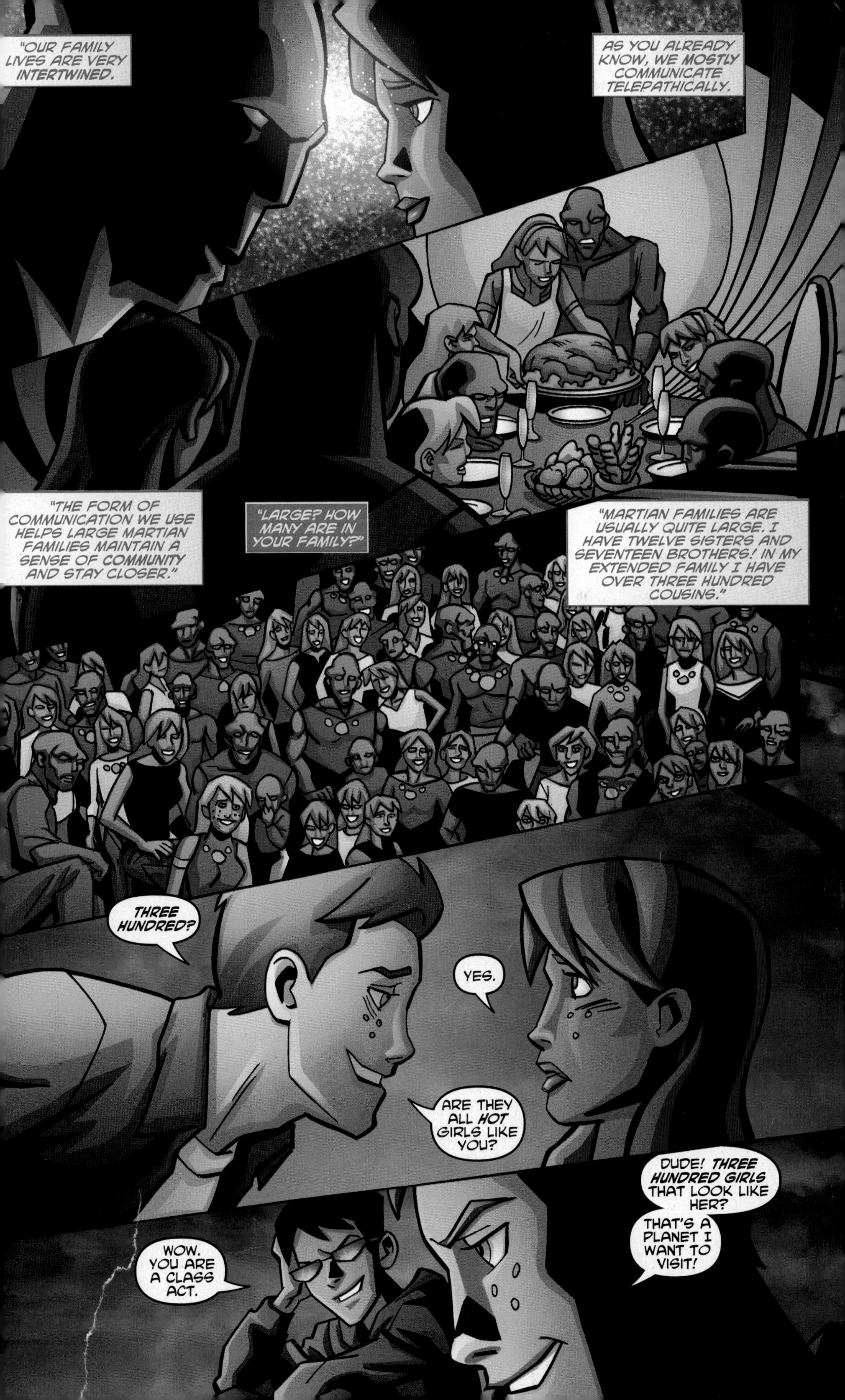
"OUR FAMILY LIVES ARE VERY INTERTWINED.
AS YOU ALREADY KNOW, WE MOSTLY COMMUNICATE TELEPATHICALLY.
"THE FORM OF COMMUNICATION WE USE HELPS LARGE MARTIAN FAMILIES MAINTAIN A SENSE OF COMMUNITY AND STAY CLOSER."
"LARGE? HOW MANY ARE IN YOUR FAMILY?"
"MARTIAN FAMILIES ARE USUALLY QUITE LARGE. I HAVE TWELVE SISTERS AND SEVENTEEN BROTHERS! IN MY EXTENDED FAMILY I HAVE OVER THREE HUNDRED COUSINS."
THREE HUNDRED?
YES.
ARE THEY ALL HOT GIRLS LIKE YOU?
DUDE! THREE HUNDRED GIRLS THAT LOOK LIKE HER?
THAT'S A PLANET I WANT TO VISIT!
WOW. YOU ARE A CLASS ACT.

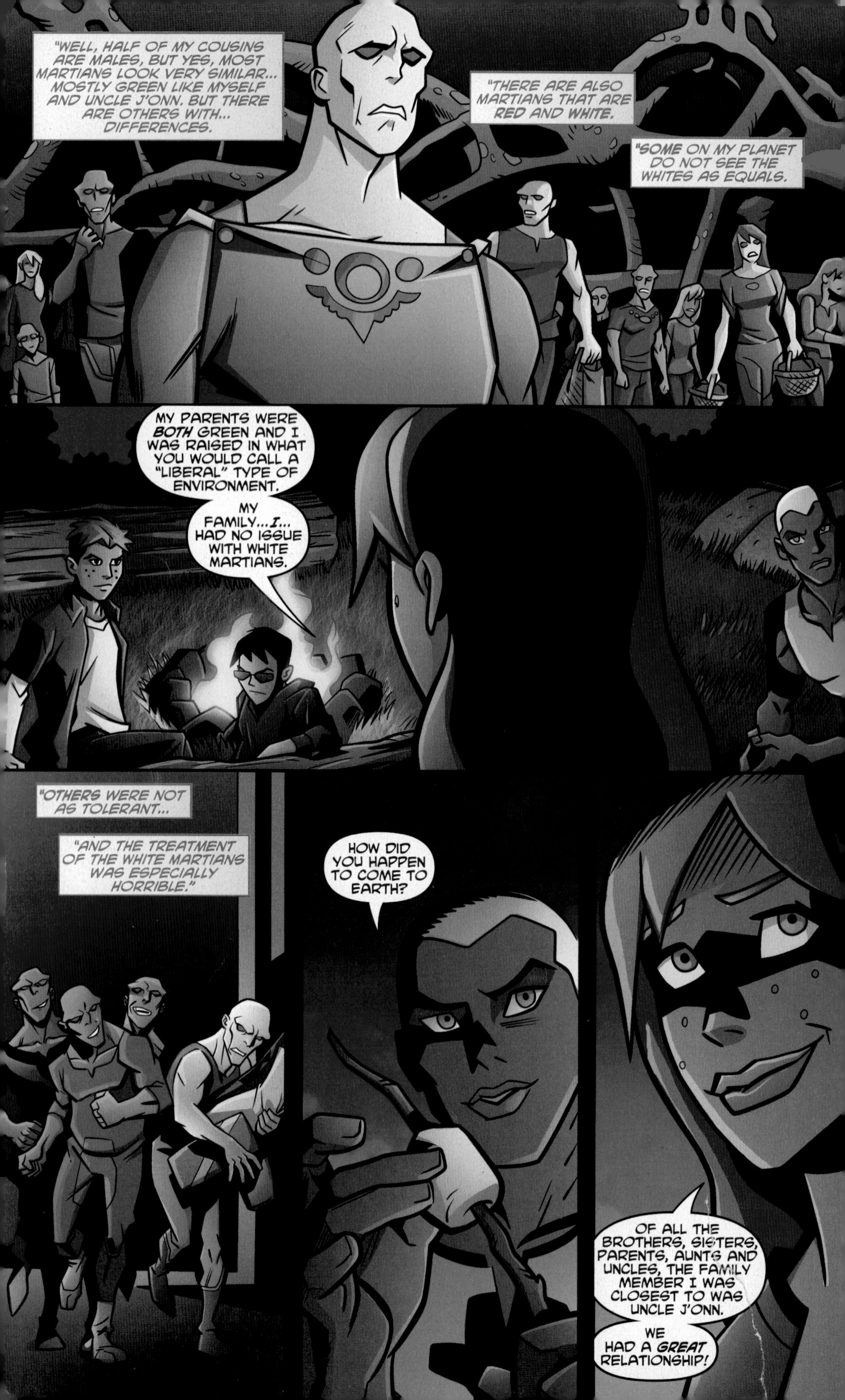
"WELL, HALF OF MY COUSINS ARE MALES, BUT YES, MOST MARTIANS LOOK VERY SIMILAR... MOSTLY GREEN LIKE MYSELF AND UNCLE J'ONN. BUT THERE ARE OTHERS WITH... DIFFERENCES.
"THERE ARE ALSO MARTIANS THAT ARE RED AND WHITE.
"SOME ON MY PLANET DO NOT SEE THE WHITES AS EQUALS.
MY PARENTS WERE BOTH GREEN AND I WAS RAISED IN WHAT YOU WOULD CALL A "LIBERAL" TYPE OF ENVIRONMENT.
MY FAMILY... I... HAD NO ISSUE WITH WHITE MARTIANS.
"OTHERS WERE NOT AS TOLERANT...
"AND THE TREATMENT OF THE WHITE MARTIANS WAS ESPECIALLY HORRIBLE."
HOW DID YOU HAPPEN TO COME TO EARTH?
OF ALL THE BROTHERS, SISTERS, PARENTS, AUNTS AND UNCLES, THE FAMILY MEMBER I WAS CLOSEST TO WAS UNCLE J'ONN.
WE HAD A GREAT RELATIONSHIP!

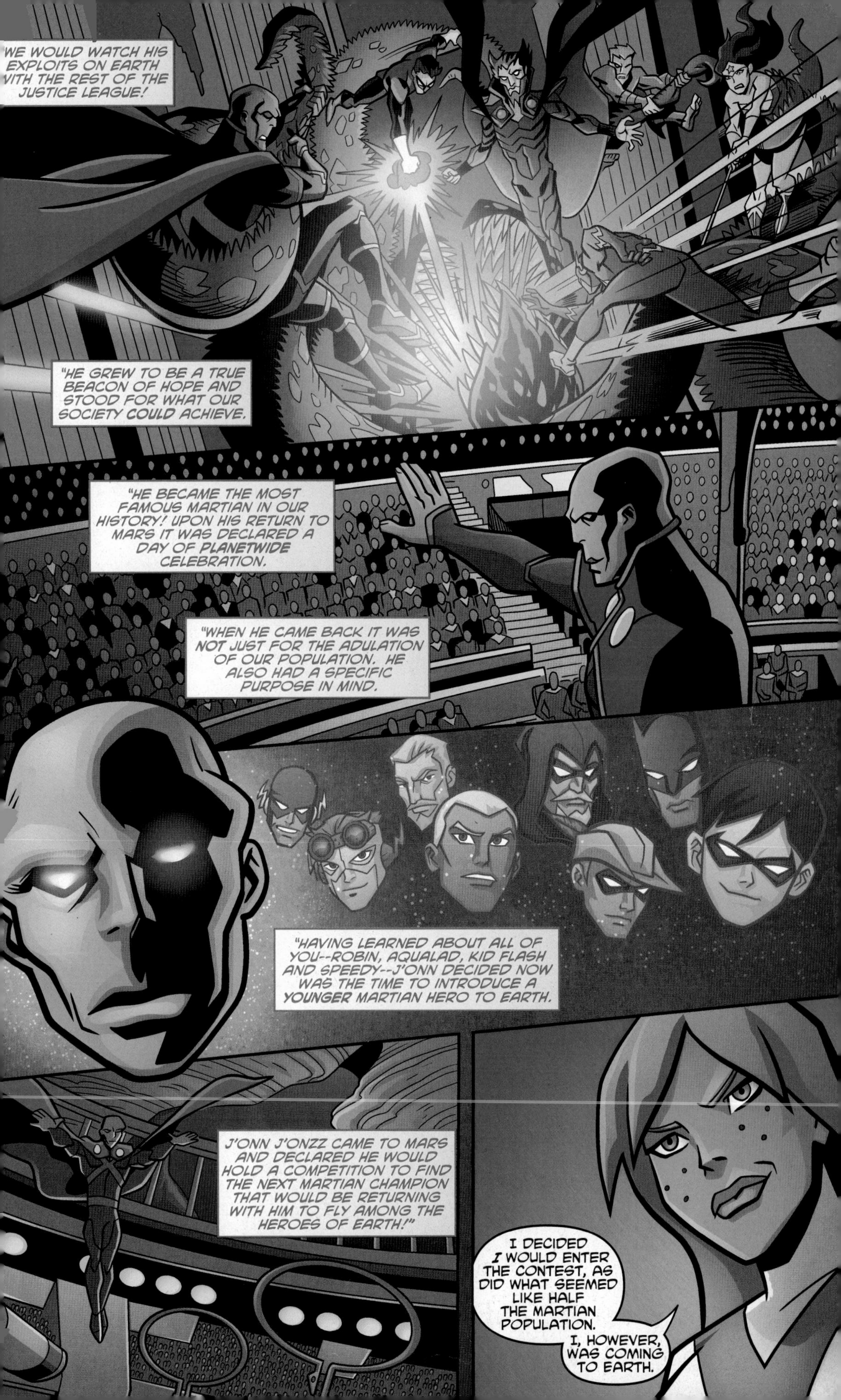

"WE WOULD WATCH HIS EXPLOITS ON EARTH WITH THE REST OF THE JUSTICE LEAGUE!
"HE GREW TO BE A TRUE BEACON OF HOPE AND STOOD FOR WHAT OUR SOCIETY COULD ACHIEVE.
"HE BECAME THE MOST FAMOUS MARTIAN IN OUR HISTORY! UPON HIS RETURN TO MARS IT WAS DECLARED A DAY OF PLANETWIDE CELEBRATION.
"WHEN HE CAME BACK IT WAS NOT JUST FOR THE ADULATION OF OUR POPULATION. HE ALSO HAD A SPECIFIC PURPOSE IN MIND.
"HAVING LEARNED ABOUT ALL OF YOU--ROBIN, AQUALAD, KID FLASH AND SPEEDY--J'ONN DECIDED NOW WAS THE TIME TO INTRODUCE A YOUNGER MARTIAN HERO TO EARTH.
J'ONN J'ONZZ CAME TO MARS AND DECLARED HE WOULD HOLD A COMPETITION TO FIND THE NEXT MARTIAN CHAMPION THAT WOULD BE RETURNING WITH HIM TO FLY AMONG THE HEROES OF EARTH!"
I DECIDED I WOULD ENTER THE CONTEST, AS DID WHAT SEEMED LIKE HALF THE MARTIAN POPULATION. I, HOWEVER, WAS COMING TO EARTH.

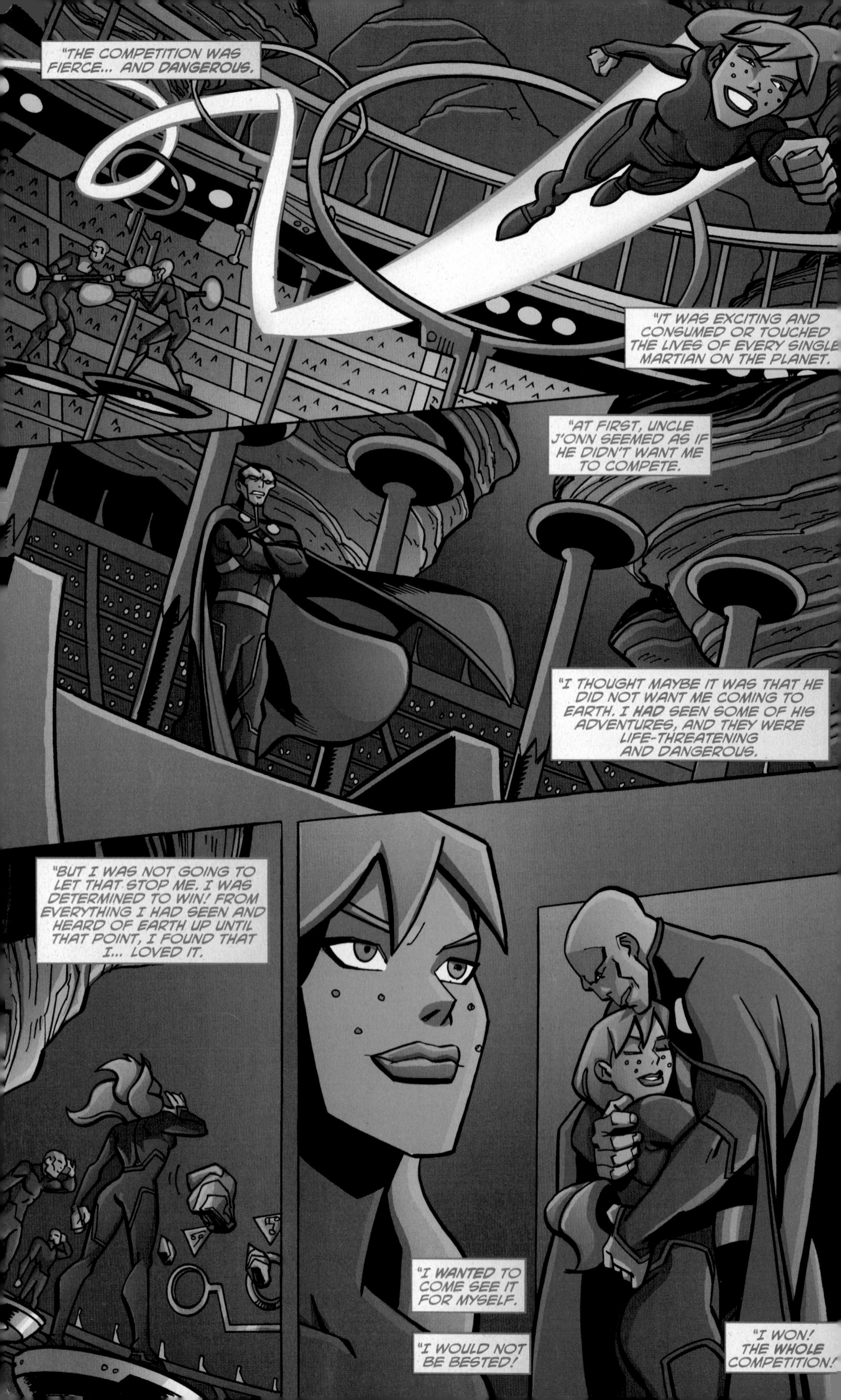
"THE COMPETITION WAS FIERCE... AND DANGEROUS.
"IT WAS EXCITING AND CONSUMED OR TOUCHED THE LIVES OF EVERY SINGLE MARTIAN ON THE PLANET.
"AT FIRST, UNCLE J'ONN SEEMED AS IF HE DIDN'T WANT ME TO COMPETE.
"I THOUGHT MAYBE IT WAS THAT HE DID NOT WANT ME COMING TO EARTH. I HAD SEEN SOME OF HIS ADVENTURES, AND THEY WERE LIFE-THREATENING AND DANGEROUS.
"BUT I WAS NOT GOING TO LET THAT STOP ME. I WAS DETERMINED TO WIN! FROM EVERYTHING I HAD SEEN AND HEARD OF EARTH UP UNTIL THAT POINT, I FOUND THAT I... LOVED IT.
"I WANTED TO COME SEE IT FOR MYSELF.
"I WOULD NOT BE BESTED!
"I WON! THE WHOLE COMPETITION!

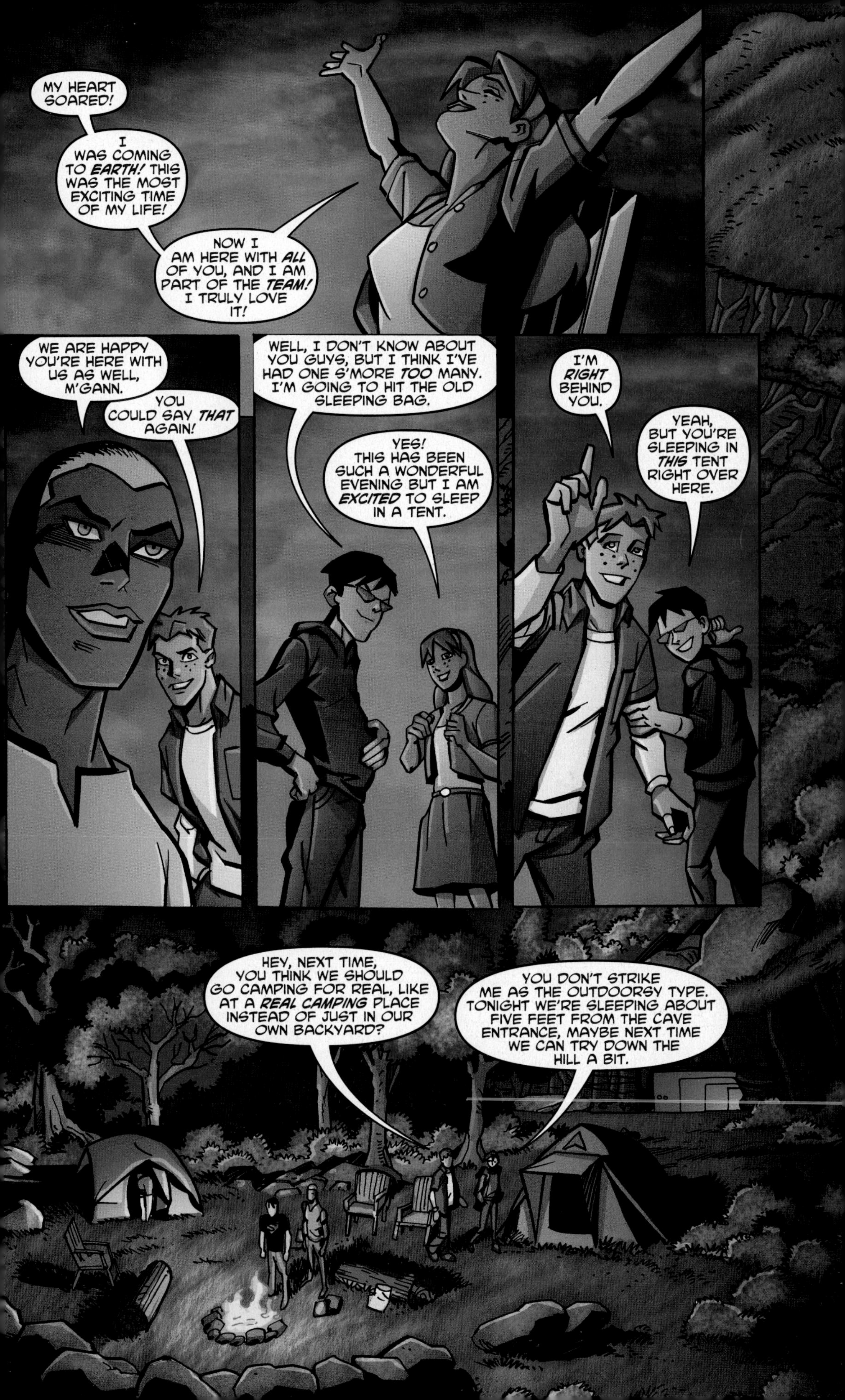
MY HEART SOARED!
I WAS COMING TO *EARTH!* THIS WAS THE MOST EXCITING TIME OF MY LIFE!
NOW I AM HERE WITH *ALL* OF YOU, AND I AM PART OF THE *TEAM!* I TRULY LOVE IT!
WE ARE HAPPY YOU'RE HERE WITH US AS WELL, M'GANN.
YOU COULD SAY *THAT* AGAIN!
WELL, I DON'T KNOW ABOUT YOU GUYS, BUT I THINK I'VE HAD ONE S'MORE *TOO* MANY. I'M GOING TO HIT THE OLD SLEEPING BAG.
YES! THIS HAS BEEN SUCH A WONDERFUL EVENING BUT I AM *EXCITED* TO SLEEP IN A TENT.
I'M *RIGHT* BEHIND YOU.
YEAH, BUT YOU'RE SLEEPING IN *THIS* TENT RIGHT OVER HERE.
HEY, NEXT TIME, YOU THINK WE SHOULD GO CAMPING FOR REAL, LIKE AT A *REAL CAMPING* PLACE INSTEAD OF JUST IN OUR OWN BACKYARD?
YOU DON'T STRIKE ME AS THE OUTDOORSY TYPE. TONIGHT WE'RE SLEEPING ABOUT FIVE FEET FROM THE CAVE ENTRANCE, MAYBE NEXT TIME WE CAN TRY DOWN THE HILL A BIT.

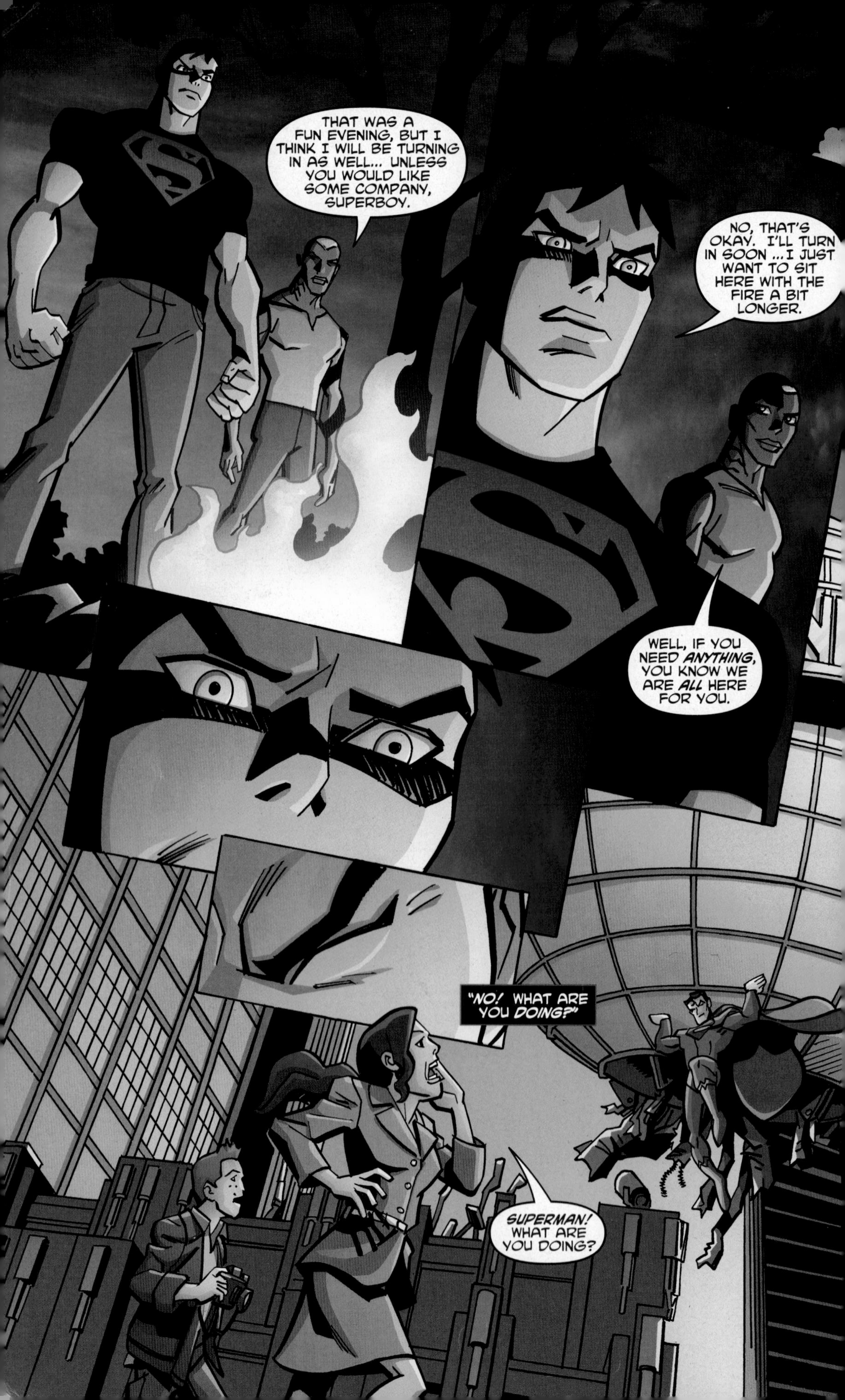
THAT WAS A FUN EVENING, BUT I THINK I WILL BE TURNING IN AS WELL... UNLESS YOU WOULD LIKE SOME COMPANY, SUPERBOY.
NO, THAT'S OKAY. I'LL TURN IN SOON ...I JUST WANT TO SIT HERE WITH THE FIRE A BIT LONGER.
WELL, IF YOU NEED *ANYTHING*, YOU KNOW WE ARE *ALL* HERE FOR YOU.
"*NO!* WHAT ARE YOU *DOING?*"
SUPERMAN! WHAT ARE YOU DOING?

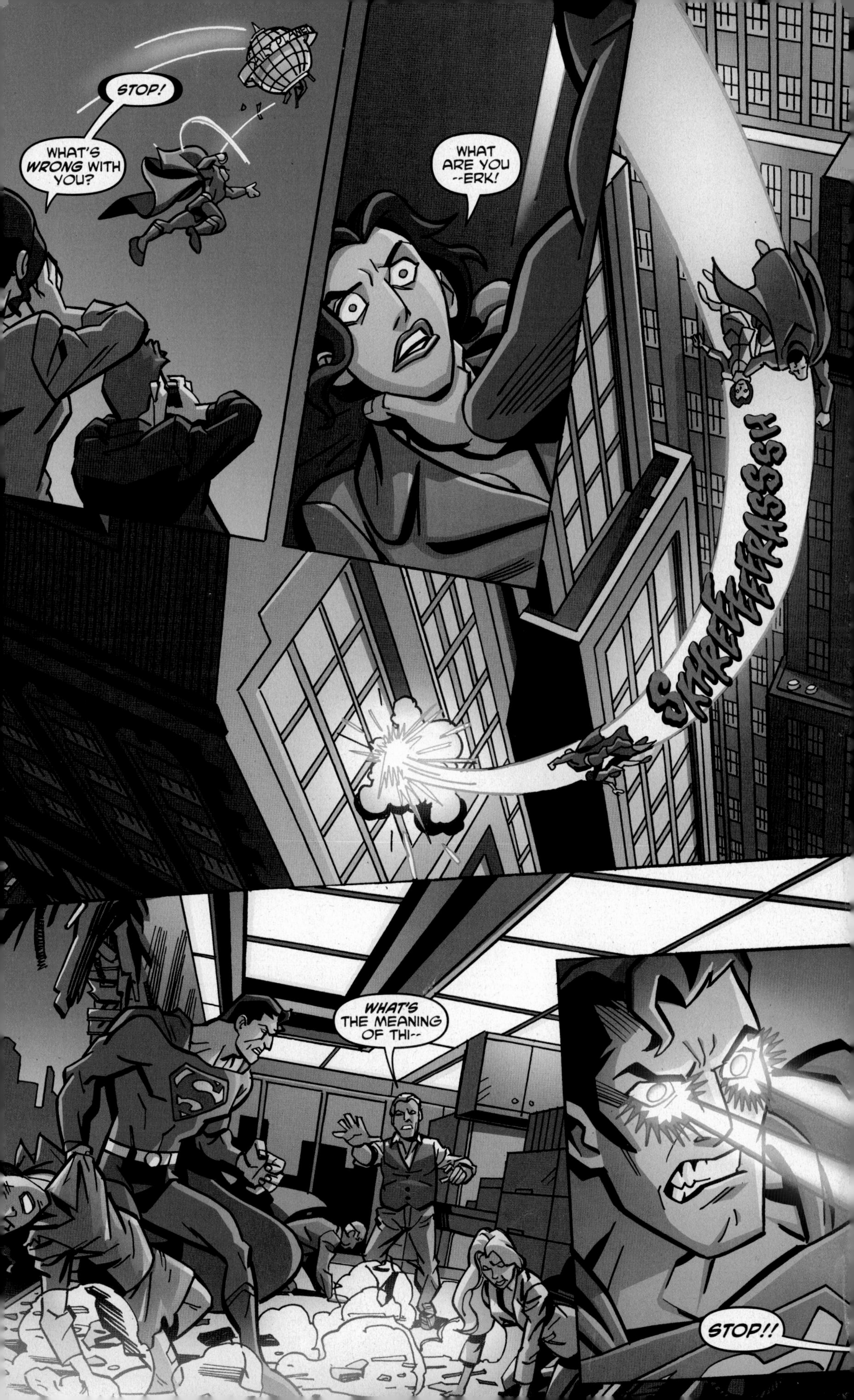
STOP!
WHAT'S WRONG WITH YOU?
WHAT ARE YOU --ERK!
SKHREEEERASSSH
WHAT'S THE MEANING OF THI--
STOP!!

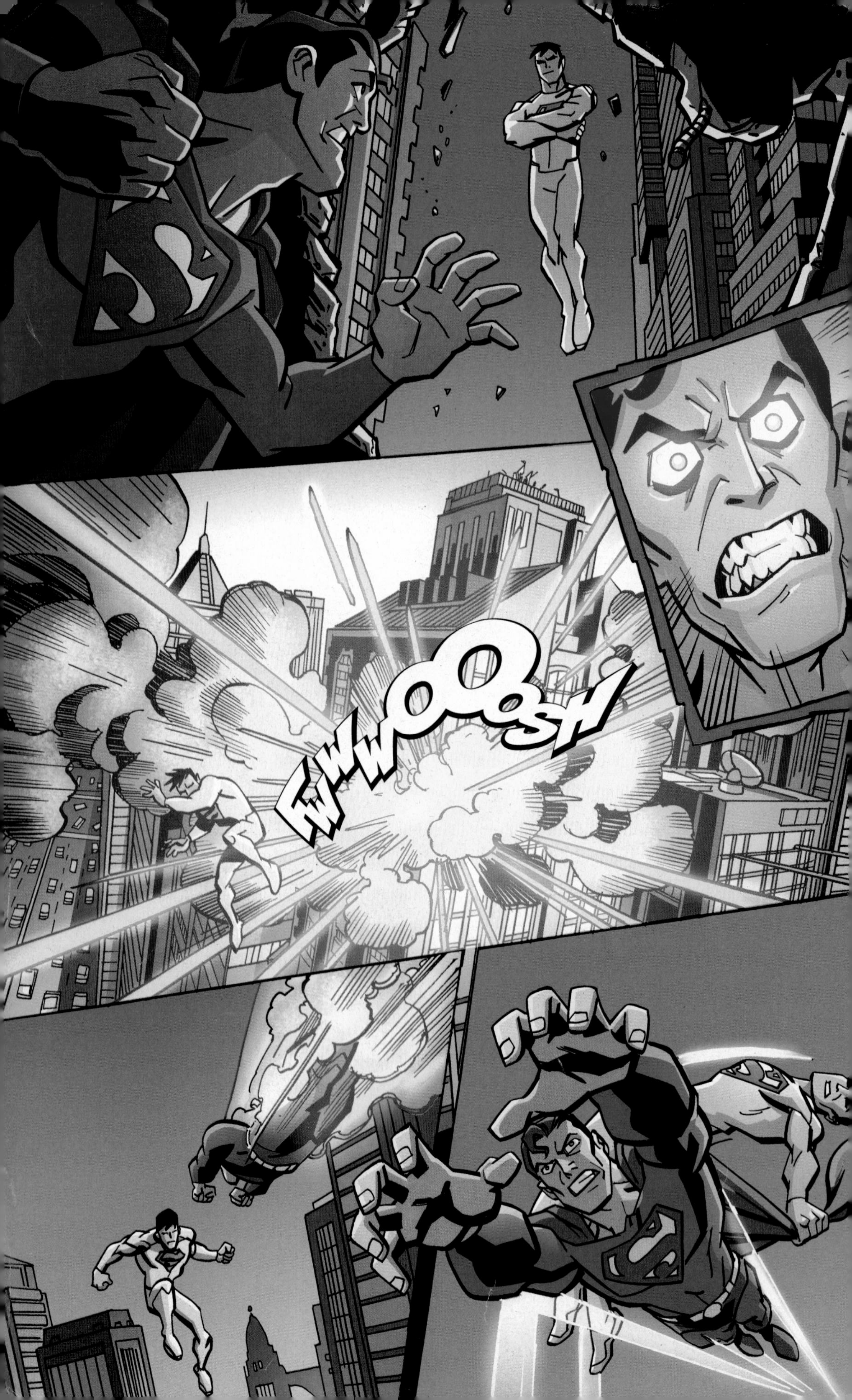
FWWWOOOOSH

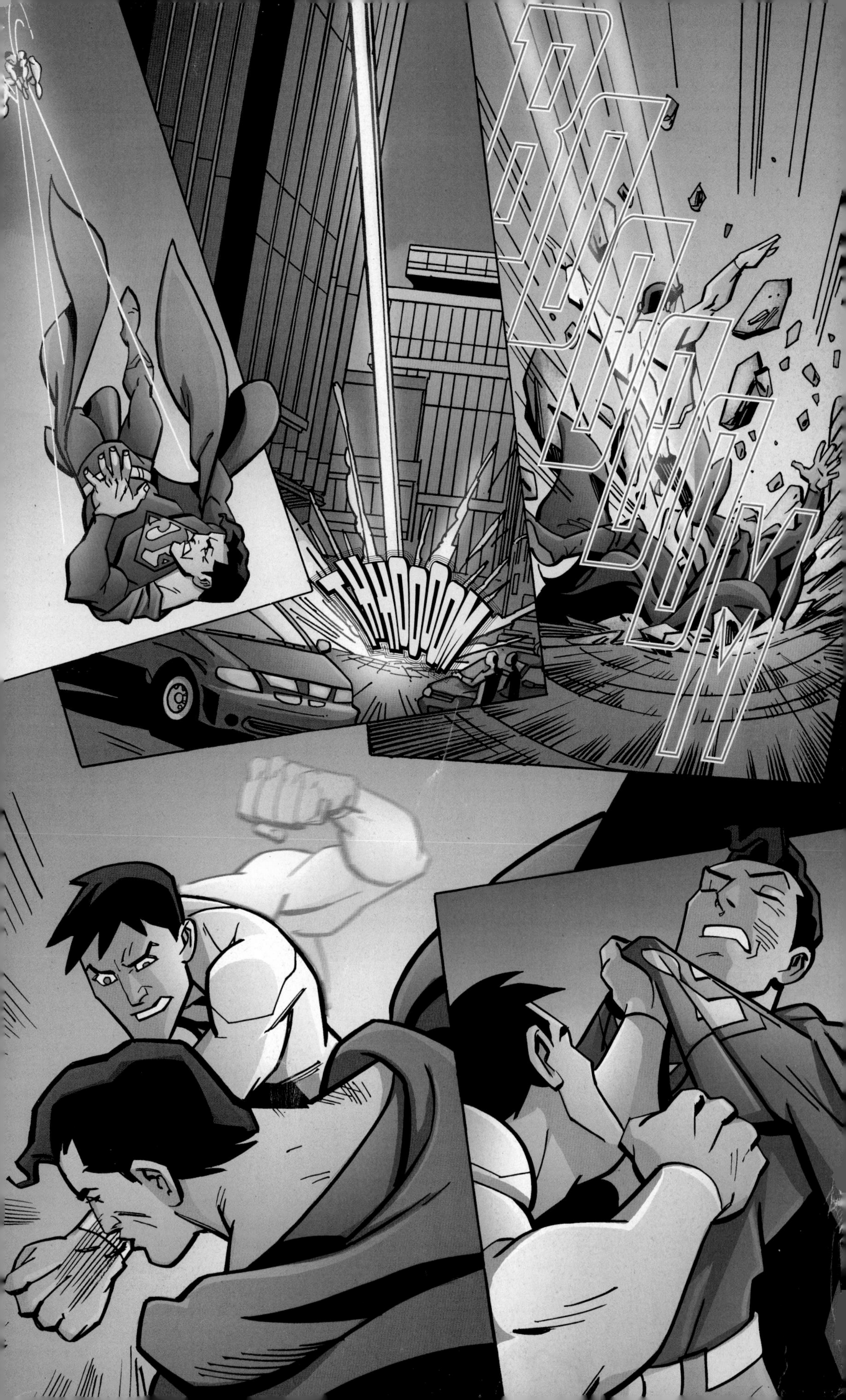
BOOOOM
THOOOOM

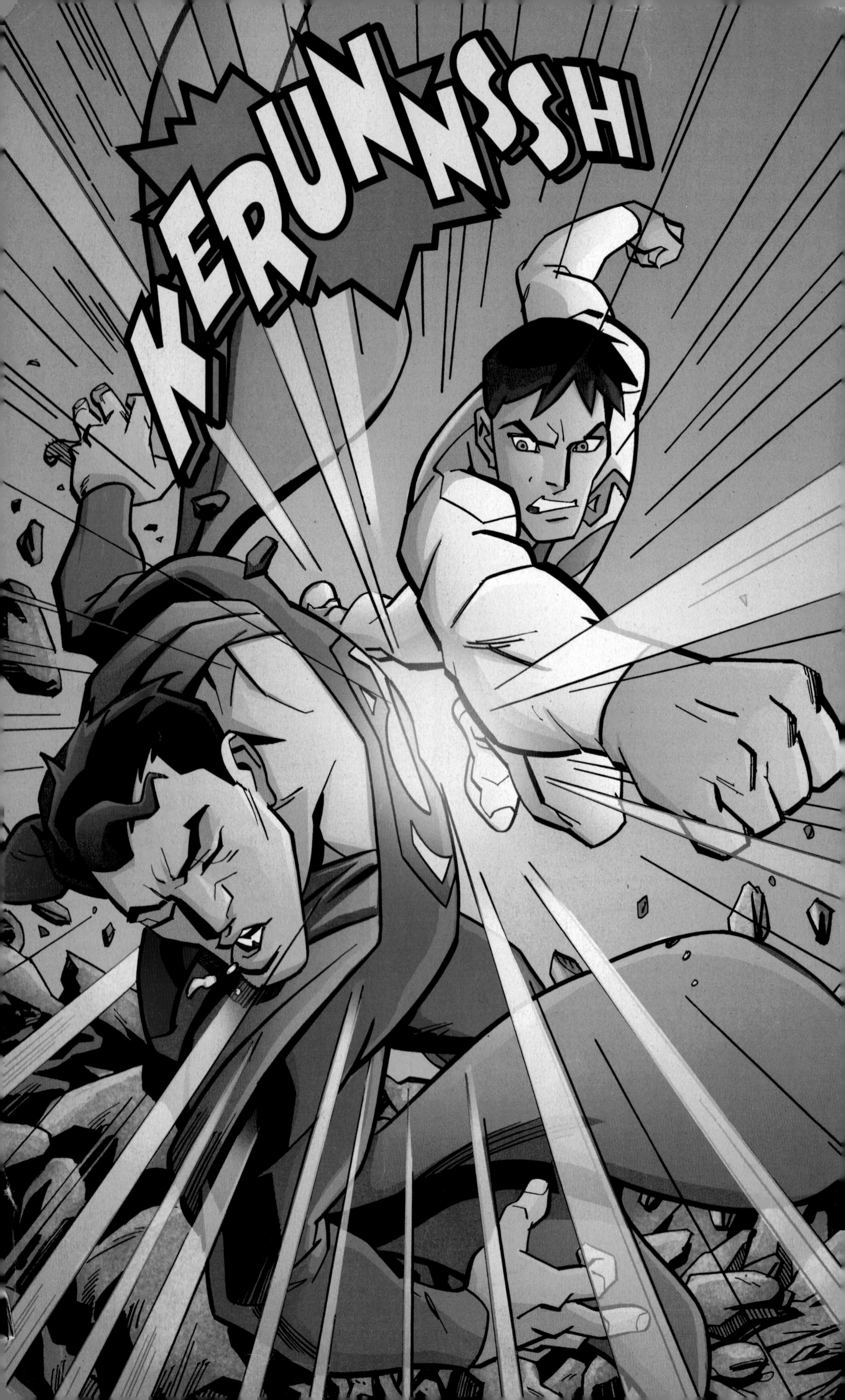
KERUNNSSH

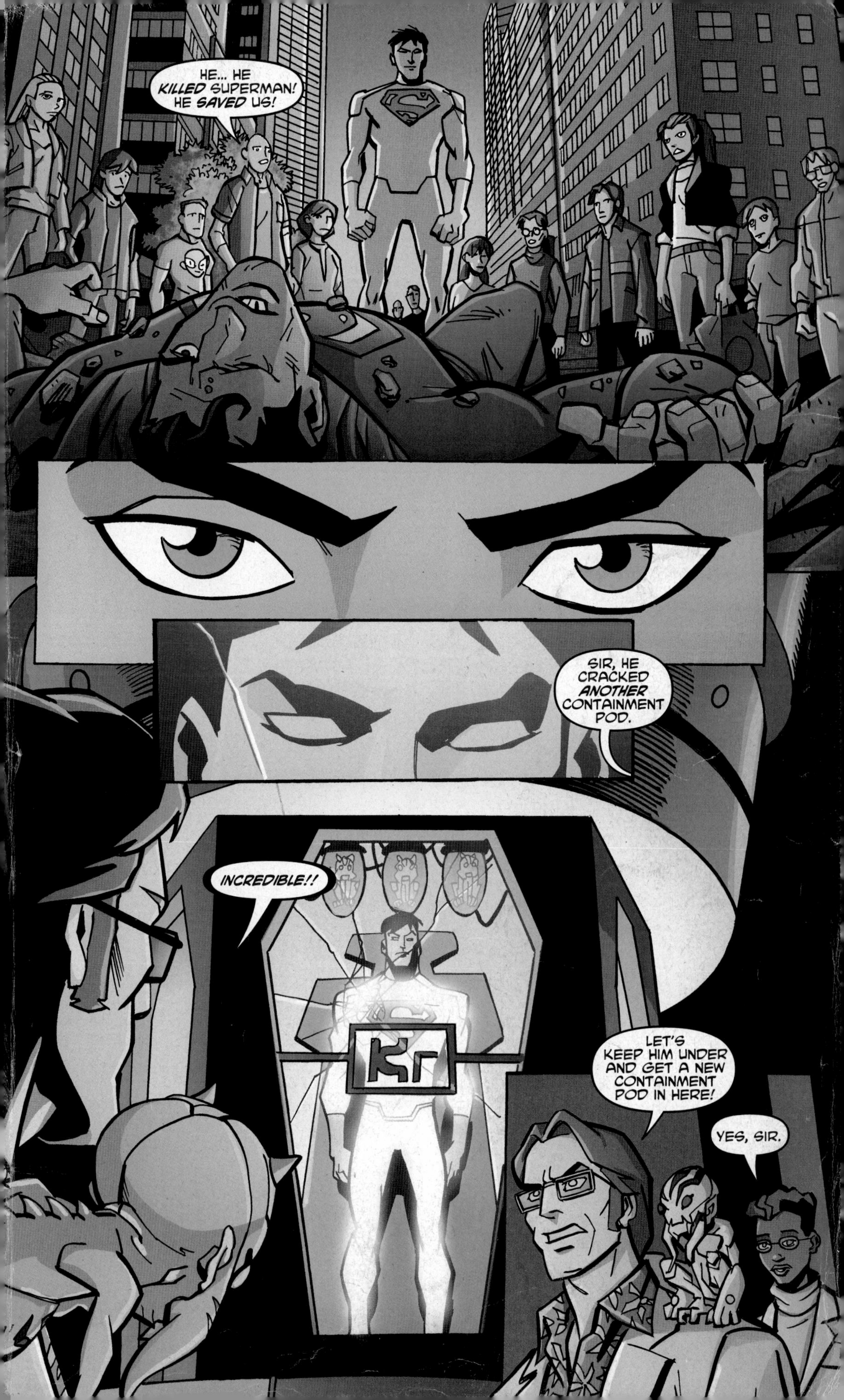
HE... HE KILLED SUPERMAN! HE SAVED US!
SIR, HE CRACKED ANOTHER CONTAINMENT POD.
INCREDIBLE!!
LET'S KEEP HIM UNDER AND GET A NEW CONTAINMENT POD IN HERE!
YES, SIR.

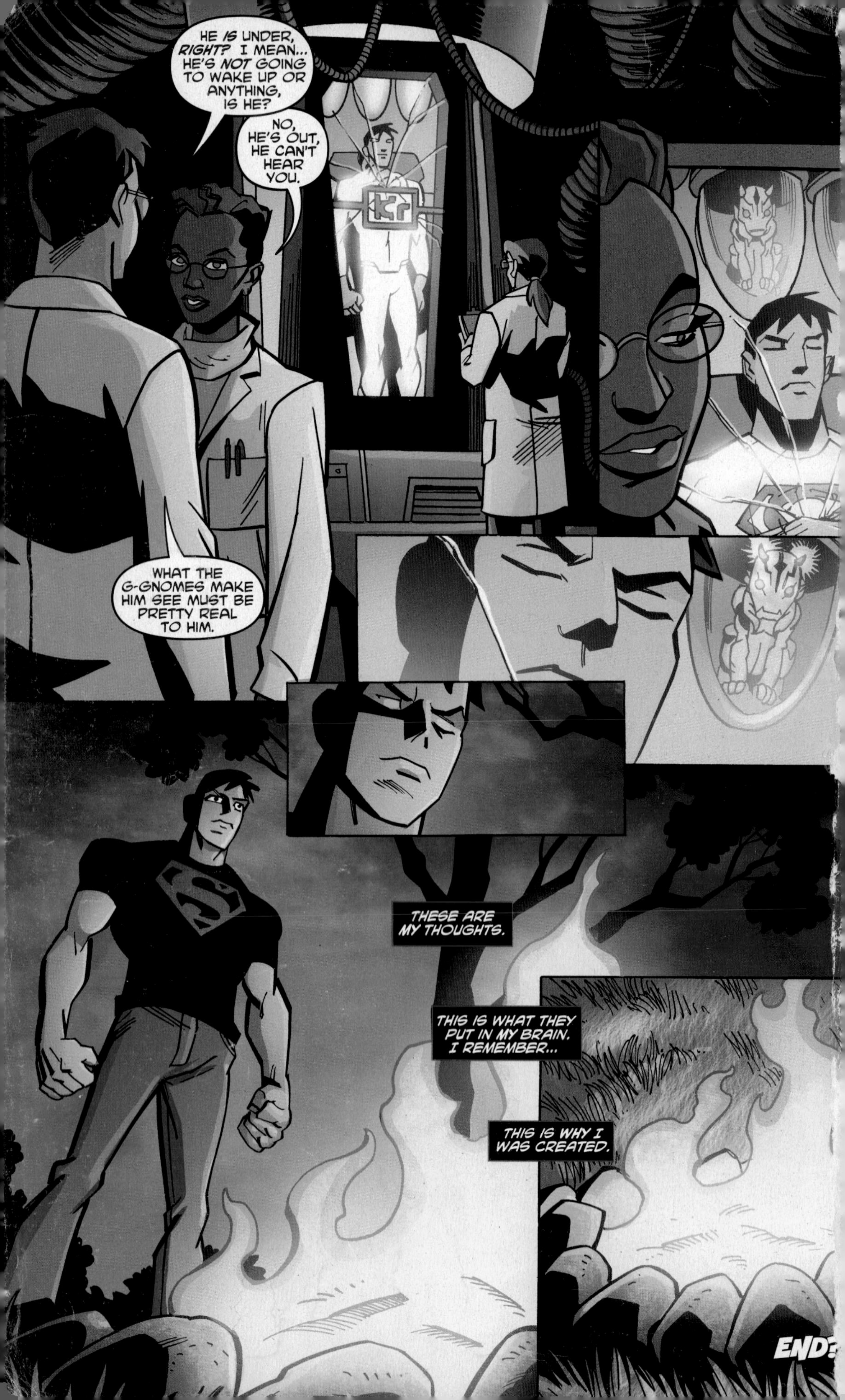
HE *IS* UNDER, *RIGHT?* I MEAN... HE'S *NOT* GOING TO WAKE UP OR ANYTHING, IS HE?
NO, HE'S OUT, HE CAN'T HEAR YOU.
WHAT THE G-GNOMES MAKE HIM SEE MUST BE PRETTY REAL TO HIM.
THESE ARE MY THOUGHTS.
THIS IS WHAT THEY PUT IN MY BRAIN. I REMEMBER...
THIS IS WHY I WAS CREATED.
END?